Editor: Stevi Mager (Instagram: @stevimager)

Proofreader: Taylor Robinson (Instagram: @tay.r.rob)

Cover Designer: Jaqueline Kropmanns (Instagram: @jaquelinekropmanns.coverdesign)

Map Artist: Zoe Holland (Instagram: @ghost_nymphz)

Character Art: Marina Ceban (Instagram: @cebanart) / Zoe Holland (Instagram:@ghoset_nymphz)

Unsplash Images: Vino Li, Jezael Melgoza, Kyle Glenn, Ivan Bandura, Wil Stewart, and Adrian Regeci.

BLOOD OF DESIDERIUM

THE DIVIDE
BOOK ONE

ALI STUEBBE

TRIGGER WARNINGS

-Violence/Gore/Death
-Grief
-Profanity
-Mental health themes
-Mention of suicidal intent
-Torture
-Overall dark themes

This book is NA Dark Fantasy Romance that is 18+ with explicit language and sexual scenes. BoD is the first book in the series and ends on a cliffhanger.

Emma may be a fictional character, but her feelings and thoughts about herself and life are real. The heaviness in our emotions can make us feel like we are drowning, and I know parts of this story can hit home in readers. If you ever find yourself in need of someone to talk to, there are always people wanting to help when you are ready.

The National Suicide Prevention Lifeline

ALI STUEBBE

Call: 1-800-273-8255
Crisis text line: Text "HELLO" to 741741

PRONUNCIATION GUIDE

Deyadrum- (De-yay-drum)
Helestria - (Hel-es-tree-a)
Asiza- Ah-see-za
Amihan- (Ah-me-han)
Asov- (Ay-sov)
Ahbainn - (Ah-vein)
Tsisana-(Tsee-sah-nah)
Masiren - (Maz-ren)
Zoraida - (Zor-ay-da)
Draven -(Drav-en)
Mauve - (Mohv)
Telion - (Tel-EE-on)
Whiro - (Were-oh)
Kaimi - (Kye-EE-me)

DESIDERIUM

des · i · de · ri · um

: an ardent desire or longing
especially **:** a feeling of loss or grief for something lost

To the readers—
This book is for the ones who were told they couldn't but did anyways.

For my husband Chris—
Because you engraved our love on your heart, a permanent declaration, for me.

To Family—
Thank you for all the love and support. This is your last warning to not read beyond this point. Respectfully.

PART I

CHAPTER ONE

Mariam

A sense of hollowness overwhelms me from the hum of power in my body growing mute.

My well of power became strained the moment I set foot on the Mortal Lands of Helestria. Centuries ago, a ward was set in place here that would cut off the tether to the power of anyone from the Fae lands who stepped foot on the mortal lands. It was meant as a way to protect the humans from those who could easily dominate them—a treaty for peace and equality. But the loss of my power as I walk through Helestria feels foreign, like I've been stripped bare on the inside.

A small coo brings my eyes to the bundle of innocence cradled in my arms. A calming smile washes over my face, a contrast against the exhaustion spreading through my body from the journey across the sea. Brushing the pad of my thumb across my daughter's forehead, I draw in a deep breath, taking this final moment of togetherness and locking it away to cherish forever.

I see a small house nestled just past the line of woods, with smoke pluming out of the brick chimney. The cool breeze brushes through the sleeping trees standing tall in the night. Walking between them, I gently recover the plush blanket over my child's head to keep her warm. I tuck her closer to my chest as I step past the treeline and walk through the open field to reach the reason I traveled so far. My closest friend. My closest *Fae* friend, who I have always considered a sister.

Lydia grew up in the Fae lands of Deyadrum but became tired of the rulers and the power-hungry individuals. I still remember the day Lydia left for the mortal lands, saying she didn't want anything to do with powers and everything that comes with having them. So, she moved here, living like a human would. An ordinary life. A *safer* life. Which is exactly what I'm hoping for.

The board on the one wooden step dips slightly when my foot presses on it. I walk up to the door, tapping the back of my knuckles against it.

Nothing.

I knock again, and this time, I can hear footsteps dragging across the floor inside, growing louder with each step. The lock unlatches with a click before the door creaks open. I stand there with so much over-whelming love for seeing my dear friend after so many years. She looks the same, hazel eyes with amber hair that's piled on top of her head from sleeping.

I can't help but smile when Lydia's eyes go wide and she cries out in disbelief, covering her hand over her mouth. "Mariam?" she gasps.

"The one and only." I gingerly shrug, stepping closer to give her a hug, but making sure not to squish my heart wrapped in the blanket.

Lydia hugs me with a soft sob that rears its way up her throat. "I can't believe it. I've missed you so much. What brings you across the damn sea?" she asks, but her words stop when she steps back and looks down at my arms.

"I need a favor, Lyd," I say, seriously. "A life-changing one."

Lydia shakes her head warily. She opens her mouth to speak but closes it again instead.

"Please, Lydia," I beg in a broken voice. "She can't stay with me."

The silver streams of light shine down upon us, casting a glow through the veiled darkness. I watch Lydia closely as she stands with her dark wood

14

cabin door slightly ajar. Her eyes remain wide as she stares back at me, never blinking.

"Mariam! How do you expect me to take care of a baby? I–I'm not cut out to be a mother, you know that. I can barely take care of my own damn self."

I stare down at the beautiful gift the universe bestowed upon me: a sweet baby girl. Wrapping the soft, wool blanket tighter around her, I gently trail my fingertips over the name stitched on top. *Emma*. I clutch her closer to my chest and squeeze my eyes shut, knowing I *have* to do this. I fight the tears as my eyes fill with sorrow, the pain in my heart unbearable, but the slight touch of a little, cold hand pulls me back to gaze down at her again. "Lydia, you are the only one who I consider family. The only person I would trust my life with, and that now goes for my daughter. She's not safe with me. She's barely a month old, so vulnerable, and I–I can't let him have her." I bring my pleading eyes to meet Lydia's, begging. "He's after me, and it's all my fault."

I watch the way Lydia's eyes fill with heartbreak before they widen even further as she sucks in a sharp breath, shaking her head violently. "No! No, no, no! How can that be?!"

I inhale deeply, letting the rose and honey scent of my daughter wrap around my senses to calm me. "When I gave birth, my power surged from the pain, and my control slipped for a moment. That split-second mistake put me on his radar. So, please, Lydia. I need you to please, please protect her. You're all she has."

Lydia glances around the front of her cabin. My eyes follow her gaze, only seeing the section of trees swaying in the night breeze and hearing the whistle in the wind before she opens her door further. But I just stand there, silently shaking my head. "I can't. It's too risky for me to stay longer than I already have. I need you to take her."

Stepping out onto the worn, wooden porch, Lydia holds out her arms to take Emma. I place a lingering kiss on my child's forehead, whispering parting words: "No matter in this world, or the one beyond it, I promise we will be together again. My heart will always be with you. I love you, my sweet child."

My hands tremble, but I try my best to mask it as I gently place Emma in Lydia's arms. I take another long look at her to engrave her in my memory, wishing I didn't have to do this. My entire body screams at me to take my baby back. After a few silent moments, I step towards Lydia and squeeze her free hand tight. "Thank you. Whether in this world or the one beyond it, I will see you again, dear friend. You are a sister to me. I love you."

My eyes become glassy as I see Lydia's cheeks grow damp with free-flowing tears, and her lips quiver as she shakes her head. I know Lydia would do anything to help and is most likely wishing she could prevent all of it.

"I love you," Lydia quietly whispers.

I give her a soft smile to hide the heart-wrenching pain that is tearing me up inside. But my heart swells seeing the way Lydia looks down at Emma, who is looking up at her with big, grey eyes. I choose this moment to silently flee to the treeline, hiding in the shadows. I witness a soft smile grace Lydia's mouth when Emma's little hand reaches up to her, and a bittersweet feeling burns behind my eyes.

Lydia swipes her hand over her face to erase the tears falling down her cheeks, then lifts her head to look for me. But I'm already gone, tucked beneath the trees and out of sight. I can't face a longer goodbye. This is hard enough—to rip myself away when everything in me is screaming to go back. To never let her go, knowing I'm going to miss every moment, every milestone in her life, as she blooms into the most beautiful flower.

Lydia's eyes widen as she keeps searching the treeline, and I feel the ache growing in my heart at seeing her panic before me. I continue to watch Lydia look around for me until enough time passes that she clutches Emma to her chest in defeat and walks back inside. I struggle to hold back the cry that wants to rip out of me as I see the door fully shut. The finality of it makes the tears break free as I take off into the night.

CHAPTER TWO

King Oren

*W*e've been sailing for hours since we departed from my kingdom, the Court of Asov. When we left, there were clear and calm skies, the sun sparkling against the waves. But good things come to an end. It's always a trick and I find it's important to keep everything in a death grip, claiming control. That way, nothing stands a chance of slipping through my fingers.

Because now, the clouds begin to darken as they roll across the sky, hindering the warmth from the sun. The ship is starting to feel restless, swaying with the change in tide, while the wind picks up speed. A warning of an impending storm.

My boots splash along the slick wood boards of the ship's deck as I approach my right-hand advisor and my fleet's captain, Calloway. He's also my Seer, but for this task, his powers are pointless.

"Keep searching," I bark over the wind that's growing louder and beating against the sails. Calloway keeps his hands wrapped tightly around the ship's helm, holding it steady as the waves start to grow stronger, pounding into the starboard side. The crew are scrambling with the ropes, stowing the sails. I'm giving these lower Fae mere minutes to get our ship ready before I unleash my wrath on them. I can already feel my eyes heating red with power at the thought of trapping them in an illusion they can't escape, punishing them so they learn to move faster next time. The storm is racing towards us without warning. I briefly wonder if that's a sign I'm *close*. If I'm angering the Gods.

I look directly at Calloway with my brows scrunched in maddening determination. "Tell the water wielders to get to the side of the ship and start pushing the waves away from us," I say through gritted teeth. We don't need the sea to swallow us whole, breaking the ship and dragging us all down into its hidden depths.

Calloway gives a firm nod right as a crew member approaches me. My annoyance is instantly provoked by his disturbance. The gall of him approaching his king and not requesting my presence first is unacceptable. "My King, if I may speak." The male takes his hat off and holds it against his chest while the rain begins pelting down in heavy drops. I stare down at him with disdain, impatiently waiting for him to continue. "We've been searching for this myth—this creature made by the Gods—for years. How do we know we aren't just wasting our time, Your Grace?"

Fury flames through me, but I keep my hard gaze searing into him. I take pleasure in seeing the tremble in his hands and in the twitch in his neck as his pulse races. But the most pleasure comes from seeing the moment his eyes widen when he realizes his mistake.

I take a slow, menacing step towards him, a smirk playing on my lips as the rain drips down my skin. "What's your name?" I speak calmly, but my voice holds a flicker of danger. A trick of my own, like the calm before a storm. The crew know how heartless I can be, but they would never dare voice a word of it to the people because they'd be dead before they could finish speaking.

He hesitates, then roughly gulps, opening his mouth to speak. "I'm—"

Before he can finish speaking, I whip my blade free and slice right through his neck, cutting his head clean off. The thump of his skull hitting the floorboards gets drowned out by the vortex of wind and the hard patter of rain. His eyes are still open as his head rolls towards the port side of the ship, while the sea sways us along the raging waters. The body slumps to the ground next, spilling blood before my feet. I watch it blend into the water splashing over the rail of the ship, washing it away and spreading it over the floor before it can stain. An easy clean up.

I notice Calloway look down at the body and then slowly drag his eyes to the head that's rolling back towards us. He brings his uncaring eyes back to mine, not a flicker of shock in them. "He was a nuisance."

I tear the cloth from my pocket and clean the blood dirtying my blade before sheathing it back on my hip. My white dress tunic with gold embellishments is now stained with specks of crimson. It's tainting my image as the merciful king I work hard to be seen as, as red bleeds into the fabric.

With an irritated grunt, I walk to the edge of the ship, staring over the expanse of the rocky sea. The sky flashes in a strobe of light every so often as thunder rumbles behind the clouds. The rain continues to downpour like it's having a tantrum. I hate the sea. Always have. It's one thing to be above it, looking down. But I don't like the concept of vulnerability when I'm in the water. It's unpredictable. Too many unknowns I can't factor in, and it's way too easy for a mishap to occur and suddenly find yourself drowning at the bottom.

I trail my eyes carefully through the waters, ignoring the sting of the rain whipping through the wind. My eyes freeze. *There.* I see a glimmer of yellow shining like a beacon in the night as two golden orbs peer back at me, skimming just above the water's surface, taunting me. I yell at my crew and to Calloway to steer the ship east and prepare the chains.

The glowing eyes disappear down under, and I let out a string of curses as I rear back and grab the spear latched near the helm of the ship. My eyes cut to Calloway. "Send some of the crew in with ropes. NOW!" I command with a roar. Without another word, I take a deep breath, hating to make myself vulnerable to the sea. But my obsession with this creature is too consuming. I take off, diving into the water below with the jagged spear in my hand.

My body plummets beneath the waves as they roll and push against me, threatening to pull me into their grasp. Underneath the sea is another world entirely, but when it's storming, it turns into chaos. A chaos that almost took my life before I reached the age of puberty. Much as I despise the sea, it seems it despises me just as much, because a storm always brews when I travel, like it's punishing me for invading its territory.

All sounds are drowned out from my hearing, but being Fae, my eyes can still see through the darkened water. I glance up when more lightning flares above the surface, but it soon fades away when I force my body to swim deeper.

The burning pressure in my lungs increases with every second I hold my breath. I pause, floating in the midst of an angry sea. I jerk my head around, looking in every direction for the creature I *know* I saw.

I have to stay on alert, for even if this creature was only a myth until this moment, one warning has always been told in every story spoken amongst the people that this creature: it's deadly; a killer.

A blur darts past me, stunning me from my thoughts, and I twist around while gripping the handle of the spear tighter. My eyes frantically search in every direction, until another blur speeds past. This time, I feel a slice graze along my skin through my clothes. The sting of it radiates up my leg when it brushes against me. I glance down and see red swirling into the sea.

The saltwater seeping into my wound burns, but it all soon becomes distant as my lungs start to tighten painfully, straining. I feel about seconds away from imploding when bubbles of air escape through my lips.

My body is begging me to swim back to the surface when the blur of grey starts racing straight towards me. I kick my feet hard to push myself upward and I'm able to slam the heel of my boot into the creature's chest. It rolls backward against the waves, only for a second before it launches into another attack.

A current of water charges from behind me, slowing the creature down as it fights against a blast of power I already know is from members of my crew who dove in to help. Before the darkness around my vision can consume me and the pain in my lungs can take over, I hurtle the spear to stab through the creature's side. Not to kill it, but enough to make it stagnant and weak so I can capture it.

An ear-piercing note wails from the creature. It's not loud, but the pitch is high enough to shatter an eardrum. I immediately slam my hands over my pointed ears, but the sound quickly begins to fade as it starts sinking further into the blackened sea. I look to my crew and point at the creature that's growing faint—a silent command.

Being only seconds away from drowning, panic grips me. I use the rest of my strength to desperately kick and push my arms forward, fighting against the torrent. The need to fill my lungs with air becomes overwhelming. When I reach the surface, I break my head free and greedily inhale the air, when suddenly, a massive tidal wave slams over my head. I'm forced back underneath the sea's assault, choking on the salty water. But I manage to pop my head out of the water again when the wave settles.

My crew reach for me from over the ship, helping to heave me back over as I grapple with the rope they tossed. Hands clutch at my saturated clothes, but not roughly, as they make sure to be careful with their ruler.

I remain on all fours when I'm back on the ship, hacking up the water that made its way down my throat. But I stand up quickly, fighting against the quiver in my muscles as I do so. A king is never beneath his subjects; they are beneath *him*.

I turn my dark gaze to Captain Calloway, noting that my right-hand advisor is already looking at me. "Have them get that damn creature locked in the iron chains." I look down at my legs, my white trousers soaked in red as the pain still ripples against the cut, but I can feel the wound working to heal itself, clotting the blood and stitching my skin back together. Even with getting what I want, my anger flares, needing to seek payback for daring to harm me. I glance back up to Calloway with cruel intent filling my eyes. "Keep the creature chained, but let it drag alongside the ship." I smirk as pleasure blooms at the image, picturing the rough waves smashing it against the belly of the ship. "I'm going to go change. I don't care if it takes a few lives to get it secured and captured. That creature will be *mine*."

Calloway dips his chin in a nod. "Consider it done."

With a clench in my jaw, I head off to make myself look like the well-kept king once again.

Back at my palace, I reflect on our journey home. Once the storm cleared and the waves settled, I could hear the creature's muffled wails all the way home. I smirk at the memory as satisfaction fuels me at the successful capture of this creature—this supposed *myth*—after years of searching. Now, as I stand on my land and stare down at the sea below me, I feel more like myself again. More in control. More powerful. Just more.

The creature is chained up in a well outside, bolted to the stones at the bottom. The well contains just enough water, but not so much that it could hide deep under. According to my crew, it can breathe easily on land, yet its body will always need to return to the water or else it will start to flail, and presumably, die.

I casually approach the well, even though I'm anxious to see what it truly looks like. But I'm more anxious for what it will say. According to the myth, this all-knowing being must answer the questions of its captor.

I reach the lip of the well and bend over to look inside. I keep my face neutral, but the battered creature staring back at me is unlike anything I've seen before. A stab of pride puffs my chest that I have it in my control. Unable to escape. Unable to attack. A powerful threat subdued.

Its weathered skin is a pale grey, and those slitted, gold eyes illuminate through the shrouds of shadows cast around the bottom of the well. Its long, boney arms and legs extend to black webbed, pointed claws. Ripples of gills trail up its side, and a tail with an arrow-shaped tip curls behind its body, swishing back and forth in aggressive strokes.

Its mouth opens with a hiss, displeased with my abrupt appearance. It bares its black, razor-sharp teeth at me, most likely wishing I would come closer. But no. Now it's time to see if the myth is true. To see if it answers me without a fight.

"What are you?" I belt, my voice echoing down the depth of the well.

Its eyes glow slightly brighter, as if its power is flaring at the question, commanding him to respond. "A Masiren." Its voice prickles against my skin. The hissing words hold an undertone of power, like a hum that floods my senses, much like the sea. Except, this sensation shifts something in my mind, deep in my psyche. I can feel my body wanting to jump into the well. Wanting to inexplicably submit to my own death. My hands slam on the ledge of the well, gripping tightly. My body wars with my mind. I squeeze the ledge harder, as bits of stone crumble, falling down the well and dusting over the Masiren. I grit my teeth as I struggle to fight off this feeling, grunting with the effort to force whatever is invading my thoughts out. Gathering all my strength to fight off this unknown power, I regain control of myself.

I shake my head, hard, fighting off the crippling effect on my consciousness from its speech. I'm hesitant to ask it something else as I stare down at it with enraged curiosity.

My eyes narrow while I unbolt my sword and toss it away from me, just in case I attempt to use it against myself. I don't know what just happened, but my mind wasn't my own. I twist my head back to look at the guard standing ten feet away. "If you see me about to fall into the well, make sure I don't," I demand in a sharp tone.

He dutifully nods with concern furrowing his brows, before shifting his eyes to look warily at the well. He straightens his spine and readies himself, per my orders. With a deep inhale, I turn back to look at my newest possession. "How do I get more power to secure my legacy?" My question falls into the depths of the well, bouncing against the stone as it hits the Masiren's ears.

It cocks its head sideways with a twitch, the gold in its eyes flaring brighter once more. "You must seek the girl with silver eyes far across the sea."

Its words cement themselves in my mind, but the allure of ceasing to exist slams into me. I could jump, but that's not a sure death. Slowly, I twist my head to see the sword I threw still on the ground. My face turns into a mask of no emotion as my feet move on their own accord, walking me closer to my own death. The hum of the Masiren's voices still sings in my head, making nothing matter except dying.

I bend to swoop the sword off the ground, admiring the sharpness of the blade glinting in the light. The hilt holds promises in my hands, ones that end with my death. My palm clutches it tighter, ready to twist the sword into myself, but a boot suddenly kicks it out of my hand. An irritated growl erupts from my throat. I go to throw my body at whoever dares stop me from delivering what I crave, but a giant palm smacks against my cheek.

My head snaps to the side, and when I bring my gaze straight, my psyche comes back into focus. Calloway stands in front of me with tight lips and a crease in his forehead. "My King." He nods his head once. "Feel better?"

I should spit words of fire at him for laying a hand on me, but Calloway has always had my back. Just now, he saved me from taking my own life while my guard still stands across the way without a clue. I give a silent nod in thanks, turning to look back at the well that holds the creature of the Gods. A hiss echoes up the well, wrapping around me, taunting me.

Nothing has ever been told of the Masiren's spoken words and their effect. But it seems, in wanting help from the Masiren, one must face the curse that clings to its truths. A boiling rage bubbles to the surface from learning that aside from the original Fae created by the Gods, this creature also holds a greater power than me. My hands fist tightly to the point of pain because this is unacceptable.

I glance down at the sword I almost used on myself, now lying beside my feet. I have killed many before, but I never once thought to end my own life. Until now. I look back at the well, and it is clear to me now: to receive the Masiren's gifted answers, you must first survive its presence... or pay with your life.

I shake off the remaining prickle over my skin from its power. I fill my lungs with a deep breath and exhale it slowly. When the sensation subsides, satisfaction bubbles to the surface as a smirk lifts the corner of my lips. I got what I wanted, and the Masiren didn't succeed in its goal to harm me.

Bending over, I swoop up my sword, sheathing it back in its holder, and walk away without giving the Masiren any more acknowledgment. But its words play through my mind.

"You must seek the girl with silver eyes far across the sea."

CHAPTER THREE

Mariam

Six months later

*R*un.
Panting, lungs burning, I sprint through the forest as fast as my body will allow. I can feel the crisp, cold air going straight into my bones. The breeze's bitterness has made my body feel stiff, and my muscles strain and burn with every step I take.

I never look behind in fear of it slowing me down. I squeeze my eyes shut for only a moment to stop the tears of exhaustion threatening to spill because I can't afford my vision to become impaired. Not now.

The final light of the day filters through the trees, flashing with each one I pass. I'm praying I can survive until darkness falls upon the land, allowing me to hide in the night. Twigs and leaves crunch underfoot as I keep up my pace. My heart feels like it will pound out of my chest, and the hair on the back of my neck prickles as I feel him getting closer. The black wisps of unnatural shadows start surrounding my path, a signal to my fear, almost like a dense fog.

He's here.

Panic seizes me as I continue racing through the woods. The will to live overpowers my body that's demanding rest. I've had to stay on the move since I separated from my daughter, never being able to stop for a moment. I left the mortal lands to misguide him, to keep *him* away from her. But the lack of sleep, food, and the constant stress on my body have caught up to me. My power is only a dull spark, unless I can truly rest. *Impossible.*

I grunt and push forward, dodging branches and leaping over roots. My lungs sting from the exertion of trying to stay out of reach from the shadows that continue to creep upon me. But before I can form my next move, pain blasts me in the back of the head, and everything goes black.

CHAPTER FOUR

Lydia

Four-and-a-half Years Later

"*A*untie, can I pweaseee go outside?"

I glance through the doorway into the main room, where Emma is impatiently bouncing back and forth on the balls of her feet. Her eyebrows are raised with her mouth stretched wide in a grin across her face, practically holding her breath. Her brown, long-sleeved cotton dress is worn and stops above her ankles to show her ratty, old black boots that she refuses to get rid of. Emma's long, brunette hair is braided and messy, with loose pieces falling out and hanging in front of her face.

Seeing her in this state brings joy to my heart, the image of a child who's unapologetically herself—wild and free. I wish I could provide more for her, but all I have is the small income I earn from selling paintings of what life looks like in the Fae Lands of Deyadrum. Years ago, I was able to build this minuscule cabin in the midst of the Mortal Lands of Helestria, a section where not many wander, and where we can remain inconspicuous to the humans.

A squeal pulls me out of my thoughts as I focus back on the little girl, who is now on her knees, dramatically begging to play outside. With a roll of my eyes, I give in. "Alright, but the sun will set soon, and I want you back inside before it does. Understood?"

Emma jumps with excitement and yells back over her shoulder as she races out the door. "You got it!"

Before I can get another word in, Emma is already gone, leaving the door hanging open. Memories of Mariam disappearing in the night four-and-a-half years ago abruptly invade my thoughts, as I stare past the empty porch to the treeline outside. I wish I knew where she was or if she was alive.

An hour passes, and I step outside to where Emma is climbing in a tree, hanging upside down by one of the branches. Where most little girls want to wear pretty, clean dresses and keep their hair neat, Emma prefers to play in the dirt and be wild. I tilt my head to look towards the sky, seeing the golden globe descending, and I know Emma will be upset that it's time to come inside for the evening. I bring my hands around my mouth and yell across the yard to my untamed niece still swinging upside down, "Emma! Time to come inside!"

Emma keeps swinging as she looks at me with a pout. "But Aunt Lyd! Can I play for five more minutes?"

I huff a sigh and slightly shake my head. I need Emma to come in before it truly gets dark. "No, Emma, playtime is ov—"

Before I can finish speaking, every bird flies out of the woods at once. The herd of flapping wings and shrieks startle me and Emma as an uneasy chill creeps through the air. I dart my eyes all around while making my way towards Emma. She fell from the branch when the birds startled her, but now, Emma is slowly pushing herself up to stand and brush the dirt off her dress.

Something's not right. "Emma, I need you to go to the cabin. Right. Now." I keep my voice low.

Emma snaps her head up to look at me, taking in my expression and absorbing the severity of my voice. She frantically starts shaking her head. "Not without you. I'm scared."

Reaching out and grabbing hold of Emma, I pull her into a tight hug and kiss the top of her head, breathing in her rose and honey scent mixed with a hint of earthiness from playing outside. Taking a steady breath, I kneel down on my knees so I can be eye level with her. "I love you, you know that, right? But I *really* need you to listen right now. Remember our safe plan I told you about?" When Emma silently nods, I continue. "Well, I need you to do that now, okay? Go to the cabin. I will be right behind you. I need you to stay safe, okay? Promise me, sweetie."

Not a question, but a demand.

Emma's eyes begin to fill with tears as she nods. She throws herself back in my arms for another hug, whispering in my ear, "I prowmise. I love you, Aunt Lyd." Then, she takes off to the cabin.

I watch her race across the yard, and as soon as she's inside, I spin around to search through the trees. I clench my hands in tight fists, readying myself for whatever might be out there. The woods are unnaturally quiet, but that works to my advantage. I hear the whistle of an arrow flying towards me before I see it and lunge out of the way.

The arrow must have been the signal to forge ahead because a dozen assailants step out from the shadows, where they were hiding. I curse to myself and sprint to grab the arrow that is now stuck in a tree and yank it free. A makeshift weapon for defense will have to do. This would be the one moment where I regret living in Helestria. Having use of my powers would be beneficial right now, a fast and sure way to take down each threat. With or without power, I don't have a choice; I must protect Emma.

I forgo running to deter them, because it won't make a difference. There are a dozen of them, and they would easily catch me. But more importantly, my back would be left vulnerable to them. Instead, I sprint towards the closest attacker, the one who aimed his arrow at me from the looks of it. I see his ears are pointed and my hackles immediately rise. *Fae.* If they traveled this far, they won't stop for anything.

I dig my feet in the undergrowth with every step as I force my body to move faster. The male raises his bow again, but when I'm a couple of feet away, I twist away from his shot, spinning my body to curve into him, and drive the arrow into his neck. A choking sound gurgles from his mouth when he drops. I don't waste a second to applaud myself; I don't have time. I rip the arrow from his jugular and face the rest of the Fae blending into the dark of night after the sun's quick descent. They begin running towards me, but then, I hear something snap from behind.

More Fae. How the hell did I not notice them? I'm surrounded now, and so is the cabin. My fear and anger combine as I tighten my grip on the smooth wood of the arrow, pressing the pad of my thumb hard into its stem. I raise my arm back, readying to throw it in hopes of getting one last, final shot, but an arrow knocks into my shoulder, momentarily stunting me. I go to lift my uninjured arm with the arrow still in hand, but another arrow strikes my thigh. I can't contain the scream that tears out of my throat, and the arrow in my hand falls limply before my feet.

A third arrow pierces my other leg before I can steady myself, and I crumple to the ground. My knees slam on the wet forest floor, seeping into the material of my pants. Once I calm my breathing down, I look up. All the silent attackers have stopped progressing and now stand around me in a wall of armor, and that's when I notice the emblem etched into their uniform. They are the King of Asov's notorious soldiers.

Footsteps sound a few feet away, and I turn my head slightly as my pulse thumps rapidly. The pain becomes more unbearable, mixed with the fear of the male before me: King Oren, the ruler of the Court of Asov.

He watches me with amused eyes but still keeps the hard gleam within them. "Well, aren't you clever? All these years, you've been hiding across the sea… Hiding her! Living amongst the mortal filth." His amusement slips for a second as his voice rises, bellowing through the trees. I remain silent, refusing to give him anything.

King Oren chuckles softly. I can tell his anger is reined in as a devious smirk creeps onto his face. "No need for conversation, I suppose. I already know she's here. I've spent four-and-a-half years searching for the girl with silver eyes across the sea. None of the girls I found before had grey eyes or any right to my legacy. But imagine my surprise when I spy a pointed-eared female buying bread in one of the mortal shops. That was you, no?" He laughs again to himself before he continues. "No need to answer that;

we both know it was. I know she's here. My soldiers spotted her just this morning, when I had them surrounding your home. She will be coming with me."

My eyes widen, and I try to push aside the pain spearing through me to stand up and fight. But I've lost so much blood already. My body is slowly weakening, and my consciousness is dwindling to the faintest glow. Intense burning gradually spreads from each arrow, making me fall back to the ground. *Iron*. The damn arrows are made of iron. Fae are virtually indestructible because, while iron won't kill Fae unless it's a critical hit, it will weaken them, slowing down the process of their quick healing. But it's excruciating, as the contact of iron itself feels like being lit on fire.

As I turn on my side to ease the pain, a heavy boot presses down on me. I slowly drag my eyes up to see the king's dark brown orbs glaring down at me.

His face holds no emotion, yet his stare slices through me. "I'm a king who always gets what he wants. And do you know what happens to those who stand in the way of that?" He pauses for a moment, and I get the feeling he doesn't care if I respond. "They cease to exist."

All I can think about is Emma and how I hope that she won't be found. I wish I could have protected her better. I think of all the memories we created since Mariam put her in my arms, as the sword in King Oren's hands comes for me, piercing straight through my beating heart.

CHAPTER FIVE

Emma

My body shakes as I stare out of the cabin window. I know I should be hiding, but I don't want to leave Aunt Lyd. She told me I must hide, but I'm scared. Aunt Lyd never looked so frightened, and her voice was shaky. She's a mom to me and I can't lose another. Auntie told me that my birth mom had died every time I asked about her. So, I have no one but her left.

I recoil behind the curtain when I see Aunt Lyd dodge an arrow. My heart falters and I slap a hand over my mouth. She's strong, my Aunt Lyd. She will fight them off. I know she will, just like I know I must hide. I want to help fight, to protect her, but I know that Auntie would be upset with me if I don't listen.

Running to the kitchen, I grab the knife strapped under the table for emergencies. I follow the plan Auntie taught me that I know by heart. I then race to the small closet in the hallway. The door squeaks slightly as I pull it open, sliding my fingers along the seam in the floor. Lifting the one panel, I continue with the next two. Underneath is a makeshift hiding spot Aunt Lyd created, and it has just enough room for my body to fit if I keep my legs folded to my chest. Clutching the knife, I tuck myself in and replace the floorboards after closing the closet door. Now I sit, waiting for Auntie to come for me.

The shouts and sounds outside stop, leaving silence. I can only hear my heart pounding, the rapid beating magnifying in my ears. I squeeze my fingers tighter against the smooth, wooden handle of the knife, holding it with both hands and pressing it closer to my chest.

The sound of boots grows louder, and the faint voices through the walls let me know it's not Aunt Lyd in the cabin. I suck in a breath, too scared to breathe. The pounding sound in my ears grows louder.

The closet door squeaks, and slivers of light seep through the cracks in the floor. My whole body freezes. Every muscle in me becomes tense as I hold my breath and squeeze my eyes shut, wishing for them all to go away.

A low, bristly voice cuts through my thoughts. "She's here."

The floorboards are ripped off before I can feel the goosebumps that course down my arms. I stare widely at the male towering above me. His big, brown eyes soften when they land on mine, and his voice is scratchy, but deep. "There you are, Princess. No need to be frightened. I'm here to bring you home."

My head begins shaking profusely, not understanding what this older male is telling me. How can I trust him? Where is Aunt Lyd? I thought this was my home.

His calloused hand reaches down, and I just stare at it. "You're safe now. The raiders who tried to find you are gone. I took care of them."

My thoughts keep shifting to Aunt Lyd and what happened to her, hoping she escaped. I'm trapped. I've been found, and I have nowhere to go but with him.

The male begins speaking again. "Princess, I won't hurt you. I'm your father."

I freeze. Auntie has never once talked about my father or said if he was dead or alive. But this male is saying that he is. My eyes turn frantic as they roam over his face before landing on his ears: pointed, just like mine.

I slide my eyes back to his in disbelief. My grip loosens on the knife as I keep my focus on him, hoping. Not knowing which is truth or lie, I hesitantly take his hand, unsure of what my future holds.

PART II

CHAPTER SIX

Emma

Nineteen Years Later

ear licks down my spine as my body and psyche protest in warning. I'm trapped. The pounding of my heart echoes in my ears, a war drum preparing for battle. Shadows swirl around my body, caressing every inch of my skin until they bind me so tightly it's hard to breathe. I try to search my surroundings, but all that's around me is darkness. I can hear the whispers of the shadows as their freezing touch crawls against my skin, making my jaw shake and teeth chatter.

The panic is setting in as I begin to scream, my lungs burning from the drop in temperature, but it's useless. My screams only echo back to me. I squeeze my eyes shut in hopes to make this all go away. But then, the whispering stops. A deep, gravelly voice invades my mind, and I can feel a phantom touch of a hand gripping my neck.

"Emma…"

Every muscle in my body tenses as I suck in a sharp breath just before the grip on my throat tightens, cutting off more of my airway. Suffocating me. Stars dance before my vision, and I try to shove down the panic working its way up my throat. The bruising pain is almost welcoming from the shadow's icy embrace that is turning my body numb. I attempt to take a deep breath but only manage a small gulp of air as his voice rattles against my bones.

"Oh, Emma…the fear I sense from you pleases me. The sight of you struggling to fill your lungs, the blue tint to your lips… Remember this feeling, Emma, because I'm on the hunt for you, and I always find my prey." *The male's deep voice reverberates around me. Then, he chuckles softly, almost like he finds this amusing.*

I shoot forward, gasping for air, my hands automatically holding my neck and resting against my heart in hopes of calming down my frantic pulse. I glance up and notice I'm in my room, the golden globe just waking up in the distance, casting a soft glow throughout and reflecting sparkles of light on the walls from the crystal chandelier hanging on the vaulted ceiling. The sheer curtains sway from the breeze drifting through the cracked balcony doors. My bedroom looks so peaceful with the soft creams and rose color scheme decorating each piece of furniture, the complete opposite of how I feel inside. Dark. Cold.

A nightmare. I've had bad dreams before but this one was different. Usually, my nightmares are just flashes of painful memories from my past and nothing more. Never have I heard a male's voice so clearly or felt a touch that seemed so real. My hands are still clinging to my neck as I look at the disaster of my bed. The plush comforter is all balled up around my feet, my feathered pillows are thrown about, while my nightgown is twisted, and I can feel the cool brush of air along my damp, sweaty skin.

Once my heart thrums at a steady beat, I dive off my bed and sprint into the attached bath. I grip hold of the sink as I nervously force my eyes to see my reflection in the mirror. Not even the sounds of the birds singing their morning tune can calm me down. My big, grey eyes are wide with fear from the lingering assault of my nightmare. My soft brown hair is tangled and looks like I waged war against my bedding. Dark crescent shadows stand out under my eyes against my fair skin. Then, my eyes begin to trail down past my nose and lips to land on my neck.

Holy shit.

Faint black marks paint my neck, spread around the choker necklace my father gave me. *How is this possible?* It was only a nightmare, right?

Running my fingertips a hair's breadth away from the inky mark that looks like a stain, I close the distance and lightly stroke it. I suck in a breath. *It's cold.* A moment later, the nightmare's evidence begins to fade, any proof of its existence gone. None of this makes sense, but I do know that sleep will be hopeless for me when night falls again.

I strip out of my silk nightgown and turn on the hot water for a bath. The white stone floor is cold against my bare feet and the steam starts to billow around me. Shifting to grab an ivory towel out of the bin, I jerk back… Frozen in a trance, my jaw clenches while I stare at the ruined girl before me. The full-length mirror exposes every part of me—the parts I let no one see. It's easy to fool the people around me, allowing them to see only what I choose to show. They may see beauty and grace, but underneath is damaged and bitter. Eleven years ago is when my soul started suffering and a poison began to seep into my veins and feast on my heart. When my life turned into its own version of a nightmare I can't seem to escape, and at the hands of the one sworn to protect me.

My eyes travel over every inch of scarred skin, skin that is supposed to be smooth like porcelain. No. My scars are anything but smooth; they are gnarled and mocking. I twist my torso to take a glance at my back, where the worst of my scarring lives, and tears threaten to spill. But I refuse to let them fall. Biting my lip hard enough to draw blood, I take in the grotesque girl before me. No male will ever want to touch me in the way I've seen lovers do. Any guy would be disgusted by one look at my back, to the slashes across my ribs and the ones on my thighs. Father made sure these healed without a healer so that I always have a reminder of what happens when I step out of line. The only markings on my skin that I feel a gut-wrenching tidal wave from are the clean lines along my wrists.

To this day, I still wonder if that was my weakest moment for wanting to escape or my strongest for trying to put an end to my torment by forcing my father's hand. Maybe one day I will figure out the answer. But until then, I will have to accept that it was fate that the kitchen staff found me when they brought food to my room after I didn't show for dinner. I was lying in a pool of crimson, almost on the brink of death, before the healer rushed in and flooded my body with her warm power. My body should be able to heal itself within moments, but my father gifted me an iron necklace that is permanently welded around my neck. The damn thing suppresses my Fae powers and the ability to heal.

He gifted it to me when the light power I was born with began growing stronger. One day, when I was walking through the corridors, a servant and I collided around the corner. The collision startled me, causing a flare of power to jolt free and hit one of the pillars, leaving a chunk missing from the side of it.

The destruction to my father's palace infuriated him, making his eyes flame red before he pulled me into an illusion, one he created just for me. A whole separate void in the world to punish me in. Except, this time, he chained me to the posts, only to bind me with this Gods damn necklace. It was sealed on me that day, its iron grip a permanent reminder of being both powerful and powerless. Turning me into a prisoner and making my mind a hell within my own body.

My father says it's to keep me safe from any more accidental slips of power, that it will hide my power signature from anyone trying to hurt me. And yet…it doesn't keep me safe from him. This *gift* of his is unforgivable.

Well, fuck him. Fuck this palace and fuck this goddamn leash.

I remove my eyes from the necklace and push all thoughts of it aside as I step into the bath. The heated water feels soothing against my bruised skin and the aches that came with it. I soak in the tub way beyond the point of wrinkly fingers. No doubt Father will be upset with my late arrival to breakfast, but lately, I'd rather deal with his wrath than please him.

After drying off every drop of moisture, I walk into my closet that he demands stay stocked full of dresses. And not just any type of dress. They all are coincidentally full-coverage, floor-length dresses. They go up to my neck with sleeves to cover the whole length of both arms. I choose a black satin dress, if only to go against my father even more. Everyone dresses in light shades of color at this court, but my soul resonates with the dark, calling to it because it wants to dance with the night. The sleeves flow loosely on my arms, the bodice is snug, and the skirt hangs softly, giving my legs a feather-light caress.

I let my hair dry in loose waves as I slip on a pair of ballet slippers because they allow me the chance to run, if need be, compared to the horrendous, ankle-breaking heels most wear. Yet, mine are collecting a thick layer of dust in my closet. I walk across my room and step out onto the balcony. The gentle breeze swirls around me and through my hair. I look up to see the puffy, white plumes blanketing the sky, giving off a calming peace throughout the sea beyond me. My father's kingdom, the Court of Asov, is the southern-most and warmest island in all of the courts of Deyadrum. The dancing waves span as far as my eyes can see; the salty sea air washes over me, with a lingering sweet aroma from the waves crashing against the shore. The beauty of the world beyond and the purity of nature are the only things that lift the darkness from my soul.

Three quick, light knocks tap on my door and intrude on my few moments of isolated tranquility. I'm disappointed by the interruption, even though I know it's only Cora, the one Fae my father assigned to assist me, who is also a healer in training in the palace. But most importantly, she's my friend. She taps the same way every time, so I will always know it's her behind the door.

"Come in!" I yell across the room from the balcony.

The door creaks open as I turn towards her. She looks beautiful, as always. Her light, sun-kissed hair is in a loose bun, with a few strands hanging to frame her face. Her ocean-blue eyes shine brightly as happiness pours from her. She's about the same age as me and only stands an inch shorter than my average height. She's wearing her cream-colored, cotton dress with pockets sewn into the sides, which she claims every dress should have.

Her slippered feet pad softly towards me on the balcony before she closes her eyes to inhale the fresh sea air for a moment. When she opens her eyes again, I see the brief sense of peace is gone. She looks like she hates what she's about to tell me. "Your father has requested your presence in his study instead of meeting for breakfast."

I can't stop my eyes from rolling, even though fear begins to creep into the back of my mind.

Before I can respond, Cora continues, "He said to come at once. That what he needs to discuss is urgent and a very important matter." A somber expression clouds her face when she is usually the light to my dark.

I stare at her as my jaw clenches, giving her a silent nod. When my nerves settle, I try to sound like the princess everyone expects to see. "Very well. We shouldn't keep him waiting, then."

She leads me out into the wide hallway filled with sunlight from the open windows beyond. The floor is smooth and has seashells embedded within it. It truly is beautiful, but beauty can be deceitful; I know evil lurks here. It is an illusion of light to mask the monstrous king within these walls.

When we reach the end of the hallway, we turn left and cross over the central, open area on the second floor that looks over the entryway at the front of the palace. We hurry past and continue to the other side that leads to my father's wing, the side where screams are silenced.

The guard outside my father's study dips his head in greeting and reaches to open the heavy, white-clad, double doors in front of me. Before I head in, Cora takes hold of my hand and gives it a quick squeeze, a way of her reassuring me that she will be here after. Filling my lungs with as much air as I can muster, I make my way through the opening of the doors as I approach the King of Asov, who is sitting regally behind his massive stone desk. I keep my shoulders pulled back and chin high as I stop a few feet before him, waiting in tense silence for him to acknowledge my presence. I clasp my hands in front of me. The perfect image of a perfect princess.

Minutes pass before he lifts his head, and his deep eyes spike right into me. Stabbing into my soul, only to pull free and leave me slowly bleeding to death. His lips curve upward, as if he's pleased I'm here—a rare reaction that unsettles me. My stomach starts churning inside, making me grateful I did not eat breakfast yet.

He leans back in his chair as he assesses my dress, his brows furrowing at the choice of color. His nostrils flare from aggravation. Yet...he's holding back. Why? As my thoughts tumble over his odd behavior, his voice vibrates throughout the room: "My dear Emma, how lovely for you to come to my study in such a timely manner."

I keep my voice steady and quiet, hoping to not show an ounce of fear. "You said it was urgent."

My father heaves a long sigh and stands up. His all-white tunic with gold embellishments glistens from the golden rays shining inside. His light brown hair is slicked back, with thin streaks of silver creeping up the side on full display, making him look more kingly. His power weighs heavily between us as he lets it stretch out, a weight trying to crush me down as it prickles over my skin. Both a threat and a warning to behave.

"Yes, you're right. It's news I'm sure you will be happy to hear. I have come to an agreement with Captain Calloway for you to be betrothed to his son."

The sinking feeling in my stomach intensifies as my father becomes blurry in front of me. I must have misheard him. I shake my head in hopes of clearing it, and reach deep down to find my voice, hoping it doesn't waver. "Is this some kind of joke?"

He tips his head back as he bellows a laugh, acting like I was the one who made the joke. "My dear, I would never joke about such things. You are past the age when you should be getting married. Captain Calloway is my right-hand advisor, and his son is your closest friend. This is a great alliance for the two of you and will secure our lifelong friendship. I thought you would be happy."

I can't find the right words to express my feelings, but I know *happiness* is not it.

Captain Calloway is the one who leads the fleet of ships when my father needs to travel, but he's always despised me. He is a cruel man, and his eyes are like daggers, always piercing into me like I'm a piece of rotten meat he wants to toss overboard to the sharks. But his son, Aiden, is my friend, mostly because I grew up around him and have never been allowed to leave the palace. I do like Aiden, but I was hoping to find love—the kind of love I read about in the books hidden away in the darkest corner of the library. A hot, dangerous, all-consuming love that ignites your soul. A mate.

I've read about mates in some of the books in the library, how it's like two halves coming together, making the other whole. My father never talked much about my mother, and I learned not to ask. But with how little he wishes to reminisce about her with me, I doubt they were true mates. Cora has told me more about fated pairs, and it's a love worth waiting for. Worth sacrificing for.

My father raises his voice as he quickly alerts the guard outside to open the doors. Right on cue, Captain Calloway and Aiden strut into the study and stand on either side of me, caging me in. Their presence invades my space, absorbing all the oxygen my body so desperately needs in this moment.

Captain Calloway bows deeply as he greets my father. "I assume you have told the princess the great news? My son and I are quite ecstatic."

Aiden's feet shift next to me as he clears his throat. "Yes, I'm thrilled to wed Emma. I promise to take excellent care of her."

My father huffs a small laugh. "I do not doubt that. You're a good guy, Aiden."

Captain Calloway reaches around to slap Aiden on the back, causing uneasy chills to erupt down my spine as his arm bumps against me. "That's my boy. You have no worries with him. He will make sure Emma stays in line and keep her close."

Aiden bristles beside me, and I can see his spine straighten and his muscles tense. He seems just as uncomfortable as I am. My whole body flares to life as these thoughts create chaos in my mind. I feel Aiden's arm brush against mine, but I refuse to look at him; he may be my friend, but this is not a decision I chose to make. This is just another way for my father to use his control over me and keep me within these walls. Another chain to add to my already collared neck. I can't help the immense frustration that's taking hold of me. It's not Aiden's fault, but surely, he understands my growing temper.

Deep down, I feel an ember inside of me spark, the power inside wanting to spread and incinerate everything near. Anger coils around every cell in my body, screaming to be set free. I hear their gasps as I feel my power of light surge against my father's restraints; the necklace starts to sting around my neck as my power slams against it. They must feel the weight of my power as I become frantic in reining it in. The depths of it vibrate underneath my skin. Demanding. Wanting to answer my call for revenge. It's too much.

My head's thrown back from the force of it. Burning light turns blinding behind my eyelids. Like needles sliding through my veins, pain ripples through me as my power is forcefully shoved back down, with no way for it to release itself but back within.

The iron collar that has my neck in a chokehold turns into a ring of fire and begins burning my skin—the punishment for not keeping my power under control. Screaming inside as the smell of singed flesh wafts up my nose, I refuse to give my father the pleasure of hearing me shriek in pain. He will use it as a reason to dole out more punishment, or worse. For I have learned to silence my screams, but that just gives my father another challenge.

Crack. The throbbing in my knees registers before I realize my legs have given out, and the hard surface becomes my focal point for drawing in my power. I bend over with my hands bracing against the cold floor to force it away completely while closing my mind off to all this agony.

My breathing is ragged and shaky when the collar begins to cool and the power inside of me starts to flicker out. I can feel their stares on me without looking; I assume I just put on an entertaining show. A puppet performing for its master.

On wobbly legs, I rise back up, keeping my fists clenched in hopes of locking my rage in. Aiden's brows are turned in, worry shining from his eyes. His hand lifts like he's going to comfort me, and then pauses mid-air, only to flex his fingers and let it fall back to his side. Captain Calloway stares at me with a cold expression, one that I am sure many have seen before they died by his hand. Then, there's my father, King Oren; his lips quirked up on one side, arms crossed in front of his chest, eyes gleaming… He enjoys my suffering; this pleases him greatly.

CHAPTER SEVEN

Emma

I race back to my room as fast as my legs will carry me, with the skirt of my dress wrapping around my legs with every step. I couldn't care less about the servants' looks as I rush past them. Princesses should never run.

The walls in my father's office began closing in on me, consuming all the air. The room hung in a suffocating silence; its pressure constricting my lungs. And I had to leave. I had to get out of there.

I have to get out of this palace.

I should be thankful he didn't unleash his power on me before I could leave. A power that makes his eyes sear red and suck me into a void of his own making. An illusionist.

A shudder rolls through my body at the thought of how he uses his power. My fists clench tighter in my skirt as I pick up the pace to get farther away from him. The slippers I'm wearing keep my feet quiet as I hurry to my room, the only sound is the thumping of my heart echoing in my ears as I round the final corner and slam into my door, only to see Cora staring at me down the hall.

She takes a step forward, "Emma, wha—"

My eyes widen as I shake my head and hold my trembling hand out. I can't find the words to speak yet, whether from the shock, anger, or another feeling that I'm not able to place. Cora seems to understand I need time alone instead of comfort. She smiles softly at me with a small nod, turning back around to walk the other way. She knows that I will eventually talk to her about everything. She and Aiden are the only two friends I have in this castle, aside from my most loyal guard, Kye. But Aiden won't be a friend to me anymore... No, now he's my *betrothed*. The word crawls beneath my skin and turns my stomach in a sickening way.

I shove my door open and slam it shut, leaning my back against it as my chest moves up and down rapidly. Turning, I plant my hands flat against the slick wooden frame, letting my head hang forward as I center my focus on steadying my breaths.

It's better to spark the smallest ember than to curse the darkness. The saying my Aunt Lyd used to tell me whenever we faced hard times, stuck with me— always bringing a sense of calm with it. I can only remember bits and pieces of her, but that one is a memory I latched on to.

I remember her telling me one night that darkness is always broken by the light... But she must not have realized that there can be no light without the dark. A friend that listens, lives in your soul, and will never leave. But if you're not careful, that darkness can become your own damnation.

There was never any hope for me, I was always meant to have a darkened soul. I had no mother to speak of—my aunt had told me she'd died. And only foggy memories of Aunt Lydia, who I know loved me as her own, but that life feels long forgotten now, with no family to love me every single day. Fate cursed me from the moment I was born. My father is all I have, but he's the reason my soul has splintered and lost its light. You might as well bury me alive, drain my blood, and send me to hell.

Once the room stops spinning, my breathing working at a lazy pace, I make my way to my bed. I lift the feathered pillow to grab my worn paperback. I trail my fingers over the cover before fanning the pages in front of my face because I love the smell of them, the coarse caress of it against my fingertips, a cherished world which could never be mine. A world where I could be free, maybe even loved.

But what would love even feel like? I've seen only the males who have come to visit my father, almost accidentally stumbling into their presence before I hid behind the nearest wall, allowing myself to take a glance before my father locks me away in my room. Some were handsome, but none made my breath stall in my lungs or made my heart beat faster.

I wonder how it would be to feel a male's touch be pleasant instead of brutal. To be accepted instead of tossed aside with disgust at my body. Someone who will see my scars as a sign of strength rather than a deformity of my being.

I secure the worn paperback—one of my most cherished romance books—under my arm. It's a lighthearted love story of a couple meeting at sea, two fates crashing together in a chance of impossibility. But the girl in the book is lonely in a way I can relate to, and I feel like I'm visiting an old friend every time I read it.

With my book in tow, I leave my room and scurry down the hall to the side door. I'm not concerned with Cora coming back; she knows I need time and will find her when I'm ready. Quickening my pace down the back spiral staircase, I hear the patter of my slippers echoing against the stone in the otherwise silent stairwell. I let my hand graze against the polished handle, until I reach the door at the bottom, pushing it open to exit out the servant's entrance. For a moment, I'm taken aback as I step outside, letting my feet sink into the warm sand while the bright light layers everything with a golden glow. My skin soaks in the warmth of the sun and the weight pressing against my chest dissipates as I devour the details of the endless sea before me.

Glistening diamonds blanket the water as it laps against the shore, the crystal blue tides cresting into mini plumes of white. Further down, towards the large rocks bordering the shore, the water soars through the air as it crashes against the boulders before retreating back, pounding repeatedly, as if it's sensing my frustration from earlier. In the distance, birds dance with the wind as they glide through the air under the sun, singing their sweet lullaby.

Subtle drops of moisture trail down my back as my black dress absorbs all of the heat. Sliding out of my slippers, I let my bare feet sink into the sand. I inhale deeply to take in the sea air, leaving footprints behind. A sensual thrill runs through the soles of my feet as I walk across the light specks of powder—the only gentle feeling I know. The grains of sand start to mix with minuscule rocks that dig into my skin.

Clutching the book tighter, I continue on. Each footstep crunches underneath me as I make my way to my secluded spot, where I go to feel a semblance of escape. A place I can call my own, and where my father never dares venture. I'm thankful I don't have a bodyguard hounding me every moment of every day, besides at night, when a guard is posted outside my door. Watching me. And preventing me from escaping in the dark of night. Unless we have guests, or if my father is angry with me, then he will have guards watching me like a hawk. But those days, I stay in my room, refusing to be monitored like a child.

I follow along the sea's border; the line separating my confinement from my freedom. I let the water cascade over the top of my feet as I make my way towards the chaos pummeling against the perimeter of the cave. The weathered rocks wrap around to the front of the cave, blocking any view of the palace, leaving only the expanse of the sea before me.

I reach the end of the shore where it meets the cave, taking one balanced step at a time, and making careful work along the slick rocks. Gripping a jagged boulder resting on the side, I duck as I reach the cave's entrance and take one small leap to the hard, smooth surface. Inhaling the serenity of the space, I head towards the back that's only a short distance, leaving wet footprints in my wake. The best part is that the water seems to be tamed by the presence of the cave, almost like the darkness scattered within is daring the sea not to upset its essence.

I slide down the cool stone, bending my knees to my chest, letting my dress fall around me in a pool of ebony. Opening my book to the folded corner, soft light streams through from the cave's opening, just enough to see the words on the page. I stare at the inked letters, but my thoughts venture elsewhere, back to distant memories of a past I can't fully remember. Brief images flash through my psyche of Aunt Lydia and her shiny, amber hair that always looked so ethereal in the wind. The way her laugh

49

was contagious as she would chase me around the yard, her hazel eyes full of light. But her laugh sounds like a distant dream. Now, only screams, darkness, and the echoing of my own heart remain. I should be scared of the dark, but instead, I find comfort in it—blanketing myself in its obsidian embrace, much like this cave. Welcoming the hum of its desire. I was warned away from it by Aunt Lyd—to never accept its promises. But it is a curse that calls to me, tempts me, and haunts me.

I drift my gaze out towards the cave's mouth, getting lost in the distant sea, and wonder what life exists beyond this island. My father ventures to the other three islands of Deyadrum from time to time, but of course, it's *too dangerous* for me. When will he realize the real danger to me is him? I would give anything to journey beyond these waters to see what exists in the other courts. A glimpse of freedom is yet another kernel of wishful thinking that will never be.

I've read some of the worn history books that sit on the shelves in the library to absorb the knowledge of the world, of Deyadrum, and the courts that live in the distance. Apparently, there are four courts that float in the sea of Deyadrum, and the ancient map inked in the middle of the book showed them forming the points of a diamond. The courts are called Asov, Amihan, Asiza, and Abhainn. The Court of Asov in the South is my father's. The beautiful island with its endless sand, lush palms that sprout along the water, white gulls that dance through the wind, and an ivory palace with light gold accents. A serene island in all its beauty, and the perfect mask to hide the hideous beast that lives within.

The scrawl that danced along on the copper pages told of the Court of Amihan in the North covered in high peaks of white-capped mountains, with pale specks that fall from the dusty clouds, veiling the island in a glacial frost. The Court of Asiza in the East is shrouded in grey mist that lies below the evergreens—a primordial forest told of dense shadows that worship the ray-less gloom instead of the light. Then, the Court of Abhainn in the West is said to have gentle, grassy green slopes that roam for miles, and a glittering river full of unknowns that twists and turns throughout, with songs that are sung along the wind.

But the history books were left vacant of the words spoken in hushed voices throughout the halls spreading myths. Stories of balls, where Fae dance until dawn is on the horizon, how every hour that passes blends together as one. Tales of secrets that are hidden throughout fog-covered forests, caves tucked in the mountains, and murderous creatures that swim in the sparkling river. But those whispering mouths also murmured about a fifth court…the Court of Ashes. They spoke of a land crawling with sins and lost souls.

I wonder if my father cares about the evil spoken of in this fifth court, or if it's just gossip being spread amongst the people. My teeth start grinding together at the mere thought of my *father*. If only people knew the devil that lurks inside him, the one that relishes in demonic torment. Horrid flashbacks suck me back in time: the slash of pain whipping across my back, the slice of skin pooling red across my thighs, and the harsh crack that sounds from the head of his gilded sword slamming into my side. But worst of all…the box. My own personal casket above the surface. When he locks me inside for days, leaving me shrouded in pitch black and curled up on the frigid, damp floor, until my wounds heal on their own. A way for my father to feed his wicked intent, by letting me rot in my own filth, all to tighten my leash and correct my shameful behavior.

Maddening thoughts start to fester deep inside as each pain-inflicted memory is displayed behind my eyes and my blood heats at the thought of revenge; addicted to its luring song. Fisting my hands tightly, I welcome the minor sting from my nails digging into my palms, bringing my mind back to the present as they leave behind crescent-shaped marks. The rage within coils into something impenetrable, a deep-seated root that has been growing with every passing day.

A chill burrows deep in my soul, nudging against my beating heart and against the shielded walls I've built around my mind. It sings to me like a siren does to its prey. Beckoning. Pleading to be let in.

Maybe if I give in to the darkness, just a little bit, only for a second…

Slightly dropping my barrier, it feels like a rush of icy tendrils streaming through me, brushing against my heart, seeping into my veins. A decadent drug cooling my boiling blood from this immense anger. A sigh leaves my lips as I let the darkness weave through my body.

So cold.

The anger dissipates, falling away to nothing as indifference settles in my bones. A hunger to take what I want, an unholy thirst for power. Eliminating all warring emotions, only to be consumed by vengeance.

So *damn* cold.

Prickles of needles stab along my fingers as I raise my hand in front of my face and gasp. Black. Twisting my hand around, I can't seem to understand what's happening. Like lines from a feather pen, injecting my skin with ink as it becomes frozen to the touch. Sharp splinters of ice track through my veins, darkening my blood to oil. Snaking down my arms, stealing my breath from the fierce chill of it. My mind is screaming at me to slam my wall up. Instead, a heady laugh spills from my lips. It sounds deranged even to my own ears.

"Emma?"

Everything halts to a stop with the familiar voice. My consciousness breaks through the vengeful haze and I blast my walls back up. My breathing is rough as I struggle to catch my breath, eyes wide and staring at the opening of the cave, working to gulp down more air. A quick glance at my hands brings me relief, where the black veins have completely receded. A million questions drift through my mind. Why didn't my necklace react, and why is this darkness coming to life within me? Does it relate to the phantom who invaded my dreams, unlocking this part of me? I don't have time to dig deeper into my thoughts as I prepare for company.

Crunching steps and the scraping of boots draw my attention forward again.

From the sound of his voice, this can only be one person.

Sandy hair peeks around the cave's curved edge as Aiden takes a final jump inside. The breeze drifts a scent that is only him, a tinge of leather and whatever soap he uses that reminds me of fresh rain falling from the sky. A combination I have become familiar with over the years. Strands of light hair fall in front of his eyes, and there's a dazzling smile stretching across his face, shining through the dim cave.

I anticipate for him to saunter over to me, but instead, his body blurs before vanishing, only to appear next to me. Aiden is a high Fae and his power allows him to teleport short distances. My eyes naturally trail down his lean form, taking in the brown training leathers he must have changed into after the meeting with my father, with his sword strapped across his chest. He must be planning to practice some of his combat training soon.

My gaze works its way back up his body, trying to see him in a *romantic* way.

Not just as a friend.

I can't deny that he's handsome, with shaggy hair that falls perfectly without him having to do a thing, and eyes the color of deep green sea glass—a shade so serene that it has always brought me comfort. A smooth jaw, toned muscles straining against his leathers, and rosy lips that look feather soft. Our eyes connect, and his briefly darken when he notices me watching him. My cheeks flush in embarrassment from being caught and how he's looking at me in a way he never has before.

He drops himself beside me, nudging my shoulder with his and unhooking his sword to lay it down beside him. "Hey." One simple word and somehow all my anger towards him rushes back out into the sea, being dragged beneath with the waves. "Sneak another romance book out here?" He teases, breaking the ice with his easy-going nature and smooth voice—a sound that wraps around me in a familiar embrace. I can't help the smile that forms and the soft laugh that tumbles past my lips.

"Ha-Ha. How did you know?" I ask sarcastically.

His smile widens further, and he answers me anyway, leaning closer like he's going to tell me his deepest, darkest secret. "Because I know you." His breath is warm as it rustles the small hairs by my ear.

Almost. If only he knew everything, would he be disgusted?

Only a handful of people know about the soul-sucking ring sealed around my neck, and Aiden's one of them. *Especially* after my little scene earlier this morning. But no one knows about my father's cruelty towards me. His threats alone are what steal my voice. And there's nothing anyone can or *would* do when it comes to going against my father.

And why would they? There is nothing special about me for someone to risk their lives in going against my father. I am already too far damaged, way past the point of being worthy of protection. Plus, I don't see how anyone would be able to stop him.

Most of the people of Asov just assume I have no power. A weak, *pathetic* princess. Mostly because I have no way to prove otherwise; I've been secluded within these walls for as long as I can remember.

The small smile on my face falters for a second as I take in the way his eyes are trying to tell me something deeper. Like the emotions are warring inside him, battling with words not spoken.

"Aiden—"

"Don't." His eyes close as he inhales deeply, fighting to keep a sense of control. "I know this is not what you want. That *I* am not what you want. But…am I so bad?" The gentleness of those last words cracks something in my chest. The sun filters in through the cave in splintered rays, reflecting into his eyes as they sear into me. Like twin emerald gems glistening.

Shaking my head, I huff a breath. "We're *friends,* Aiden. But you know it's more than that. I want to find love, not be *forced* into it."

My heart suddenly feels heavy, and tears threaten to spill at the thought of never truly having the kind of love that steals your breath. Consumes your soul and burrows itself in your bones.

I can feel his gaze as I mindlessly fidget with my fingers, suddenly unsure of what to say. My teeth scrape against my bottom lip as a fleeting distraction. The silence between us becomes heavy, a pressure in my chest gradually building. My breath stalls when a large hand covers my restless fingers, ceasing their frantic movements. I turn my head slowly to peer up at him, finding his eyes already locked on me. The tender sway of his thumb begins to rub across the top of my hand, while his green eyes gradually work their way to my nervous lips.

On a whispered breath, he disrupts the silence: "Emma…if you don't stop biting your lip, I'll have no choice but to make you stop by sinking my teeth into it."

I think I stop breathing, my lips parting in shock.

Aiden's *never* spoken to me like this before. In all the years we've known each other, he's never crossed the line of friendship. But here he goes, slicing through our boundaries without an ounce of uncertainty. I seem to have lost any coherent thought and the ability to speak, just wide eyes and staring.

The left side of his mouth quirks up in amusement, but his other hand comes up to cup my face. His thumb leisurely swipes across my cheek. Trailing the pad of this thumb to the corner of my mouth, his heavy-lidded eyes meet mine. "I want…" Aiden pauses to clear his throat, clenching his jaw as if he's fighting to say what's on his mind.

"Want what?" I say softly. I can barely form the words, sounding breathier than I'd like. I've never been this close to a guy, a few breaths away. Only inches separating us, the slightest movement could steal my first kiss from me. Unless…

Do I want him to kiss me?

I realize with stark clarity that I wouldn't stop him. I'd let him take something I'd never shared with anyone, even though I told myself I'd never let any male take what they wanted from me anymore.

But with Aiden…I *trust* him. And I'm curious to know what a kiss would feel like.

Even if he doesn't know the depths of my father's hatred towards me, he is still one of the only people that knows bits of the real me. Not just the Princess of Asov, but the girl, Emma.

A long-strained breath leaves his parted lips as he tips his head forward to rest his forehead against mine. The small touch alone sends a shiver of heat down my spine. "Fuck what I want, it's what I *need.*" The low-pitched timbre in his voice wraps around my body, igniting a pleasure deep within.

His palm blanketing my hands squeezes roughly, and as he draws his head back, his heated stare freezes me. The air around us pulses with every bated breath, craving for more.

"You. I *need* you, Emma. From the moment I saw you, I knew I had to be near you. Give me a chance because this—*us*—can work," he implores.

I furrow my brows as I absorb the words he's saying.

I subtly begin to shake my head. "But we're *friends,* Aiden. That's all we've ever been. I don't see how—"

The sudden jerk of my head stuns me silent as he grasps both sides of my face, his fingers wrapping behind the nape of my neck. "Damnit, Emma, I don't want to be friends with you anymore, I never have. I restrained my wants because of your father, but now, there's nothing holding us back. I want you, all of you," he growls.

I still, letting the jagged cave wall dig into my back, confirming this is real.

Right now.

Aiden wants *more…*

He doesn't move as my mind continues to spin out of control.

When I start to speak, he cuts me off. He pulls my face towards his, until we are a hair's breadth away from one another, sharing the same breath.

"Please," his voice cracks on the word. "Let me show you."

I suck in a shallow breath, my lips parting when all I can do is nod as I keep my eyes on his. Relaying a message of me waving the green flag.

A throaty growl escapes him as he closes the distance between us. The warmth of his lips pressing against mine, soft and sure. He pulls back too soon but keeps his lips just barely grazing mine. A small smile tugs on his lips. His scent once again swirls around me, this time with a hint of mint mixing in, making my head buzz with pleasure. The caress of his hands holding my face sparks goosebumps along my skin, as he pulls me in again. But he doesn't have to, I lean in willingly. Soft lips brush against mine, causing a tremor to shoot through me.

His tongue swipes against my lips, an unsaid question hanging in the air as I answer back with fervor.

That's all he needs as he drives his tongue in, tasting every inch.

Gods.

Heat pools between my thighs as he devours my mouth like it's the most delicious dessert he's ever tasted.

Is this what I've been missing?

His minty taste consumes me as I kiss back with a desperate need.

More.

I need more.

My clit begins to throb as I feel a slickness gather between my legs when he starts to trail his hands down my arms, leaving sparks against my skin, until they settle on my thighs. He spins my whole body to face him fully as my book slides to the ground, spreading my legs and yanking me onto him. My dress covers any proof of sinful contact as I straddle him, with his back against the rock-covered wall.

Oh, Gods.

There's no denying his crazed lust at this moment, the hard length of him lines up perfectly between the center of my thighs. His hands find purchase as they rest on my hips, gripping. Clutching me to him.

A spellbinding pulse beats in the air around us, as he continues to ravish my mouth. A moan pours out of me, but it's lost in him when his mouth covers mine.

A scratchy moan escapes him. "God damn, Emma, this is——"

He breaks off his own words as he slams his mouth into mine again. A sigh gets lost between our frantic breathing. I shift my hips, trying to rid myself of the ache pulsing through, making Aiden grunt and lift his own hips. The movement places more pressure on my center, and a sweet whimper of relief breaks free.

More.

I must have spilled the plea from my lips because he starts to move his mouth across my jaw, nipping down my neck as he takes hold and guides the rocking of my hips.

My eyes roll back from the feeling as my hands cling to the back of his head, gripping his hair.

He continues to lick and suck above my necklace, slowly gliding lower, his right hand sliding across the collared neck of my dress as he dips his fingers underneath the fabric and begins to pull down.

NO!

Slamming both palms to his chest I shove myself off him with full force. Twisting away to brace my hands on the hard ground, my legs become tangled in the length of my dress.

"I—I'm sorry," I say quietly.

The passion is cut with a sharp knife, dissolving the heated energy between us.

Aiden clears his throat, confusion lacing his words. "What just happened? I thought… I *know* you were enjoying that kiss just as much as I was."

Standing on wobbly legs, I brush my hair from my face, watching him rise to his full height and latch his sword strap across his chest. "I changed my mind," I mumble.

Taking a full step towards me to close the distance, he grabs my chin between his fingers, making my gaze meet his. "Don't play dumb with me, I can *smell* your arousal."

My breath catches in my throat at the shock of his vulgar admittance, and the flaming in my cheeks burns brighter at the thought that he can *smell* me.

I push trembling words through my lips and hope I sound stronger than I feel at this moment: "This is too much, too fast. I need time for just…for all of *this*." I wave my hands to motion between us.

It's all I can offer him.

Aiden, to my surprise, releases my chin and takes a small step back. "Of course, I shouldn't have moved so fast." The soft features on his face challenge the clipped tone of his voice, and the stiffness in his posture tells a different story.

I wrap my hands around myself, letting my fingers cling onto the fabric of my dress, unsure of what to say as a murky silence falls between us.

My heart shatters at not being able to speak the words he wants to hear. To tell him I want this, to place his mouth back on mine and give in to temptation. My first taste of desire, the taste of *Aiden*… But my mind can't seem to catch up to the dizzying feelings lingering from his mouth, hands, and lower…

He deserves to find his mate and to have someone who won't question marrying him.

He deserves someone whose soul is not fractured.

Unlike mine. I feel only fragments of myself exist, as I fracture further with each loss. With each new scar I receive as *punishment*. With each day I'm held prisoner in my own home.

I stretch my arm out, about to provide some type of comfort to what I can't give him, but before I can reach him, he takes another step back. Swallowing hard, he shoves his hands in the pockets of his brown pants. "I know you don't want to be my wife, to be *mine*. I want to give you time because it's what you asked, but it will be hard, Emma. I've waited a long time for you already."

What does that mean?

I can't even begin to process his words. Was he promised me before I ever knew? Did he plan this? I don't see how or why, since he's not innocent when it comes to intimacy. I've seen all the girls hanging off his arm since he's grown into himself. It's a painful reminder that I'm the innocent one, and that he may have been my first kiss, but I was not his. A sudden urge to ask if my kiss was memorable hangs on my tongue, but he shifts his feet to face the cave's opening.

He stands momentarily still, and I see his shoulders lift and fall back down as he takes a deep breath. Nerves flit under my skin, unsure of what he's about to say or do. Aiden's head twists back to look at me, but the frustration stirring in his eyes is gone, replaced with playfulness. "Race you to the water."

My mouth falls open at his change in mood. In how he always finds a way to keep a smile on my face. He's waiting, staring at me with a dare glinting in his eyes.

I chew on my lip, considering his challenge. "I don't know, Aiden, I'm dressed in— " I don't finish my sentence as I take off in a full sprint, startling him. I'm hoping my dull words of acting like I was going to say no will throw him off guard, and luckily, they do.

I leap onto the stones, racing past him as a giggle leaves my throat. I can never turn down a challenge; it kicks my adrenaline on high. A rush of excitement shooting through my veins.

A tide comes rolling to me and I manage to dive over it and let my body glide into the sea. My dress floats in a beautiful dance beneath the water when I duck under the surface, right before Aiden jumps in beside me. I open my eyes, watching him swim back up towards me, bubbles whirling around him. His green eyes shimmer under the iridescent rays cutting into the water, sparkling as they hook on mine. He smiles and pushes up to the surface. I follow, letting the water smooth my hair back, wiping the drops lingering from my eyes.

I let a smile soften my face when I look at him, my eyes falling to his lips of their own accord, remembering how they felt. Our breaths and the lapping waves are the only sounds I can hear at the moment, with both of us lost in this effortless connection we have.

Aiden smirks. "Watch out."

I crease my eyebrows in confusion. "What are you talki— " Water splashes against my face and drowns out my words. I shake it off only to find Aiden laughing at me, clearly finding it amusing to splash water at me. He just started a war. We continue this game for a little longer before he stops, holding his hands up.

"It's nice to see you smile," he says with affection. "I have to go train before it gets too late. Father won't be happy if I miss a day." He looks down at himself, sliding his hand through his wet hair, slicking it back. "But I clearly need to change first," he says with a laugh. I swim back to the cave's opening with him, as he holds his hand out to help me up on the rocks. He grabs his sword—which I didn't see him take off, since I was too worried about winning—and hangs it over his shoulder. He gives me a chaste kiss on the cheek before he turns to walk away. Only for him to pause his movements, his muscles tensing.

"I can't promise you the love of a true mate, but I can give you love, Emma, and a good life with it," he says, his toned back facing me as his head twists around to speak. Confessing that he could give me love, even if it's not the earth-shattering kind, he can give me something. Which is better than nothing in this life.

Before any words can leave my mouth, Aiden walks away. Taking a small, graceful leap to the single stone, he peers back at me one last time, offering me a tight smile, and disappears. His parting words linger in the empty space around me.

CHAPTER EIGHT

Emma

*T*he echoing rumbles of my stomach force me to head back to the palace and retrieve some food. My dress is partially dry from staying in the cave to continue reading after Aiden left to train, but the soaked soles of my slippers leave behind a shiny, reflective trail as I sneak into the kitchen. Telion, the cook, hates when I invade his space and snatch morsels of food between mealtimes; though I think he secretly isn't bothered by my presence.

I stayed in the cave past lunchtime, and without eating anything for breakfast, I left myself no choice but to come back before I ate the pages of my book. Because that would be a sin.

I make quick work of scouring for bread, some cheese bits, and the savory meat covered on the counter. I pile it on a tray and poke my head in the hidden cabinet, knowing a special dessert would be in there. The scent of something sweet and fruity fills my nose as I spy a raspberry tart prepared. With a devious smirk, I snag a slice before heading back to my room. I may be a grown adult, but sometimes, I feel like a child when it comes to the games against Telion.

When I make it back to my room, I gobble down every crumb of food on my plate, easing the hunger pains that were building in my stomach. The delicious flavors burst against my taste buds, wishing I would have eaten it more slowly, if only to savor every bite.

Another agonizingly slow day of being stuck within these walls, but I'm grateful the cave offers a sense of reprieve. Some days I dip into the water just to float and erase my troubling thoughts. Now, I wonder, when I go back to the cave in the future, if the memories of Aiden's mouth on me will rush back and flood my brain. The need to go to him and fix whatever is strained between us intensifies, knowing he only buried his feelings about what happened before we swam, but the subtle need for space halts the urge.

I quickly change into a clean dress before I let my body fall back on the top of my bed, sinking into the feather-filled blanket. Closing my eyes to the world, I wish I could escape into a different reality. The unbreakable choker around my neck is stifling, often making my breathing feel compressed by its constricting weight. Bringing my hand up to hold it over the iron ring, I focus on the pace of my breaths. *In. Out. In. Out.* There is a constant dull ache from keeping the power of light at bay. It creates an empty void within, a hollow hole where an orb of strength should be.

Aggravation rattles my bones from the memory of my father sealing my fate to hell.

Stealing my power, stealing my voice, stealing my *life*. Only, instead of running from hell, I plan to walk right through its gates.

Tap. Tap. Tap.

Cora.

I sit up, straightening my dress before I tell her to come in, hoping she can't tell that only hours ago, I was devouring Aiden's mouth as if the air was stolen from my lungs and his lips were oxygen.

The door opens wide as she steps inside, closing it softly behind her. The blue irises of her eyes meet mine in a silent question: *Are you okay?*

I offer a nod for quick reassurance, tipping my head back and looking up at the ceiling as I inform her of the news. She doesn't need to say a word before I clear my throat to relieve more of her worry. "I'm fine, Cora. My father just feels that announcing a betrothal to Aiden is news worth celebrating." I cast a quick glance at her just in time to catch her shock.

Then, her brows scrunch slightly, stepping further into the room and making herself comfortable in the cushioned chair by the balcony. "Is a marriage to Aiden such a bad thing?"

Heaving a sigh, I walk over to her and plop myself into the seat beside her, a very unladylike action for a princess. "I suppose not, but he's not my mate, not my *choice* for love." I sneer, unable to tame the immediate disgust of my father's show of control over me; a doll to play the part, but a slave to his punishments.

Cora nods in understanding. "I know, and I hate that he's forcing you into this. But you and Aiden have been friends for years. Surely *some* feelings have developed?"

I narrow my eyes, staring intently at her. She's digging. She can't possibly know about the cave. So, she's questioning if I've ever thought of him in that way.

"Ugh, you know I've never seen him as anything more than a friend. Not my mate, remember? But I can't deny that I feel *something* for him because, besides you, he's been one of the few I hold close. I just don't think those feelings can develop into love." I shrug with uncertainty.

I may have had a moment of weakness earlier because I'd never felt such a strong coil of heat wrap around me and it made me lose all sense of reason, but one moment can't determine if there could be love in our future. The feelings I have for him still linger in friendship, but maybe that heat between us I felt can grow into something more. Into something Aiden was telling me we could have—a good life.

Cora offers a soft smile and twists her mouth to the side in thought. "I know, and I wish there was something I could do. A marriage with Aiden could still be good, Emma. On the bright side, he's not some old bastard with a potbelly." She giggles. "At least Aiden's nice to look at, and you're already close to him in many ways."

If only she knew how close we got today.

I give her a look but can't hide the feeling of how my leash has only shortened. "I want a choice, Cora. Or, at least, choose to marry Aiden of my own free will."

She takes those words in, knowing I've had zero control in every aspect of my life. "Then, what are you going to do?"

At the moment, I don't know how to answer her question. I let my eyes drift towards the open balcony doors, admiring how the sky is ablaze with the fire of the setting sun. With marriage to Aiden, I will still only be here, in these walls, never to see the beauty of what's out there. I won't survive. I would stop my own beating heart before being stuck here any longer.

I look down at my hands, a rebellious determination lighting up inside.

I feel a padded foot softly kick my leg. "Hey, where did you go?" Cora asks.

Staring at her with wide eyes and a hint of recklessness, I ask, "Can you do me a favor?"

Her arms fold across her chest as she narrows those cobalt eyes at me. "You know I always will, but why do I have a feeling I won't like what's about to come out of your mouth…" She suspiciously narrows her gaze on me.

I can't help but laugh at that, a rare smile widening across my face. "Because you won't," I say with amusement. "I'm going to go into town, see what Asov is all about. To have a semblance of freedom for a little while. But…I'd need you to distract the guard outside my door for his nightly shift." I wince.

Cora tips her head back and lets it fall to the back of the chair, groaning in a very unladylike way. I have to bite my lip to keep my laugh from escaping. Lifting her head back up to take a serious look at me, her facial features relax, signaling her white flag. "I can't say no to you, but it's not pretty out there, Emma. Not safe like it is in here. What if you get hurt? What if someone recognizes you and tries to harm y—"

"They won't," I promise. I reassure her the best way I can. "You know I've had secret training sessions with Kye for years. I'll be able to defend myself and sneak around without notice. Plus, I'll wear my hooded cloak, even though that doesn't really matter, considering nobody knows what the Princess of Asov looks like," I say cheerfully.

Kye has been one of the bodyguards here for as long as I can remember, and we seemed to click. He was one of the only ones who would talk back to me and treat me like a normal person, not give me one-word responses and stare everywhere but into my eyes. I made him become my friend, whether he wanted to be or not. One day, he witnessed my father grab my arm during breakfast in the dining hall, and from then on, he has made me meet him in secrecy to train. He told me that he wants me to have the option to protect myself, and I never fought him on that. I *wanted* to become strong, able to fight off my father and the demons that torment me in the future.

The glare burning into my soul from Cora is one that says she's not convinced, but she won't fight me on this. "*Fine.*" She sighs. "When do I need to play sidekick?"

I smirk at her words, and a ball of excitement forms in the pit of my stomach. "Tonight," I say with pure determination.

A night of freedom.

CHAPTER NINE

Emma

I slip into a pair of flexible, black pants with a long-sleeved shirt that hugs my body. Walking into the bathroom, I grab the brush and tame my tangled strands of hair before pulling it all to the side and making quick work of braiding it, letting it hang down past my shoulders. I stare at my reflection for a moment as I silently pep talk myself.

You're doing this. No one will ever know you left.

Shaking off the last of my doubt, I head for my closet. After walking inside, I drop down to my knees, pushing past some clothing and shoes to the hidden chest underneath. Running my hands over the top of the delicate, silver swirls that cover the top, I relish in the smoothness of it. I open it up and my heartbeat picks up in pace, a thrill bursting through me as I stare longingly at the most stunning weapon I have ever seen. A gift from Kye, my very own dagger that glints black with the silver swirls wrapping around the handle, shimmering when the light catches it as I wave it in the air. The weight of it balances perfectly in my hand, bringing a sense of comfort.

I grab the holster for it and tighten it around my thigh, sliding the blade in place as I stand and find my black leather boots to pull on. As I exit the closet, I grab the dark-as-night cloak hanging on the wall, letting it fall around me as the hood shadows my face, with the tail end of my braid dancing free from the side of the hood. The cloak hangs down to my knees, only showing my boots at the bottom.

Once I'm ready, I head to the balcony and wait for the signal of Cora's knocks. About thirty minutes have passed since she left my room. I told her to be back when the orange glow sinks halfway in the sky, casting more shadows on the land for me to camouflage myself in. Any minute, she should be here.

Knock. Knock. Knock.

The smile that plays on my lips can't be helped. If Cora is anything, it's punctual.

I reach the door and only open it a sliver before peaking my head out. Cora's there, looking absolutely bored. "Way too easy. I told the guard that Kye requested his assistance for a moment and that I'd keep you company until he returned. On top of that, I told Kye to keep the guard busy so we can have a girl's night in peace and not worry about nosy ears listening. Honestly, these guards are *way* too comfortable with their jobs to just believe little ol' me." She winks.

I let her in, and she makes herself comfortable. The plan is for her to stay here in case anyone comes knocking on the door, so she can divert them. I walk up to her and pull her into a tight embrace. "Thank you, Cor," I whisper.

She wraps her arms around me, squeezing me back before we both release each other. "Of course, just promise to come back in one piece."

"Promise." I beam.

Leaving my room, I slink down the empty hall on silent feet. Aside from my guard, no one should be down this way, because why would the king need more guards on his whipping post when I never leave my room in the evening? The ever-obedient daughter.

I strain my hearing to make sure no one is near as I work my way to the door that leads to the same stairwell I take to go to the cave, using quick feet to race down them. As soon as my feet hit the bottom, I dart for the servant's door and race outside, cutting the corner to press flat against the palace wall. I look down and realize my attire stands out like fire in the dark, with black clothes against the white stone. *Shit.* I sprint down the side and around the corner to the small alcove that is tucked away next to the pillar, secluded in darkness as the sun makes its final descent, taking its golden light with it.

The palace seems to be quiet; no one would dare defy the King of Asov, who is all smiles for his people but strict and demanding within the confines of his palace. Creeping along the edge, I look ahead to the trees in the distance, the ones that divide the island of Asov from the palace and its people. I may not be able to leave this island and venture into another court, but I can at least explore my court and see the life my people live.

Crouching down, I gauge the distance and the guard standing at the entrance of the palace. All I need to do is make it to that first tree. A few moments pass as I watch the guard's movements, calculating his steps, which ways he turns, the path his eyes travel. But the Gods must be secretly working in my favor, because he steps around the side of the building.

I let my ears strain to where he walked, hearing the sound of a zipper... Ugh, males.

But I don't waste a moment as he relieves himself. I charge forward on soundless feet to my first checkpoint. The tree gradually increases in size with every step. My legs are straining, arms pumping, slicing through the wind, heart pounding, and my cloak billows behind me like a phantom floating in the breeze.

My body scrapes against the rough bark of the tree and I sidle behind it. Tucking my arms in tight as I press against the base of the tree, I swallow hard in an attempt to catch my breath from my burning lungs. The adrenaline coursing through my veins continues to pulse frantically as I stare at the path beyond. The sun drops below the horizon and the light of the moon casts a soft glow, but darkness still shrouds everything in sight.

With small movements, I peer around the tree to the palace entrance. The guard must be done relieving himself because he's settled back into his station. I will be unseen now as I creep from tree to tree and stay in the shadows, blending into the night as I make my way through the small border of woods and into the town of Asov.

I peek around the final tree and can't help sucking in a breath at the sight. Wooden ships rock with the sway of the darkened sea along the dock, creaking with the movement. A stream of glistening gems shimmers on the water from the reflection of the moon. The whispering of the wind spirals around, delicately brushing against my face with its cool caress. Its a gentle but welcome change from the harsh life behind me, and I let my feet step around the tree, walking into the soft light of the moon that creates a majestic glow on the homes of Asov.

There are white and tan stucco homes lining up along the cobblestone road that travels the length of the coast. Shrubs line the front of the homes in a perfect order, the decorated doors peeking out behind them in an array of vibrant colors. Painted rocks adorned with rainbow colors and tiny handprints trail to the houses.

Family.

The word dances along the edge of my mind. Family should be filled with happiness and love. It should be beautiful like the brush of colors that paints the sky from the setting sun. Like the stars in the night that will always remain. Their love should burn brighter with each passing day... But mine burned to ash. A brief flame extinguished before I could make a wish on it, its stain coating my heart, turning it black. A colorless organ that pumps poison into my veins and slowly drives me towards corruption.

Following the cobblestone road, I stick to the edges of the homes, tiptoeing around shrubs and making my way towards the inner city. Faint lights are radiating through the windows of some homes as I shuffle past. After a few blocks of ducking and prowling on silent feet through a neighborhood of Asov, I finally reach the city's center. Tall buildings loom down the streets; shops and bars are open for gatherings, among an endless number of other places. Many Fae still mill about, out for some evening fun, it seems.

A couple meanders down the path to the bar, his arm around her shoulder, pulling her in tightly. She looks up at him, eyes shining with enough emotion to plunge a knife into my heart. Her heartfelt laugh carries through the air, as she rests her head against him. A deep longing for some type of love to treasure fills me, and I yearn to feel the bliss they seem to be lost in. Their freedom is never a worry as they walk side-by-side together in the open, enjoying a simple evening in each other's company. That carefree joy they have is something I've experienced only a handful of times in life, only brief moments that are impossible to cling to. That kind of life, it's not in the cards for me.

I decide that I'm disguised enough that no one would even look twice at me, let alone question the girl under the hood. So, I step out from the shadows and walk down the side of the road, just like everyone else. Voices carry from the open doors of shops, music drifting through the air and making my heart feel lighter than it has in years.

I lose track of time as I walk through the town, cutting through an alleyway as a shortcut back to the sea. I can see the treeline and boats rocking in the far distance at the opening of a path; it must be a sure way back to the palace. I pad down the stone alleyway, welcoming the chill of the night breeze as the temperature continues to drop throughout the evening. Pulling my hood down more and wrapping my arms around myself, I inhale the fresh moment of freedom into my lungs.

Scrape.

My whole body seizes from the sound of metal sliding against stone. Halting my steps, I take a quick glance around at both ends of the alley but see nothing. Just a momentary silence before the sounds of people enjoying the night drift in from the distance.

Heaving a sigh, I continue to make my way down the passageway, shaking off the paranoia that sent a wave of prickles down my spine.

Halfway down the back alley, I hear another set of footsteps.

Scruff. Scruff. Scruff.

This time, I don't bother to stop my trek, and decide to pick up my pace. The sound of footsteps speeding up to keep pace with mine grows louder. My heart starts to pound a little harder as the hair on the back of my neck raises; my body's warning to me to *move*. Without questioning my intuition, I take off at a full sprint, racing down the musty, sewer-filled path, my legs straining as I fight to keep out of this person's grasp.

As my feet pound on the ground, I take only a second to peer over my shoulder and see a monstrous figure closing in on me. Its eyes are shrouded in black, zeroing in on its target...me. My stomach drops as I spin my head back to focus on the opening that's getting closer. But before I can register what's happening, I'm thrown into a brick wall. The air whooshes out of my lungs as I fall, my head flying backwards, until it smacks down hard, slamming into the rough ground at full force. Sharp pain blossoms at the point of contact on the back of my head, and stars dance before my vision as I try to peel my eyes open.

My palms scrape against the pebbled surface as I struggle to regain control. The darkness of my surroundings becomes a blur of shadows, swaying to the thumps of my heart. With shaky arms, I try to push myself up a little, in a desperate need to find the threat.

Scrape.

Behind me.

Ignoring the raging pounding in my head, I leap up and spin, coming face-to-face with a burly male looming over me. The scent of death wafts through the air, filling my nose with ashes and something bitter. The air around us becomes freezing within moments, my breath visibly puffing out before me.

Taking a small step back, I reach for my dagger. At that same moment, he lunges, taking hold of my throat and slamming me against the building's wall. The tips of my toes just barely touch the ground, preventing his grip from hanging me and delivering me an untimely death within the palm of his hand. A bloodthirsty growl leaves his chest, turning the blood in my veins to ice.

His hair is wild, dirt covers his skin, and torn fabric hangs from his body. His head dips enough to show his features in the moonlight, and my heart stops.

Those deathly pools target me with oil-stained veins traveling along his skin, creeping from the edges of his irises. Drops of inky blood trail from his eyes and nose, dripping onto his ragged shirt. The bitter smell intensifies as more blood seeps out of his body. The foulness of it makes me want to gag, as bile threatens to creep up my throat. The hand on my throat tightens, constricting my airway. He leans in and inhales deeply. His other hand comes up to touch the slickness that formed on my head and brings it to his nose. A stronger inhale this time, and then, something flashes in his obsidian eyes. Pure terror engulfs me as he lets out a high-pitched shriek that rings through the night sky.

I can feel my lungs convulsing within my chest, desperate in their need to fill with air. Black starts to creep around the edges of my vision until my head gets whipped forcefully to the side, his claw-like hand pounding against my jaw. A burst of metallic consumes my tastebuds as blood fills my mouth. His hand releases my throat, causing my body to curl forward, and I gasp for air, gulping it down greedily.

I snag my dagger from its sheath as I stand back up, but his claws are already descending at lightning speed, ripping my clothes against my torso and lighting a fire against my skin. A silent scream echoes in my head. Never show any sign of pain; a technique I learned when my father punished me more for any noise that would fall from my lips.

His clawed hand comes swinging back, this time aiming for my neck. Planning to silence me forever and take my life that should have been taken years ago. But I won't give in that easily, not after seeing the life of my people tonight and gaining hope of one day joining them in their happiness. I tighten my grip on my dagger, ready to deliver sweet agony until it stops his heart. Before I can thrust the dagger into his chest, his hand freezes in mid-air, dropping down as his eyes widen, staring into nothing. Silence.

My eyes drag down to his chest. Pools of blackened blood flow down and the sharp point of a blade peeks through, only inches from my own chest. A second later, the silver point disappears, as more blood gathers and the monstrous being falls to the ground with a thud.

My chest rises and falls in a deep rhythm, the sounds of my breathing filling the silence. A slight tremble wracks through my body as I fist my blade tighter, squeezing so tightly I begin engraving its intricate design into the palm of my hand. While staring daggers into his body, wishing he had a slower death, by *my* hand. But who stole my kill, yet also saved me…?

I can feel eyes burning into the side of my face, daring me. Without a second to guess, I push off the wall and spin, my body protesting the sharp pain radiating across my ribs from my wound as I knock a hard mass of muscle into the stone. I've learned to embrace pain, no matter how gruesome the wound is. My father taught me well when it came to that.

My eyes focus and land on a male. I ignore the warmth seeping from his body into mine and the pain barking along my ribs as I push my weight into him. Swinging my arm up and aiming for his throat, I let my blade press against his pulse, feeling the flutter of it. His neck resists my dagger as it must be indenting his skin to the point of pain. I'm almost craving to spill some of his blood.

His face is veiled in shadows from his hood, like staring into a black abyss. My hand disappears within it, but I know I have him by the neck. He's not deranged like the male before. His skin is not ice cold. There is no atrocious smell, just something heady I can't seem to place. Something sinful, wrapping around me, calling to me. The blood in my veins faintly buzzes with our proximity.

The sound of crackling draws my attention away from the male before me for a split second, zeroing in on the lifeless form sprawled on the ground. Smoke begins to trickle from his unseeing eyes, and then his entire body crumples to ash. The shock tears through me at the sight. How is this possible?

Breathing becomes a little difficult as I turn back to my other threat. "Who are you?" I ask in a dark tone, hoping to not let it show how much he's affecting me. The way my body is sparking to life.

A deep chuckle rises from his throat, the vibrations of it coursing through my knife and into my hand, raising goosebumps along every inch of my skin. "Wouldn't you like to know," he says with a voice that spikes my pulse.

"Oh. Apparently, you're an asshole," I deadpan. I have no idea where this choleric side of me is coming from, but his presence is affecting me more than I care to admit or can even understand. It's irritating.

His pulse stays steady against my blade, never wavering. As if being held by knifepoint is nothing new to him, or maybe he simply doesn't fear death. Does it purr a sweet release to him as it does to me? Does the darkness fill him with wicked desires? Then again, it seems he can control the shadows as he keeps them masking his face. So, I wonder if he does hear the sweet song of darkness, but maybe he can conduct the tempo of its music within himself.

The silence stretches between us as he lets my words fall into nothing. Never responding, neither confirming nor denying. But I think the answer is clear.

I push up on my toes and lean into him more. "Tell me why I shouldn't kill you right now," I whisper.

I can't see his eyes, but I can feel them. Daggers piercing into me with spiked ends. I don't think he will answer me again, but then, his voice slices through the quiet: "You won't," he says with confidence.

Anger bursts deep down within me from his words. I press the sharp-edged knife harder into his neck and hear a faint hiss leave his lips. I can't hide the venom in my voice. "You don't know what I will do."

I go to press my dagger even harder against his throat, but at the same moment, he grabs hold of my wrists and spins us around, shoving my back to the wall and pinning my wrists above my head. His large frame cages me in, blanketing a dome of shadows around us, blending into the night.

"You won't kill me, because you never had a chance, little demon," he growls.

Who is he calling *little demon*? Yet, the name beckons to my shattered soul.

The urge to rip his hood back rakes through me. As if he can sense my thoughts, his hold on my wrists tightens to a bruising grip. His other gloved hand comes up and takes my silver-and-black-etched dagger, bringing it close to my face. The sharp edge is slick with red, tainting the shiny blade with a deep crimson.

I nicked his neck. A deep pleasure blooms at the thought, followed by a tinge of regret.

He brings my steel blade to my own neck and twists his hand to place the cool, flat side against my throat, pulling back and wiping his blood on me. "Vicious little thing," he growls, staining me with my own wicked deed. Once the smear of his blood paints my skin, his movements freeze.

But only for a moment, as he drags the point of my dagger down my neck, tracing along the edge of my necklace. The hood that covers his head tilts slightly, as if he's curious. The pounding of my heart echoes in my ears, unsure of what to do. I should be scared, trying to run for my life. Yet, I remain in his grasp, wanting to see what he does next, daring him.

Dropping the knife, he presses his hooded face next to my ear. "You shouldn't be wandering around dark alleys alone, he would have killed you." His breath feathers against the shell of my ear before pulling back so we're face to face. Even inches apart, I see nothing but black.

A shiver shoots straight down my spine, making my body want to arch into him. I push the impulse away, locking my muscles in tight. "And you won't?" I question. Pinning him with my hard stare, tempting the shadowed beast before me. "I had it handled," I spit back.

A huff of amusement brushes against my hair. "If that's so, then you think too highly of yourself, or are just ignorant of what he was."

I push against his hold but fail miserably as he keeps my wrists locked in place, with no room to escape. I've had enough of his shit. He might not know I'm the princess, but he's still speaking this way to a lady.

But then, my thoughts get snagged on the word *what*. I know the male who attacked me was not a normal Fae, that something was consuming him, controlling him, turning him into a heartless creature. Devouring his soul until nothing was left, but… I have a *wary* feeling that once I learn about this, there is no going back.

He seems to sense my turmoil, because he leans an inch closer, bringing the shadows with him. "He's what we call the Corrupted, little demon. Cursed from the mark of a Scavenger that was sent from death itself."

CHAPTER TEN

Unknown

*T*he furious look on her face is quickly replaced by one of confusion. Her hands go slack in my hold, the fight in her slowly fading away. She says nothing as her eyes flicker around, trying to make sense of the truth. This vicious, little female smells of roses and honey—an intoxicating scent that is beginning to drive me mad. Commanding my shadows tighter to me, I stare into her eyes. They are wide in disbelief, but the swirling, grey storm within them is begging me to dive in. Reminding me of a raging sea that will drown me if I'm not careful.

Her eyes finally begin to focus back on me, her eyebrows scrunching with uncertainty. "I—I don't understand…" she stammers.

I look deep into her, trying to find her lies. But my gut is telling me that this is the first time she's heard of this, that she's clueless about the curse that could kill her so easily. *Pathetic.* How can someone be this oblivious? My mind is still warring with the internal instincts of her honest words. If she truly doesn't know, then what hole did she fucking crawl out from?

"What's there to understand? Curse. Corruption. Death," I muse. "Go back home, little demon."

Her mouth snaps shut as the nickname slips past my lips. Her hands jerk in my grip, while she simultaneously making an attempt to kick me in the balls. *Clever.* Nice use of a distraction, but still won't work on me. I lean my entire body right up against hers, pressing in and trapping her between me and the wall even more. Her chest is rising and falling rapidly, like she's trying to cage in her anger. Her nostrils flare, and her stare is like an arrow of fire burning straight through me.

"Stop calling me that!" she seethes. Her voice echoes down the dark alley, scaring away any critters lurking about.

"No," I say plainly. I find it amusing that this feisty, little savage of a female is getting worked up over this. The longer the silence around us grows, the more I can see her wanting to push her stubbornness to the side and relent in this battle of wills. Unlucky for her, because I never lose; I know she will crack.

Her shoulders sag as she mildly shakes her head, releasing the heaviest sigh. "How long has the Corruption been happening?" Her face almost looks pained, like the thought of these people suffering and fighting such a curse hurts her. I briefly look her over, not quite able to figure her out. I'm usually good at reading people, but I can't seem to think straight as her body fits perfectly against mine. Her every curve is visible in that tight outfit and molds right into me. A body made of sin. Dressed in all black, looking like a cloak of shadows. The thought of my shadows caressing her skin sends heat to my spine, making my cock twitch.

The loose strands of her brown hair gently graze against her face as the wind flows around us. Her face is lit by the moon as the ring in her pointed ear glints in the silver light. She has a rosy lips that are begging to be tasted, and eyes that squeeze the air from my lungs. The purest grey that reminds me of the lustrous darkness of fog that blankets the forest before dawn. The hue of her eyes is calming, like the clouds before a storm, yet as dark and melancholy as the ashes of death. I break away from her gaze before it muddles my sense of thought.

I slowly let my scrutiny travel to her fragile neck, one I could snap in an instant. My whole palm would fit around her neck, constricting her breath. The mere thought of stealing her air makes my cock so hard that it begins to ache. *Fuck.* I go to take my eyes off her, but they snag on that damn necklace. It clings around her throat like she's its life source; a prey that it's captured. I have the urge to rip that fucking jewelry off her slender neck, knowing my hand would make a better necklace. Declaring her as my capture. Gods. What the *fuck* am I thinking? Feeling jealous over a damn necklace on some hellish female. I can't help but feel curious about it because it doesn't seem like a piece of jewelry a girl would wear to decorate an outfit that screams she's sneaking in dark alleys.

Her throat clears, and I forgot she asked me a question. I look hesitantly at her, preparing for her to attack like the violent creature she is, as I let go of her hands. The bulge of my cock pressing along the seam of my pants has become painful at this point, and I don't need her body rubbing up against it.

I take a deep breathe to clear my thoughts, remembering she asked me a question. "This curse has been spreading for years, but it was under control before, when only a few were Corrupted and could be handled before they got worse. But…" I pause, thinking about this past year and the hundreds that are making their way throughout the land of Deyadrum. Every court has been trying to fight them away from their borders, but it's not enough.

"But…?" she prompts.

Impatient little thing. "But they're becoming bolder, and more Corrupted have been created, enough to start a war."

She leans against the wall, tipping her head back to it. "Why?" she asks.

One simple question that holds so many unknown answers. "Nobody knows. They act on pure primal instincts; they're death incarnate with their cold hearts and cravings to kill."

Her hands begin to tremble as she looks off into the distance, but something in her eyes shift, like she's clearing away the unease wracking through her small frame. As if she shoved her feelings deep within and locked them away, hiding the part of her she let slip out. She pushes off the wall and bends down to retrieve her dagger, her gaze locking with mine as she comes back up. A slight smirk lifts the left side of her mouth, twirling the blade in front of her before she sheathes it on her lean leg.

"Thanks for cleaning it for me," she says, as I shoot my eyes to the smear of red against her soft skin. The claim of crimson I marked her with was beyond my control, it was the need to have my scent on her in some way and see if she would shy away from someone holding her life in their hands. I could have easily swiped a neat line across her smooth skin to take her breaths for good. The skin I want to see more of, but she's almost completely covered in her attire. Most females show off as much skin as they can get away with, wanting to score attention. But this one doesn't need to do that; she can lure males in just by looking at them, and she doesn't even realize it.

"Anytime," I reply. Walking away to the far end of the alley, I keep my senses on high alert in case she tries to sneak an attack, but for some reason, I feel she won't.

I can feel her eyes searing into my back as I gather more shadows around me. The cool glow of the moon absorbs into me, shrouding everything near into darkness.

"Who are you?" she yells. I don't pause my movements as I continue to grow the distance between us. A ghost of a smile forms on my shadowed face.

After a few more steps, I take a quick, subtle glance over my shoulder and give a smug smirk she won't see, but I'm sure she can feel. When she huffs and turns her back to me, I make that my cue and disappear into my shadows.

CHAPTER ELEVEN

Emma

The night air becomes chilly, the layers of my clothes doing nothing to shield me from its numbing grasp. I can't help but blow out a sigh of relief as I enter the warmth of the palace. My mind is reeling as I sneak along the back stairway of my home, but I pause on the landing and brace myself on the railing. My mind drifts to the mysterious male who uprooted my entire thoughts of this world.

The world where people continue to sing, dance, and drink together in each other's company. But I wouldn't be surprised if it's because they believe the lies I'm sure spill from my father's lips about how he has everything under control. But surely some know. So, why has no one bothered to mention the curse to me? I can feel the anger rattling in my bones, the sensation causing the darkness to swell inside me. I wanted to ask the male of shadows more, but my pride took hold of me and I couldn't let him see how truly little I knew, or that my heart began bleeding for everyone fighting this Corruption, while I sat in a cushioned palace without a damn clue.

Before I had made it to the end of the alley, I wanted to chance one more look at him, but when I turned he was already vanishing into the night, and swallowed by the shadows he wields.

I make my way back to my room, and still, no guard is in sight. Cora did good with her convincing plan, which means I truly do owe her. Knocking three times, she lets me in.

I keep my cloak wrapped tightly around me to hide my still bleeding wound as I look at her. She looks exhausted, with the lids of her eyes falling every few seconds.

"Thank you, Cor," I say as I stifle a wince when I hug her. "Go get some rest now." The sun is only hours away from lighting up the sky.

She gives me a sleepy smile and a quick thumbs up as she turns to leave, before pausing in front of the door, her hand resting on the polished doorknob. "I'm glad you're back safe," she murmurs sleepily. And with that, she leaves.

My room has a warm glow that is cast by the fire crackling across the room.

Heading straight towards the bathroom, I shuck off my clothes and crank the water in the massive tub to a temperature that is probably close to the fiery pits of Hell. I flinch when I peel the fabric from the torn skin across my ribs. The slickness of my blood seeps from the open cuts, burning like a heated iron singeing skin. I reach to grab a towel, soaking it in the hot water streaming from the faucet of the tub.

Taking a deep breath in, my lungs fill with air until it becomes painful. I hold the breath, readying myself for the unpleasant, fiery pain that I know will jolt through me as I clean this wound. But if I don't, it could get infected, since my body can't heal like a normal Fae. Or what if... What if a cut from the Corrupted could change me? He never said anything about them being able to spread their poison, but he may not have noticed that I was sliced deeply by the black points that grew on the Corrupted's hands.

With a steady hand, I press the warm towel to the open flesh, letting it soak up my carelessness for not being quick enough in defending myself. At least not quick enough to have dodged the Corrupted's hand. I swallow down a whimper of pain and continue to wipe delicately across the ripped marks. I toss the bloodied towel on the floor, looking like I cleaned up spilled wine, and retrieve the salve I secretly keep stocked. I have to sneak through the healer's pantry and grab a bottle every so often, because my father would have her head if I went to her for healing his brutal punishments. The salve is a thick cream that brings immediate relief as I spread it over my open skin. The healing effects soak into my ribs until the throbbing pain starts to fade. I let the breath I was holding free and relish in the numbing effect the healing ointment offers.

Steam starts to swirl around the room, fogging up the mirrors and slicking against my skin. The sting of the water laps against my skin as I sink into the tub, the water burning in the most delicious way.

I shut the water off once it covers my breasts, letting my head rest against the curved side of the tub. My thoughts stray to the male dressed in shadows again and the conflicting feeling that took hold of me in his presence. I wanted to cut him, to hurt him, but the small ember deep inside me wanted to arch into him and let his warmth consume me. I wanted to pull him into my darkest desires, maybe be the cure for my poisoned soul. My body has never reacted like this before, but I've also never been around another male intimately besides Aiden.

Then, I remember the way he spoke to me, and the truth that spilled from his shadowed lips. The frustration I felt towards him begins to boil my already heated blood, anger bubbling within me towards this male. The male who just opened my eyes to how blind I have been, how oblivious I am to what is happening in Deyadrum. I feel like my world has been turned upside down. I know what he speaks is true; I saw firsthand how death flowed through the Corrupted's veins when I was attacked, and I can't ignore the curse the people are battling. I'm forced to watch this messed-up reality from behind my prison, but if I do nothing… I may as well shove the sharpest blade straight through my heart.

I let out a sigh as the heat of the water relaxes my muscles as I sink deeper, enjoying a moment of tranquility from such a long evening. My eyes start to close of their own accord as exhaustion settles into my body. The pounding of my heart slows to a steady rhythm as my mind drifts.

Swirls of smoky claws pull me under, clouding the water as dark as death. Its icy grip freezes my blood as I'm forced to hold my breath. Fear consumes me as the surface of the water in the tub starts to freeze over. A thick layer of black ice forms to trap me. I thrash against the hold of the shadows, needing to break free before the top becomes completely solid. I twist and jerk, but it's no use; only the loss of air that slips through my lips makes me stop. A tear sneaks free as my eyes begin to burn, but it gets lost in the water. As if it never existed.

The temperature of the water keeps dropping, feeling like pins and needles against my skin.

"Emma…"

Every muscle locks up and my eyes widen at the deep voice that causes warning bells to ring in my head. I try to scream with my mouth closed, but the sound is muffled underneath the dark liquid.

"You don't seem happy about my visit," *he snickers. The pressure on my lungs gets heavier with every moment. I won't be able to hold my breath much longer, as my head begins to feel light, the rhythm of my heartbeats becoming farther and farther apart.*

Thump… Thump… Thump…

"You have something I want, Emma, and I'm going to get it. I always get what I want," *he sneers with the deepest, fury-filled undertone. His voice slithers through the water; the shadows squeeze tighter, and my stomach starts to churn. Black edges blur around my vision as white spots start to float in the dark abyss.*

A phantom hand slams into my chest, causing the remaining air to release from my lungs. I begin to gasp for air from the shock of pain, but only water slides down my throat.

"Sweet dreams," *he whispers. His shadowed breath grazes me, and his vile voice stops my heart as more chills shoot down my spine. I buck harder against the restricting hold on me while I keep sucking down water. The moment the grip on my body is released, I lurch upward to the surface.*

I smash through the top of the water, sending waves of liquid cascading to flood the bathroom floor. Both hands clasping the edge of the tub in a white-knuckle grip, I choke on the water that was drowning me. It gurgles from my mouth, making me heave forward as my body rejects it.

The moment no more water comes, I greedily start gulping down air, desperate for it as I claw at my chest from the painful pressure. The pounding of my heart hurts with every thrum, straining to find its rhythm again. My saturated hair clings to my face and chin as agony throbs across my chest bone. Looking down, the water sloshes around at my breasts, but a faint, oil-stained handprint marks my skin from where he slammed against my chest. The area is still cold to the touch.

As soon as my body begins to settle and my breathing steadies to a normal rate, the pain lessens as each minute passes. I take everything in: the floor shining from the layer of water coating it; my chest marred with red slashes as beads of blood form against my skin; and the water…clear. Another fucking nightmare. But…are these still dreams? Because what's happening is very much real. I can't just declare it a figment of my imagination anymore. Unless it's him taking advantage of my vulnerability the moment I drift off to sleep, slithering through my mental shields and taking hold of the darkest parts of my psyche.

I almost *drowned*. I can't fucking die this way, not without a fight. The panic I felt earlier rushes to the surface in my mind, the feeling of being forced under the water. But I refuse to let someone else destroy me. If I'm going to drown, then I'll do it on my own by drowning in my own self-made Hell.

I'm not scared of death, but I fear this phantom male who invades my sleep and takes hold of my mind. I fear the unknown of not being prepared to fight. But death? No. If anything, death would rid me of my suffering and send me where I belong for always bringing destruction to others' lives. My whole life, I have felt out of place, a burden on those around me. I'm a walking curse who disrupts and ruins others' lives. So, death would turn me into nothing, but my lost soul could at least roam free.

If this guy wants to kill me, then he has to find me in the flesh first. He said I have something he wants… I don't know what that is, but I'll have to play his game and dance with the devil.

CHAPTER TWELVE

Emma

*A*fter my escape from death *twice* last night, I chose to forgo sleep for the rest of the night. My eyes scream at me, with their dark circles that hang heavy underneath, desperate to rest. I let my brown waves curtain my face to hide the proof of the hours my psyche has been battling between truths and lies, figuring out what is real and what is only a figment of my imagination.

I stare out at the majestic deep sea, blending blues and greens with a wavy haze of heat shimmering along the horizon. Leaning my elbow along the balcony's edge, I let my mind dive down into its darkest corner, until it brushes against the chilling darkness stirring inside, and images flash of the monster who attacked me in the alley. Unease trickles in and I have to shove it deep into its box and seal it shut. Dread coils in my stomach at the thought of my father finding out about my rebellious adventure in the night. I snuck out, being aware of the consequences if I'm caught. Without a doubt, he would ruin me until I was decorated in a blanket of crimson, then throw me away. Seal me in the caged iron box, chained to the bottom to suffer in silence.

But the information I learned about life outside of these walls makes it worth it. I may have no worth, aside from being a pawn in a marriage, but maybe I can do *something* to fight back against the curse. The guilt of not knowing is overwhelming. The people are suffering, and I can't bear the thought of it. Something needs to be done.

Maybe I can find a cure or a way to put an end to it.

I have to visit the palace library and search for books that may tell tales of Scavengers and death itself. I just can't get caught searching for such things, so I'd have to visit when the moon is high in the sky. But that leaves me with the problem of having to find a way to divert my body-guard again. *Ugh.*

The gulls drag my focus to the puffy clouds shifting through the sky, bringing a soft breeze swirling through the air. The pure bliss of the birds soaring around only to dive down and swing back up has my heart clenching for a feeling I will never experience. The carefree lightness in life that has no weight to it, unlike my heavy heart made of stone. Dragging me down until I'm forced to sink into my misery.

I often wonder if my mother was alive if my life would have been different. Would she have brought love? The kind that could make me feel safe and protected from the horrors unleashed on me, and be the light in this endless void of darkness? I've been trapped for so long, my powers buried for years, and aside from my pointed ears and heightened senses, I'm essentially mortal. Powerless like the humans in Helestria, who can do nothing but yield to a Fae with power.

I only have a few distant memories of my Aunt Lydia, who offered me affection. There's one that often plays in my mind of her tucking me into bed one night and kissing me on the forehead. Or when the last real smile she gave me that softened the features on my face in a moment of pure happiness. My hope of receiving love from my father died a long time ago. It was the kind of hope that bloomed like a spring flower, only for the petals to fall and shrivel into nothing. Something that could have been beautiful, but ultimately became withered from rejection and lack of love.

Now, I'm haunted by a phantom being who wishes to steal my final breath, and by whispered voices that call to me from deep within, begging me to let their darkness seep through my veins and numb the pain. Promises of ecstasy and a way to bleed out the grief and agony that screams in my blood. While also fighting my father's rotten heart and the wounds he inflicts on me. My fists clench at the reminder of how his leather whip feels when it carves into my skin. The way it slices through the layers, sinking deep as he swipes it and readies for another blow. The burn and sting combine into a blinding pain I refuse to make known. My eyes start to burn as I remember, feeling them fill with tears I don't want to shed. Not for him. I squeeze my eyes shut hard enough to create a mix of black and light flare behind my lids. The self-pity is hard to swallow, but I ram it down my throat, refusing to let him take any more from me.

I resist the pull I feel to be outside of these walls and tread back into my room. The light colors and fluffy pink pillows make me nauseated, another way to mask my blackened soul.

I head back inside as I get ready for my routine, under-the-radar training session with Kye. I applied more healing salve to my ribs earlier this morning. They're only slightly tender, but manageable. My mood starts to lighten as I feel a little more like myself since I am dressed in my training leathers that cling to my body but stretch with every stroke of movement. I'm looking forward to having a reason to release some of this pent-up anger, but also a way to help me have some form of protection on my own without access to my powers.

The black leather snuggly fits in a sleek design that has extra hoops to strap blades, but my favorite is my own personal dagger from Kye. The one that always stays strapped against my thigh, but now holds a memory of a shadowed male wiping his blood on me. I push the memory of him away and sheathe it in place, which, to most, is very unladylike for a docile *princess.*

I unhook the pale blue cloak that matches perfectly with how everyone dresses in light colors in the palace—a perfect camouflage to cover my attire. I drape it around me and snap the front together, blanketing every part of me. As soon as I clasp the second button, a short knock raps against my door.

"Come in!" I raise my voice to be heard, knowing it's not Cora, and nervously wait to see who's on the other side. The handle turns and light filters through from the hallway as the door gets pushed open.

"A little help here?" A raspy voice says, and I let out a breath of relief. *Telion.*

I hurry to the door and swing it fully open. The cook has his full-length apron on, with the floppy chef's hat hiding his bald head. A dark mustache speckled with red covers his upper lip, and his wide, burly frame squeezes through the door as he pushes a breakfast cart into my room. The smell of cinnamon swirls in the air, causing drool to form in my mouth. Piles of fruit, cinnamon buns, orange juice, and a covered dish lay in wait for me.

The moment he enters, his eyes widen a fraction, assessing me and my surroundings before releasing the breath he was holding. Every once in a while, Telion will bring meals to my room when he gets the chance, but I know it's from his fear secretly eating away at him. He was the one who found me three years ago, when I was pale and bleeding out on this very floor.

He pushes the cart of food to the couch near the balcony, before turning around and raising a bushy eyebrow at me. I suck my lower lip into my mouth and quickly look around the room, noticing the specks of dust gathering on the crown molding of the ceiling, suddenly finding it interesting.

I can feel his stare digging a hole into my head, and when he clears his throat, I shoot my eyes back, only to purse my lips and narrow my gaze on him. The war of holding each other's stare turns competitive as he dips his head and stares harder, his eyes almost protruding out of their sockets. The scene before me and the vein swelling in his forehead almost makes me huff a small laugh, but instead, causes me to blink and give him the win.

His stomach shakes as a rumble of laughter leaves him. "Points for effort, girl, but you can't beat the ol' champion," he muses.

I roll my eyes and walk towards him and the heavenly scent of breakfast that's calling my name. "One day, I will," I chide. "How come you're bringing breakfast to my room today?"

Usually, food is prepared and then set in the dining room, ready to eat when we choose to come down. Unless my father commands my presence.

"Well, I thought I'd ask you in person if you've seen a rat runnin' around. One that sneaks food from my kitchen, maybe even has a sweet tooth..." he says, nonchalantly, as he side-eyes me.

Again, I purse my lips and narrow my eyes on him. "Hmm... Let me think... Nope!" I plaster the biggest, fakest smile I can manage onto my face as I pop the *p*.

The corner of his lips lift, raising the mustache with it. He leans forward to lift the lid of the silver tray. I hold in my laughter and surprise as I stare at a delicious slice of raspberry tart topped with a swirl of whipped cream.

"Well, if you see the rat, please tell it that I'm onto it," he says. Facing me with an amused smile, he pats my shoulder and walks to the door to leave. It clicks shut behind him and his footsteps become faint down the hallway. I hold in the brief feeling of warmth that his kindness gives. An unfamiliar feeling, but one that I wish wouldn't disappear after only a few moments.

I greedily take in the food before me and devour it, chewing every bite to savor the flavors. Groaning at the sweetness that sends a surge of sugar straight into my bloodstream. I force myself to eat as much as I can, so I have plenty of energy to fuel my training with Kye for the next hour.

———

Kye and I train on one of my father's ships that is docked far behind the palace; the one with a broken mast. A few years ago, the ship was out at sea traveling to the Court of Amihan, where I heard the water becomes layered with sheets of ice, and white powder falls from the sky. Mid-travel, a storm wracked and tossed the sea to frightening heights, and monstrous waves cascaded over the ship, slamming into it with an endless assault. My father had to abandon that trip and chose to redirect the boat home, but not quickly enough, as a bolt of lightning snapped from the sky, striking the wooden mast and cleaving it in two. I heard the journey back was slow and rough, but ever since, this ship is permanently tied to the dock, remaining in constant motion with the rocking waves.

Kye likes to meet here to train, not only because it's far from prying eyes, but because the sway and motion of the ship helps me focus more on my stability. The sun-faded sails billow against the breeze, as the wooden frame of the ship knocks against the dock, creaking with every tip as it rocks.

I scurry past the line of ships and veer left down the final strip of the dock towards our hidden gem. While racing up the pegged ramp as my cloak cascades behind me, I hear the sharpening of a blade as I turn the corner, reaching the back deck of the boat.

Kye sits atop a barrel, one foot resting on his knee as he balances his sword on top of his leathers, scraping his steel stone along the sharp edge. Hunching over to inspect his work, his shirtless torso shifts, his thick muscles rippling with the movement. The sun beats down on his skin, turning him a darker shade of gold with each second that passes. His long, tousled dark hair is partially pulled into a bun, putting the long scar that runs down the side of his face on display, fading behind his beard. He told me he earned it in battle before I was born, but however old Kye is, he only looks about ten years older than me. Then again, most Fae look centuries younger than they are. He still won't tell me his true age, but maybe he will if I win a friendly duel against him.

The tan skin of his back is decorated with other small wounds earned in battle, leaving behind spots of blemished skin scattered throughout. If only I could say my damaged skin was earned from battle. It's impossible to fight when my father ties me against a post to punish me, but one day, I will get my revenge. I will win that battle.

"Right on time," he says, his deep voice rumbling over the sounds of the waves crashing. Kye glances up at me as he stands up to begin our training, pleased that I'm never late. He's at least 6'3, with broad shoulders, bulging muscles, and abs carved from steel. Kye's bulky frame is pure strength that makes any male cower in his presence. His tight leathers stretch at the seams along his hard thighs and sit low on his waist, making the lines of his deep V extremely visible. He approaches me barefoot. He once mentioned that he's a primal male who feels that boots bring too much cushion to training.

"You know I'd never disappoint you," I tell him. He's helped give me back so much of my strength that I lost over the years, giving me a reason to keep fighting, to destroy my father. But for me to do that, I need to learn every fighting skill out there to make me unstoppable and to see if there's a way to get this necklace off.

I shuck off my cloak and toss the nauseating powder blue cover to the other side of the deck, feeling more myself in my all-black training attire. But the sun is radiating an intense heat today, soaking straight into me. The dark thread of my clothing is drawing the sun's fiery rays into me like a moth is drawn to a flame. Beads of sweat are already forming along my hairline, forcing me to tie my hair back into a high ponytail as the gentle breeze cools the cluster of moisture that's on the back of my neck.

"You really should wear lighter clothes, unless you want to faint from overheating," Kye states, raising his eyebrows at me and my choice of training attire. But he should know I'd never do that and haven't since he's known me. He may not know about the scars I keep hidden, but he should be used to my stubbornness and doing things in my own way by now.

Sighing, I regard him with an annoyed look that's hardly convincing. "I'll be good. Let's just begin so I can kick your ass," I tease.

He shakes his head, and the loose strands of hair fall from his bun from the movement, tickling the side of his face. "In your dreams, Princess."

I hold his gaze as his amusement slides away, being replaced with a taunting glare, which challenges me to make a move. I smirk at his change in demeanor as he tosses me an extra sword and I begin readying my stance, arms in position.

Kye's feet shift into defense, knowing I won't hesitate to make the first move. He tests the weight of his sword in a graceful movement as he finally grips the hilt and steadies it in the air. Watching. Waiting.

I push off on my back foot and lunge forward, swinging my sword to the side, ducking and swinging my leg low to the ground to knock him off his feet. But he sees the sword as the distraction it is and leaps over my leg, readying his stance again as I straighten my form and instantly fall back into position.

This time he twists to the side, while simultaneously striking his sword towards my chest. I dive and roll, springing back to my feet as he swings again without a moment's pause, causing a string of curses to fly from my mouth.

We tango to the sounds of clashing steel and curse words for the next hour. With swords in our grasps, we strike, block, and dodge until we're drenched in sweat, our chests heaving as our muscles scream with exertion.

As the bright orange sun drifts across the sky, growing hotter in the passing hour, I drop my body to the ship deck, sucking in the salty air as slick strands of hair stick to my face. My parched mouth is in desperate need of a drink, and my clothing is clinging tighter to my body from absorbing the moisture coating my skin.

Kye crouches down beside me, handing me water from his canteen. I guzzle down as much of the liquid gold as I can, but make sure to still leave plenty for him.

He regards me as silence settles between us. The white birds chirp in the distant sky, and the wind softly whistles as the sails clack against the gusts of air. I can feel him observing me, and I already know what he will say before he even begins to open his mouth.

"Why aren't you sleeping?" he asks softly. Concern fills his voice as his eyes turn gentle, clearly noticing the dark circles that live under my eyes, the fatigue and slow recovery in-between each swipe of my sword. But mostly, I'm given away by how I stopped training to rest instead of demanding him to keep going.

I don't want to tell him about the nightmares and how sleep drags me under into the hands of some devious phantom. The way an icy grip wishes to stop the air entering my lungs and tint my lips blue for eternity. Or how sometimes my own darkness stirs inside me, slithering through my veins, feeding off the fury that simmers deep down. The darkness wants to devour me whole as it wraps around my mind, body, and soul. Promising to end my misery, but I feel it will only smother every sliver of light as I become trapped in a bottomless pit, an endless void. How I can feel the strength in me wanting to demolish every evil soul in this world, but then the moments I feel weak, tired from the war raging inside, is when the darkness seems like an escape. A way to slip under and make this grey world fade into nothing.

Turning my head lazily, knowing I can't lie, because this life is already tearing my soul to shreds, I offer him a different answer. "I know about the Corruption." I stare deep into his dark brown eyes.

He jerks his head away and stares out at the sea, his eyes glinting with specks of amber in the sun's beams. The muscle behind the scruff on his jaw jumps as his scarred, strong hands clench and unclench.

"You're angry that I know," I say.

"Damn right I'm angry!" he seethes. Shooting up to stand, he starts pacing back and forth, carving a path on the wooden deck. He blows out an aggravated breath, scraping his hand down his face and roughly rubbing his jaw. "I almost lost my whole family when they started digging into the evil of this world, too curious to let it be. To let someone else handle it. They wanted answers, to help the people, and they paid for it. They were just lucky I was able to help lessen their punishment." His eyes squeeze shut as the painful memories roll through him. "I can't have you met with the same fate as them." Then he freezes.

Shit.

Turning on the soles of his feet, his body becomes rigid and his darkened eyes pin me to the spot. "*How?*" he growls. "*How* do you know about the Corrupted, Princess?" His eyes darken even more, already assuming what he knows to be true. If I tell him, I will have to deal with his words of outrage, but eventually, his anger will burn out. If I don't tell him the truth, I'll lose his trust. He's one of the only people I can rely on and the thought of that makes my already black, hardened heart crack. Splintering it in the center. The idea of him knowing I lied to him would be unbearable.

Kye's height is frightening when he's standing, and I'm still flopped on the floorboard. Pushing up onto fatigued arms, legs shaking as I force them to hold me up straight, I raise my light eyes to his dark ones, clashing against each other.

"I left the palace," I say with a strong steadiness that even I am proud of. But the frustration and fury coursing through Kye could vibrate the ship, splintering the wood and sinking it for good.

I hold my ground, never breaking eye contact to let him know I will tell him whatever he wants to know about my evening of rebellious freedom. That no matter how mad he is at me, I'm not going anywhere, and he won't either.

The tension in the air intensifies around us as some of Kye's power signature leaks out, a ring of cobalt forming around us. Each power has its own color based on the Fae's ability. The lower Fae is determined by what element they possess, and the high Fae have a different color that ties in with their special power. After a Fae's power takes root and begins to show at a young age, they are placed in the class ranking that matches their power. The lower Fae tend to have weaker levels of power and usually work around the palace or become masters of trade throughout Deyadrum. Many use their elemental powers to help their Royal Court and the high Fae they work under. Even high Fae's work under the Royals, because they are descendants to the bloodline connecting to the Elders— the beginning of our race.

Kye's ability ignites brightly with the sheer force of his strength. The pressure of his power feels heavy against my body, the weight almost too much for me to remain standing. But I keep my eyes locked on his, never wavering, no matter how hard my body shakes and rages against his power. His eyes look crazed as more power slips free, but the moment he sees my body dip a little, the surge is snuffed out. As fast as it came alive, it's pulled back as he tames his power and enraged feelings.

Our eyes are still connected, still holding onto one another. Guilt flashes in his deep eyes. He looks away from me as he stalks back to the barrel he sat on earlier.

"I'm sorry," he breathes out, turning back to look at me with pleading eyes. "I lost control and just snapped. I didn't mean to use my powers on you." His gaze trails down my body and back up, assessing. It's absurd, really, but I understand why. The magnitude of his power of strength can easily snap bone if he willed it, and I have this treacherous necklace that won't allow me to heal quickly. "Did I hurt you?" he asks.

This giant of a guy has the most caring heart when he opens it up to

94

someone. A stark difference from the broody asshole he becomes around the fellow guards he leads. "Pft. In your dreams," I say, throwing his earlier words back at him, hoping to smooth the worry that creases between his brows.

A slight twitch of his lip lets me know it did the trick. The anger that put him in a frenzy seems to dissipate with the fear of possibly causing me harm. But in a way, he did, by neglecting to share the curse spreading throughout Deyadrum and keeping me in the dark. An ache in my chest spreads at the thought of Kye, someone who I thought would always keep me safe, leaving me feeling vulnerable.

"Why didn't you tell me?" I murmur. Sorrow coats every word as my voice cracks, forcing the words out to drift across the breeze.

By the look in his eyes, you would think I just pierced his heart, ripping it out and holding it in the palm of my hands. As if keeping this information from me was slowly killing him, knowing it would hurt me in the process.

"I couldn't, Princess. The king demanded it. But I also know you, and I didn't want your stubbornness to risk your safety. I couldn't stop my parents from their own stubbornness, so when I saw an opportunity to stop you from yours, I took it."

The fissure in my chest rips further apart at the mention of the *king*, or the fact that he chose my father over me. A secret he's kept that I hope has tasted bitter for as long as he's withheld it. The space between us grows heavy as every bone in my body wants to close the distance separating us, only to hurt him like his words are hurting me. "Since when do you choose my *father* over me?!" I scream. "Has he offered you pounds of gold to weigh down your pockets? Females to bed every night? Freedom from this hell?!" I'm seething.

He was forced to sign a contract years ago in order to save his parents from a death sentence ordered by my father. To clear them from false accusations of rebelling against him when they were trying to help others. The sliver of darkness curls out of the crack in my heart, wrapping around it to take hold and free me from the outrage and devastation wracking through me. I can feel it feeding off my rising rage, fueling its icy hunger. Kye's frame begins to blur as the haze of my emotions contorts everything around me. I feel my eyes darken as I lose my sense of self, spiraling into a vortex of obsidian as my heart starts to freeze over.

"Emma…" The softest voice penetrates the wall of shadows, sparking the ember in the expanse of darkness. The voice of the male who always gave me strength, who found a way to keep the small flame inside me burning. My name echoes in my head. Distant. But I'm clawing my way back, swimming through the shadows, becoming angry with myself for being so weak and letting this poison consume me so quickly. For giving in to its desires.

I demand my powers of light to come forth, to disintegrate the dark and bind it back to the hole it crawled out from. A deep warmth grows inside me, melting the coldness hardening in my chest. Burning brighter and flaring out in a forceful blast. Waves of white light scorch through my veins and spark against my fingertips, as I feel myself internally screaming at the agony.

My eyes begin to burn hotter, glowing white as I push my power further, but the pain of it ricocheting off my necklace is overwhelming. The iron ring singes against my skin, dragging my nails down my neck, clawing, begging for it to stop. But the pain brings me back to the present. As my vision clears, I find Kye in front of me, gripping my upper arms tightly and staring at me with wild eyes.

I look down at my nails, layers of my skin and blood caked underneath from clawing at my throat in an attempt to stop the pain. The fingers that are wrapped around my arms turn bruising, demanding me to look up and explain. But how do I explain something that I don't even understand? The leash on my powers is nothing new. Kye knows about the collar that feels like a ring of fire when my power overreaches, even if seeing me fight against it never gets easier. But how am I supposed to explain the black poison that sings in my blood? To voice the part of me that likes its sweet whispers and wants to dive underneath its waves of ebony and drown myself in the dark promises. To accept an offer of devouring my emotions so I don't feel the broken parts of me that I can't mend, to be set free from the endless suffering.

I lift my grey irises to him, as he is still frantically roaming over my face. "Your eyes went black," he whispers. Speaking so quietly, like he's nervous to snap the string that's holding my control and, ultimately, myself together. "What was that?"

Jerking my head back, I step away from him. Not able to look into his endless pits of worry, shame flaring to life in me. Ashamed I lost control over my psyche so quickly, leaving my soul vulnerable to the clutches of evil that lurk inside.

"I don't know," I tell him, refusing to face him. Acting like a coward when my mind is screaming at me to use the strength I know I have. But I know Kye. He wants to protect me from everything, and now there's something burrowed into my soul that has caught him off guard. An enemy he can't protect me from. If he could, he'd shove his hand through my chest and rip its vile claws from its grasp on me. But there's no way of tearing this demon from my being without wrenching my heart out with it.

"When did this start?" he demands, turning into every bit of the commanding bodyguard that he is.

Sighing, I fill him in on all that I know, but refuse to tell him about the nightmares. There is no saving me from those, and I can't ask him to try, because I'm already too much of a burden to those around me. This game the phantom started is one I have to play, and play alone. "Just the other day, when I became enraged with thoughts of my father. It calls to me when I'm angry, as if my raging thoughts are a drug that it craves. I've managed it so far, but it would be easier if I had full access to my powers."

I finally turn to look at him, keeping the few paces of distance between us. I've always lived with some type of nightmare, but the new ones with the phantom male are recent and the feelings of the darkness whispering to me didn't start stirring until he invaded my sleep. "Everyone says they want to protect me, but imprisoning my powers leaves me wide open for someone to end my life. Yes, you've been training me, but there will come a time when self-defense won't be enough. My death is inevitable because even my own body wants to attack itself. To suck the essence from me and turn me into something darker."

"We will figure it out. We'll find out what this darkness is and tear it from your body," he declares, standing tall, chest raised, fists clenched, and ready for a battle he can't fight.

A sad smile stretches across my face with a slight shake of my head. I knew this is what he would say. He can't help himself. Even if he kept the secret of the Corruption from me, and listened to my father's orders, he still will always be my knight in shining armor, cutting down and shielding me from everything that would do me harm.

"Kye," I plead, needing him to *hear* every word I'm saying. "There is no ridding me of this darkness." I take a steady breath and stare deeply into him, so he hears the truth in my words. "Because this darkness… It's a part of me, and in order to free me from it, you'd have to kill me." I know it in my gut. I can *feel* how this darkness is one half of my soul. Something that has been with me since I was born, growing stronger with every passing year. Finally coming to claim me, because now its strength is spilling over, wanting to swallow every spark of light I have inside. He can't save me from something that *is* me.

The look darkening his eyes tells me he would say damn my words because he'll try anyway, but I just don't see how. I can tell he's refraining from bursting out and throwing his words at me, like usual. He's scared to push me towards the shadows of my mind. I save him the anguish by changing gears.

"Forget it, please. At least for now. But I need you to tell me about the Corruption." I urge him, walking towards the shadowed space underneath the top deck's railing, desperate for some reprieve from the scorching rays. My clothing feels like it's melted into my skin at this point, making the rolling waves look like the most refreshing sight.

Kye joins me in the cooler section of the deck, letting the slight breeze dry the heated beads that drip down off our skin. "Only if you promise we'll talk about this *darkness* and let me help you find a way to destroy it."

The determined look on his face tells me he won't back down from this or tell me what I want to know until I agree. "Promise." *Lies. There is no way to destroy it unless you destroy me.*

He scrutinizes me for a moment, not quite believing my quick agreement, but he seems to accept it for now as his body settles with contentment. "First, you *have* to know that I didn't want to keep this from you. But the king was very stern in his orders about keeping it from reaching your ears and, at the time, I saw it as a way I could protect you from the true evil of this world. As time went on, the urge to tell you was eating at me, but it felt too late to tell you the truth, and I didn't want to see the look of betrayal cross your face. I never chose his side; protecting you was always the priority. I know that my choice to keep you unaware was wrong."

I hear the truth in his voice as he bleeds out the pain from keeping this from me. He leans against the deck's beam as he continues. "I also want to know more about *how* you found out about the curse." He squints his eyes at me, pinning me to the spot. "But I will explain what I know first because you desire an answer. Nobody knows why the Corruption started or why it's growing so quickly. Some point blame at the two Gods, and some swear it's the ill-fated Elder."

I stare at him as I rack my brain about the Elder he's speaking of. I know of the first Fae, but I can't seem to recall the cursed one.

Kye waves his hand in the air. "I'm sure you've read about this in ancient texts your father made you study, but the Elders were the first Fae to be created by the Gods 12,000 years ago, and some would say they are the most powerful in Deyadrum. But none mention the sole Elder who was believed to be cursed. Wiping the Elder's history from existence—an outcast from the rest and abandoned on the island we know as the Court of Ashes."

He pauses, rubbing his knuckles along the scar running down his face before he sighs. "Nobody knows the truth, though. It's all just speculation. The myths about this Elder creating the curse only began once we learned that the Corrupted originate from that court. The court where those sentenced to death for their wrongs are sent, a place where there are Scavengers that look like giant, shadowed wolves, a black fire coating their phantom limbs, crimson eyes, and teeth sharper than any blade." A shiver travels down my spine that such a creature exists, and I am just now finding out about it.

"Any bite or scratch of any sort from a Scavenger will turn a Fae feral, monstrous, and savage. When someone gets a Scavenger's poison under their skin, it turns their blood dark. Like black roots covering their body as the venom charges through their veins. Sharp, pointed claws grow from their fingers and every one of them develops black eyes. But only the Scavengers can transfer the curse, not the Corrupted." He stops and looks at me after he says that, clearly still concerned as to why my eyes changed to a soulless pit of nothing, just like the Corrupted's.

"The way to kill them is with an iron blade stabbing straight through their heart, sending their deathless souls into a mound of ash. We haven't been able to figure out how they are traveling over the mass of the sea and intruding into every court. Let alone come to a conclusion as to what they are after, unless it's solely to kill the people of Deyadrum. But that's all I know, Princess, and if I learn more, then I swear it to the Gods above that I will tell you," he promises, placing his giant hand over his heart and dipping his head for my honor and respect. "The kings and queens will be having a meeting during the time of the ball that's approaching, to strategize the next steps in how to end the Corruption for good. Now, Princess…are you ready to tell me how you found out about it?"

"I suppose if I don't, you'll tie me up to the mast and force me to cook under the sun until I give." I roll my eyes as I catch the slight smirk of his lips. "The night Cora sent the guard outside my room to you, so we could have a girl's night—"

"She told me to keep him busy until the sun rose over the horizon so you and her could pillage through Telion's hidden sweets and wine, and not be stopped by your guard. Also, for you to not have prying ears outside your room, as you two planned to gossip and laugh through the night." His eyebrow raises at that, then falls the moment I feel the chuckle form low in my belly and tumble free. I have to give it to Cora; she can fool any male with a blink of her eyes. "So, instead, you left the palace like you said— "

"Yes," I interrupt. "I *had* to get outside of these walls and see what the people of Asov are like. I know nothing else but the palace and the sea that it sits on. Especially once I officially marry Aiden, I'll be stuck here for eternity." Taking an enormous inhale to prepare for the worst and ready myself to say the words as fast as possible. "I ended up running into a Corrupted Fae, who then tried to kill me, but before he clawed me in two, a shadowed vigilante stabbed him through the heart and turned him to ash." Cringing, every muscle in my petite frame tightens in anticipation of his wrath for putting myself in such a dangerous situation. Except he's silent. Staring. Absorbing the words I fired at him.

Yet, his masculine body is utterly still as he stands frozen before me. "A shadowed vigilante?"

Out of everything I just told him, that's what he gets stuck on? "Yes…" I say with caution.

He looks stunned, as if I'm speaking a different language. "There are myths of a male who has been hunting the Corrupted since the beginning of this curse. It is said that he uses no ships to cross the sea yet appears in every court to strike his sword through the hearts of every Corrupted he finds, leaving ashes in his wake. Only whispered words that travel against the raging sea tell of his shadowed face and his cloak of night. Nothing more, because he vanishes and speaks to no one, but everyone calls him Shade."

The air in my lungs is punched out of me as chills wrack my skin. If Kye was nervous and shocked to speak of this myth of a male… The male that *saved* me. *Spoke* to me…

"Shade," I test out the name the people call him, but no bile rises in my throat. No vile taste coating my tongue, just a satisfying flavor as I finally know who the cocky asshole is.

CHAPTER THIRTEEN

Emma

*a*fter my training with Kye, I came back to my room to clean the sticky sweat that was clinging to my body. The golden globe looms far across the clearest blue sky, signaling dinner, since I trained through lunch. I've been summoned to dine with my father when the sun drops halfway to the horizon. Usually, meals are prepared, and I eat alone with only a bodyguard lurking behind me, and my father tends to eat his meals in his study. So, him requesting my presence has me on high alert.

The devil summoning his enslaved demon for dinner.

In my bedroom, I stand before the full-length mirror trimmed with swirls of gold, delicately crafted atop the polished wooden frame. As I stare at my reflection, I take the kernel of strength that's rooted inside of me, keeping it close, and giving myself comfort as I lock it away for the evening. With my actions these past few days—from leaving my father's study before he excused me to my nightly explorations through Asov—I shove down my pride and wear a dress my father would approve of. The tight corset top connects with a shimmery, thin nude fabric that covers up to my neck and trails down my arms, with a loop to hook over my finger.

Hiding my disgust at the way the light dusty pink washes me out, my eyes scan my reflection once more. Sweet, charming colors to appease his false fatherly love. But if I hope to stay under the radar through dinner and not displease him, then I have to play the part of the delightful princess. The dress spills around me from the waist down in sheer layers of pinks and champagnes, hiding the murderous weapon that's tightly secured around my thigh.

Always prepared.

I slide my hesitant feet into champagne silk slippers and take a second glance over my hair, making sure no strays are out of place or stick out in unwanted areas. I decided to pin my hair up in a low, twisted bun, leaving my neck on display to show off the gift he'd so generously bestowed upon me for the rest of my life. The necklace occasionally makes me feel like I can't breathe, with its heavy weight and the tightness of it. Feeling more insane with each passing day that I can't get it off. Although I've now somewhat grown used to its heaviness, the desperate need to rip it off still lingers.

I continue to get ready as I slide a gold satin clip atop my bun and stare at my reflection. Anger simmers and a pang of sadness kicks in at how I appear, but deep down, I know this is strength. Facing my unknown hell every day, pretending to be someone I'm not in order to protect myself. That's not weakness. Just another game—one I plan to play my own way and rewrite the rules to.

I exit my room, steeling my spine; ever the noble princess. My steps are sure, unhurried, leaving a trail of fire in my wake. Minutes later, I descend the grand staircase that widens at the end, veering right as I approach the swarming scents of roasted chicken and garlic. Drool pools in my mouth and hunger pains stab me, my body demanding to be fed as I take in the savory intoxication.

The open archway that leads to my father's presence looms in front of me. Straightening my shoulders back and jutting my chin up, I enter. Ready for battle.

My shields are raised around me but falter at the sight of Aiden and his father, Captain Calloway. A dent in the exterior of my barrier, as arrows are shot from the cold depths of Calloway's eyes. Calloway is a threat. One of many. But he's the most menacing here, the most unknown of them all, and I don't have an inkling as to what is lurking in his mind.

Sitting on my father's right, he's dressed in a sleek brown tunic, brocaded with copper stitching, and the emblem of being the King's Right Hand---an honorary position he abuses—glistens on his chest. The colors of a captain whose sole love is the wooden beauty that rocks at sea. He leans comfortably in his chair, a mocking behavior in a king's presence, but my father doesn't seem bothered. In fact, it seems he couldn't care less, as his gleaming brown eyes never leave me, following every step I take. I make it towards the empty seat to his left, which happens to be on Aiden's right, who I have not seen or spoken to after the incident in the cave. I've been left unsure of where his thoughts are at after he masked his feelings before racing me in the water.

He shoots out of his chair with graceful ease and stands behind mine, pulling it out for me. I halt before him, wanting to read his expression, but his face is neutral. Bored, even. Wearing a navy tunic with silver clasps, his golden hair is slicked back along the sides, and his green eyes battle against the blue of his attire.

Cautious not to draw attention, I let him slide the cushioned chair to the backs of my knees as I lower myself. The stillness and utter silence in the room are smothering, but I seal my lips, not daring to break them.

The King of Asov takes hold of his wine, swirling its contents before bringing it to his lips. "How is the lovely couple?" he asks between mouthfuls of ruby liquid.

Staring straight ahead, I keep my eyes focused on everything and nothing. Not giving in to his teasing questions, which I assume he already has an answer to, based on his smirk and the rigid posture of Aiden. I'm not sure if this formal dinner with our fathers is making him uncomfortable, or it could be my presence, now that he's had time to think. I worry my reaction in the cave made him upset with me. But surprise jolts me back as Aiden's smooth voice fills the space.

"Magnificent." He lays his hand on top of mine, taking hold. "We're looking forward to the ball in the Court of Asiza."

My eyes seem to be glued to his hand grasping mine, confused at the display he's putting on and trying to keep up with the switch in his demeanor. His large fingers wrapped around mine give a tight, quick squeeze, alerting me to the present.

"Ball?" I ask. Pondering the words that fell from Aiden's lips. My father has never sent me to another court. He couldn't possibly…

"Yes, Emma. Now that you're betrothed, it's best for you both to make an appearance as a couple. Of course, it has been themed as a masquerade ball. So, your face will still be secret to the people of Deyadrum, aside from the ruler of Asiza. It's courtesy to know each guest. But for everyone else, they will be able to know your existence is true. Every court will be in attendance; it would look bad if you weren't there."

I knew a ball in Asiza—the land of mist and evergreens—was fast approaching. Kye mentioned it during our training. I assumed I would be stranded here, staring out at the endless sea, longing to join. No words could form in my head as chaos erupts in my mind, with every thought coursing through me at the declaration that I will be journeying out of Asov.

Calloway leans forward, resting his elbows on the table. For someone dressed in such finery, his body language lacks proper etiquette. "Don't get any ideas though, Princess." The way he says *Princess* is laced with disdain. "This will be the only time your pampered feet step foot on my ship. Keep in mind that I'm *allowing* you this courtesy because the king needs you at the ball and to showcase your engagement to my son by letting the people see you two together. Any wrong moves, and you'll be tossed underneath the ship until we reach shore."

I slide my hand from Aiden's and move both of my hands under the table, clutching the material of my skirt. I'm squeezing so hard that the edges of my nails pierce through the sheer fabric, digging into my palms and carving half-moons in their wake. I welcome the slight sting as I reign in the irritation flooding me. Shoving down any retort that would result in a hand whipping across my face, I choose my words carefully.

"Understood, Captain, but that won't be necessary."

I feel a nudge against my knee. Aiden's gentle attempt for my attention as I hold Calloway's determined stare. Not allowing him to see any fear his words tried to create. A challenge.

"Now, now," my father interrupts. "My dear Emma will be on her best behavior, won't you?"

A warning.

A threat.

"Of course, Your Highness." Addressing him by his title will please him, enough to get the target off my back.

With the puff of his chest, along with the high and mighty look that crosses his face, I would say my attempt worked.

Another move in this dangerous game.

"The ball will be held in two days' time. Tomorrow at dawn, we will set sail to make it to Asiza by nightfall," my father says sternly. A twinge of excitement bubbles in my chest at how soon we leave. I can't help the lightness in my mood at knowing this palace will be in the distance soon. "It won't begin until evening the day following our arrival. Therefore, you are to rest in your rooms that morning. I have a summit I must attend, so don't roam about like some child, and you will speak to no one. Your appearance is needed at the *ball*, not wandering aimlessly through the castle in Asiza. Your identity still needs to be kept secret." The harshness in his voice washes over me, drowning me in promises of torment if I go against his demands. "Remember, this is to protect you."

I can't help but question his remark. It sounds like a worthless attempt to show he cares. A con artist tricking his victim. I'm tired of his lies, his words that are infused with his own brand of poison.

The urge to leap over the edge of the table and drag my dagger across his jugular is almost unbearable. My fingers twitch on their own accord. Wanting to take. To claim revenge. To see how he likes it when I spill *his* blood.

Whispers come forward, promising me his death will taste sweet. Silencing him would bring great pleasure. A pleasure I've never felt before.

Another nudge knocks the side of my knee, stomping on every murderous thought and disintegrating them to ash. I give a quick glance at Aiden from the corner of my eye. His emotionless eyes dart to our fathers before slamming into mine. The weight lessens in them, briefly offering me a tender smile in understanding before it drops, becoming neutral again. He's playing a role, not only for us, but for himself.

I drag my eyes back to the table, extending my arm over the top, reaching to grab the ruby wine demanding to be sipped. But I need more than a taste. It needs to flow down my throat until a numbness settles in. Calming the nerves racking through me from how close I was to unleashing this demon within.

I take a breath and look at my father. "I understand, Father. Your concern is greatly appreciated." Bile shoots up my throat, souring my tongue.

I wish I could tell him to go to hell instead. Only…we're already here and have been for many years. I bring the glass to my lips to help swallow my retorts back down. Playing the compliant daughter screams against everything I am. But in order to win the game, I must discreetly move the pawns on the board while I figure out my plan. To keep mastering my skills at training and keep playing my role as princess, while seeking his weakness. This hunger growing in me to take him down is becoming stronger each day, wanting to be fed.

A prickling sensation crashes into me from across the table. I know Calloway is skinning me alive with his eyes. Trying to find the lies under my sweet, docile responses. He won't find any in the obedient mask I wear. The ability to keep an impassive expression is all thanks to Father Dearest and the years he's had to rip the emotions from me.

"Very well. Cora is preparing your luggage as we speak." I give a slight dip of my head to offer my acknowledgment. "I expect you to be ready before breakfast. We need to start our travels early, for a storm may approach and roughen the sea. Aiden, you will make sure Emma behaves appropriately, yes? We don't need a scandal on our hands, especially at her first gathering with the people."

"I promise, Your Highness." Aiden's hand rises to his heart, delivering the promise of being my babysitter and personal bodyguard, something no grown female should have. I should show them how well I can wield a blade; how precisely the point of my dagger can hit its mark. But that knowledge will ruin my chances of surprise. They need to only see me as the weak Fae princess who possess none of her powers.

"Eat," my father commands in an exigent voice.

The rumble of my stomach tells me how hungry I am, enough to eat every bite in one breath. But instead, I delicately hold my fork and knife, taking my time slicing the meat into perfect bite-sized morsels. I place the knife neatly next to my plate before stabbing a small piece of chicken, gently placing it in my mouth.

Perfect. Fucking. Etiquette.

The rest of dinner is lacking. Aiden and I remain completely silent, only focusing on the food before us. But I feel his knee brush against mine every so often. A silent comfort. My father sits at the head of the table, turning in towards Calloway as they chat amongst themselves, ignoring us as we sit on my father's other side. Fine by me.

My eyes flick to the table. I'm almost finished with my second glass of wine and the now-cleared dish sits before me as I wait for the king to announce the dinner's end. Should I go for a third glass? With the taxing atmosphere, I don't bother waiting for the server as I swoop up the bottle and fill my empty glass to the brim. The magical liquid already flowing through my bloodstream is erasing all thoughts of annoyance. Slight tingles course through me as it continues to numb me from within.

Fuck it.

Taking hold of the bottle, I pour the rest of its remains into my waiting glass. Sliding my tongue over my lips, I bring the rim to my mouth. I don't dare take only a sip as I relish in the fruity scent before tipping the glass all the way back and chugging down the wine in gulps.

A scoff comes from my father. "Aiden, it seems the *princess* is too indisposed to continue dinner, clearly unable to handle her drink. Escort her back to her rooms." The disgust in his voice is clear, but it gives me an excuse to leave dinner early. I can feel the irritation rolling off him in waves, but it has no effect on me, for the wine is singing in my blood, blocking out everything.

"Yes, Your Highness," Aiden replies without hesitation.

The scrape of his chair vibrates around the room as he stands, grabbing hold of the back of my seat. I slowly rise when I feel the chair start sliding away from me. Before I'm fully standing, Aiden's hand clasps mine, with his other resting on my lower back, and offers a quick bow to the king and his father. I manage to tip forward, a slight wobble to my bow before Aiden pulls me up and guides us to the exit.

The wine takes over as I dramatically let my eyes roll in their sockets at the façade he's playing. I allow him this moment to play the doting betrothed, ignoring the warmth of his palm pressing into my back. When we cross under the archway and enter the hall, his steps start leading us towards the staircase. The steps that lead me to my prison inside a prison. Once I'm tossed in my room, I'll have to remain there until morning. The thought unsettles me. I'm not ready to pace around my room or restart the book I just finished.

Whether it's the wine or my desperate need to steal more time away from my room, I twist out of Aiden's arms. Casually walking down the far hallway without warning. An amused huff sounds behind me, followed by the tapping of footsteps.

"It seems you must have misplaced your room. If I remember correctly, there are no bedrooms down this hallway," Aiden speaks to my back, as I allow a smirk he can't see to grace my lips.

"Your memory would be correct," I chide, still not giving him any explanation for my impromptu route.

"And where, pray tell, are you going?"

"Not my room," I sing-song.

"Well, that's *blatantly* obvious. Do you care to indulge me with your destination?"

I keep my pace, ignoring his question and, therefore, ignoring him. It's pointless, really. If he keeps following me, he will find out where I'm headed.

Another huffed laugh leaves him, but he says no more, knowing I don't plan on indulging him. Really though, with how close we have been over the years, I would think he would already know, or at least have an inkling. Maybe he doesn't remember the tiny details of me as clearly as I thought.

When we near the end, I turn right, crossing through the open court-yard that's blooming with flowers, vibrant trees, and the greenest grass. The moon has just started to rise in the sky, shining down to offer a soft light. Little lanterns decorate the pathway through the courtyard. A warm glow casts over the route to the other side of the palace. A cool breeze skates over my body, crashing against the warmth in my blood from the wine. A sweet concoction of warring sensations.

Aiden remains a few steps behind, trailing after me as I reach the other side of the courtyard, turning left. Only a bit ahead of me are the double-winged doors that open to my favorite room in this palace. I open the doors, stepping into the other world that is the library. Rows of books stretch far and wide, towering high above me. The heavenly aroma welcomes me, transporting me into a world of pure ecstasy. White pillars stand tall at the end of each row, and the white-shelled floor expands throughout. Where the bright light usually beams through the glass panes along the ceiling, only a subtle glow shines from the stars glistening above.

Cushioned cream couches furnish the center room, facing the glass doors of the closed-off balcony. Even being on the first floor, this end of the palace sits against the cliffside. Usually, the view of blue against blue is all that can be seen for miles. But at the moment, the sun is asleep. Darkness with glints of silver shimmering on the waves is all I see.

"I should have known." Aiden's voice penetrates the calmness that took over me, while getting lost in my own slice of bliss.

"I'm surprised you didn't," I say, without looking at him.

I walk away and gravitate towards the farthest row, where my favorite books are hidden. The ones that collect the least amount of dust from my frequent use. I can feel him following me, invading another one of my favorite spaces to hide away. This evening was the first time we spoke since the kiss, and even that was vague. No true discussion on the future or what transpired between us. I'm also not sure I'm ready to. But I suppose with the ball fast approaching, I have to end the silence and give in. I refuse to let anything get in the way and rip my first journey to another court from me.

The delicious view of my favorite romance books appears, and I bend down when I get to them. Running my fingers across their spines, I relish in the texture against my fingertips. I glance over them as I try to figure out which book I haven't read in a while. I've read each one numerous times, but I continue to rotate through them. New romance books never stock these shelves. I'm surprised these few are here. If my father knew, he would rid the library of them.

I grab the one that's a faded black, with bent edges and pages that are turning a shade of yellow. It's my favorite one. The title is scrawled in a dull white along the spine: *A War of Hearts*. When I open the book, the words consume me, pulling me into a heartwarming story of love won and love lost. A battle of wills with the character's beating heart. Deciding if she should guard it or let it bleed. I stand up and flip through the crisp pages, taking a step back—

Oomph. Solid. I bump into Aiden's heated frame; all space between us…gone. Why is he standing so close?

I freeze when I feel his fingers touch the side of my neck, brushing the strands of brown that fell from my bun. Goosebumps rise along my skin, the contact rushing in awareness that every inch of his front is pressing into my back. He lets his fingers trail down my spine, leaning forward and dipping his mouth to the junction between my shoulder and neck. Such a sensitive spot. I can't conceal the shiver or the shallow hitch in my breath. His hand latches onto my waist while skimming his lips along my slender neck.

"Don't fight this," he whispers, placing a soft peck under my ear.

I close my eyes in hopes of controlling the lust brewing inside me. The desire that's blocking out all rational thoughts. I need to tread carefully. I want nothing to hinder me from traveling to another court. I don't see Aiden telling my father to leave me here if I upset him, but I don't want to take that chance.

"We should talk," I force out. I'm barely able to handle his slight touch.

I know of lust and desire. The lovers in my books share many details on that. But the only experience I have is by my own hand, trying to seek pleasure and ease the ache that builds and builds, but a solo thrill never seems enough anymore. The ache only returns with a vengeance, nagging me to the point of insanity.

He turns me around and guides me towards the closest pillar, pushing my back against it.

"Okay, so talk," he says, staring at my lips with half-lidded eyes.

A rush of air comes out of me in a sigh, relieved that he's willing to talk about us and our impending future. "I think—"

My words are cut off when he slams his mouth to mine. A squeak escapes me as shock takes over. The hand still on my waist squeezes harder, pulling my lower half closer to him. The book falls from my hands in his rush to consume me. He seems to always let my books get in harm's way, neglecting the care they deserve. His other hand takes hold of my face and tilts it to the side, allowing him to slant his mouth over mine. Coaxing my lips apart as he plunges his tongue inside, swirling. Tasting.

The muscles in my body remain tense, but only for a few moments. The clean scent of Aiden cascades around us. The wine zings through my body and his heat ignites that kernel of desire inside me, loosening all sense of control. A pleasure-filled sigh passes through me, kissing him back with just as much force as I give in. Licking, tasting, teeth clashing. I can't get enough. The feel of his mouth is intoxicating. I never knew what kissing felt like before, but now I never want to go back. I could kiss Aiden for hours, it seems.

The darkness of the night shrouds us, the lit moon draping its dim glow over our heads, casting us as shadowed silhouettes.

I let my hands track up his muscled arms, over his shoulders, until my fingers slide through his hair. The blonde strands are slightly stiff with the gel he used to slick it back, but my fingers break through the mold, curling into the softness underneath. My nails scratch his scalp.

He groans. It seems he likes that.

I do it again.

Our mouths never part. His groans seep into me, and the vibration coming from his chest melts into mine. The hand on my face vanishes. The warmth is gone.

He roughly grabs my leg through my skirt, lifting it up to wrap around his waist. I'm thankful he grabs the leg that's bare, lacking any type of weapon. He presses his hardened length against my core. The pressure spurs on the ache, causing a moan to tumble free. His grip is bruising as he tries to press into me harder, eliciting another moan from my throat. Heavy breathing and pleasured moans fill the air around us. Until my body decides to have a mind of its own, starting a sensual grind against his cock. Needy. So *fucking* needy.

"*Fuck*, Emma," he groans. "You're killing me."

112

No words. I have no words to say, just a desperate plea to find release as I grind harder against him.

The hand on my leg tightens and his other hand leaves my waist, landing on my hip, before it slides to my ass and grips it. Pulling me closer to him, he hooks a thumb around my hip to help me rock faster against him.

A coiling heat forms in my stomach and my body burns with need. His mouth leaves mine, licking and nibbling against my jaw. Then, a zap of pleasure shoots to my core when he skates his teeth along the side of my neck, above the necklace, followed by his tongue. My pulse pounds harder, begging for more.

The point of friction between us is winding the pleasure tighter inside me. I can feel how wet I am as it drips down my legs, wanting to be filled.

"Aiden," I whimper, concentrating on his hot breaths that caress my skin.

He teasingly nips my neck, making me yelp in surprise. I expected pain, but none came. With one final squeeze, the hand clutching my ass leaves abruptly.

"Let me feel how wet you are," he growls.

In the next moment, his hand ruffles the hem of my skirt, trying to get underneath.

Panic seizes me in awareness.

What if he feels the mangled skin on my thighs, or finds the dagger hidden there?

In a flash, I shove him back again, my palms using as much force as they can muster against his solid pecs. He stumbles a couple of steps, not expecting my reaction. My chest heaves in rapid movements as he stares at me in crazed confusion. Still high on lust.

The effects of the wine and the desire Aiden sparked go out. I'd been blinded by the feelings of his hands, the heat of my blood, but all of it gets doused in cold water in a heartbeat.

The male standing before me straightens to his full height. Taking one step closer, the muscle in his jaw twitches. "Why do you keep pushing me away?" he asks in a wounded tone.

I shake my head, feeling the sense of deja vu slam into me all over again. "I'm sorry. The wine is affecting me more than I thought." *Lies.* A lame one, too, but I can't tell him I don't want him to know what's beneath my skirts. The weapon, the scars, or seeing how wet I am. This is Aiden, my friend of many years. Now, the lines between us are blurring, becoming fragile. And if I'm not careful, it will shatter.

By the look he's giving, I can tell he doesn't fully believe me. Yet, he doesn't question me further. I can still see the hardness of his cock straining against the seam of his pants, most likely aching for release as much as me. But I can't give him what he wants.

With a dip of his waist, he gives me a curt bow. "Goodnight, Emma."

And with that, he takes his leave. Still, no actual conversation transpired between us. He just chooses to leave me alone, aching, and confused.

CHAPTER FOURTEEN

Emma

Fae are milling about, readying the ships. At one point in time, there used to be Fae who didn't need to travel by sea. Fae may be powerful, but none can fly. Not unless you go back into ancient history, when there was a rare breed of Fae who lived throughout the courts with traces of dragon blood running through their veins. I can recall one ancient text that said that the God of Darkness became unhinged when creating the first Fae, that with an uncontrolled surge, the God accidentally created the dragon Fae. They were a lineage so rare; it was scripted they could transform into a dragon themselves, soaring high above the clouds and owning the sky.

I imagine the freedom that comes from being that far from the world. A beautiful silence that must exist that high, settling the soul.

It's a shame they're extinct. Killed off from years of being hunted with a special brand of iron, since the common iron did nothing to their thick blood. It doesn't weaken them or absorb their powers as it does to Fae like me. The history book in my father's library didn't specify what kind of iron harmed them, only that it's impossible to find now.

Feeling the rocking sway of the deck beneath the soles of my feet, I brace my hands against the rough exterior of the ship. The cushioned feel of knee-high boots with black trousers encases my lower half, with a cream blouse flowing on top. My hair is tied up in a low bun, and I'm wearing a wide-brimmed, soft leather hat that's folded up on one side and embellished with light feathers, giving me the appearance of a pirate. Cora was instructed to paint me as part of the crew, picking out my clothes for me to change into so that I blend in, rather than standing out in a gown that would have every male staring or draw attention to the Princess of Asov.

I couldn't have been more pleased when she told me the news. I'm delighting in the comfort of being covered in clothing that wouldn't tangle around my legs. The feeling of not needing to look like a princess excites me more. A subtle smile slides across my face as I take in the iridescent sea before me, ready to claim the miles ahead.

Shouts bellow across the ship as crew members fasten the ropes, prepare the masts, and raise the chains. Calloway stands in navy trousers and a cream shirt, a similar fashion to mine. A dark brown, three-point hat sits upon his repugnant head as he commands orders from the quarterdeck. I watch as the members work in uniform precision, prepping the ship for her journey.

The warm rays of the rising sun start to heat my face as the sea breeze glides through the heart of the ship. Adrenaline surges through me when I feel the ship move forward, and I race towards the figurehead at the front of the ship to look out beyond. Leaning over the edge as I step up on the wooden board a foot above. The water parts as the ship begins to glide, and the sea-green waves cap and roll, as if parting at the ship's command. I let the salty air rush against my face, breathing in deeply to inhale its refreshing freedom.

A small laugh squeaks behind me and I whip my head around to see Cora staring at me in hilarity. She's dressed in the same fashion as me, if only to please me in case I felt uncomfortable.

"You're like a child," she teases, no trace of bitterness lingering in her words. Her playful tone makes me hop down and land a few feet before her.

"It's amazing," I say. Still in disbelief that both of my feet are off the island of Asov and moving farther away as we speak.

She looks over my face and sees the true bewilderment shining through. The smile she gives me is a mix of her own happiness and a hint of sorrow, knowing I've been stuck in the palace.

Cora has family in our court that she visits but she lives in the Palace with me and is able to venture to the other courts if she wishes. She told me she went to each court once, but is now content to remain in Asov, to be near her loved ones, her parents, and younger brother. Her goal in life has always been to master her healing abilities, wanting to travel across the lands to teach those with the same power. Her job as my handmaiden at the palace provides her with a large sum to help keep her family comfortable and a way to train with the top healer of Asov.

Yes, she's joining this journey at the request of her king, but she told me that it never feels like that for her. Technically, she is here to keep me properly assembled and, if anything, act as another set of eyes for the king. Though, I know Cora would never tell the king a word. Her loyalty is to me.

"It's more than amazing," I proclaim. Still not able to fully fathom the journey ahead.

She wraps her arm around my shoulders, a comforting gesture as we begin to walk back towards the belly of the ship.

"Have you spoken to Aiden today? He's looking quite striking," she says as she glances sideways at me.

My shoulders sag at the mention of his name. I should tell her what happened between us, but I don't know the words that could possibly explain the hot and cold feelings of conflict. I know my reasons, but he seems so forward, wanting, and then shuts down without showing any willingness to talk. To be anything other than just mouths clashing together.

I feel the sense of someone watching me. I look up, and there he is. Green gems dazzling back at me from the light of the sun. Piercing me with his unreadable stare, not giving a hint of any joy at seeing me. He's wearing the outfit that brings memories of us tossing rocks on the shore a few years back when everything between us was easygoing. A loose white shirt that splits at the chest, with brown pants and matching boots.

I watch his chest lift as if he's taking controlled breaths and I wonder if he's frustrated with me. He looks like he's struggling to not storm over here and take what he wants. But I've never seen Aiden look at me with such discontent. We've had little bickering fights throughout the years, but he always brushed them off, never holding a grudge. In fact, he would be the one to come up to me with a smile and act as if nothing happened. Like he did at the cave. But now, there's no trace of a smile. No glint of happiness in his eyes. The stillness in that stare reminds me all too well of the glares his father gives me.

I stop my feet, rooting them to the wooden planks as our eyes battle against the friction and mess of emotions.

Those endless emerald eyes blink, washing away the coldness in them. Only for him to dip his head in acknowledgment before he continues to walk, never coming to greet us. He just passes by. I suppose this is the *time* I asked for, but why does it sting so badly?

The tension in the air is so strong that Cora shivers, tugging me forward and guiding me back towards the front of the ship.

"Want to step up there and become the wind together?" she asks. I'm thankful she changed the topic, seeming to pick up on the strain between us and dropping all talk of Aiden. Hoping I will forget him, too, if only for a moment in feeling the pure bliss of the sea breeze flowing through me.

"I'd like that." I offer a small smile. I hope whatever is going on between Aiden and me can be fixed, because I already miss him. I feel like our ships of friendship are sailing farther apart in different directions, with no rope to keep us together.

I close my eyes as I once again relish the air hitting my face, letting my worries drift away and get lost in the wind.

Hour by hour ticks by, and Cora is taking a nap, but I'm too in awe of the journey to risk missing anything. We continue along the deep sea; the light hidden behind the blanket of clouds, darkening the sky in foreboding shadows. A dense fog settles over the water, the waves flattening into an eerie stillness, creating a dark sheen of reflection along the surface. The crew aboard the ship halts their movements in wariness. Silence invades the air around us, as if one sound will shatter it. Our ship cuts through the fog, hauntingly almost, like a ghost ship creeping through misty air, invisible to any eyes looking out in the distance. A shadow of wide boards and high masts cloaked in black.

I quietly work my way down the side of the ship, heading towards the back end to look at the sea left behind. The fog becomes thicker and the gaps between the grey plumes close in together, slowly blocking the rest of the sky beyond. The shades of grey swirl together, blending to make the most beautiful sky I've ever seen. Something about the serene gloom settles my soul, calming the raging war inside, waving the white flag. My chest feels lighter as I inhale a deep breath, letting the misty air fill my lungs before I release it. I tip my head all the way back to stare off into the shrouded sky, reveling in the protection it gives from the blinding sun.

A moment later, a dark blur disrupts my peaceful gaze at the clouds. I snap my eyes to it, but it vanishes as quickly as it came. Are my eyes playing tricks on me? I swear it was…

No. That's impossible.

Through the final space between the clouds, it looked like a shadow of black wings zoomed overhead as quickly as lightning. I strain my eyes, wanting, wishing for another glimpse. As I search, nothing shows again. I must have imagined it. My wish for such freedom shining through is so incredibly strong that it's making me see things that are not real. Illusions of my longing and desires to be set free. I huff in annoyance, even as my heart pulls towards the open air above. A pull so strong it feels magnetic.

I lose track of time as I lay on the floorboards along the back deck, a few feet lower and behind the quarterdeck, where Calloway still remains as he guides the ship. His voice booms against the quiet evening sky.

Hours must have passed, for the sun is nowhere to be seen, signaling our destination. I can hear the scraping of chains as the anchor is lowered into the deep depths of the sea, jerking the ship to stop as we approach the lit-up docks ahead.

I hurry down the ship, keeping out of the way and veering around each member working, in a desperate need to lay my eyes on the Court of Asiza. I dart to the side and hitch a leg on the ledge as I grab hold of the shrouds, scaling the ropes to reach a higher vantage point away from the bustling crew below. No moon offers any form of light as the dense clouds still cover the night sky, but the lanterns scattered around allow us to see everything nearby.

I'm sure Cora is waking from her nap. I told her I'd be fine by myself, and I could see the dark circles beneath her eyes from the hours she spent preparing our things for the journey. Aiden has yet to speak with me; in fact, I haven't seen him since that one moment when we began our travels. Part of my mind has been telling me to go find him, but there's a huge part of me that doesn't want to. Why should I make such an effort, when it seems he couldn't care less? He's one of my closest friends, but now, our relationship just feels strained. He wants more than I'm willing to give, at least right now. But confusion flares within me at how he's shutting me out, something he never did when we were just friends. We used to talk about everything, and he would always listen.

A deep-rooted sadness blooms in my chest, but I do my best to ignore it as I wrap my foot through the opening of the shroud, coiling my arm around the rope to hold myself steady. Letting myself lean away from the rope to peer through the thinning fog, I can see small lanterns glowing down the path of the dock, fading into the pines beyond. The sharp, crisp fragrance of evergreen wafts through the cool breeze.

Water splashes along the sides of the body of the ship as we hit our mark for the awaiting dock. A few people of Asiza wait on the edge of the dock and reach out to help tie the loose ropes tossed overboard to the knot around the metal pegs. Even with my enhanced vision, I can't see beyond the forest and the blackness that surrounds it. Once the boat is officially shackled to the dock's post, I hop down and weave through the chaos on the ship as everyone prepares for our arrival. I head straight for Cora, wanting to let her know we made it.

Before I can get to her, my path is blocked by the king himself. My father stares down at me, hating my presence, surely.

"We will be greeted by the Royal Court, and I expect you to stand behind me and not make a sound. Do you hear me?" He raises his voice.

"Yes, Your Highness," I mumble.

"Good. You will act accordingly, and only speak when allowed. Your presence may be required for the ball and to display your engagement, but no other attention needs to be drawn to you."

An order, and one I plan to follow so I don't get sent back home. He demands me to become a walking puppet, as he holds the strings in a death grip. I'm nothing but a vessel in his bloodline who needs to become one with the shadows and stay unseen. I am nothing to him and he surely doesn't seem to care when he connects the end of a leather whip to the skin along my spine.

"Go find Cora. You are to change into an appropriate gown for when we step off this ship." With that, he turns and leaves, making his way to the quarterdeck to speak with Captain Calloway. As my eyes glance up to where my father heads, Aiden appears next to his father, looking out at the forest ahead.

He stands tall; the wind dancing through his golden hair, his chest out strong and spine straight, a male ready to take on the world. His mouth is set in a hard line, the same mouth that trailed up my neck and consumed me with a burning need. A small tremor racks through me at the memory of how his hands felt on me and the need he caused to pool between my legs.

As if he can feel me staring at him, those deep green orbs dart to me, pinning me. I suck in a quick breath, overwhelmed with thoughts of wanting him, and I immediately rip my eyes from his so he doesn't notice. Frustration peaks inside at the tug of war of emotions he's created within me. So, I choose to give him a taste of his own medicine and walk away without another glance and go find Cora.

CHAPTER FIFTEEN

Emma

The crew stays on the ship as we walk down the wooden ramp to the dock below. I found Cora just waking, and she immediately began handing me my dress. I stand behind the changing divider and make quick work of getting ready. When I step around the divider, she busies herself with smoothing out the nonexistent wrinkles in my pale lavender silk dress that is now flowing beautifully around my slippered feet.

The color is to keep my father content, but I can't deny I like the way it hangs on my body. The dress is lightweight, not bulky by any means, and it conforms to my body in a single layer of fabric. The gown veils all of my skin with a high enough neckline to cover the hideous choker sealed around my neck, keeping it hidden from sight. The flowy skirt hangs loose and dances in a graceful rhythm as I walk, still allowing me to conceal my precious dagger underneath.

With the lack of time, Cora lets my hair down and grabs a small clip she brought to secure the top half of my hair in the back, letting the rest hang loose.

"Ready?" she asks. Even though nerves are plaguing me, knowing I'll be near Aiden and meeting the ruler of Asiza, I still feel a sense of lightness from being somewhere new. The trees, the smells, and the crisp air are calling to me. Singing a seductive melody that makes my blood hum. Taking a deep breath, I nod. "As ready as I'll ever be," I tell her with a slight smile.

I walk to stand behind my father and Captain Calloway, with Aiden's masculine presence next to me. One small lift of my finger and it would brush against his, but I refrain from being the first to gloss over this uncertain distress between us. He walked away when I wanted to talk, to pause the lust forming between us and face our situation head-on. He told me he needs me and has been waiting for me to be his, yet his *needs* seem to be driven with his dick. What happened to the friend I could rely on and talk to about almost everything? The one who would listen and just sit with me for hours? I miss that friendship, so why does it have to be one or the other? Why won't he just talk to me?

More confusion rattles through my mind as I mindlessly fight with the seam on my sleeve. Footsteps sound ahead, making my head snap up. It's hard to see past my father's bulky frame, and I dare not peek around him.

All of a sudden, a humming in my blood surges, growing stronger and causing my breath to hitch. I close my eyes to embrace the intoxicating heat surging through my veins, a fire that burns away all my fears, all my pain, and leaves them in the dust.

What's happening?

I slowly peel my eyes open and hear voices speaking to each other, but even more so...I feel Aiden's intense gaze on me as I angle my head to look up at him. His eyes are questioning, and that's when I wonder if he can sense this feeling, too. If something here is calling to him or if I just look completely insane to him at the moment. Probably the latter, with the probing look he's directing towards me. There's that slight coldness in his eyes again, and I don't think even the hottest flame could melt the icy exterior he created. But then, it's gone with another blink of his eyes, leaving me utterly confused as he raises his eyebrows at me in question.

A subtle nod forward is his way of telling me to focus.

A tinge of irritation starts building, fueling the anger of his sudden demeanor towards me. I steel my spine and raise my chin as I face forward, being the ever-loving Princess of Asov. I wish Kye were here as well, but he won't be arriving until tomorrow, when the next ship sets sail for Asiza. He promised he would be here for the ball, and it looks like I may need the extra company.

"And this is my daughter, Princess Emma of Asov." My ears catch on my name as soon as my father steps to the side to allow all eyes to fall on me. Nausea churns in my gut, but I force it away as I take a small step forward. Placing my hands in front of me and clasping them together, I slightly dip my head in a show of respect as I greet them.

"A pleasure to meet you," I say in a smooth, yet strong voice to be easily heard as confidence drips from my words. Trying my best to not allow others to see me weak.

When I bring my head back up and set my eyes on the Fae before me, I can't help the overwhelming surprise I feel. *A female.*

She's dressed in a deep burgundy gown that's fitted perfectly to her lean frame. She's a few inches taller than me, with raven-black hair that hangs down straight, going past her shoulders. The points of her ears poke slightly through her shiny curtain of hair, as a silver crown with black crystal roses sits upon her head. The soft orange glow from the lanterns warms her skin and sharpens her high cheekbones. A pleased smile graces her perfectly painted lips, while the deep plum color makes her pearl teeth glimmer through the night. Her eyes are striking, with long lashes framing her deep blue irises. It's hard to tell in the dark, but they almost look black because they are such a heavy blue.

"Such a beautiful girl. It's my pleasure to meet you as well. We have only heard words spoken of the Princess of Asov. So, it's nice to finally put a face to the name. I'm Queen Zoraida of Asiza, and these are my sons, Prince Draven and Prince Emil," her voice has a tone of magic and beauty, swirling around the space between us.

Her hand gestures out towards her two sons and my eyes land on the younger one, Prince Emil. Pitch black hair and matching deep ocean eyes, just like his mother. With a welcoming smile, a playful "hello" falls from his slightly thin lips. He's wearing a brown tunic paired with black pants and boots. Perfectly threaded clothing, yet simple for a child his age to run and play. If I had to guess, he's around the age of thirteen.

My eyes slide to her other son, Prince Draven. Such an interesting name. *Drah-ven*. I have the sudden urge to say it aloud, to see how it would taste on my lips. My heart stutters in my chest as my power surges inside. I snuff it out before I lose control, but the male before me is strikingly handsome. Jet black hair that's short on the sides, longer on top, as a small piece falls in front of his face. Straight nose, full lips, and a jaw that looks like it was cut with a knife. Slightly darkened scruff is perfectly trimmed on his face, and the urge to rub my fingertips over the hair is shocking. His muscled frame is covered by a black tunic that is unlaced at the chest, opening up to show off the deep line between his pecs and the tattoos that are engraved on his skin. They cover every inch of him I can see, from his exposed chest, up his neck, and even the visible skin on his wrists, with a few inked marks on his hands. A canvas of art.

His tunic is tucked into black pants that cinch his narrow waist with a black leather belt. A silver bracelet and rings decorate his wrists and fingers, and a long silver chain falls down inside his shirt. My greedy eyes trail back up to his face and my pulse starts to race. An eyebrow ring glints against the glow of the lanterns and his eyes are a piercing blue.

Never looking at me, he keeps his focus straight ahead. It's infuriating that this prince—who is made from sin—refuses to acknowledge me. The way my body is reacting just from looking at him is maddening, and I instantly hate the effect he's having on me. My body feels hot all over and I'm unsure if it's from the appreciation of this enticing male in front of me or from the anger boiling my blood at the bored look on his face. The look of a guy who wants to be anywhere but where he is at that moment.

I turn to look back at the queen, the one ruling Royal of Asiza. All royals are considered to be the most powerful in their courts; even though our race is split from the high Fae and lower Fae, Royals are above them. The only thing more powerful than a high Fae are the Gods, but they are never to be seen, just written about in the ancient books I found buried in my father's library. The ink on the pages mentioned a Goddess of Light and a God of Darkness but offered no more than unclear myths and broken words.

I steal a final glance at Prince Draven, still noting the disinterest on his face, before turning back to Queen Zoraida. "Quite charming," I tell the queen as her mouth lifts on the side, stifling a laugh. She clearly knows all too well how *charming* her son is.

A throat clears next to me, and Aiden takes a small step forward, bowing at the hips. "Thank you for meeting us this late in the evening. I'm Aiden Calloway, Princess Emma's betrothed," he adds on that last part with a ring of finality to it. Deep in my heart, I hope this is him showcasing himself in front of our fathers and this Royal Court. Not declaring me as his possession or claiming me.

My eyes unwillingly slip to Prince Draven. His eyes are still locked straight ahead of him, but the muscles in his jaw flutter against the warm glow, and his posture seems tense.

"Yes! Yes, of course." Queen Zoraida claps her hands together. "Everyone is excited to meet the newly engaged couple," she cheers.

Aiden gives another slight bow at his hips in thanks as my father once again steps in front of me, blocking my view of anyone and anything. A way to belittle me and make my lack of importance to him and the conversation known.

"It's been such a long journey. Please, let me show you to your rooms so you may rest." The queen's soft voice and kindness shoot an arrow right into my chest, cracking the hardened organ from years of neglect and cruel intentions.

"Thank you," both my father and Captain Calloway say simultaneously.

My eyes roll at that. Both of them have the same ungodly heart, and Calloway believes he's a king himself. My natural reaction didn't go unnoticed, though. I feel eyes on me from across the way, and before I can locate the source, my father grabs my upper arm. I hiss in a breath as his unexpected hold brings a surge of pain. To those around us, it would look normal, almost fatherly, in him simply directing me to follow. He keeps such calm facial features and a relaxed posture, but his eyes are burning holes into me.

Waiting until everyone starts walking away, he leans in close to my ear. His cigar ridden breath fans around my face, suffocating me. "This is your only warning. No snarky comments, and if I see you roll your eyes again, I'll make sure to pay extra attention to them when we get home."

Fear seizes my lungs at his threat and I gulp down the breath that froze in my throat. His face lights up with a huge grin as he subtly yanks my arm forward, causing my body to follow suit. "Come, my dear Emma, you must be exhausted," his voice raises for everyone to hear, covering the venomous words he spits in quiet.

I reluctantly follow, not wanting to cause a scene. But my eyes drift towards the burning sensation, the same one I felt before. Like my blood is vibrating under my skin, heating a warmth that makes my skin feel like it's lit up from within. Making my heart race a little faster. When my eyes land their mark, it's Prince Draven, who still remains unmoving. I keep my face neutral, but my whole body ignites at those eyes. Like ice. They are the palest blue I have ever seen. The dim orange glow from the lanterns still cannot mask the pools of liquid light. Sharp diamonds pierce into me with a hardness that is impenetrable. I follow his line of sight and realize he's glaring at the contact of my father's hand on my arm, never straying. Looking about three seconds from firing sharpened icicles at him.

I tear my cloudy eyes away while we keep walking, until I feel a softer, more gentle hand take hold of my other arm. "I've got her, My King. I'll make sure she gets to her room safely." Cora's eyes are strong as she looks up at my father, noticing the tension in my body.

He barely pays her any mind when he releases his death grip and walks ahead. "Make sure you do," he demands. Another threat he weaves under his words if we don't do what he wishes.

I quickly turn to face Cora and rest my palm on her hand. Offering her the biggest thank you I can without speaking. She nods, knowing how much I despise my father. "Let's go," she says softly.

I stay quiet as we follow along, spying Aiden in line with my father and his, not even waiting for me. Some show of partnership and love, the way he announced himself as my fiancé with such certainty, and then left me behind without a second thought. If this is some sort of game he's playing, I'll play. I'm already in the midst of many; what difference does it matter if I add another?

CHAPTER SIXTEEN

Emma

*L*ast night, I was directed to one of the suites located in the guest wing and Cora was sent to a room in the wing reserved for workers. A room that, I suppose, she will be sharing; unlike mine, which is enormous for just one lonely person. I wonder if I can sneak Cora up here, anyway? There's plenty of room for her to be comfortable.

I wasn't able to get a good look at the castle when I was escorted outside, but I know that it's huge and expands farther than my eyes can see. When I was shown to my room, I only absorbed little glimpses of darkened floors and intricate chandeliers. The candles in the fixtures burned, their flames dancing in a welcoming sway.

As soon as I was led inside and left alone, I stripped bare, tossed on a loose linen blouse, and fell on the bed. My eyelids practically forced themselves shut with the level of exhaustion I'd reached. I was even too tired to acknowledge the hunger pains coursing through me from grazing on food during our travels and not having a full meal. Unluckily for me, the hunger pains never left and woke me up with a vengeance.

The dull light streaming through the floor-to-ceiling entryway gives the room a gloomy glow. A cool breeze drifts in, prompting a layer of goosebumps to pebble on my skin. The room itself is curved stone, with an archway that leads directly outside. There's no door, no windows, just an opening that leads out to a small sitting area that overlooks the forest. Its a high point in the castle that offers the most stunning view. Green ivy veils the stone archway, blanketing the surface down the wall and into the room, bringing the outdoors inside. The floor is solid black stone with a cushioned silver rug near the bed. The bed itself could fit five of me, layered in satin ebony sheets with matching sheer curtains that hang on the sides.

A huge contrast to the room my father has decorated for me that looks like spring and love had a baby.

I pad along the chilled floors and step easily outside on the opened balcony. My room is high up above the trees, and the wind catches the hem of my shirt so that it flutters around my thighs. My hair remains in place from the messy bun I put it in last night. The forest before me goes on for miles. The sea must be on the other side of the castle, where the ship is docked, but all my eyes can take in is the fog clouding around the tops of the trees. A fresh, woodsy scent mingles with the dew in the morning hours.

The way the silence settles in the air, the intoxicating scent that burrows deep in my soul, and the hauntingly majestic forest before me...I feel drawn to it. Drawn to go explore outside and stand in the middle of the pines, for my feet to sink into the soil and inhale the pureness of nature.

After taking a few uncounted moments to enjoy the peace, I head towards the tub placed just before the open archway. Luckily, this room is high and far away enough that no one would ever be able to see in. I let the tub fill as I realize, for once in my life, that I feel rested. No nightmares plagued me, no phantom hands tormented me to my near death, just... nothing. I stare warily at the streaming water falling from the ceiling faucet, looking like rain on a stormy day.

Since almost drowning in the tub, I have become hesitant right before I bathe. But I just need to remember that I fell asleep then, letting myself become vulnerable. Falling asleep isn't an option today; I need to clean up and fill my stomach before I start to eat the greenery on the walls.

Not long after, Cora arrives in my suite with a dress in hand, ready to make me look presentable for breakfast, which she tells me is almost ready in the main dining room. She chose a forest green velvet dress with loose sleeves, a high scoop neck, and a seam that brings the dress tight to my waist, showcasing my sleek curves defined by my training with Kye. A pair of silver slippers finishes the attire, only peeking out when I walk. I brush through my hair before she can get to it and leave it down in its natural waves. I turn to see she's a few feet away, staring out at the expanse of the forest.

"What do you think of the queen and her sons?" she asks, a knowing glint in her eye when she faces me.

"The queen was very welcoming, and so was Prince Emil," I say happily, not giving in to what she is so desperately wanting to gossip about, even though she's only scratched the surface. But sure enough, she jumps right into the deep end. This girl has no patience when it comes to talking about guys.

"Mhm…and what about Prince Draven?" The innocent tone is nothing but a ruse as she knowingly cocks an amused eyebrow at me.

I can't help but get sucked into her trap. "He's… Well, he's rude."

"C'mon, you can do better than that, Emma," she teases.

"Ugh. *Fine*," I drag out the word. "He's a cold-hearted sociopath who is unwelcoming with his '*I've got better things to do*' look. And how attractive he is, is even more infuriating. He looks like he was sculpted from the Gods' powerful hands, sent here solely to wreak havoc on a female's senses." I shake my head, irritated that I exposed the maddening thoughts running through my mind since last night, and how I just admitted to finding him hot. *Damnit*. My palm meets my face instantly as I hear Cora's laugh, heaving over to catch her breath as her cackles explode out of her.

"Yes, yes. Get your laughs out now." I walk towards her in the outside sitting area.

"Don't worry, almost *every* girl feels the same way. I've heard about the notorious Prince Draven, or as others call him, the *Dark Prince*." She raises her eyebrows up and down as if that's supposed to mean something to me.

With a huff and a roll of her cobalt orbs, she continues, "He's known to be harsh and not care about anyone besides his mother and brother. Apparently, he doesn't commit either, tends to be known for leaving a trail of broken hearts in his wake as he finds a new female to bed. He may be next in line to rule, but no one is forcing his hand to marry, probably because of his hard exterior and inability to settle down." She shrugs her shoulders, as if she is indifferent either way.

I raise my eyebrow and turn the tables. "And what do *you* think of him?"

The smirk she gives tells me all I need to know. "He's the Devil himself, all wrapped up in sin and, like you said, has the body of a God. It's easy to see why so many females fall on their knees for him, begging to give him pleasure. I bet he knows exactly how to work a girl's body to the point of screaming without control."

I blush at her words, only experiencing a couple of heated moments with Aiden and the release from my own fingers. Talking about sex and imagining what Prince Draven's hands and mouth could do… The heat burns hotter on my cheeks, tinting the skin a bright red. I know Cora has more experience than me. She may look innocent, but she enjoys the warmth of another body against hers when she can find it, hoping she will find a love strong enough to steal her heart away. I envy the freedom she has and how she embraces her sexuality.

She sighs. "There are so many unknowns in life that could end us in an instant. Finding someone to fill the void of loneliness helps pass time. But I understand why the prince is the way he is, being 500 years old and still never finding a mate. Whether he chooses to be alone or not, the cobwebs on his heart must be suffocating. Probably why he's so cruel; I bet all the weaved silk has hardened from the acid of being so bitter 24/7."

Reaching over, I place my hand on hers. "Cora, you are stuck with me, even after death and in the world beyond. But if you believe Prince Draven to be so bitter, why don't you try to sweeten him up?" I wink.

"No, thank you. He's too broody for me." I go to speak up and say none of that matters when she continues, "Plus, I don't *want* the Dark Prince. Sure, he's nice to look at, and I will never deny my eyes the pleasure his physique brings, but he's not the male I'd want to sweeten, as you so put it." She giggles.

"Coraaa… Is there a guy you are on the prowl for?"

She looks up at the still cloudy sky, endless waves of milky grey that stretch far past the horizon. "Oh, would you look at that! We must get you to breakfast. I suppose we will have to put a pin in this." She prances into the room and heads straight for the door.

My hands fall to my hips in exasperation. "Fine, I see how it is. But know this, I *will* find out about this mystery guy."

Her head twists back with a playful expression that looks like a dare. "Mhm. Sure thing." A dramatic wink is all she leaves me with as she dips out of the suite.

Breakfast is uneventful but delicious. The room is moody, with grey stone that rises to towering heights and open-arched windows lining the walls, allowing the dim light from the gloomy day to stream throughout as small candles decorate the long black table. This whole castle seems to be the opposite of Asov in every way. Where our floors are light with shells, theirs are sleek with polished black marble. The walls of our palace are white, and here, it's grey, camouflaged by the foggy mist that decorates the court in a tranquil haze.

During breakfast, I eat my way through the platter of fruits and jellied buns piled high on the trays, listening to bland conversations of meetings and ball preparations between Queen Zoraida and my father. Nothing of major importance is being brought up that piques my interest, and it seems to be the same for Aiden, who sits across from me, paying extra attention to his food. He spoke to greet me with a seemingly genuine smile, but nothing else is said throughout the remainder of the meal.

Part of my heart doesn't know whether this should cause a fissure or not, but the strain on our relationship is painful. I feel like my friend is slipping through my fingers and I'm not sure if I can get that part of us back. But the other side of my heart wants to harden even more, as anger that's dark as soot coats the organ, staining the bond we grew over the years.

That's what seems to happen to those who are close to me: they die or become tainted. Eventually, their inner demons take hold and use their bodies as a vessel. My father used to be nice to me, but when I turned fifteen, I watched him change, seeing how that smile towards me turned into a sneer.

Cora and Kye seem to be immune to me, but I'm waiting for the day my presence ruins their spirits as it's beginning to do with Aiden, it seems. I don't know if I will be able to survive losing Cora or Kye, who keep me grounded when I feel myself slipping away into the dark abyss of depression.

I wonder if my heart will become as hard as Prince Draven's, who was absent at breakfast. His mother didn't seem to mind, as if skipping out on dining with guests is normal behavior for him. Who knows, maybe he's busy taking care of matters with this court, but I can't help wondering what other matters he could be handling in his room…

Snap out of it! I internally smack myself out of the thoughts that were forming. Clearly, I'm tense, in more ways than one. Not only have I had no sense of relief after the blistering moments with Aiden—which is my own fault for stopping it—but I also haven't pleasured myself to cool off the fire that won't die down. I'll have to find some sort of release for myself later, enough to bring the inferno down to a simmer before I explode. Right now, I'm desperate to find a secluded spot outside, some-where deep in the forest, to read more of my favorite book I stashed in my bags.

I meander back to my room, as a new guard follows my every move. Right when I go to enter my suite and grab my book, I'm stopped by a soft echo of my name. The voice caresses down my spine, leaving tingles everywhere it touches. I twist at the sound and see Aiden approaching me from down the hall, sauntering towards me in his crisp, blue tunic and ink-painted pants, the sound of hardened leather padding on stone with every step.

I turn to face him, rising to my full height to prepare for whatever he's about to say. He stops less than a foot away from me, closer than most would dare, and doesn't hide the way his eyes trail down my velvet-covered body. "Leave us," he orders the guard, and I watch him bow quickly before disappearing out of sight. I connect my eyes back to Aiden's in a questioning look. "I forgot to tell you how beautiful you look."

Not blinking, I tilt my head sideways and stare deep into his eyes. I let his words hang in the air between us for a moment as I try to figure out this hot and cold behavior. He's giving me whiplash.

"Hmm. Seems you forgot how to speak altogether," I say calmly, with a twinge of irritation lacing my words. Just enough to note my displeasure.

His chest rises high as he inhales deeply before letting out a long breath, the fabric in his tunic stretching against the muscles hidden beneath. He takes a full step forward to close the space, but in the spirit of being spiteful, I take a full step back.

His eyes dart back and forth between mine before sharpening as he refrains from taking another step forward. "What's that supposed to mean, Emma?"

Does he really not realize how he's been acting towards me? "You tell me, Aiden. One minute, you're lifting up my skirts, and the next, you turn into a complete stranger who's barely able to look at me," I hiss. "Ever since you left me in the library, you've chosen to give me the cold shoulder, and apparently, the coldest one you've got."

"I'm trying to give you space, Emma! You told me you need time and anytime I try to get close, you push me away. What do you want from me?" His hackles raise and I can see the turmoil flaming in his eyes.

"I wanted to talk! With *words*, Aiden, not with your dick."

A growl vibrates up his throat, but one that sends chills to rise along my arms. "I'm a guy who has *needs*, Emma. I lose control when that need becomes overwhelming, especially around you. But you keep denying me, even when I *know* how willing your body was for me. Your arousal was so strong I wanted to taste it, live off it."

I feel the blush creep up my neck and blanket my face. He must notice because his hand stretches out and holds the side of my cheek, rubbing his thumb gently against my now pink skin. "Aiden…" I pause, trying to figure out how to tell him. "That's too fast for me. I'm still—" I look down shaking my head as my skin heats. "I've never—" I sigh and internally curse at myself for not being able to voice it. "I'm not ready for what you want. I just want to talk about us and how we will venture into this new role of being betrothed, because I'm not fully ready for marriage, and you and I are still not mates."

A look of surprise streaks across his face, and then his jaw clenches tightly, his thumb freezing in the middle of his back-and-forth caress. He tips my head back up as he stares down at me. I don't know why he would assume I'd be able to have sexual trysts, being kept within the palace walls, unless the thought just never crossed his mind.

His other hand grabs my waist and pulls me in roughly against his hard stature. "You're innocent. Untouched by another," he says the words so clearly, even though confusion seems to cling to them, as if he can't believe a girl of my age would still be innocent.

"Yes," I sigh.

The fingers he has wrapped around my waist tighten, exhaling a deep breath. "Now you really will be mine," he says in a low voice. "Fuck mates, I won't allow any other male to have you."

"But—"

"No," he interrupts. "You'll be my wife, Emma." He leans down slowly, pressing a soft peck on my cheek. A strong contrast to the rigor in his voice. He must see the slight resistance from my body when he softens his tone. "We will have a good life. We can talk more about us and our wedding once we get back to Asov. For now, let's just focus on the ball tonight and celebrating." He tucks a loose piece of hair behind my ear, the tips of his fingers brushing against the silver ring near the point of it. "I'll let you get ready. I'm sure Cora has a whole afternoon planned to prepare you for the evening festivities. I'll see you when the sun begins to set." He places one more kiss on my cheek, letting his lips linger for a second longer, then leaves me at my door. He walks away again without allowing me a moment to speak.

I can't seem to keep up with his waves of emotions, as I'm left stranded at sea again, having to navigate through unpredictable weather. At some point, I'm going to give up and let myself drift away and leave him to suffer in his own whirlpool.

Aiden was right; Cora did have plans to prepare for the ball tonight. I step into my room in hopes of stealing some time for myself but walk into stations for my hair and makeup, the gown sprawled across my bed, and the tub warm and ready for me. I told her this was too much, but she insists it has to be over the top and that we need every second of the day to get ready to make it special. My first ball.

She puts a folded screen divider between the main part of the room and the tub, allowing me to soak in the bath that has the head of roses floating on top. I see the peaks of green out in the distance, with the grey plumes folding and parting across the sky, letting slivers of warmth fall through.

Most high Fae have someone to help them get ready, to help them wash their hair, and everything in-between. But Cora knows I like my privacy. She just doesn't know it's to keep the scars along my body hidden. When she first started six years ago, she once asked me why I always wore such conservative dresses. I had to pause, only then to tell her it's because I find them comfortable and that my father wishes it so. That seemed to keep her from asking again.

I dry off the heated drops that slide down my fair skin, after scrubbing with soap and making sure every part of me is smooth, per Cora's instructions. She told me, "You never know what could happen at a ball."

As I finish drying, I hear the ruffle of a dress. An all-black gown is swung over the top of the divider and draped over for me to squeeze into after I remove the water from my body. I lift the gown and hold it out before me, marveling at the intricate designs stitched into the lace.

"Let me know when you're fully dressed, you goody two-shoes," Cora teases, even though I stifle a wince at the joke.

I drag the ebony lace lingerie up my thighs and hook the bralette, looking edible enough for any male, even though these will only be seen with my own eyes. I will admit I have a weakness for fashionable lingerie; the way it forms to my curves as the fine material lays against my skin makes me feel desirable. I won't ever voice how it makes me feel, though, because Cora would have a party. She gets me the most sensual undergarments, despite how conservatively I dress, saying it will make me feel sexy for myself. I can't help but agree with that.

I step into the gown next, and the skirt poofs slightly below my waist in a whimsical swirl of glittering black. The gown is a midnight embrace, with a kiss of stars that sparkle. I slide my arms through the lacy sleeves, as the top of the dress swoops across my collarbones in waves. After a few exhausting minutes, I'm able to zip the back and hook the clasp. I step around the divider and find Cora busying herself with picking out a pair of shoes for me to wear, since slippers might not be suitable for such an extravagant event.

She stands up with a pair of silver heels that look like diamonds under the sun. When she sees me, she gasps. "Holy Gods, Emma. You're gonna turn the heads of every male at the ball. You're like a Goddess of the Night. Aiden won't be able to resist you now." She winks at me, and I can't help the soft laugh I let loose with a shake of my head. The wet strands of my hair stick to my face and Cora huffs in amusement. "Come on, let me do my magic."

Cora takes her time getting me ready with hair and makeup while gossiping about everything, including me spilling the secret of the moments I shared with Aiden, crossing over the line of friendship.

"Shut up!" she squeals. "How are you just now telling me?! Wait! Don't answer that, I don't care because you're telling me now. But then, why was he acting so strange before?"

I stare at her through the mirror as she finishes curling some strands of my hair. "That's the thing." I sigh. "He's been sweet and all over me one minute, and then the next, he practically shuns me." I explain the parts of me shoving him away and wanting to just talk, as well as what he said before I walked into my room today.

"Well, there's a difference between giving you time and being an ass. But there's one thing I do know…" She stares at me with a huge grin stretching across her face, taking a dramatic pause. "He won't be able to ignore you when he sees you. You're like a walking dream of promises in the night."

"Gods, Cora." I bury my head in my hands in embarrassment, wishing I could be half as confident as her.

She gently smacks my arm. "Alright, I'll stop, for *now.* Let me finish this last section, because the ball is about to start." She shrieks with excitement.

Cora was able to get herself ready and spruced up in between our conversations, when I needed to pause and snack on some of the treats that were sent up from the kitchen.

When I'm all done getting ready, I look myself over in the mirror. Long, dark lashes frame the grey pools looking back at me. My hair is lightly curled but twisted up in an elegant updo, letting small waves fall to frame my face. I looped a dark, sheer scarf around my neck to hide the hideous necklace from sight, and it lays gently against the lace top of the gown that hugs my torso, curving over my breasts. The skirt flares in a waterfall of dark promises as the glittering heels peek out from underneath. My lips are painted a deep ruby wine.

Cora completes the look with my mask. It's a masquerade ball after all, and mine is as dark as my dress. Like the feathers of a raven, mysterious and cloaked in night. It ties around my head with a ribbon but fits comfortably as it covers from my hairline down to the top of my nose. In a shimmering black lace, decorated in glints of silver and onyx stones. I'm unrecognizable.

She places a small, dark silver tiara on my head, absorbing the light into it, and I'm officially ready for tonight.

CHAPTER SEVENTEEN

Emma

I'm standing in the hallway outside the ballroom, fidgeting with my fingers as I nervously pace back and forth. Unconsciously chewing on my bottom lip as the nerves of walking into a room full of curious people get to me. I've never been in such a huge crowd, let alone to a ball to dance and mingle. What if I stutter my words and say something completely ridiculous, or trip in these shoes and fall face-first onto the hard floor…

The chaotic thoughts keep whirling into a vortex in my mind as I feel panic inching its way into my chest, tightening. I face the double doors, where an intricate design overlays the black wood in swirls. I see the soft glow through the crack at the bottom and feel the pounding, rhythmic pulse of the bass as music floats out from within.

"There you are." I spin around to find Aiden walking towards me in a white dress tunic and matching pants. His top has gilded embroidery, starting from his shoulders and framing his lapels down the center as they end at a point. Dragging my eyes down, I see his white shoes that shine brightly against the dark floors. His mask is pure gold, shimmering with every small movement he makes. "Wow," he breathes. "You look amazing, like the moon to my sun, since we're dressed like night and day." A chuckle rises from his throat. As he raises a hand to scratch behind his neck, I notice the gold pattern bands around the cuffs of his sleeves, shining in the light with the movement.

If I didn't know any better, I'd say he seems shy, but Aiden is never one to feel nervous about what he says. My mind begins to question if this is a part of his on and off actions towards me, throwing me off by acting bashful. But this is Aiden here, my friend for most of my life. He has no reason for any ill intent towards me.

"I suppose we are dressed quite differently," I say softly as I peer down at my gown. "Ready to do this thing?"

An amused smile flits across his face. "It's a ball, Emma, not a high Fae meeting. No need to be nervous—we're just going to prove our betrothal, dance, drink, and eat."

Sounds so simple when he puts it like that. "Yeah, okay," I breathe out. "Where's my father?"

"Here," a deep voice skates down the hall as I see him approaching us. On cue, my body immediately becomes tense, preparing for pain. My father is dressed very similarly to Aiden, both representing the Court of Asov with masks that look like melted gold painted on their face, unlike me, with Cora dressing me to fit in more with this court. She knows my love of darker shades of color, given away by my disgusted face anytime I have to don a pastel gown.

It seems my father doesn't approve of the dark essence of my attire, but he refrains from voicing it with the ball only moments away. I internally remind myself to thank Cora later for not priming me to look as stiff and aloof as Aiden and my father, to represent a court that I've been kept a prisoner at.

Once he's next to me, he leans down to my ear to speak: "Remember, your actions here will determine the fun we'll have when we return home." He stands back to his full height, embodying the power of a king. "Time to announce our arrival."

He stands in front of the double doors, while Aiden and I sidle behind him. Aiden grabs my arm to loop it through his, the perfect image of a couple united in *love*. But at the moment, we couldn't look any more different, both at opposite ends of the spectrum.

The door separates as it opens into a massive room with hanging chandeliers that softly glow and skylights lining the ceiling, offering a perfect view of the moon and the stars that twinkle through them. The stone curves high at the top, and heavy ebony curtains drop along the sides of each arched window as they skim the black and grey marbled floor, a sea of shades that blend majestically together. Bordering the edge of the room are white pillars coiled in deep forest vines with black roses, bringing more life to the space. My heart swells at the touch of roses, because I remember Aunt Lyd always telling me I smelled like them when she found them in the woods in Helestria. Then, she would place them in my hair when she got home. Since then, they have always been my favorite. But I'm suddenly finding these ebony roses to be my new favorite; they're breathtaking in their beauty.

I startle when a voice booms next to us and spreads across the entire floor of the ballroom. A male of average height stands a few feet away, speaking into a horn that amplifies his voice. Everyone stops what they're doing and turns their gaze upon us. "Presenting King Oren of Asov, Princess Emma of Asov, and her betrothed, Aiden Calloway from Asov." The crowd down below is full of every level of Fae, and all of them bow as we stand at the top of a grand staircase, the steps looking more daunting with every passing second as I curl my toes in the pointed stilettos.

I find myself putting one foot in front of the other as Aiden tugs gently on my arm. Lifting my chin high, I straighten my posture to show confidence and regal grace as I begin to glide down the stairs, turning into an enchanting shadow as I float lightly down to the main floor.

When my heels touch the bottom, the people throughout begin to mingle, toast with wine, and twirl to the notes of music. The ruby liquid is calling my name as my nerves continue to linger.

"Dance with whomever asks for your hand and let them quench their curiosity of the princess," my father says with disdain. "But before all, you must dance with your betrothed. Now go."

His order is demanding me to please any male who wishes to get a glimpse of me like I'm some sort of prized mule. My father's retreating form disappears in the sea of people as I'm left standing next to Aiden.

"Shall we?" he asks, hopefully.

"Do I have a choice?" I sneer. I see the flinch before I can stop myself from spitting those words at him. A kernel of guilt bubbles in my throat for taking my anger at my father out on him when he's showing his softer side. Aiden's sun-kissed hair is glowing under the dim lighting, and his emerald eyes stare deep into me through the golden holes of his mask. The gleaming green and gold bounce off each other in a mesmerizing vision, like the yellow rays that wrap around the vibrant green leaves, or how the sun shines on a fragment of sea glass.

His eyes have always brought warmth, but recently, they've been sending a different type of heat into my body. I'm still unsure of how to tread, as I'm stuck in between two seas crashing into each other.

I can see his jaw clenching below his mask at my words. Without a word, he leads me to the middle of the marbled floor as a new song begins to play. The tempo is fast enough that I force all my concentration into the steps, as I gracefully move my body to the sound. Years of training have also taught me how to let my body naturally flow as I control every movement. Aiden's hand is on my waist while the other is holding my hand up as we begin to spin in circles and then step back and forth. The beat pulses in sync with my heart as I twirl and let the music consume me.

A smile stretches across Aiden's face as he notices my body relaxing more the longer we dance, getting lost in the rhythm. "You and I are a good match, Emma. Don't fight something that's not broken. We *are* good together." Then, suddenly, the song ends. He steps in closer to me, leaning down a hairbreadth away. "I have to share you now, but I'm looking forward to our next dance." With a soft touch of his lips to mine, he walks off towards where his father, Captain Calloway, is standing. He's beside my father and Queen Zoraida, plus a couple of others, who I am assuming are the other rulers of the courts in Deyadrum. All of them look deeply invested in the conversation. But I stand frozen for a few seconds at his easy-going kiss, as if it's the most natural thing in the world, while I'm still hesitant every time.

I lift my skirt an inch off the floor as I hurry to the platters of food and wine. I need some sustenance and liquid courage to get me through the rest of the night. With small bites, I eat a few of the delicious chocolate treats, and then pour wine to the brim of my glass. With a huge breath, I stare at the glistening, crimson liquid, debating if I should sip it or down the whole damn thing. After only a moment, I choose the latter and chug it down in a few big gulps. Not very princess-like, but I couldn't currently care less.

As the last sweet drop falls onto my tongue, a tingle spreads along my skin. I dart my eyes up and see piercing blue eyes on me from across the room, digging deep into my soul through the gaps of dancers swirling around the floor. I stop breathing. They stay locked, unmoving, on my silver ones, turning it into a battle. A couple walks in my line of sight, and when they pass, those cold diamonds are gone. I glance around the room and see nothing but wine-hazed faces and blurs of color as guests dance in a sea of twirling gowns, like colorful brushstrokes on a painting.

Unnerved, I go for a second glass of wine. I follow through with the same action of filling my glass and downing it in one go. I make sure to turn my back to the room as I relish in the warmth flooding my blood as the alcohol buzzes through my system.

"May I have this dance, Princess?" I turn to see an elderly Fae, waiting with his hand outstretched before him. I give him a smile and dip my head. "Of course, you may," I tell him politely, as I set my glass on the table beside me and let him guide me out to the floor.

A song starts to drum in quick beats as he grabs my hand to spin me around and pull me back in. For someone of his age, he sure seems nimble. I laugh out loud at the thought, and the wine intoxicates my nerves with every breath. The carefree feeling bubbles up to the surface as I see him laughing with me. We continue our dance throughout the entire song, and before I know it, I'm being passed from one male to the next.

Song after song.

Yet, I don't mind. My body is humming and light as I glide around the floor. Getting lost in the high of bliss and music, completely losing track of time.

My mask is still securely in place, and I begin to feel glad that my face isn't fully exposed and on display for everyone to drink in and judge. It keeps an edge of mystery to the princess with deep-red lips.

The music shifts to a slower, more sensual song, and I'm expecting Aiden to be collecting his next dance. So, I didn't expect the deep, velvety voice behind me: "A Princess of the Night."

The male I was dancing with bows with a satisfied smile and takes his cue to hastily leave. *Huh.* Why the rush? A bolt of warmth vibrates through my veins, a feeling of awareness.

As I face the voice that slithers down my spine in a seductive touch, my breath catches. Pools of clear blue simmer before me, intently watching my every move. Prince Draven. His ink-black hair is tousled in a sexy way, with a black mask that makes his blue eyes pop. I allow myself a brief second to take him in, the wine still singing in my blood. He's in a black tunic that has a silver design stitched in beautifully, with matching silver epaulets that decorate his shoulders. The ink on his skin peeks above his collar and spreads up his neck and down the tops of his hands. A silver trim traces the edge of his black pants, and dark as night shoes complete his sultry ensemble, painting the perfect image of the *Dark Prince.*

His stare unsettles me as it never leaves my face, and the pulse in my neck starts to quicken. Holding his gaze with a bold one of my own, I steady my voice. "Oh. He speaks," I snark as the wine loosens my tongue.

A cruel smirk lifts the left side of his mouth, making those lush lips look less inviting. Without asking, he takes hold of my hand, and the cold kiss off his silver rings bites against my skin, while he slides his other arm around my waist, pulling me in close. "What are you doing?" I ask suddenly.

"Dancing," is all he says.

"*Ass,*" I mumble under my breath.

The *nerve* of this guy. Ignoring my arrival and now forcing a dance with me without even a simple *hello.* Most likely he's expecting me to grovel at his feet, hanging onto his every word, like I'm sure most girls do. I don't blame them—he is strikingly handsome. But how can they get past his arrogance? It's revolting to see yet another male believe he can take what he wants.

As he begins to lead us in smooth, slow movements, gliding us across the room, I make a point to step on his foot. He shoots me a glare that would send most begging for forgiveness. I simply shrug my shoulders and plaster an innocent look on my face.

"Oops," I say sweetly.

His nostrils flare at the sugary tone of my voice and I feel his hand tighten around mine, glaring daggers at me as he continues to guide our steps to the melody. My eyes hold a malice that I hope burns him as I can't wipe the smile off my face, the wine still numbing me. I must seem like a siren, with a look of sweetness that comes with devious intent. I won't bow down to his commanding presence, no matter how sharply his eyes slice into me. I've fought worse monsters than him, but what he doesn't know is that I might be the darkest monster of all.

The silence between us only adds fire to our burning tension, the fire I want to burn him with and wipe away his air of prejudice. His crystal blues trail down to my ruby-painted lips. The way he's staring at my mouth shoots heat to my cheeks, and I turn my head to look anywhere but in his direction. I glance along the side of the ballroom in hopes of ignoring this suffocating air he's filling with displeasure. What I don't expect is to see a pair of light brown eyes glaring at me from a blonde, who looks about ten seconds from blowing her reddened face to bits. Her hair swoops perfectly around her face, hanging down in shiny waves. She looks more fitting to be a princess than me.

But then, it hits me: this must be one of the many girls who would drop before him and offer him the world on a gilded platter. I huff. Then again, maybe this one is his girlfriend, and he's decided to settle down.

The way her fists are clenching together makes me go on the defensive, but I don't believe she would cause a scene at such an event. I let my eyes assess her. The girl looks like she lives solely to sit and look pretty, not a defined muscle anywhere on her body. This leaves me to assume she lacks any sense of fighting skills or defense. That thought settles some of the unease that was beginning to fester.

But if his girlfriend is so upset, then why is he dancing with me? It's not like the prince and princess of each court *have* to share a dance, and I know it's not out of the kindness of his heart, or an attempt at being gentlemanly. This male doesn't have a polite bone in his sculpted body.

"Your girlfriend doesn't seem too pleased; you should probably go and console her," I tell him, not wanting to be a thorn in someone's relationship. "She's glaring with her arms crossed, looking about two seconds from attempting to rip my hair out."

I glance up and see his dark brow rise, which only makes me zero in on the silver ring glinting through it. A slight tilt of his lip makes me think he found that amusing, but I doubt that. I'm sure this male finds nothing funny, let alone something *I* said.

Without warning, his hold tightens as he dips me back, leaning over my body and sending his scent washing over me. Such a heady scent that I savor as I close my eyes for a moment, the hints of woods and maple mixing with the wine swarming through my body. A deep warmth caresses inside me, making me want to melt in his arms. His breath fans over me and I smell bourbon coating his lips. *Shit.* He would smell good.

I open my eyes when I realize he hasn't lifted me back up. Frozen, mid-dip, he stares at my neck. That's when I realize my scarf must have slid off while I was being consumed by his masculine smell and held under his spell. And hating that I love it. I can't seem to read the look in his eyes as he starts to bring me upright again. I feel the blood rush from my head as the dim bulbs above begin to sway and blur. I have to take a moment to allow my body to center itself before we start our sinuous movements once again.

I feel the heated touch of his hand slide up my back as it reaches the base of my neck. "Not the style of a necklace I would have chosen for a princess," he says in a low voice. I feel the tickle of his fingertips brush against the neckline of my gown and up to my collar now on display.

In a flash, a hiss escapes him as he yanks his hand back. If I wasn't already looking at his face, I would have missed the shock flashing across his eyes before he shoved it down, with his neutral, cold appearance back in place.

Prince Draven places his hand back on my waist as we continue moving with the slow rhythm to what seems like a never-ending song. His posture is tense, and his gaze darkens as he stares down at me.

"You really know how to flatter a lady. It's just a necklace. No need to act as if it bit you." I roll my eyes to hide the embarrassment bubbling inside me. I hate this necklace and the attention it brings, making me wonder if he knows my power is locked away, or if he heard about the powerless Princess of Asov from any of my people who travel to his court for trade.

But I also can't seem to shove down the retorts that keep spilling out from me.

He doesn't say another word. The song *finally* comes to an end, and I make that my cue to quench my thirst. It's polite to offer a dip of the head or part with thankful words, but when he drops my arms and steps back, the prince just leaves without a sound.

Gods! Such an arrogant prick! I scream inside my head. Pure, aggravated fury.

No wonder the prince has a thick layer of cobwebs on his heart when he acts like *that.*

I could use another glass of that delicious wine to help me forget this *charming* dance. I take a steadying breath and sneak through the sea of people as I work my way over to the sweet wine that's calling my name. I don't indulge in this much wine often, but tonight, I think I can throw my concerns over the damn cliff.

I need space, somewhere quiet to calm my pounding heart and the enraged heat coursing through my body.

CHAPTER EIGHTEEN

Shade

*N*ews spreads of an attack on the south side in the Court of Asiza. The border of the court, farthest from the queen's castle. The place where a few locals live to stay out of the village's center, building cabins on the outskirts of the forest. I let my shadows blend me into the night as I increase my speed to the location of the attack. It's the perfect time for one, as Asiza's famous ball is in full swing, where all of the rulers are focused on entertaining for the evening. I feel balls are loud and overcrowded, with too many people sharing the same air.

The moon emits an ethereal glow all around, casting the land in a magical light that's too delicate for the evil that lurks. The frigid air is a blessing, keeping me alert and on guard. I drop down and brace both feet in the undergrowth, tightening my shadows as I glance ahead of me.

The cabin before me is eerily quiet, but the Corrupted still know how to hunt for a kill. Their logical thinking in strategy still exists, even as the venom turns them animalistic.

My boots crunch as a twig snaps beneath my foot, and I curse myself for not noticing it. As I cautiously creep forward a metallic scent drifts to me, causing my nostrils to flare.

I decide to hell with it and throw caution to the wind as I take off in a full sprint. I pass through the broken-down door in a matter of seconds and swipe my sword from its sheath as the pungent smell of the Corrupted blood mingles with the red blood of one who is sane. The room has a dim glow from afar, as the fireplace is still roaring. Slowing my movements, I see a lantern with an unlit candle in it lays partially smashed on the floor, the smoke still streaming from the wick. The wax melting from the candle is still warm as I dip my finger into it.

They're close.

I silently pad my boots across the floorboards and into what looks like the kitchen area. A blur flashes to my right and, without hesitation, I stretch my arm out, latching onto the Corrupted's throat before swinging my sword down and driving it up through his stomach, angling it into his chest. A gush of oily liquid floods from the wound when I yank my sword back. Soulless black eyes with dark veins slithering in every direction look back at me, unseeing as the body drops to the floor. My eyes begin burning with the foul smell protruding from the corpse, but within moments, the body disintegrates into ashes. As if he never was.

I feel a stab of sorrow for the person who used to have a life before it was ruined by a Scavenger, but then I'm flooded with hate towards the monsters they become. Killing innocents, tearing them apart bit by bit, draining their blood. It's almost like they aren't satisfied with the person they kill. Maybe they are searching for something else, but that part is still a mystery to me, driving me mad trying to figure out the root cause for their everyday invasion.

A shriek tears me from my thoughts and I race out the back door, not bothering to clean my sword, leaving my kill's remains dripping from the tip as a warning. The moment the cold air smacks against my face, I leap towards a Corrupted holding a female Fae in the air by her throat. When I get close enough, I slam the hilt of my sword into the back of his head. The force causes him to drop the female and spin menacingly towards me. The dark veins trail up his arms, neck, and around his eyes. Eyes that look like the endless pits of death digging deep into my soul. With another shriek, he launches forward with a pure, primal instinct to kill. They may be smart when it comes to hunting and staying hidden, but once they find their target, they become unhinged.

He goes to swipe his razor claws at my neck, but I block the blow with the bracer on my leathers. I thicken my shadows to form a tougher shield and disappear in the night air.

The monster pauses in confusion while I pierce my sword straight through his chest. This one doesn't drop so easily. He stares down at the source of pain, and still shadowed in the dark, he stumbles backward. A snarl leaves his cracked lips before I glide the silver blade free from his poisoned heart.

I let my shadows lighten for a moment. My mistake.

I'm blasted from behind with force. Flying forward, I manage to tumble and roll, leaping back onto my feet to see a Corrupted female fueled by a crazed strength. She crouches, cocking her head unnaturally before she darts forward at a high speed. I spread my feet, draw on my shadows, and hold my sword in front of me.

The moment she's before me, she ducks, aiming for my feet. I push off the ground and she misses, flying underneath me. When I land firmly, a wicked gleam shines through her coal-black eyes. A promise of death. Yet, I'm the one holding the oil-stained sword, leaving ashes in my wake. I smirk, daring her to try again.

The primal side of her seems to be more restrained, but not fully, as she comes straight at me. When she's a couple of feet away, I drive my leg up and slam my foot against her chest, sending her flying backward. Her body slams to the forest floor. I stalk to where she lies unmoving in the dirt. I know she's not dead—these suckers can't die unless you stab them through the heart.

I raise my sword the moment she tries to leap up and rake her claws through me. I drive the sharpened point down, crunching through bone and going straight through her and into the ground. Pinning her death to the damp soil.

Her black blood leaks out and absorbs into the ground she lies on. I wrench my sword out the moment she turns to ash.

A buzzing fills my ears at the kills tonight, my heart racing with adrenaline. A high from ridding the world of three more Corrupted in one night.

A scream startles me as I look for where the sound came from. The Fae female who must live here is cowering next to a male on the ground. They slowly inch backward, away from where their frightened gazes are locked. I look beyond them and—

Gods.

A Scavenger prowls out between the trees, lowering onto its haunches. A hellish growl vibrates from its chest, sharp mangled teeth on full display as its lips are peeled back. Bright red eyes focus on them like two orbs of fire as it seems to feed off their fear.

Its body is a mirage of shadows and black flames, morphing together into the shape of a monstrous beast. It is wolf-like in the lethal grace of its movements. Precise. Strong.

How did a Scavenger get over the seas? This is the first sighting of one outside the Court of Ashes. They typically stay behind their borders, but Deyadrum is clearly taking a turn for the worst.

I'm not even sure how to kill one, or if these phantom creatures even have a heart to pierce, but it would be the best option to try. Driving a blade through the heart seems to work for everything else. But I can't stand here and let it live, or worse, turn these two innocent Fae into Corrupted.

Without a second thought, I take off and strain my legs to reach the monster. But it chooses that moment to launch from its hind legs and pounce on the Fae male, locking its sharp teeth around his forearm. A throaty scream leaves him as I push my shadows out to wrap around the Scavenger's body.

"Nooo! No, no, no! Oh, Gods no!" the female screams, horrific sorrow lacing every word as she breaks, knowing what happens when someone is bitten.

I blast another round of shadows at it as I ignore the sobs behind me. I cord them around its neck, tightening. Vile hissing threats sound as it tries to escape my hold, seething, drops of black venom spraying with every jerk of its head. I charge my sword at it but...nothing.

The iron sword goes straight through it...

What the fuck?!

I toss my blade aside and focus all my strength on wielding my shadows, wondering if I can strangle the damn thing to death.

Groans of pain still fill the midnight air behind me, but then, something thuds by my boots.

"Try that!" the male forces out between ragged breaths. "It's made from wyvern iron. It might do the trick."

My eyes widen at the blade laying in the soil as I tentatively pick it up with my gloved hand. Wyvern iron is the strongest material, but it's rare. It was used specifically for hunting groups that would scour the land during the time dragons roamed free. Basic iron has no effect on dragon shifters; it's just a piece of metal to them. But wyvern iron is different—it's the only way to kill one, which the hunters learned fairly quickly and used to their advantage, killing the dragons off. But now, not having been forged in centuries, this type of iron is so rare that few in Deyadrum possess such a weapon.

I put the questions of how this male has something so deadly in his grasp out of my mind, as I carefully tighten my hold on the sword's hilt.

The Scavenger is still savagely snapping its mouth, twisting and turning to free itself from my hold, but before it can, I drive the sword down through its head.

The hissing and snarls are silenced as the Scavenger turns into a plume of smoke and particles of black embers. I stare wide-eyed at the empty space before me, then at the weapon in my hand. I tuck the knowledge of how to kill a Scavenger in the back of my mind, knowing I will need it for another time. But first, I need to secure some wyvern iron of my own.

I turn to approach the couple on the sodden forest floor, the soil dampening their clothes as the male is still whimpering in pain. The female's tears are continuously flowing, but her heart-wrenching sobs have stopped.

The male's arm is bleeding crimson, the punctured bite marks darkening as the venom seeps into his bloodstream. It will only take a matter of minutes for it to reach his heart and completely corrupt him. Streaks of black begin to spread from the wound as I watch the female's face turn into a look of horror.

"Shit," he grunts. "Toss me my sword, mate." I reach down where I dropped it and hand it to him, unsure of his intentions. But before I can even form a question, he lays his arm flat and takes in a deep breath. Without a second thought, he slices the sharp steel through his limb, cutting it off clean before the elbow.

His bellows ricochet off the trees around us, loud enough to scare the birds resting, their wings flapping in sync as they flee. The female leans over the side as bile shoots up her throat, heaving her disgust into a puddle of vomit.

Surprisingly, the male before me is still awake; that pain would make most faint. The detached limb continues to grow black veins, and the blood tints to liquid death as it leaks from the open end. I look over the wound on his attached arm, seeing no black veins. No black blood. In fact, his body is already starting to clot the blood oozing from his severed limb. This Fae just saved his own life, preventing a cursed death. He will only have one arm, because even though Fae can heal themselves fairly quickly, they can't regrow limbs. But he will live…

He sits up and slowly takes deep breaths in and out. "What's your name?" I ask. "Your quick thinking will allow you to live." Respect for him is flowing from my words and he can tell, because he gives a grateful smile and a sharp nod.

"Vincent, and oh fuck, did I just luck out, mate." He starts laughing in disbelief as his face scrunches in pain. "I didn't know if that would actually work!" His laughter rumbles from deep within, and this son of a bitch just saved his own life by the skin of his teeth. I can't help the small huff of incredulous amusement at the ridiculousness of it all.

The female beside him, who must be his wife, wipes her tears away as a huge smile lights her face. Pure adoration shines in her eyes as she wraps her arms around his neck, holding him to her. But that's when I notice the markings on the left palm of her hand as they hang loosely from his neck.

"You're mates," I blurt. My heart stutters at the sight.

No wonder she was distraught; losing a mate is losing half of your soul. A lightning bolt to the heart. A mate is fate's way of offering a love that's pure, and one that can overcome anything. It's the stars guiding you through the darkest of times. The embrace of magical bliss and promises of dreams coming true.

There is a ritual performed to intertwine the couple's souls, fusing their blood together in a bond so strong, not even wyvern iron can break it. Only death ends all bonds. But a gaping hole will be left in its place—a heart torn in two, never to be repaired—after the loss of your other half. The loss of a mate is gut-wrenching and damaging, leaving you wishing for death yourself.

The mating mark only shows on the left palm, and by pure fucking luck, Vincent cut off his right. Their marks are so beautifully designed. Every mated pair gets one with a unique style of inked swirls that are only identical to their mate's. They both hold up their hands and press them together. Their love for each other courses through the space between them.

"We are," the female says, a serene smile softly mirroring his.

Vincent breaks their moment and looks over at me, but he does a double-take and truly looks at me and the shadows that are still blanketing around me. "Gods. You're supposed to be a myth," he breathes.

"Sorry to disappoint," I joke. But I say it with gruffness because I've heard this before when someone recognizes me as Deyadrum's vigilante. But they will never be able to see who I truly am behind the shadows I command to hide my identity. My face is always masked behind my hood as I cloak it in darkness. A mask of secrets and hidden truths.

"Thank you…Shade," Vincent says as he palms his left hand to his chest, dipping his head in thanks.

I nod. "Just don't go cutting off any more limbs." And with that, I disappear into the night.

CHAPTER NINETEEN

Emma

*A*fter snagging another glass of the sweetest wine that's ever met my lips, I sneak off to the back corridor that's tucked into the corner of the ballroom. I'm hoping I'll find my way to a balcony or garden, where I can feel the crisp air across my heated skin. Gods only know how warm my blood is still boiling from Prince Draven grating on my nerves, plus the wine's continual buzzing through my system. Let alone the irritation coursing through me from the way his touch ignited a fire against every nerve ending.

Even through the smooth fabric of my gown, the heat of his hands scorched straight to my skin. I'm going to blame my lack of physical touch from others, or at least the gentle kind, for why my body is reacting the way it is to a guy who acts like his balls are twisted and shoved up his ass.

I take a huge gulp of wine as I continue down the dark hallway, heels clicking with every step, creating an echo of my presence. I pause and slide them off, holding both straps in one hand as I continue on. The cold stone is refreshing on the soles of my bare feet, cooling the ache that was starting to grow.

I turn left at the crossway, but jolt to a stop. Panic consumes me as I scurry back around the corner and press my back against the wall, holding my breath. Heart pounding heavily, I firmly hug my wineglass to my chest, demanding it to slow down. I *have* to be dreaming.

A moan bounces off the stone walls.

Definitely not dreaming. A crack in my heart skitters through its center. How can this be? I thought... I thought wrong, apparently.

I slam my eyelids shut, trying to erase what I saw.

Aiden. A girl. Kissing with mangled breaths. Her hands holding onto his neck.

I squeeze my eyes shut tighter as they begin to burn with the tears threatening to spill. I'm frozen in place, willing my feet to move so I can be anywhere but here, but they remain cemented to the floor.

A grunt echoes followed by a whimper. One heart-shattering drop falls from my eyes before I swipe it away with the back of my hand. *No.* He doesn't deserve my tears. What started out as a close friendship began to morph into uncharted territory for me, but I needed time. I have no say in his extracurricular activities, but the sting of his actions still hurts. Saying he's been *waiting* for me, that he *needs* me, only to go shack up with some random female in a dark corner.

Gods, we're *betrothed*. I know I haven't been on board with marrying him and ruining my chance with fate, but it's still the promise of a union between two people.

I need to leave, to get away from here before he sees me. Even though a part of me wants to confront him head-on and have it known he was caught.

I swivel softly on my feet, glass in one hand and shoes in the other. The quick turn briefly throws me off balance, the hallway swaying like the waves at sea, or at least it feels that way. I lean on the wall with one hand for support, steadying myself, trying to call on my training from the rocking ship to work to my benefit.

I pray his sensitive hearing is tuned out by the distraction with fiery red hair before him. I go to tiptoe forward, but as I push off the wall, one of the heels in my hands gets caught in the tulle of my gown, tugging it free from my grasp. I watch in slow-motion as the crystal-coated shoe curses me by falling to the floor, crashing to the stone with a loud smack.

I halt. All other sounds are silenced in repercussion.

I hear Aiden's voice mumble, "Get off," as a feminine gasp sounds in response.

I could make a dash for it, but a strong urge to confront him keeps me planted in place.

"Who's there?" Aiden's voice rises and I can hear the concern laced in the question.

I manage to chug down the rest of my wine, appreciating the way it glides down my throat. With the steel of my spine and determination set into place, I turn to face the corner he will come from, ready to take on whatever comes my way.

I'm curious, though. How will he act knowing I found him? Will he beg me for forgiveness? Say it was a mistake and that it will never happen again? Maybe he will ignore me as he did before, and act as if none of this ever happened.

As I bring my eyes forward, Aiden appears around the corner. The button on his tunic is undone. The gold strands of his hair that were styled neatly before the ball are now ruffled in every direction as he attempts to smooth them down. I raise a single brow at him as he finally sees me, even though it's probably fruitless with my mask still in place.

The apprehension in his eyes shines brightly, but the moment those green orbs connect with my grey ones, shock fills them as they widen, making him stumble a step. The girl with auburn hair flounces from around the corner next, huffing as she tries to fix her lipstick.

I flick my eyes away from the girl and hold Aiden's gaze. But where I thought I would see guilt of some sort, I find shocked eyes turning into a promise of damnation, just like his father's. The pools of green harden before me, as he hesitantly begins to prowl closer. I can't help the confused look that crosses my face at his change in character. The hairs on the back of my neck are rising, but I hold my ground, nonetheless, refusing to be walked over or scared away. And the dagger strapped to my thigh suddenly feels soothing.

The girl behind him starts untangling her hair as Aiden inches closer to me. He stops a foot away. "Leave, Margaret," he orders, never straying his rage-burning eyes from mine.

She squeaks at his blunt demand, but then she saunters to him, reaching up to press a quick kiss on his cheek. Only, he turns his head out of the way, denying her. Her mouth falls open, then she shifts her brown eyes to me with a challenge. I ignore her as I keep my sight plastered on my friend before me, still trying to figure out how this conversation will go.

After she realizes she won't get a reaction out of me, she walks past without a sound and makes her way to the ball that's still alive and in full swing.

When Margaret's footsteps can no longer be heard, I watch his eyes settle. The sharpness in them dulling. "It's not what it looks like, Emma," Aiden says, still standing a foot away from me.

"Isn't it, though?"

He shakes his head. "It's not. What did you see?" His lips press together, waiting for my response as he slightly sways on his feet.

I roll my eyes at his denial, even though I see an ounce of remorse. I word vomit my reply as the wine suddenly has me not caring what I say: "It looked like you were about to get your dick wet. But why?" I ask. No need to beat around the bush when we both know exactly what was happening just moments ago.

He heaves a painful sigh, like he knew that would be my answer. "Then you missed the part where I pushed her off me," he says on a hiccup.

"You are a male who is supposed to be *betrothed*," I try to say calmly, but a small snarl accompanies it.

"I am!" he swears. "Margaret used to be a girl I fooled around with way before our betrothal. I pulled her aside to end it, for you. But she refused to believe that and threw herself on me. Anything I've ever done with her meant nothing."

I can't contain the flare in my voice as the wine buzzes through me a little stronger, offering a helping hand in speaking my mind. "So, did it mean *nothing* when you told me that you *needed* me, that you have been *waiting* for me?! Did it mean *nothing* when you promised that we would be good together?! Or how about when we kissed…" I pause, sucking in a steady breath. "Did those mean *nothing* as well? Just lies and words to try and win my heart over?"

He shuts his eyes on an inhale, before opening them and stunning me with how splintered those green gems look. I go to tell him it hurt to see him with another, but before I can even finish that thought, his hands pin me against the wall. One hand is on my waist and the other presses against the wall beside my head. The back of my skull softly thumps against the stone as a dull ache starts to form from the abrupt contact. His face is so close to mine, I can feel the brush of his breath that smells like stale booze, mixed with the hint of cherry lingering on him from the girl's perfume.

"Aiden, wha——"

"Emma," he says on an exhale. "You really think I would cheat on you? To fool around with another? You are *mine*, and I am yours. You must believe me, because Margaret is never happening again. I told her as much. She just didn't take it well. But there needs to be trust. You have to trust me." His every word guts me, guilt forming from my outburst and the sinking feeling that he's not being completely honest. Hearing him say her name only drives the knife deeper into me.

I jerk my head to the side, not able to look at him. My head feels cloudy. Spreading his legs on either side of me, he presses more of his weight into me, brushing his nose along my cheek.

I could easily twist my body with a quick raise of my elbow to knock him back, then duck to free myself. But I don't want my skills to be known. Especially with the feeling of uncertainty that Aiden won't hurt me. I worry he might turn into an enemy more than a friend because the sting of betrayal punctures my heart, making it bleed by his own doing. I can feel a fragment of my trust for him shattering into a million tiny pieces that will never be able to come back together.

"You're so beautiful, Emma." He moans, a dark lust filling his eyes as they begin to trail down my body, even though most is hidden behind the layers of my gown.

"And you're evading," I snap. If he thinks I'll let him share any more heated moments with me right after another girl, he's lost his mind.

A drunken chuckle leaves him as he turns my head and slams his mouth on mine. My heart stalls and a muffled squeal leaves me from the contact. On instinct, I drive my knee up with force, hitting my mark as it slams into his unprotected balls. His mistake for leaving an opening and not anticipating that docile Emma would retaliate. I can see it in his eyes as they widen with surprise.

His hand drops from my face, immediately palming the source of pain. He grunts in agony, and I stare down at one of my closest friends, who I thought could be worth ignoring my hope of finding a true mate for. But the male before me is drunk and insincere.

I can feel the cold caress of the darkness within me begging to be set free. Whispering to do more, savor his pain, and promise him hell for making me feel like a fool. Promising to take away the ache that stabs through my heart. I almost give in, wanting to let them take over and do their worst.

But I don't. I shove them down deep, holding onto my sanity, while I keep my stormy eyes on the male I'm beginning to not recognize anymore. His handsome face and sweet words are a mask—an illusion to play tricks on the eyes. But I see clearly now, and I won't be so easily played by him again.

I shake my head as I glare down at him. "You *smell* like her," I declare. Before he can find his voice, I walk away, leaving him to suffer in his own destruction.

CHAPTER TWENTY

Emma

*T*he ball is still blazing with loud laughter and cheers, drinks splashing in glasses, and frantic words shared between friends. The room spins and the floor feels like I'm on a ship sucked into a whirlpool at sea. The combination of wine, my boiling blood, and my pounding heart all seem to be playing tricks on me.

A small touch on my elbow startles me and I turn to see Kye standing there, with Cora right alongside him.

"Everything okay, Princess? You look like you've seen a ghost." Kye stands directly in front of me now, assessing every inch in trying to get a read on me.

"Yea—yeah, I'm fine." I blow off everything that just happened as I force a tight smile onto my face. I'm still fuming with frustration towards Aiden, but I've decided to bottle it up for tonight. I'm not ready to dive back into the rough waters of mine and Aiden's relationship before it could even really start. If I tell them what happened, Cora will ask me a million questions, while Kye will hunt Aiden down, only to rip his dick off and shove it down his throat. A little extreme, but the thought slightly lifts my mood. I'm sure I'll regret thinking that once the alcohol wears off. "I was just looking for some fresh air but got a little lost on the way. Also, I'm afraid I may have indulged in more wine than food. At this point, I think I'm just ready to lie down."

"Well, I'm afraid you have to briefly indulge Queen Zoraida and your father with your presence first. But then, I'm sure we can sneak you away to the comfort of your room," Cora says with a wink. Promising she will make it happen, even though I know she'll make quick work of my escape so she can return to the ball. The beads of sweat glistening on her forehead tell me she's been getting lost in dancing, most likely devouring the treats for a moment's break before diving right back into the music. I envy her carefree way of life when she's not under orders to get a task done. She never complains. She just lives.

Kye's lips briefly lift looking at Cora. He shifts his eyes away quickly, right before he shoves a glass of water in my face and gives me a knowing look. I gratefully accept it, wondering what that momentary look was, and chug half of the water down in one go, then hand it back. "Wish me luck," I plead.

"You don't need it," Cora says with adoration in her eyes.

The conversation with the other high Fae was bland. I was enraptured every time Queen Zoraida spoke, but kept getting lost in my own thoughts when she, my father, and the other courts' rulers spoke about the meetings they have in place for the next two days. I did catch the part when they momentarily said the Corrupted have progressed in their courts and that an attack took place tonight. But what seemed to bring pure terror in their eyes behind their masks was the news that this time, there was a Scavenger sighting. The monstrous beasts that turn Fae into the Corrupted. I can't help but wonder where the Scavengers come from? How did they come to be if they are the only creatures like them to exist in Deyadrum?

It makes me curious if the high Fae of the courts have any clues for putting an end to the Corruption or if there's a cure to save those who are scratched or bitten. They stop all talk on the matter, not answering any of the questions floating in my head. But if there was a cure, those Corrupted could be freed from the poison invading them and be able to return to their lives. To their families.

My grief slams into me, lodging my throat with emotions at the thought of a mother I never met or aunt, who only shows up in distant memories ever since I was taken by my father. If they were turned, I would give up everything, even myself, to find a cure and release them from death's grip.

I bite back the sudden need to cry as my eyes begin to burn. The wine only fuels the intensity of my feelings, but I can't break down here. I'll let myself drown in my misery for a little while, when I'm alone with no one to witness it. Once they finally manage to finish a full glass of wine with only tiny sips, I take that as my cue to leave. I've been sitting here long enough to appease their want of my presence. I can tell my father doesn't want me here at all, with the way he glares at me, then ignores my presence, only to interrupt anyone who attempts to direct conversation my way. I have a feeling Queen Zoraida requested my company, if only to make me feel more welcome.

My father starts a conversation with the queen, letting his words swerve around me as if I'm not even here. "Where are your sons, Queen Zoraida?"

She waves her hand in the air, a light-hearted twinkle glinting in her eyes. "I'm sure Emil is off enjoying the music and food, the simple pleasures of being a kid." The gentleness in her voice as she speaks of her younger son warms my heart. I'm curious to know how that feels and am completely in awe of her as she plucks a black rose off the vine decorating the pillar beside her, placing the stem in her hair behind her ear. "And Draven, well, he does as he pleases. He doesn't need his mother breathing down his neck," she says with a chuckle.

My father grunts with a small nod, as if he understands what she's saying. But that is so far from the truth, and I'm sitting as proof that he doesn't understand, since he controls all aspects of my life. My father turns, leaning in to speak to Calloway sitting beside him.

A perfect opportunity and a break in conversation to speak. "Excuse me, I'm feeling a little faint and am going to take my leave," I address them in a soft tone.

"Are you alright, dear?" Queen Zoraida asks, and I can hear the concern in her voice as she studies me.

"Yes, Your Majesty. If I'm being honest, I think my dress may be trying to suffocate me." I try to lighten my departure with a small joke.

She chuckles and nods, setting her empty glass down on the table beside her. "I know all about that, dear," she says with a sweep of her hands that trails over her bodice. "But of course, these males are clueless about the confines of females' clothing. I hope you rest well." A dip of her head and a gentle smile grace her regal face. A queen, indeed.

"Your Highness." I curtsy when I face my father, and lower just enough to inflate his ego and show his power over me, even as bile rises up my throat at belittling myself. But I must continue to act how he expects, never letting him see my true motives as I slowly get stronger in hopes of one day watching life leave his eyes.

I wake up to slivers of sun peeking through the dense clouds before the light is swallowed whole. It's refreshing to wake up somewhere that horrid memories don't plague me, where I don't picture blood-stained floors or hear faint echoes of snapping from a whip. Never screams though. Never any screams.

I desperately need some time alone. Time to catch my breath and figure out how everything I've come to know has been a lie. How I assumed the land of Deyadrum was full of peace and protection, not expecting the reality of a war brewing between life and death. Then, there is Aiden, someone I considered a close friend... My heart clenches at the thought. I counted on him, shared many parts of who I am with him, and he was always there with caring eyes and gentle words. But last night Aiden grew a set of horns.

This is just more proof that those who are close to me eventually become tainted. Their pure, good hearts stain black as their souls sour. The darkness within me, the one that shadows my every thought, seems to slither into the people I care about. Who's to say I am not the reason for my mother's death? Or the reason why Aunt Lyd's home was raided that led her to getting hurt?

Guilt stabs through me, twisting with all-consuming grief at the thought that losing them is my fault. It would not surprise me. I am the disastrous common factor in both of their lives. If I am the reason, then there will never be any punishment harsh enough to make up for the damage I've done.

I choose to toss on a pair of fitted black pants with a tight, charcoal long-sleeved turtleneck shirt, grab my darkest cloak to drape over me, and slip into a pair of black knee-high boots to truck through the forest in. The final touches: grabbing my book and securing my dagger around my thigh, so it's out of sight once I close my cloak together.

The air may be thicker here, but the temperature is colder. There's a welcoming chill in my lungs as I take a deep breath in, causing a slight burning sensation that triggers a small cough. It's just cold enough to see the puff of air when I release it.

I'm grateful for this time of leniency. My father couldn't possibly pin his guards on me all hours of the day, for it would raise suspicion. More than there already is with me never attending any events in all my life. I hurry out after breakfast to find a quiet place to read, wanting to be outside of the castle walls. But it's more than that... I feel drawn to the forest, or something primal in it. My blood buzzes with the urge to venture deeper within it, blocking out the chilly air from freezing my veins. Even with the gloomy sky above, walking beneath the trees darkens the already cloudy day. They only allow slivers of cool light to glow in-between the branches.

The forest here must be centuries old, as the ancient trees guard its spirit. The fog clings to every crevice in the forest with its ghostly blanket, covering everything in a milky white. Its weightlessness is an eerie vapor that can envelop you in a soundless embrace.

I take a few steps into the woods, noting that the light fog seems like a mirage that would discourage people from venturing further. But I find the mist almost...ethereal and comforting. It swirls and dances in streams of grey as it weaves between the tall, magical pines.

I hold my book tighter to my chest as I trudge through the dense undergrowth, a soft breeze nipping against my face as it whistles through the trees. The forest is quiet, except for the wind's song and every crunch under my boot as I step on leaves and twigs. The trees stand tall, watching.

The rough caress of their deep brown bark feels peaceful when resting my palm against it, like they are welcoming me to their home. The trees were purely made from nature, yet guarded the shadows that seemed to worship this dark forest.

When the castle is far off in the distance, I find a place to rest against an old tree that has sprawling limbs, its leaves dancing with the wind. A glimmer of morning light peeps through the opening above, just enough for me to read. I'm anxious to open my favorite book and get lost between the pages, escaping this messed up life for at least a little while.

I slide down to lie against the base of the tree, propping my head against it as I hold my book up on my knees, already being consumed by the words before me.

I lose track of time as I devour the story in my hands, but I only break free from its hold when I look up in fright and see a dark figure lurking between the trees.

CHAPTER TWENTY-ONE

Draven

I stride into my mother's parlor this morning, just as the sun crests over the horizon. Emil is still sound asleep in his bed. That kid can sleep the day away and nothing can wake him. Not even a blast to his window would alert him and bring him to rise from his dreams.

The door clicks shut behind me as I let myself in, comforted by the sleek, dark floors and champagne drapes edged in gold that line the windows. Velvet-cushioned lounge chairs rest in the middle of the room, a color of red that reminds me of Princess Emma's smart mouth. I shake my head to clear those unwarranted thoughts, even though it's hard to wipe the image away.

An elegant chandelier hangs above the sitting area, reflecting designs of light around the space. I head towards the floor-to-ceiling windows on the far side, with my hands behind my back, and look out at the chorus of silvers and golds as the clouds blend with the morning light.

"There you are!" My mom rushes in with her eyebrows raised, taking note I'm here on time. She's still wearing her cashmere sleep set. It's one of the things I admire about her, that her title and riches don't change who she is. She puts herself together to look like the regal queen she is, but she would much rather lounge in comfy clothes and slippers.

"Here I am," I say, a small smile lifting my mouth. She sent a message asking to see me and I headed straight over. She shouldn't be surprised I'm here, just that I'm not late tying up loose ends from an evening of empty pleasure. I chose to forgo company, a first for me. But a small part inside of me didn't like the thought of another's hands on me or hearing whiny moans that some think are sexy. It's like a high, ear-piercing screech that goes on and on, only to leave you with a bland orgasm and a pounding headache.

My mother can't seem to ever hide her enthusiasm towards seeing me and my brother. Her face lights up as she settles in a chair, folding her legs beneath her. "How was your evening at the ball?" she asks, hedging for any juicy gossip because she can't help herself.

"It was uneventful."

"Hmm, even dancing with that sweet Emma of Asov? Or did she scare you off with only one dance?" Her voice turns playful as she teases me.

I wanted to tell her that *princess* has not one sweet bone in her body. A devious little thing with her petite frame, thinking she can play with fire against me. But I'm surprised my mom noticed my dance with her. I thought it was brief enough, even though it makes no difference to me either way.

I ignore her taunt about the mysterious princess, who is just now appearing to the public. That tells me she's up to something, or her and her piece of shit father are plotting something against the other courts. Many love King Oren and his friendly presence, but I see past the bullshit. He's nothing but a snake underneath stitches of finery and a crown to mask it.

"She wasn't the only female at the ball." I raise an eyebrow at her with a sly smirk, hoping she takes the meaning behind it.

"Ugh, Dravennn," she drags my name out with a frustrated sigh. "I love you more than you will ever imagine, but must you keep slumming it with all these ladies? I know you are still waiting for the chance of finding your mate, but…" She stops speaking as she notices the drop in my expression, seeing pain etched in my features as I glance away.

I've been alone without a mate for centuries. I thought I found my mate, a girl who I grew up with named Sienna. We were inseparable, always climbing the trees and running through the forest around the castle. As we grew older and reached our twenties, those feelings morphed into more. Into love. We were each other's firsts and accepted being together in hopes of a mate bond forming eventually. Praying for the stars to align our souls together.

But one day, a traveler from the Court of Abhainn came to ours. Visiting an old friend, he said, when he bumped into Sienna at the art shop in town while looking for a painting. The second their eyes connected was the moment our love cracked in half and sailed separate ways. Those fifty years spent with her, gone. He was her true mate, and she left with him. Not before she apologized to me, begging me to forgive her. I did, for her sake. I wanted her to feel no regrets in leaving. My love for her didn't want to break her heart, just because she wasn't mine. It's been 425 years since that day.

If there's anything in this life I will be selfish about, it's holding out hope that fate will bring my other half to me. I bring my eyes back to my mother and find regret filling her eyes as they begin to get a watery shine. "I'm sorry," she breathes out. "I shouldn't have said anything. It's none of my business."

I slowly approach her, needing to comfort away the sadness creeping in. I sit next to her on the cushioned chair to her right and lay my hand on her arm. "It's okay. I know you only want the best for me and everything you say comes from your heart. I could never be upset with you." I give her arm a quick squeeze. She has taken what life has dealt her and ran with it. My father, King Irad, never came back when he journeyed to the Court of Ashes to confront the ruler. He wanted to form a connection, some type of alliance, so the court wasn't set as an outcast. A court of death, as it has become, where those who commit unspeakable crimes are sent and never return. Yet, the power held there must be immeasurable, for my father was the strongest out of the high Faes, and he, too, did not return.

We learned of his fate five years ago when, one moment, my mother was sipping her morning tea during breakfast, and in the next second, her cup smashed against the floor, shattering. Her eyes went wild as she fisted her heart. My parents were true mates, and that day, she felt his life ripped from hers.

I block the rest of the intruding thoughts from my mind as I see the smile that lights up her whole face, taking away any guilt she felt from prying. "Can you try and show Emma around?" As she sees my smile falter, she quickly tries to add another alternative to make it seem less daunting for me: "Or maybe just a small conversation with her to make her feel more welcomed? That girl wasn't feeling well last night, and she seems a bit lonely," she says as she scrunches her brows together in thought.

"Why would you say that?" I ask, curious.

Staring off into the distance, she takes a moment to respond. "By her eyes, or rather, what she's trying to hide in them." Her face turns serious before she lets out a small chuckle to lighten the mood. "Just something a mother would notice, but then again, I could be wrong. Anyway...will you welcome her a little more?" She looks up at me, holding her breath for my answer, even though she knows I can never say no to her.

"Yeah, I can do that, but I make no promises about how it goes."

She shakes her head, eyes crinkling at the corners as she laughs. "Try to rein in your dazzling personality." She nudges me with her elbow, teasing me with her all-knowing look.

I made sure I got everything I needed to get done first before tracking down the menace of a princess to please my mother.

I got my morning training in after breakfast—the training I do solo to focus on my strength and agility. In the afternoons, I spar with others who want to practice their combat skills, but there are many times it ends up being Emil and I challenging one another. That kid thinks he'll win every time, and I hope one day he does. But he still has a long way to go in learning strategy while he builds muscle.

It saddens me that Father won't be around to teach him. He's still so young. It's hard for Fae to have children, and on a fluke, my parents were blessed with Emil after they assumed my mother would never become pregnant again, since it had been so long. But I will be forever grateful.

I take a shower and look over the information I've been gathering on complaints filed in our Court of Asiza, including on the Corrupted sightings. I insisted my mother let me do what I can to help, to assist in serving Deyadrum. But I can't help the obsession that has snowballed in me and the desire to figure out everything I can about them. There's something I'm missing. Well, that everyone is missing. Even the high Fae and rulers of every court.

They have gatherings often, yet, no set solution by the end, still just as unsure of what to do as when they walked in. But I have heard them mention Shade, the one who walks in shadows and hunts those with poisoned hearts. What I don't understand is why not try to reach out to him as allies? Instead, they want to interrogate him, find out what he knows. The only thing is…they have to catch him first.

As the heir of Asiza, I have attended quite a few of the gatherings. But lately, I have chosen to skip them, because nothing comes from them. My mother will come back and give me all the information I need to know, which is usually lacking.

Once I look over the maps a few times, engraving each detail into memory, I read through my notes in hopes of something crucial sparking. I drink a glass of my favorite maple bourbon as I get more frustrated with the standstill of information. I need to take the edge off of my stress from the task my mother asked of me: to exchange pleasantries with the enigma in a dress.

The princess that crawled out of a hole has a mouth on her, and one that I find myself staring at more than I'd like. I imagine her smart mouth being silenced as I shove my cock between those lips. I've slept with plenty of females to keep my needs at bay, but none of them ignite a true need in me. They don't make me go mad at the thought of them; they're forgettable and unfulfilling, and I make it clear I want nothing more. I won't lose hope that I will find my mate one day, but every year, it's getting harder and harder to hold onto that hope.

But I can't stop wondering about Emma and the inferno she stoked in me, because I *know* she's not my mate. The bond would have snapped in place and consumed us both the moment we were near. But I still can't stop thinking about her at the ball, with those dark painted lips that matched the color of wine I watched her sip. I had to dance with her to get a closer look, picturing her mouth staining my dick as she sucked me deep in the back of her throat. Especially after she acted like stepping on my foot was an accident. I wanted to teach her a lesson, because she was riling the beast inside of me, tempting it. I could feel my cock straining, hardening against the seams, but fell limp when she brought up Katrina, like a bucket of cold water was doused over me.

Forcing myself to clear my head, I feel it's time to keep my word to *welcome* the princess. Tipping back my glass, I let the final sip of my drink slide smoothly down my throat, contemplating another if it may help with the annoyance I'm about to deal with. I set the empty glass back on my desk, slip on my boots, and start towards her suite.

When I go to head up the steps towards the guest wing, I pause. Hand gripping the polished banister as I catch the flowery scent of roses. *Her* smell. It swirled around me and invaded my thoughts during our dance, leaving its mark for me to never forget. I take a few more steps up, until I realize the smell is growing fainter as I head towards her room. That can only mean one thing: she's not there.

There are many visitors staying at the castle from every court—maybe she made a friend. I mean, you would *think* this girl would have made friends with someone, or at least be busy, so I wouldn't have to personally deal with her. Then again, she is betrothed to that uptight golden boy. They could be having a romantic picnic together.

I almost heave up the contents of my stomach all over the stairs at the thought of them being close. Imagining his hands on her surges a feeling of possessiveness, the need to break his fingers and crush him.

I clench my jaw hard, shoving away that unsettling feeling.

But I have a strange hunch that she's not with him, as I recall what my mother said about thinking she's lonely. Not to mention how she's been staying under the radar her whole life. Being the only person to hide from everyone for so many years, I suppose that's what she does best. She's hiding somewhere.

I feel a sliver of delight at the thought of finding her, like a game of cat and mouse. Taking joy in hopes of interrupting any semblance of peace she was planning to get.

Using her scent to guide me, I follow her trail that leads me outside and into the forest. Already, my overheated body appreciates the chilly air as I'm wearing nothing but a loose, black tunic, matching slacks, and a pair of boots. The cold never bothers me, it only calms me and cools my constantly heated skin with its frigid touch.

I weave in-between the trees of my home, knowing how to navigate through every inch of the shadowed forest. But instead of going my own way, I follow her sweet, intoxicating scent that grows stronger with every step I take deeper into the woods. I will say, the girl has some balls for coming out this far and away from anyone who would hear her scream for help. Although, the fog and shadows themselves would silence her pleas, not even allowing so much as an echo. Only me and my brother delve this far in. Even the guards here stick to the outskirts near the path. It's pathetic. But this girl…she walked straight into the core of darkness.

I stick to the dark silhouettes of the trees as I finally have her in my sights. She seems oblivious that someone is so near to her. I'm able to see her turn the page of her book greedily, as if she can't read fast enough. The way she's rubbing her feet in anticipation of the part of the story she must be excited for, so lost in a different world and not a care for the one she lives in.

Her hood is down, and her hair lays in waves over her shoulders. She's wearing all black, like a princess of the night again, and I can't help but focus on how she's sucking her bottom lip. The immediate desire to taste her and claim her mouth burns through me, but I snuff it out as quickly as it came. This girl is nothing to me. A nobody I have to make nice with for a couple of days. I don't need another female, one who is challenging, when I have so many willing as it is.

She's fully laying on a bed of leaves, not caring if the damp soil seeps into her clothes, which is odd for a princess. A speck of dirt usually makes regular girls have a panic attack, let alone a princess.

The book is held high above her head, arms stretched out before her, and it looks uncomfortable.

I decide to make my presence known but hope to instill fear in her unsuspecting body.

This princess needs to learn a lesson. She needs to learn to not venture into dark woods and be mindful of the beasts that lurk in them.

CHAPTER TWENTY-TWO

Emma

A loud snap sounds as Prince Draven steps out from the shadows he was lurking in. Fear jolts through every nerve in my body as I startle and my muscles jump. Before I can react, my book slips from my fingers, landing hard on my throat.

I heave forward on all fours, gagging while trying to catch my breath from the book's spine practically throat chopping me with a force I didn't realize a book could have. Raising one hand, I hold my neck as the initial pain begins to fade, but the soreness still lingers. I drag in steady breaths as I feel my heartbeat drop back to a normal pace.

A slow clap fills the air and silences the sound of my breaths. "That's one way to lure a male into the woods." His smooth voice sends tingles down my spine, but I let my irritation for this arrogant prince stop them before they go deeper.

I lift my head to stare daggers at him, steam shooting from my nostrils as I huff in aggravation. He's like a leech that sucks any ounce of happiness right out of me. "Wow, and here I thought you ran out of words in your vocabulary after our dance." I push myself up so I'm at my full height, not wanting to be on my knees for him. "But if I were to lure a male into the woods, you wouldn't even be on the list to choose from." I do my best to keep my voice calm, but I'm sure he can hear the anger burning through it.

I bend down to snatch my book off the ground and brush off the loose bits of leaves on me. *What is it with these males making me drop my books?*

I do a quick inspection of the book, making sure there's no damage before I bring my eyes up to finally look at him, and *Gods*, I wish I hadn't. A warmth is already spreading across my face at the sight, even with him giving me a disgusted smirk.

His gaze hardens as I stare at him, letting my final words hang in the air. I'm sure no female has ever told him they aren't interested in the Dark Prince, even though he looks sinfully divine. But I can't get past his distasteful personality.

I can see his corded muscles beneath his clothes as the wind makes his shirt cling tight against him, and how his pants hug his strong legs. The tattoos that trail up his neck make my heart skip a beat as my eyes snag on the silver piercing in his brow. His raven hair falls perfectly in place without even trying, but his eyes... The icy depths within send shivers through me, and I can't help but want to let them freeze me over. Maybe it will numb the heat that coils deep in my belly.

He takes another step forward, raising his eyebrows as his eyes scrutinize me. "Are you sure about that?" he asks, and by the way his smirk lifts higher, it tells me he damn well knows I was taking in every inch of him.

I hold his gaze, hoping he sees I'm not threatened by him. I have no interest in him beyond admiring him from a distance. But he better be careful, because that cockiness of his is going to earn him a dagger to the throat.

Mine, preferably.

My eyes blatantly assess him before I scrunch my face like I ate something horribly bitter and then turn to start walking away.

I hear a slight chuckle leave him. "You're not going to answer my question?" he continues, as his deep voice skates up my back.

"Nope." I pop the *p* as I keep trudging forward and wave a hand in the air, hoping to brush him off or shoo him away. "It's just that your degree of ignorance has rendered me speechless."

I usually tramp down any outspoken thoughts, but for some reason, I can't seem to bite my tongue around him. He irks me in a way that no male ever has, and I just let the words fly out of my mouth. Maybe it's the frustration over Aiden's actions mixed with Prince Draven's annoying presence intruding on my little bit of tranquility. But I need to seek some control of my mouth, because if my father finds out…

I internally flinch at the thought.

But this male… This *prince*, doesn't know the difference between how I speak now vs when I'm around my father. It's too late now, anyway. But if I become the docile princess, he would just walk all over me, and there is no way in hell I'll let that happen.

I don't turn around as I keep my footing steady and sure, setting a pace quick enough to put distance between us. The cold wind picks up as it bites through my clothes. I wrap my cloak tighter around myself, hanging onto the little body heat I've trapped within, and hold my book closer to me. The temperature must be dropping as the day passes by. That's what I get for losing track of time.

Suddenly, a heated touch snakes down my arms and around my waist, sliding its way up my spine and into my hair. My muscles tense as I stop walking. A simmer of terror freezes in my veins. The touch feels like the phantom hands of my nightmares as I remember the feel of their icy grip and unbreakable hold. My body starts to shake until I realize this touch is *warm*. Gentle.

I spin around as fast as lightning, expecting Prince Draven to be right behind me. But he's still standing where I left him. Hands in his pockets, staring at me with a dark expression.

I give my head a shake. Maybe I'm so cold that I'm simply imagining things at this point. Simply wishing I had someone's heated hands on me, now that I have an inkling of what it feels like. But who? As for Aiden, I'm done, and I refuse to marry him. I just need to figure out how to make that happen.

Then there's the Dark Prince, who's still staring at me with an expression I can't identify. And even though those masculine hands would probably feel good, I wouldn't be able to handle the cockiness on his face. So, I guess that leaves…no one. Gods. My own hands will have to do.

Just as I settle the decision to release some of my frustration later, I turn back around to leave the prince behind and go to take a step forward. But a faint wisp of air tickles against my neck.

I gasp in shock. Frozen, as my mind is trying to catch up.

"I came all this way to find you, and you're just going to ignore me?" Prince Draven says in a deep voice from behind. Why didn't I hear him approach? I may not have access to the well of my power, but my heightened senses are still normal. How did he get right up against my back so quickly?

I don't move, keeping perfectly still as I focus on calming my racing heart. I'm silently praying to the Gods he doesn't notice how uneasy he has made me by catching me off guard.

His warm scent of cedar wraps around me. Yet, I smell a sweet, intoxicating note of maple as his breath fans against my face, and suddenly, I want to know if he would taste like that.

His nose brushes behind my ear, taking a deep inhale. "No one walks away from me." There's a hard edge to his words. "But I find it ironic that you call me ignorant. Seems you're projecting something about yourself. It's unbecoming, really." His soft baritone voice drifts around me, soothing the momentary fright before annoyance bubbles in my throat.

I spin, whipping my hair around and hoping to Gods it smacks him. "What the *hell* is that supposed to mean?" I seethe, clenching my jaw as a scowl washes over my face and narrowing my eyes at his ludicrous words.

He's anything but amused as we stand inches apart and I can feel the heat radiating off his body. It's a welcoming warmth that wants to thaw out the cold nipping at my skin. The challenge brewing between us is enough to keep Hell's fire blazing for all eternity.

His mesmerizing eyes look like they glow in the shadows cast beneath the trees, pulling me in only to drown me in pools of blue. I can't look away; I'm too stubborn to back down. I feel drawn like a moth to a flame. Skirting on the edge of danger and temptation, with a hint of curiosity, becomes overwhelming

He invades my space more when he closes the remaining inches between us, making me tilt my head back to hold his gaze. "Because here you are, finally *claiming* your title to the public after not giving a shit about Deyadrum your whole life. Waltzing into a ball with a pathetic excuse of a fiancé on your arm, while you have done *nothing* to help the people. *Ignorant.*" He sneers.

I'm fuming. Not so much at his words, but how true they are. I'm mad at myself. I know I have been shackled to the palace, ordered to stay hidden, but I've only recently begun to understand the chaos this world is in. The suffering and on-guard nature in which the people have to live.

It's like a bucket of cold water is dumped on the boiling anger that wants to burst inside me, being replaced by guilt. I feel a prickling sensation behind my eyes as tears threaten to spill, and I dart them away to hide the pain I feel for doing nothing all these years. Not caring if I lose the battle of wills in our stare-off. I can't stand to show my weakness in front of him.

But I need to stay strong and not let him see the soft, fragile spot in the wall I've built in case he strikes again. So, I steel myself, blinking the tears away as I bring my grey orbs back to him. His hard eyes are softer, and it irritates me to think it's because he took notice of the way his words were shredding my heart apart. I choose to throw him off by smirking, allowing him to see the devious glint in my gaze.

I ignore his words on Deyadrum and cling to him mentioning Aiden on my arm. "You sound…jealous." I widen my smirk to show a hint of my white teeth. "Of having a little less attention on you at the ball, or because of the male on my arm…" I raise a quizzical brow. Taunting him.

He leans in to tower over me more, daring me to back away. But I don't give him the satisfaction as I stay put. The scruff on his jaw deliciously scratches against my cheek, his heady scent wrapping around me, and a deep, raspy chuckle vibrates up his throat. "Trust me, you would know if I was jealous. And for all I care, he can have you." He pulls back, giving me a once-over and letting it show how tasteless he finds me.

I try not to squirm under his scrutiny as I begin fuming. Not from the lack of interest he has in me, but for acting like I'm a possession that can be tossed around and claimed. I inhale a deep, ragged breath to calm the strong urge of wanting to bring my palm back and aim it up to strike his nose. Not like he wouldn't be able to heal it right away, but I think his momentary pain would make me feel a bit better.

He steps back as if he can read my thoughts and narrows his eyes before trailing them down to the book in my hands. "You like to read," he says. I notice he's not asking; he's stating what he already knows.

I'm hesitant about his change in tone and in the conversation as I rear my head back.

But what the hell. I go with it before I get a headache from the pounding I can feel creeping inside my skull.

Shrugging, I hug the book a little closer to my chest. "I do."

I'm curious as to where he's going with this. I slowly tilt my head to the side, waiting for what he'll say next. But he simply nods, not elaborating more on the out-of-context question. Then, he starts to walk away.

I stand there, slack-jawed, as I look at his retreating back. What... What just happened? He may as well have just stomped on my foot and then gave me a hug. I'm so confused as I stare at his broad frame expanding the distance between us with every step.

I'm still staring in shock and standing frozen when he twists to look back at me. "You coming?" he yells, his voice bouncing off the trees to reach me.

I furrow my brows until they're almost touching. He wants me to follow him? I was hoping this would be the end of whatever this little confrontation was between us. This is the point where we *should* part ways.

Rolling my eyes, I raise my voice to yell back. "Where?"

"You'll see." And then he turns back and heads towards the castle.

With a dramatic roll of my eyes, I give in and follow. Not because I'm *curious*, but because I was planning to return to my rooms anyway and seek the warmth my body is so desperately craving. I quicken my feet to catch up to him, but not fully. Even though that furnace of a male has plenty of heat to share. I choose to stay a small distance behind and suffer in the frigid air a little while longer until we're back inside.

CHAPTER TWENTY-THREE

Emma

*H*e leads me through a back passageway that wraps around the castle, dipping down and curving until we reach a set of double doors. The sleek, wine colored doors are carved with such intricate gold markings that I can't help but run my fingertips over them, wondering if what's behind the door is more beautiful than this. The design shimmers like it's full of magic and possibilities.

"Are you done ogling the door?"

I jump, momentarily forgetting Prince Draven is right behind me. I must look utterly ridiculous, feeling up a door, and it's clear that's what he thinks.

As I back up, he steps around me to reach the handle, but not before he adds on more of his lovely commentary. "I didn't know you had a door fetish, but I promise you it won't satisfy what your body needs." And with that, he twists the handles and pushes them apart. An angry retort is sitting on my tongue before I bite it back down. The irritation vanishes as I finally get to see what's on the other side, and it truly is magic.

I step into the room, but it's not a room at all…it's like stepping into another world. A glass dome ceiling expands high up, with a full view of the gloomy sky as the fog swirls around it. There's a soft stream of light peering down into the room, casting everything in an enchanting glow. I bet on a clearer night the view is mesmerizing. I imagine the dark sky glittering with white stars that dance before the moon.

More windows wrap around the curved room, offering the serene beauty of the forest surrounding it. Rich brown bookshelves tower high above in rows, all completely filled with endless stories and ancient history. Sleek, black ladders are attached to every section that roll against the polished onyx flooring. I turn to peer at the backside of the library and see a massive sitting area with deep midnight sofas and a plush rug I want to sink my feet into before the wide fireplace. A low fire is crackling within it, providing a subtle, dim light throughout, with a warmth that sends pleasure to every frozen, numb part of my body.

"Wow," I breathe out. No words can describe this hidden gem. It's so much bigger and has more than double the amount of books my father has. I wonder if they have any romance books hidden in the back, or if they keep them out in the open. But what amazes me most is that there's not a speck of dust as I walk farther into the room.

Some books lay on the table before the cushioned seats, left behind by someone in the midst of reading, with a bookmark poking out between the pages. I'm in awe. This library is cherished, used, and cozy. Especially compared to home, where I'm the only one who seems to make use of the library, even though I have to sneak around to read the kind of books I want.

All I can hear is the crackling of embers in the fireplace and the steady beat of my heart as I keep surveying the room. Until Prince Draven's voice disrupts the peace: "I take it that means you like it?" The roughness in his voice brings me back to focus after I got lost in my own thoughts.

I turn to face him, taking notice that he stayed put by the doors while I move around the room. His dark stare latches onto me as I bring my grey eyes to his blue ones, crashing against each other like waves in a storm.

But I can't seem to let my dislike for him boil over in this room; it feels wrong to bring spiteful energy in here. I take a deep breath and sort through my thoughts, throwing away every single one that wants me to bite back at him and strangle him.

"It's amazing," I say on a breath, peering up at the whispering veil of clouds above.

He nods, shoving his hands into his pocket. "Well, my mother will be pleased. You're welcome here at any time, day or night."

Free rein of all these books for the rest of the day, and I still have an entire day tomorrow! I internally shriek in excitement. I may never leave this room.

Prince Draven clears his throat as it echoes throughout the space. "If that's all, then, and you have a way to occupy your time, I'll take my leave."

I snap my neck back to him, although it desperately wants to tip back and stare longingly at the evening sky, even if there is no way to see the sun drop behind all the gloom.

"Wait!" My voice echoes down every row of shelves, skating up the walls and back down. I didn't mean to yell, not realizing how this room would magnify it.

Before his booted foot crosses over the threshold, I wonder if this small moment of ceasefire will allow me to ask for help. "Any chance you'd mind showing me if you have any books on curses?" As his eyes widen in shock, I add, "Oh! And if you happen to have any romance books…?" I wince, a little embarrassed about that last one, but I also don't want to walk mindlessly around for hours trying to find them. I plan to look at every rack of beautifully placed books here, but I don't want to waste precious time in finding the ones I want first. Even if I have to deal with the judgment from this God-like prince before me.

"You want…curses?" he asks, skeptically.

I tighten my lips and nod. "Mhm."

"And romance…?"

"Yep. That pretty much sums it up," I say quickly.

"May I ask why?" he hedges, looking at me curiously, like he can find the answer if he stares long enough.

"I'd rather not," I state plainly.

The last thing I need is to tell him how I think *I* may be cursed. I'm not sure what else could explain the darkness lurking deep inside, begging to be set free. Even though its whispers taunt me, I can't deny the feeling of euphoria as they wipe away all the pain, heartbreak, and loneliness. Then, what about the phantom who haunts my dreams, or rather, steals them to trap me in his hold? Is this part of some curse placed on me? To forever be visited by a monster people only tell stories of?

If I'm cursed, it would explain why those close to me suffer. At some point in their lives, they will be thrown overboard and left to be washed out to sea.

And the romance... Well, that's self-explanatory. I like to read the love told between pages because I know I will never have that. But that's just another thought I'll keep to myself.

As I've been deep in thought, I realize he's still staring at me. He narrows those glacial blues at me, seeming to not be happy with the fact I'm refusing to elaborate. But what's new? We seem to have already established we don't like each other, only this brief moment is neutral ground. Yet, I have a feeling that won't last much longer with how his eyes look, like they're trying to freeze me over, to trap me beneath an icy sea.

The cords in his neck twitch before he turns on his feet and starts heading between the rows of books. I reluctantly follow behind him, until he stops abruptly, making me collide with his back.

Oomph.

Gods, what is he made out of? Pure rock? Maybe the hardest steel ever to have been forged? I stumble back as I rub my forehead to lessen the slight ache. But the contact sends a bolt of electricity into my veins, vanishing the moment I put space between us. I stand rooted in place by confusion, as the remaining tingles that erupted in me begin to fade. I look up at him, his large frame tense as I see the way the muscles in his back bunch together.

I wonder if he felt the same thing, or if I'm just so deprived of any kind of contact that my body immediately lights up. Then again, it didn't feel like this when Aiden touched me, this feels...different. Unless it's my hate for him fueled by and warring against how devilishly handsome he is. My subconscious is telling me no, but I choose to ignore it.

His shoulders lift as he takes a deep breath in, and I see the inked black swirls that extend to his hands tighten in a fist before flexing his fingers. My eyes suddenly notice a symbol that stands out from the rest of his tattoos. It rests on top of his pointer finger, looking like a black circle with a crescent moon connected inside. I furrow my brows to concentrate more on it, wondering at its meaning.

Clearing his throat, the gruffness in his voice penetrates the silence. "Any books on curses would be in this section."

He keeps his back to me as I stare at his thick, black hair, suddenly imagining my fingers gripping it from the roots. He glances back at me before fully turning around. The prince takes a large step toward me, closing any semblance of normal distance as I once again feel the heat rolling off his body, coursing into me like a drug. He dips down just enough to see the long, dark lashes that frame his eyes. He's so close I can see the blur of my reflection in the ball of his eyebrow piercing.

He lifts his arm to point his finger to the opposite side of the room, directly at another set of shelves. "The romance books are over in that section."

He stays inches in front of me, waiting for me to give him a snarky response, but I can't. Even with the way his voice is teasing, I'm feeling a little exhausted from fighting at the moment. I see his gaze trail down my face, past my lips, and land on my necklace. His face gives nothing away as to what he's thinking, so I choose to break the tension swarming between us.

I blink and take a small step back. "Thank you for showing me."

He snaps his assessing eyes back to mine. "You seem to like that necklace."

My mind spins as I try to keep up with the sudden change in conversation. I also don't like that he keeps bringing it up, and I need to deter him from it. "It was a gift," I say, inching back some more and raising my hand to it, covering it as if I was protective of it.

I'm clenching my teeth so hard they might crack. Acting like I cherish the shackle on my neck makes me want to savagely claw it off me and let all the pent-up tears flood free.

The storms in my eyes and the raging waves in his push against one another as I feel the energy shift between us. The peaceful reprieve has ended, and it seems we're back to hard glares that promise hell.

"Draven?" A chirpy, high-pitched voice slices through the thickness of the air, but we don't move. Neither of us is willing to stand down this time.

Heels clack against the floor, growing louder as they pass by rows and rows of shelves. Until they stop abruptly.

"Oh! Uh…there you are." Whoever this girl is, she seems shocked, but covers it up with a sultry note in her words.

He stands fully upright, about a good foot above my 5'4" frame and drags his eyes to the female behind me.

"Katrina," he greets her, not making a move to go towards her. I hear the sound of the *clicks* and *clacks* of her shoes again before she stands next to him.

I should have known it was the blonde from the ball who looked like she wanted to rip me from his arms during our dance. So, I was right, this is his girlfriend. Or at least, she wants to be. She has sleek, light hair that falls just past her shoulders and she's wearing a pale, yellow dress that has white petals decorating the top layer, paired with a nude heel. Her eyes are brown and have a thick layer of mascara on, along with fuchsia-painted lips. She is the epitome of a spring day. The flowers' first bloom under the golden rays.

I briefly remember the changes in season when I lived in Helestria, the only one that never showed was winter. But mostly, I recall how the flowers bloomed during spring because it was Aunt Lyd's favorite. The seasons don't change in Deyadrum, and a small part of me wishes it did.

I watch as she wraps her one arm around his and presses in to put her other hand flat against his chest. Her fingers play with the buttons he chose not to close, as she occasionally lets the tip of her finger graze the tattoos on the sliver of his chest peeking through.

"I've been looking all over for you. I should have known you would be cooped up in this stifling library." She finally glances at me and acts innocent, even though it's clear she's not happy finding him with another female. She probably can't tell who I am without the mask, and I'm not dressed how a princess should be. But I recognize her. She had a mask on at the ball, but one that was attached to a holder so she could drop it at any point, giving anyone a clear view of her face. My guess is so the Dark Prince could spot her easily. "And who are you?" She tries to make it sound sweet, but she sprinkles too much sugar on her words, making her voice sound nauseating.

Prince Draven opens his mouth. "This is Pri—"

"I'm Cora." I cut him off before he can give her my name. I know my friend won't mind if I borrow her identity for a moment.

Prince Draven looks utterly lost. This cold, completely put-together male looks like this is the first time he's been thrown through a loop and doesn't know what to say. But I don't want to be known as the princess. I wore a mask that covered most of my face last night, the main reason why my father was more accepting of letting me come at all. Now, the castle won't be as crowded in the next couple of days, and no one will look twice at me. But then, it makes me wonder how Prince Draven recognized me if he never even had the decency to look at my face when we first arrived. Unless he did, and I was unaware.

Katrina's lips lift up in a tight smile, but I can see the sneer she's hiding beneath it. "Well, a pleasure, really," she says with annoyance. My mistake, she may be beautiful as a fresh spring flower, but she's ugly inside from the constant rain that wilts them. "Draven, babyyy, I thought we could go eat dinner together and maybe have some dessert after."

I suck my lips in tightly, doing my absolute best not to let the laugh bubbling up my throat break free. Her whiny voice mixed with flirting is amusing. I know I don't know much about how to flirt, aside from what's in my books, but I now know what *not* to do. I squeeze my lips harder together to the point of pain, hoping it will extinguish the laugh about to spill out of me. She's staring up at him with such longing and something must be in her eyes…? She keeps blinking rapidly and I almost feel the need to ask if she's okay.

I slide my eyes to the male in her arms, curious to see how he's reacting to all this. But instead of looking at her, he's looking at me. My breath catches, and Katrina doesn't miss it either as she snaps her head in my direction, glaring. Her eyes drift down my body, taking in the pants and shirt combo, combined with my black cloak, which now seems oddly out of place since we are inside.

Her nose scrunches in revulsion. "Don't you have somewhere to be, or work to be doing?"

I cock my head to the side, my eyes locked on Prince Draven's, until I slide them to hers again. She thinks I'm a lower Fae worker, here to serve. But at the moment, I'd rather be that than the title that weighs heavily on my shoulders. Maybe if I didn't have such a deep well of power that my father believes needs to be restrained, he would have gotten rid of me. Tossed me to the Scavengers. Yet, the idea of being free from his hold and having a chance for survival on my own is a wish I will never have granted.

I offer Katrina a small, tight smile. "You know, I actually do have things to do. I just need something in that section over there first."

With that, I dip my head in good riddance and slip past them to walk towards the other side of the library. I turn once more to look back at the two of them and see the prince's eyes following me. He gives me a confused look as I turn my back on them and head to where the stories of undying love and fated mates are told.

***

I'm happy when I make it back to my room without being seen. I've been able to avoid my father and Aiden for the entire day, and I'm assuming neither of them care to see me. I know my father is busy with meetings and who knows what else, probably plotting the punishments he can enact on those who go against him. My stomach coils thinking of what demented methods he would use.

Then, I think of Aiden, still torn on how he acted towards me last night. I didn't want to face him today, worried I'd see something different lurking in his eyes. I want to believe that he had too much to drink, or that there was at least some *reason* for acting out on me. At the time, I hadn't wanted to find out; I'd just reacted.

There's a part of me that is holding on to a sliver of hope that when I see him again, he'll be his normal self. My friend. The one telling me everything will be okay, the one who would always challenge me in a race down the halls, or crack jokes about how wild my hair would get from it.

The male I saw last night… I saw a glimpse of my father in him, and that alone terrifies me. My racing thoughts try to understand everything as I make my way to change for the night.

I slide my boots and socks off, padding to the closet where Cora arranged my clothes. The cool touch of the stone floor feels soothing against the heated soles of my feet. I strip from my clothes and toss my cloak over the hook on the wall, as I grab the silky lounge set folded on the rack.

I pull the pants on and tie the little strings to slink them tighter against my waist, then button up the loose, long-sleeved top that hangs down. It's a deep navy blue, reminding me of the night sea back home when lightning strikes against it, illuminating the deepest shades of blue.

After taking a few deep breaths in, I finally settle the storm that was brewing within, shifting the direction of the wind so it will drift away the unnerving thoughts. Earlier, I browsed the titles in the curses section of the library for anything on internal darkness or haunting nightmares, but nothing was there of any use. It seems no one else suffers the same way as me, but I shouldn't be surprised that their fate is brighter. No storm clouds weighing above their heads every second of the day.

Reaching into my cloak, I pull out the book I ended up choosing to borrow. I've never seen so many romance books that I could choose from, and as much as I want to keep reading the one I brought with me from home, I may never get the chance again to dive into a new love story. I have no idea what it's about, but the design on the cover lured me in, and here I am, padding over to the bed so I can escape for a little while.

The sheets feel cold but smooth against my skin. I look out to the open wall across the room, knowing the chill that must be in the air. But…I don't feel anything. The fireplace is on, but it wouldn't give off that much heat or block the cold from whipping in.

Excitement bubbles up at realizing that Fae in the castle are using their powers to keep the rooms heated. Shielding the opening from letting the dropping temperature creep in, but still allowing it to feel like you're open to the land beyond. The barrier is basically nonexistent; you can still hear the wind whistle and the brush of the leaves as it swirls through them. It's amazing.

It doesn't get very cold at my court. Ours is similar to what summer would feel like every day, and here must be the equivalent of fall.

I settle down under the covers, leaving only the light beside the bed and the steady glow from the fireplace to light the room. I open the book, noticing the crack in the spine and the folded corners of the pages. This must have been someone's favorite, for it looks very similar to mine, and a comforting feeling washes over me at the thought of someone cherishing a book like I do. I sink into my pillow and begin to read. But then, hours pass, and I start to feel the weight of my eyelids as they begin to fall.

Something's not right. I can feel myself slipping, falling into a pitch-black vortex of whispers and dark intentions. I somehow know I'm asleep, but I can't seem to wake up as I claw against the shadows pulling me under. It's no use. They already have me in their unrelenting hold, and now I have to face the nightmare I know is waiting for me.

The shadows swim around my body, surging their icy touch along my skin. The feeling of a million needles pinching every crevice, only to pull out and sink back in again. Chills start to race down my spine when I feel another presence nearby before he even speaks.

"I can sense you are somewhere new, but where is the question." *His voice brushes against my mind, attempting to push into my thoughts.*

I squeeze my eyes shut, forcing all my willpower into building up whatever mental walls I can. "How can you be here? How can nobody sense you?" *My mind races with so many questions I know will go unanswered as I wonder how to put an end to these nightmares.*

He clicks his tongue. "Darkness is undetectable, Emma. I thought you would have figured that out by now." *Suddenly, a million whispers invade me, growing louder as the words intertwine and become unintelligible. Just as fast, they stop.*

That grave voice cuts through the dark, sounding demonic as it reverberates throughout the void. "Tell me where you are."

I keep quiet this time, hoping if I stay still and act calm, the shadows won't restrain me. They continue to slither around my body, swirling and twisting in warning. I let my eyes fall shut as I feel him coming closer, his phantom claws assaulting my mind, dragging me under like quicksand. He can make me feel pain here, even force me to the brink of death, but I'm starting to think he can't actually kill me. Not without consequence. It takes an immense amount of power to invade the dark part of one's psyche.

A shadow latches around my throat so fast, like a snake striking for a kill. "Silence will only anger me," he growls.

I begin to open my mouth to speak but find my voice is cut off as I snap my mouth shut. Then, the pressure lifts and I can breathe easily again. I stare at nothing and everything as I sense where he lingers.

"You're delusional if you think I will tell you," I spit. Fuck calm, the torture he put me through last time boils my blood with rage that tunnels my vision. My pulse is pounding so loud it starts a steady echo in my ears.

I hear him snicker before I can register the shadows diving down my throat, stopping my breath. Like ice being poured down my airway, I start clawing at my neck, desperate to bleed them out. But my hands are yanked back, the darkness swirling around my wrists and tightening them behind me.

"On second thought, silence is better if you can't be nice." His breath skates over my face. He's close, but he blends into the dark, invisible to the eye. I struggle, my chest beginning to heave, my body begging for air.

I feel a finger trace down my tear-stained cheek. "Weak." He sneers.

My body drops, knees slamming on the shadowed ground. My legs give out as my muscles begin to spasm, but he can't kill me. I don't think he can, but I'm trapped. Stuck in his hold until he wants to release me. My head drops forward, feeling weaker every moment that passes without a chance to fill my lungs, the cold touch of the shadows slowly freezing them.

A rough grip on my jaw jerks my head up, but my eyes are unfocused. He squeezes tighter, his hold turning painful. "I will take back what's mine," he growls. In a flash, the shadows holding my wrists and blocking my breath evaporate, right as they form into a sharp blade that drives straight through my chest.

For the first time in years, I scream.

The metal slides out slowly before it stabs through me again. Another tear falls, trailing down my cheek and leaving behind proof of my weakness. Then, I remember, the darkness doesn't frighten me; it calls to me. I always push it away, but maybe I should welcome some of it in, just enough to numb the searing pain. Maybe enough to push this monster out of my dream and force him back to where he belongs.

I smack my teeth together and hiss when the knife pulls back out again, leaving a *trail of fire in its wake. I reach deep down inside, not able to touch the ember of light in me, but the necklace doesn't restrain the dark. I grab hold of it, letting the whispers turn louder.*

The depths of it rise, crawling through my veins as the pain in my chest begins to numb. I only let a small amount of the darkness come through, blasting my eyes open the moment I release it. It flies out of my hands as I raise them in front of me. A chilling ecstasy washes over me as I disintegrate the phantom before me and every last trace of his shadows from my mind.

CHAPTER TWENTY-FOUR

Draven

I lean back on my arms, looking out at the forest stretching under the midnight sky. My legs hang over the edge of the roof as the wind whips by, wrapping the fresh scent of pine around me. Moonlight shines through small gaps in the clouds, only providing a small semblance of light. The roof here is my sacred place. Its a spot no one ever comes, where I can breathe in comforting silence.

There's no one to come knocking on my door to summon me or ladies visiting the castle who sneak by to try and woo me up here. But a heavy grief weighs down on me, because my father used to join me sometimes. I rub the rough exterior of the ledge, feeling it scrape against my palm. He would sit next to me as we took in the stillness of the forest before us, the only one who truly understood me. Every part. The good and the bad.

I let my mind drift to the most recent memory of us here.

I feel his gaze on me as I stare out into the night. "What's on your mind?" he asks. I remain silent, not knowing how to explain what I'm feeling, but I don't have to. My father already knows, as I feel his power tingle along the edges of my mind.

He pats my back with attentiveness. "I know you feel like you have the weight of the world on your shoulders. But you don't need to carry it alone. Open up, my boy. You will be surprised by what you find." *His hand squeezes my shoulder as we fall back into a peaceful silence.*

Opening up to someone meant trust, and I swore to myself to never let someone have it again, unless it was my mate. Yet, as I sit here, a part of me wants to listen to his final words he spoke in the dark to me. A crack in my shield guarding my vulnerability, and it's filled with so much pressure it's about to burst.

I let my lungs fully deflate and tip my head back. My jaw clenches as I try to block the feelings of sorrow that always sweep through me when my mind travels to my father. The grief of not knowing that would be the last time I would hear his voice.

I scrape my palm down my face, thinking of earlier. I fulfilled my mother's wishes when I found Emma. I made small talk and took her to the library, where she can pass her time, since she seems to prefer to hide away. I huff a small breath of amusement. It doesn't slip past my notice that hiding away is exactly what I'm fucking doing now.

I lean forward and white-knuckle grip the rough edge again, unable to wrap my mind around this *princess* that came out of nowhere. I assumed she was reveling in the attention, with all eyes on her, when she stood at the top of the staircase, looking down at everyone before her.

When she first arrived off the ship with her father, I dismissed her. She's someone who refuses her duty to take care of the people who are scared of the Corrupted increasing, never taking action to find a way to help or protect them, didn't deserve my welcome or acknowledgment of her presence. I only stood there for my mother's sake, who asked if I could at least show my face and support her as family. So, that was all I did.

I made it a point not to look at her face, not offering her even a little bit of my respect. But I couldn't stop my eyes from zeroing in on her father's hand. I saw the way the muscles in his hand flexed around her arm, a telling sign he wasn't being gentle. Then, the way his eyes held an underlying threat that didn't fit the words he was speaking. I've never liked King Oren. I always thought he was more of a snake than anything. I don't know him enough to believe he may hurt his daughter, but then, she could have just been being a brat.

She does have a sharp tongue, so it's not surprising. Hell, I had to hold my hand from smacking her behind when she called me an ass. I even had to bite my cheek when she assumed Katrina was my girlfriend and told me that she looked like she would attempt to rip her hair out. The princess was not wrong though. Katrina was fuming, but she is more likely to strike with her perfectly polished nails in secrecy.

I slept with that girl one time and it was an uneventful night for me. According to her, it was the best sex of her life, but I couldn't get her out of my room fast enough. There was no thrill or even a powerful orgasm to make it worthwhile.

Her parents are friends with my mother. So, they are often at the castle and stay when they visit. But Katrina wants *more*. She wants a relationship, a ring, and a whole future with me. But I see her like a plague I can't get rid of.

Her parents keep pushing her on me with small comments about how amazing we would be together. Katrina acts like I'm already hers. I allow it sometimes and play nice because I want no bad blood with her parents. But when Katrina interrupted the semblance of peace between Emma and me in the library... I wanted to tell her to get the fuck out.

But Emma's reaction confused me and made me question *everything* I thought about her when she hid her identity of being the Princess of Asov. If she really was seeking attention, she would want everyone to know, and use her title as power. It would have put Katrina in her place, but Emma never did.

Then, there were the clothes she was wearing when I found her sitting under the trees deep in the forest. She wasn't in a gown, strutting around the castle and requesting food and drink. She cloaked herself like a shadow to hide away, keeping silent and venturing far away from another soul.

I shouldn't let it bother me so much, but I can't keep her from getting under my skin, and it's maddening. It had grated on my nerves how transfixed she was when she stepped into the library. Watching her expression morph into one of awe sent a wave of a different kind of pleasure through me. A softer kind that I had to extinguish immediately.

I was surprised and disappointed that she didn't snipe back at me when we were in there, because her feistiness feeds the beast in me. She's challenging and unpredictable, and at the moment, I can't tell if that's a blessing or a curse.

I let the rest of my thoughts fade away as I absorb the hushed night. Not a soul should be awake. No birds chirping, no crickets giving themselves away, just the tangle of wind between the branches of the trees and my own steady heartbeat.

But that all ends when a piercing scream slices through the silent air.

My heartbeat triples as I twist my neck towards the sound.

Nothing.

I jump to my feet and take off at a sprint along the rooftop towards where the sound came from. Pushing through the wind and leaping down on the lower section of the roof, I pause when I reach the other side, listening as the night grows silent again. My ears strain, waiting for the sound to come back.

Another shriek echoes out into the night, coming from inside the castle below. My mind takes only a moment to register it is in the guest wing.

I grab onto the ledge, hook my fingers in the groove, and fling my body over, hanging for a second before I drop onto the outside terrace of a room. My boots slam on the stone with a solid *thud*.

Roses and honey hit me. *Emma*.

A whimper fills the room as I walk in through the opening, heading straight to her bed, where I can see her restless body move. She's asleep. My eyes scan her room, but she's alone.

I look back down at her. Another shriek tears from her lips as she claws at her neck and chest.

Nightmare.

I remain beside her, seeing her brown hair spill over her pillows, sweat dampening her porcelain skin, while she's tangled in a ball of her sheets. I decide to try to wake her as another whimper of agony falls from her lips. But then, I see something that freezes my movements. She still has that necklace on, almost as if she can't part with it.

But that's not what really catches my eye.

I lean in closer to examine her jaw and see a black-stained handprint painting her skin there. I reach out to touch it, and as soon as the tip of my finger makes contact, the room disappears.

I'm sucked into a vortex of nothing. When my obscured vision adjusts, my eyes allow me to take in my surroundings.

I see her.

Emma.

On her knees, her lips are tinted blue as shadows have her in their hold. I begin to take a step forward to help, but I can't. My feet are frozen to the ground, like a statue. I can see what's happening, but I can't interfere... as if I'm not really here.

I cup my hands around my mouth and yell her name. Nothing happens. My voice is only heard by my own ears.

My pulse is frantic as I become aware of what's happening. She's gasping for breath as the shadows take on the form of a long, sharp blade, driving right through her chest. Over and over again.

I helplessly watch the way her screams become quieter as she pulls in on herself. I want nothing more than to just jolt her awake. To wake her up from this nightmare.

When I try to scream her name again, her eyes pop open, but the stormy grey that usually accents her face is gone. They've become soulless black pits, while her veins run dark.

What. The. Fuck.

She looks just like the Corrupted, but not feral. My mouth falls open at the sight.

In the next moment, a final scream ricochets from her as a black fire flares from her, and the whole void disintegrates into nothing.

Suddenly, I'm back in her suite, hovering over her with my hand on her jaw. She rid herself of her nightmare, but she's not yet awake.

Her chest is rising and falling like normal as her body lays relaxed. I stand up straight, staring down at her as I furrow my brows. Why did she morph into something that looks just like the Corrupted? Is she a part of them? Is that her secret? Why has she been in hiding? To rule them? I know she *isn't* one fully, otherwise she would be on killing sprees and not sleeping soundly, attending balls, and hiding away to read.

I can't get the image of black veins and deadly eyes out of my head, even as I see her long lashes curl, and a few freckles that dot her delicate face. The black mark on her jaw is completely gone, wiped from existence.

I'm starting to question what I saw, but I know it happened. So many questions keep bubbling to the surface. I planned on never speaking to her again, letting her go back to her court and parting ways for the rest of our long lives. But now, I'm not sure what to do.

I instinctively grab the dagger I stashed in my boot. I should kill her now. I could use my powers, but if she's one of them, she wouldn't be worthy of dying so easily. She deserves to bleed out.

I raise the dagger and point the tip of the blade in front of her neck. My conscience is yelling at me to stop, that there's a chance she may be the key to the spreading of the Corrupted. I want to brush the thought away, but it's nagging at me. It pesters me enough that I flare my nostrils in frustration and pull the knife back, tucking it safely in my boot.

I take one long look at her before I disappear back into the night.

CHAPTER TWENTY-FIVE

Emma

I wake to sunlight streaming into my room from between the clouds. Its not as gloomy today, but a layer of fog still veils the trees, like smoke swaying to a sultry song that glides effortlessly through the air.

I sit up and look around the room. A calming quiet hangs in the air as I take a deep breath. I feel…rested.

I remember the nightmare and the burning pain in my chest before I allowed the darkness to take it away. To show me their whispered promises held true. Everything blew up in black light, sending waves of shadowy fire into every crevice, until there was nothing left. They got greedy though, banging against the wall I put up to block the rest of it from seeping through. I could feel the tether on my shield becoming shaky as I struggled to hold a scant amount of control. To conceal this dark power before it became ravenous and waged war against me. I don't want it to consume me. To consume my soul. I just wanted help dealing with the monster who haunts my dreams, and it worked. After I managed to shove it back down, my body settled, and I fell into a deep, serene sleep.

I stretch my arms above my head, enjoying the moment of feeling refreshed. I breathe in deeply, feeling a yawn about to crest, until it gets caught in my throat. A heady, lingering scent of cedar with a swirl of maple catches my attention. I *know* that smell. I *recognize* it. But why am I only getting the remnants of it here?

There's no way Prince Draven was in here. I look at my door and see it's still locked. That would only leave the balcony and there's no way someone would dare leap down from the roof. I looked up the side of the castle the first day I arrived, and it's too high. Only someone with no care for themselves and a death wish would attempt that.

I inhale deeply again, trying to consume every speck of it before it completely fades. Wow. What is wrong with me? When have I become a girl who sniffs the air because it reminds her of a guy…? And not just any guy, one who is an asshole. I must have conjured his scent and am going crazy.

Once I officially force myself out of bed, I take a soothing bath. When I'm done, I toss on a fresh pair of black pants and a matching long-sleeved tunic and slide my dagger into my boot. I have to conceal it there, since I would look out of place wearing my cloak around inside of the castle. The plan is to find Cora, since I didn't get to see her yesterday; she had to help clean up after the ball and get things in order.

I make my way down the corridors until I get to the ballroom, where she's finishing up a few tasks, and wait outside the door. I lean against the wall, acting completely un-princess-like, so I don't draw attention. I am just a random face to anyone who passes by.

Footsteps sound to my left, and I glance down the hallway. I suck in a sharp breath, suddenly on edge. Its none other than Aiden, walking my way with…

Gods. Why do the stars punish me so?

Katrina is beside him, giving him all of her attention as her mouth moves at a mile a minute. His eyes are glazed over like he's been up all night, and he's not fully giving her the time of day, which sends a trickle of glee through me.

But the memories from the other night turn my dose of amusement bitter, and suddenly, I don't want him to see me. I go to make my way into the ballroom, but it's too late. His gaze latches onto mine. *Shit.* A smile stretches across his face, showing his straight, white teeth. Katrina notices he's no longer paying attention and follows his gaze, finding me the target of it. Her eyes narrow as he pats her arm, sending her away before he shifts his direction to approach me.

"Hey," he says hesitantly, unsure of how pissed I am at him.

I don't say a word and just stare. What does he expect me to say? I caught him with another female, and then he tried to come on to me while I could still smell her perfume clinging to his clothes.

He sighs and steps closer, looking deep into the storm brewing in my eyes. "I'm sorry, Emma. Gods, I'm so sorry." He brushes both hands through his hair in anguish. "I don't know what came over me the other night, and I know I have no excuse. I drank too much, I got wound up, and I lost control. You must believe that I would never want another girl or force you into something you're not ready for. You know that, right?" He pauses, eyes pleading as he searches mine.

One breath.

Two breaths.

Three breaths.

He sighs. "I deserve your anger and the silent treatment. I deserve it all." He slowly brings his hand to gently rub the side of my arm and I watch that hand show tender affection, when just the other night, it was on *Margaret.*

"You do." I bring my head back up to face him, staring hard into his emerald gems that look like they are filled to the brim with remorse. The kind I was looking for when I caught him the other night, but couldn't find. I couldn't even tell if his words were genuine.

He nods in understanding, and I'm stuck standing here in confusion. This is the Aiden I know, the one who has been by my side for so many years. I saw a different side of him the other night, and it twists my gut thinking about it. Part of me wants to give him the benefit of the doubt. One night of acting out of character hardly compared to the years of being kind. The years of joy that helped me get through all the torment from my father. He never knew, and still doesn't, but the times we shared shined a light that helped guide me out of the darkest corners of my mind.

I fight for words as my heart and mind go to war. I give in, as my heart aches at the pleading look he's giving me. My conscience wants to smack me, but my heart wants to try to forgive.

I keep my eyes locked on his. "I've known you for so long, Aiden, betrothed or not, and that wasn't like you."

He doesn't blink. "I know."

I raise my arm to press my palm along the side of his face. "But I don't want to lose you from my life. I need to still process it all, but I won't let one night ruin the friendship we've built." As the words come out of my mouth, his face lights up and it spreads warmth through me. But a small twinge of uncertainty still hangs in the recesses of my mind. I let my hand drop. "But I can't say the same thing if something like that happens again. I can't be treated like that. I deserve better as a friend and as someone you're betrothed to."

"You're right. It won't happen again, promise." He pulls me into his chest, holding me as if the ball of regret was too much and I was the one who crushed it, setting it free. He presses a kiss to the top of my head, and then another on my forehead. "I have to go assist my father with a few things, but maybe we can catch up later?"

"Yeah, maybe. I'll be spending the day with Cora." I stay still, only offering a small smile.

He grins, and before he walks away, dips back down to kiss my cheek. "Don't have too much fun." He winks and leaves me to wait outside the ballroom doors.

I stare after him as I watch him leave, and an unsettling feeling remains.

A few minutes pass before Cora pops out. "Boo!" she yells as she tries to scare me.

I give a blank stare, not a flinch in sight. "Gods, Emma!" she huffs, tossing her hands in the air. "I can never scare you. You're like a gargoyle, phased by nothing, I swear. It's no fun."

A smile tips my lips at her fake pout, but if only she knew what I've gone through and the monsters I face. "Ready?" I ask her, looping my arm through hers, feeling energized after such a good night's sleep.

"Heck yeah, I'm dying to explore this place. Maybe we'll find a hidden room full of secrets or one that has shirtless guys in it." She bumps her body into mine, laughing at her own words.

"There's only one way to find out."

She smirks at me. "And we are most definitely going to find out, my friend."

Hours must pass between wandering around the halls and sneaking snacks as we go. We find endless amounts of the most enchanting artwork on display, many sitting rooms, a garden, music room, and I take Cora to show her the library. She had to practically drag me out of there and tell me she'll bring me back after if I listen. To which I smack her on the shoulder, a small giggle escaping me. She's unbelievable and such a damn good friend. I don't think I'd survive if I ever lost her.

We venture through every inch of this castle, except the Royal Wing, where the queen and her sons' rooms are. We are on our last hallway of scoping out the rooms down here, and after a few paces through, laughter bellows down and out of an open door ahead. We share a look as we silently tiptoe towards the doorway that has light spilling out of it. Clanks of swords smacking together can be heard beyond the voices.

Peeking in, we see both Prince Draven and Prince Emil in the room, along with another Fae I have not yet seen. They're in a room that looks like a gym, with a whole section made for sparring and mats on the other side for hand-to-hand combat training.

The entire room is closed off from the outside, which seems unusual for this place, since every other room is wide open or has massive windows. But not this one; it's all faded stone with lanterns hanging on the walls.

Prince Draven and Prince Emil face each other inside a circle drawn on the floor. Brother versus brother. Watching the other's every step as they continue a dance along the circle's edge, waiting for the other to make the first move.

Cora and I watch with rapt attention as they dive at each other at the same time. They block blades and swing them around in artful combat. Not too long after they begin, Prince Emil's sword gets knocked from his hand as Prince Draven holds the tip of his blade to his brother's heart, claiming the win.

Their chests are heaving and I'm left gaping at the Dark Prince's face. He's...*smiling*. A true, genuine smile that softens his hard features, showing off his white teeth and... *Gods*. He has a dimple in his left cheek that dents in the center right underneath his trimmed scruff. My heart pounds hard and I feel a delicious warmth pool in my belly. There's a fascination I feel towards this male. I'm afraid I'm caught in his web, for I can now say I have a weakness for dimples.

When he drops his sword, I choose that moment to pull Cora by the bodice of her dress and walk in to join them. I ignore the clamminess in my hands as I begin a slow clap that causes all three of them to snap their necks towards us.

"Pretty sure Prince Emil let you have that win." I snicker, and once again, I am unable to control my mouth around him.

Prince Emil faces me fully, giving a slight bow as recognition fills his eyes from seeing me when we first arrived. "Please, call me Emil, Princess Emma."

I smile softly at him. "And you can just call me Emma."

His face brightens at that.

"What can we do for you ladies?" Prince Draven's voice cuts through the happy moment me and Emil are sharing, for his little brother is always so welcoming. Him and his still-gentle heart. I slide my eyes to the Dark Prince and see his eyebrow arched, causing the piercing there to stand out even more.

I fold my hands behind my back as I glance around the room. "Oh, nothing. Cora and I were just exploring and happened to wind up here." My eyes land back on his and I bring a hand forward to motion towards the mat. "But please, continue. We would love to see you lose."

He looks over at Cora, then back at me with a smirk. "So, this is the notorious Cora?"

I narrow my gaze on him, damning him to hell when Cora whispers to me, "What does he mean?"

I hold his stare as I suppress the urge to roll my eyes at him. "Ignore him. He's just being an ass, but that's nothing new."

Cora gasps next to me. I called the infamous Dark Prince an ass instead of falling to my knees for him. But I can't seem to refrain, my thoughts just tumble out. Finding ways to tick him off excites me, and it's a challenge I gladly accept.

The male I don't recognize behind Prince Draven clears his throat, stepping forward and breaking the ice building through our stare-off. His hair is a light blonde and is pulled up in a bun with loose pieces flying out. His hazel eyes remind me of fallen leaves against the soil. A small scar nicks the side of his top lip, and I see he shares the same liking for tattoos as Prince Draven. His entire left arm is coated with beautiful ink.

He beams at us as he throws an arm around Prince Draven. "Hey there, I'm Fynn, and being Draven's best mate, I can attest to him being an ass." Prince Draven's face snaps to his friend's so fast, glaring at him before shoving him back a step. "Hey man!" Fynn huffs on a laugh.

Prince Draven only smirks. "That's what you get, but you're an ass, too."

Fynn's chuckle leaves his throat. "That is also true," he pushes out when his laughter dies down. I'm not surprised that Prince Draven's best friend is just as tall and muscular as he is, both of them looking like solid walls of strength. But I'm shocked to see Prince Draven behaving *playfully*, as if the ice around his heart has melted.

"I like you," I blurt out, looking straight at Fynn, because anyone who tells Prince Draven he's an ass automatically scores a point in my book. Cora snickers beside me, finding this all very amusing, even though I see the slight tint on her cheeks when I glance at her. Those blue eyes of hers keep darting to Fynn, seeming to like what she sees.

Fynn raises his eyebrows up and down, a playful smile pulling on his face. "Well, why don't I walk you around and be your tour guide for the rest of your exploration?" He dramatically winks, and I can't help but laugh. This one's trouble, but I'm drawn to his light-hearted nature.

"Not going to happen," Prince Draven cuts in. "The princess wants to see me lose." I already know where he's going with this before he speaks it, just by the way those pale eyes stare down at me. "So, make me." There's a glint in his eyes and a dare lacing in his words. A challenge.

"Brother, she's a *princess*. You can't ask her to fight." Emil looks appalled at his brother's words. But Prince Draven seems to think differently, knowing I'm a far cry from how a princess should behave.

"With swords or hands?" I ask, letting the excitement show at taking him on. I don't miss the shock on Emil's face at my willingness to fight. But if he's offering me a chance to show him I'm not some weak girl he can walk over, then challenge accepted.

Prince Draven folds his arms over his chest. "Hands. It wouldn't be fair to have you holding such a weighted weapon."

Annoyance is an ugly feeling that crawls into my skin and bites. I narrow my eyes to slits, wishing I could ram a sword up his ass to show him how that would feel.

"Done," I proclaim.

Cora squeals in anticipation, clapping her hands together. She's fully aware of my years of training. Both of us think they are all assuming I've never fought a day in my life, unless I consider battling the skirts of a gown when walking. Cora winks at me. "Well, I'll sit over here and watch the show." She gestures to the far wall and makes her way to the other side of the room, where the mats are laid out on the floor.

Emil and Fynn follow her as Prince Draven and I stay cemented in place, staring each other down. I lift the side of my mouth up, looking forward to catching him off guard. I give him a once over before I leave him behind, heading to where a challenge awaits me.

CHAPTER TWENTY-SIX

Draven

She's wearing a tight little outfit that shows every slender curve in her body. How can this girl make my cock twitch with clothes that are so concealing? Not a sliver of skin on display, yet I have to adjust myself before I head over to the mats.

I strip my shirt off, pulling it over my head, and I notice the way her eyes dilate at my inked skin on display, and the slight swallow that moves her throat, as her eyes make their way back to mine. I give her a knowing look and those cloudy eyes narrow, understanding shining through that I'm trying to make her uncomfortable.

I bend down to take my boots off and notice she's still in hers. "No shoes on the mat."

Her glare hardens before she turns away to remove them. Only to return a moment later in fucking socks. She may think that's going to piss me off, which it fucking does, but it will only work as a disadvantage to her on the mat.

"Ready?" I ask, watching her face change from annoyed to determined as she readies her stance and places her arms in front of her.

"Woo! Kick his ass, Emma!" her little blonde friend cheers from the sidelines.

A slight twitch to her lush lips signals she heard her friend but is too consumed by the impending fight to break her focus.

The whole room and everyone in it fades away as we start a dance, circling each other before one strikes. Her body is alert, her movements are smooth with silent steps as she glides around the mat. I push off my back foot and charge at her, but she's quick. She drops to the floor as my arm swings in the open air above her.

Her leg kicks out from a low crouch, but I leap to the side before she can knock my leg from under me. I truly take a good look at her when she gets back into her defense position. This feisty princess is *trained*, she's no damsel in distress, and the socks don't make a lick of difference in her skills.

In a flash, she's by my side, followed by a trio of attacks. I block two, but the third makes me stumble back as her foot slams into my chest. I spring forward, grabbing her foot before it falls to the floor, twisting her leg and making her hit the mat hard.

She yanks her leg free and rolls to the side, jumping up to land gracefully on the pads of her feet. She's all lithe and quick-thinking, dressed in promises of your own demise. Like a little assassin wrapped in her own brand of crazy, who would slice someone's throat in a heartbeat and bleed them out to dry.

She catches my assessment, a jaunty grin spreading across her face. "Is that all you've got?"

I don't let her catch her breath after finishing that sentence as I spin around her and double back in a series of blows that she blocks. I use her assumption that I'll throw my arms around a few more times, and instead duck to slip my arm behind her knees, knocking her back to the floor. I quickly move my other arm behind her to soften the fall as she smacks down onto the mat. My body covers hers as our pants of exertion mingle together.

My jaw clenches as her sweet scent invades me, with the feeling of her sinfully firm body pressed underneath me, wrapped in my arms.

"Give in yet?" I taunt.

Her nostrils flare as she wiggles beneath me. *Fuck.* "Get off me and find out."

I press into her a little harder, both of our bodies aligned in a perfect fit. When her mouth falls open slightly, I'm tempted to taste what's not mine. I jump up before I give in and hold out a helping hand for her.

She smacks my hand away to stand up on her own and readies herself again. I should have known she wasn't done; she's not so willing to submit. I might have to change that.

It feels like an hour passes and we continue going at each other. I've pinned her down every time, but not without a fight. She's a vicious little thing that seems to never tire. We throw more fists and swoop low to knock the other's feet out. My final twist backfires when she loses her balance and my elbow knocks into her face. She falls back and palms her mouth.

"Shit," I mutter.

I race over to her and drop to my knees. Moving her hand, I see her bottom lip sliced open and bleeding. Thank the Gods I didn't break her nose. That would take a little bit longer to heal, but a busted lip should heal in a couple of minutes.

I pull the hair away that is stuck to the pooling blood. "I think that's our cue to stop. Your body's getting weak and causing you to be unsteady." She nods as Cora, Emil, and Fynn rush over.

Fynn sees her lip and huffs a breath of relief. "Lucky it's just a hit to the lip. You're tough though, Princess. Didn't think you'd last that long in training." He pats her shoulder in a respectful way as he helps her sit up.

Cora helps Emma stand on her feet and stares at her lip. "Makes you look badass."

"Thanks, Cora, you always know how to find the light in any situation." Emma laughs, but winces as she speaks.

I look at Emil, and his brows are furrowed, staring intently at Emma. I glance back at her, then slide my gaze back to him. He's quiet. Assessing. Not how my little brother usually is with his sunshine attitude and pure heart.

"You good, Emil?" he doesn't look at me, just keeps staring at Emma.

"Why aren't you healing?" he asks Emma as he ignores me completely.

I turn back to look at her lip, noticing that it's continuing to bleed. Her skin is not clotting the cut or stitching itself back together like it should.

She stares wide-eyed at Emil, at a loss for words. I step directly in front of her and grab her jaw, tilting her head up. I swipe my thumb over her lip, causing her to grimace. I clean some of the blood away as more begins to spill from the opening. I glance down at her necklace and then look back into her eyes, which are swimming with secrets.

Those silver irises hold mine, waiting to see my next move. But I have a distant feeling that I already know the secret that's freezing her lungs and causing a glimmer of fear to shine in her eyes. I hold her jaw for a moment longer as our eyes battle against each other, and the heat buzzing at the contact becomes overwhelming. I want to slide my hand around her neck, down her spine, and grip her hips. I pull my hand back quickly before more lustful thoughts take over.

"She'll be fine. It's healing, just really slowly. But I'll take her to the healer just to quicken it. She used a lot of energy just now." I turn back to look at Emil, who doesn't seem fully convinced, but accepts my answer anyway.

Fynn squeezes my shoulder when he walks by. "I'll see ya later Drav, I got some things to take care of." He looks to Emma. "One hell of a fight you put up."

Emma just dips her head. "Thanks," she says softly.

Cora yells to Fynn, "Mind helping a lady back to the main floor of the castle?" Fynn's answering smirk is all she needs. "Go get healed up, girl. I'll see you later." She leans into her ear. "By the way, you totally kicked his ass." She winks and catches up to Fynn.

"Want me to come?" Emil's voice is steady behind us.

"I've got it handled, little brother. Go get cleaned up. I'm sure mother will want you to join her for dinner, but tell her I might be late."

He nods. "Sure thing." His eyes go to Emma. "Not many girls take on my brother in a challenge. So, I'm glad you did," he says shyly.

Emma smiles a big toothy grin for him, even with the smear of red on her skin. "Someone needs to show him he's not hot shit." Seeing her fighting spirit eases some of my concern for her.

Emil breaks into a fit of laughter and turns to me. "Be nice, I like her."

My jaw drops as she seems to have won over my little brother so quickly, and I watch in stunned silence as he leaves the room.

"Kid's got spunk," she says, pulling me from my thoughts.

I squint at her. "C'mon." She hesitates for a moment, but then follows me out.

CHAPTER TWENTY-SEVEN

Emma

I follow him to the healer, walking side-by-side through the maze of corridors. We walk in a heavy silence as he leads me down a dimly lit hallway, turning left and taking a set of spiral stairs.

"You gonna tell me why you can't heal?" He doesn't look at me. He keeps his eyes hard and ahead as we continue up the steps.

"I'd rather not." There's no way I want this news to spread. My father would go after anyone who found out who doesn't reside in our palace. He would wipe them from this world, maybe even the one after. But not before he punished me for not keeping it hidden. "Look, I'm fine. It's hardly a scratch. I don't need to see the healer," I say, even though having this healed would keep my father and Aiden from asking questions, wondering what happened to me. Which is the only reason I keep walking with him. My father can't find out I know how to fight. But I don't want Prince Draven to feel he *has* to take me. I can handle a cut, it's nothing compared to my father's wrath.

It was an accident, anyway. So, I wouldn't be completely lying if I told my father I *accidentally* slipped on the steps or something.

As soon as I finish speaking, he steps in my path and crowds me. Pushing my back against the cool stone wall, he places both hands on either side of my head. He's caging me in, with only inches between us, and I thank the Gods that he put his shirt back on before we left the training room.

I couldn't resist looking at every tattoo sketched along his body earlier. The ink swirls over his chiseled chest, down the cuts of his abs, and the V that forms before disappearing below his waistband. He's all hard muscle that goes perfectly with his striking face and powerful presence.

Like right now. The heat radiating off him is overwhelming, and I find myself wanting to lean in. But the jump in his jaw and his arctic stare keeps me from melting into him.

I feel my pulse jump as he leans in closer, stealing my air. "You think I will let you walk around and go back to your room with a busted lip?" He growls.

His hand comes down and rubs his thumb over the cut, smearing the fresh blood. I hold back my wince as a sting of pain shoots through me from the contact. He stares at his thumb, coated in crimson, like it's a narcotic. I watch his nostrils flare and the muscle in his jaw jump before his eyes flick back to me. "It's still bleeding, so it's not just a scratch, Emma."

My eyes widen at the use of my first name. Hearing it fall from his lips is like the first sip of sweet red wine as it explodes on your tongue. He shows me his thumb, and my blood coats it, a single drop trailing down. It's like slow motion, the way he brings his thumb to his mouth and licks it clean. Why did seeing him taste my blood arouse a deep need in me? I should be disgusted. But I can't tear my eyes away from him.

A growl of pleasure vibrates through his chest as he savors my taste. My mouth falls open as I draw in a gasp.

His now clean hand slams back on the wall, caging me in again. He leans in next to my ear, his breath fanning along my neck as it sends shivers down my spine. "You taste as sweet as you smell." His voice is husky, and the sound sends an aching pulse straight to my core. Goose-bumps pebble along my body, and my heartbeat quickens to a frantic pace.

His head dips down, and he runs his nose along the juncture between my neck and shoulder, never touching my necklace. I fight the urge to submit by arching my neck to give him better access as he breathes in deeply, as if committing my scent to memory. When he draws back, his eyes bore into mine, darkening as they travel to my parted lips.

He just stares at me, deep into my soul, searching for the core of who I am. But the longer we stay in this heated moment, with no air to breathe, except for his intoxicating scent, the more I begin to think of that tongue licking the blood right off my lips. How he would taste and feel if I closed the small gap between us and pressed myself along the hard ridge of his body.

More heat starts to pool deep down, and I struggle to resist the need that builds as my breaths turn shallow. I'm desperate for a release, even if the male before me both ignites something inside me and irritates me like no other. I squeeze my legs together to stop the pulse that's growing stronger with him so close.

His nostrils flare again, and right then, I *know*. He can *smell* that I'm aroused.

His eyes dilate as his hand grabs the back of my head, fisting my hair and making me look up at him. My scalp prickles as he forces my head back, but I don't care. Not when I'm witnessing heat flare to life in his usually cold eyes.

So much restrained strength is coursing through him. His head twitches to the side as if he's battling for control, slowly coming unhinged right before my eyes. He looks like a beast that wants to devour me. Having already cornered his prey, the feverish want takes over all reason-ing. I wait, letting him drink me in as I watch with quick breaths and heavy-lidded eyes. I still don't understand this vehement pull my body feels towards him.

He presses all the way against me, every hard line of his body pushing into me. I arch my back off the wall involuntarily as a hiss leaves his lips. I feel his hard length press into my hips as I rock forward. My cheeks flare with the warmth of timidness at the motion, but the thought vanishes in the next second, while his grip tightens even more in my hair, making my breath hitch. The heat building around us is threatening to set fire, and I'd willingly burn at this moment. Let him consume me and turn me to ash.

I don't know why I feel so drawn, but my body temperature is rising with every passing second.

I close my eyes, letting them roll back when he inhales deeply and slowly trails his nose up my jaw until the warmth is gone. *He's* gone as he withdraws himself from me. A cold rain douses the fire burning, extinguishing the flames licking against my skin as they turn to steam, evaporating into nothing.

Now feet apart, he stares down at me like I'm compelling him against his will. I don't miss the annoyance and confusion that flickers in his light blue eyes.

He turns and continues up the stairs, and I just stare. Stunned. Still leaning into the wall, I try to wrap my mind around what the hell just happened between us. I slowly take one step at a time until I reach him waiting at the top in front of a white door. It's so out of place in the dark grey and black hallways.

He refuses to look at me as he opens the door, and a bright white light shines into the dim corridor. I glance up at him once more, but he keeps his eyes level with the room before him. I force myself to let it go with indignation as I walk inside and see an elderly female digging around in supplies.

"Good evening, Galena," Prince Draven says in a cool, collected voice, announcing our presence.

She turns to look at us and lights up at the sight of Prince Draven. "Oh, welcome! Welcome, my dear boy."

Her hair is white, pulled up in a bun. She's short in height, with fine lines creasing around her eyes and the corners of her mouth. An apron is tied around her waist as she comes over to greet us.

"And who might this be?" She looks me over as if trying to figure it out for herself.

"I'm Cora," I quickly say, dipping my head to greet her.

A knowing glint shines in her golden eyes as she gives me another once over before a small smile plays on her lips. "If you're Cora, then I'm the notorious Dark Prince, who's standing behind you right now."

All I can do is gape at her.

"My dear Princess, I've been around for a while and know many things. You can't fool an old lady like me." She chuckles and walks over to a table, where she has different healing salves and medicines lined up. "Come here, girl, and let's get that lip fixed up." She taps her hand on top of the table, wanting me to hop up and sit.

I do just that as I see Prince Draven staying by the doorway, leaning on the edge with his legs crossed at the ankle and his corded arms folded over his chest. His eyes are on me now, but he's glaring at me like all of this is *my* fault.

"Let me take a look at ya, girl," Galena says right before she grabs my face to look closer at my mouth. "Hmm..." Her eyes squint. "I would ask why you aren't healing on your own, but I don't think you'd tell me, anyway." She gives me a concerned look, seeming to know the words I refuse to say. I thought she would use a healing salve, but instead, she places her palm in front of my mouth and closes her eyes. Warmth tingles against my lip, while a soft light glows from her hand, and I feel the sting fading away.

"There you go." She pulls back and takes a cloth to wipe away the remaining smears of red left behind. "As good as new."

"Thank you, Galena," I say kindly, not being able to truly explain how grateful I am for concealing something that would light a match inside my father.

"Of course, my dear. I'm here anytime." She turns to Prince Draven. "Why don't you kindly walk her back to her room so she can rest? Be a gentleman, hm?" Her teasing tone sparks amusement in me. She seems to know him all too well.

"Anything for you, Galena." He gives her a soft smile before it vanishes, replaced with tight lips as he looks back at me.

We exit her room as he silently leads me back to my suite. The air between us is heavy, weighing me down with thoughts of what happened earlier. A small twinge of guilt creeps in. Here I am getting pissed off at Aiden for being caught with another girl, when I'm getting aroused by another guy. But that small fissure of doubt in Aiden's words still plagues me, still has me questioning if he lied to me. But what just transpired between Draven and me, no part of me can deny that in the heat of the moment, I would have let him do what he wanted.

After minutes drag by, we near the end of the corridor that leads to the main staircase in the castle. It's an easy route back to my suite from here, one I can manage on my own. But before we are exposed to the open room, he hangs back in the darkened hallway.

"It's your necklace."

I freeze. My spine is rigid, but I refuse to turn to look at him as he stands a foot behind me. I can feel his eyes imploring, demanding an answer. It wasn't a question, though. It's almost a relief he guesses correctly. It means I don't have to voice it against my father's commands. But I still give him nothing as I stay still. Neither confirming nor denying the truth, even if my unspoken words hang blatantly in the air.

He's beside me in the next moment, realizing I won't speak about this.

"Have a good night, Emma." He saunters off, heading back from where we came from. I ignore the urge to watch him walk away. So, instead, I move my feet forward and head to my room. Never looking back.

The sun disappeared hours ago, while I lay in bed, staring at the ceiling. I can't seem to push my raging thoughts aside long enough to read, let alone fall asleep. I'm flustered and an intense need has been simmering, putting me on edge. I'm desperate for release at this point, aching to give in to my body's demands.

I let my hand travel down along my stomach, sliding it under the band of my pants. I feel the lace garments and dip my hand further beneath. I can feel my pulse quickening as I get closer to where I need my fingers, anticipating the high to come.

My back arches off the bed the moment I reach my clit, putting pressure on it as I begin circling my fingers. Heat builds in my lower belly as I feel myself getting wet. I bring my other hand up to my breast, grabbing hold before tugging at the rosebud puckering through my shirt.

My mind drifts to raven hair that hangs over a silver piercing, strong hands that threw me down before softening the blow, and tattoos that bleed into skin. Tattoos I want to run my tongue over and trace in a sensual dance.

Chasing after my pleasure to thoughts of Prince Draven feels forbidden, with his arrogant mouth and cold stare. But I couldn't hide the adrenaline I felt from his challenge earlier, freely using my skills against him on the mat and pushing my body to the limit against his strength.

I noticed the beads of sweat that formed on his skin as they slowly trailed down his shirtless torso. It took extra focus to not be distracted by all that muscle on display.

A small moan escapes me as I quicken my pace before dipping my fingers inside. The wetness drips between my legs as I thrust my fingers deep. I keep a steady rhythm as I glide my fingers in and out, using my other hand to continue the needy assault on my swollen clit. My breath hitches as the warmth in my core coils tighter. Remembering the feel of his body pressed on mine during our challenge on the mat, and then the image of his tongue licking my blood in the staircase causes me to quicken my movements. Chasing. Needing. *Demanding* my body's release.

The memory of feeling of his hardened cock along my core makes me fall over the edge. My orgasm smacks into me as my inner walls tighten until it releases, clenching around my fingers in a brutal pulse. I keep circling my clit to prolong the feeling, wanting to stay in this free-falling ecstasy for all of eternity.

My chest is heaving as my orgasm fades away, leaving me breathless and hot all over. No matter how hard I make myself come, it's never enough. The ache just begins to rise again and sets my nerves on fire.

As my breaths even out, I walk to the bath to clean up quickly, and then curl back under the covers. Contrasting thoughts of Prince Draven war against my mental walls. A battle of ice and fire rampaging against each other.

My eyes fall shut as I sink further into the after-effects of my release. I feel myself drifting off to sleep, but not before my thoughts snag on the picture of the Dark Prince smiling with a dimple.

CHAPTER TWENTY-EIGHT

Emma

Cora knocks on my door when the moon still hangs in the sky to pack every bit of my clothing, even though I demand her to stop. I'm not helpless and have two hands to do that myself. Of course, she refuses and tells me to go clean up because I look like I was mauled by a savage animal.

I ignore how my mind instantly went to wishing I was mauled by a savage Dark Prince instead, but that would make me like every other girl here. The girls who would willingly lick the bottom of his shoes. That thought alone makes me want to gag. So I do as Cora says, making myself look presentable before we board the ship to head back home.

Queen Zoraida waits for us in the grand entrance at the bottom of the massive staircase, as we all gather for our departure. I can't help but notice how neither of the princes are here, but it's still only an hour or so until the sun crests over the horizon. I swallow the disappointment of them not bidding us farewell when I see my father standing next to the queen. Some

221

of his guards are taking his things out of the double doors to load them onto the ship.

My steps falter when I see Aiden appear with his father from a side corridor into the open room. Images of yesterday flash in my mind of how close I got with a male who is not him, but I push it deep down before my expression gives anything away. Aiden's father, Captain Calloway, heads straight to my father's side. But Aiden doesn't follow. Instead, he walks right up to me, until he's at my side, taking hold of my hand, which I instinctively want to pull away. His touch is warm, but it lacks the comfort I used to feel with him. I told him I would let the other night slide, even if I have a feeling that choice will stab me in the back when I'm not ready.

Plus, to rip my hand out of his in front of everyone would raise questions and leave me under the angry glare of my father.

We head over to the queen, our shoes tapping against the floor as we make our rounds to say a final farewell to her. When it's my turn, Aiden releases his hold on my hand and trails after his father and mine as they go to stand by the door.

"I hope you have safe travels back to your home." The queen offers me a soft smile as she pats my hands.

I dip, offering her a small curtsy. "Thank you, Your Majesty, for welcoming us into your home. It's beautiful."

Her teeth shine through the dimly lit room as she smiles at my words. Then she motions with her hand for one of her guards to come to her. I watch when he slips a book out from under his arm. She takes it from him and then holds it out to me. "I want you to have this. It's about time someone took an interest in a romance book besides myself." She winks.

I stare down at the book in her hands, the one I borrowed but never finished. How did she get it or even know…?

"A queen has her ways," she says, seeming to know where my thoughts were going.

I delicately tuck the book inside my cloak. "Thank you, again. You don't know how much that means to me." A well of emotions builds inside of me with this unknown feeling.

"Just promise me you'll read it."

"I will."

With that, I dip my head and make my way to the doors. Seconds later, we walk down the path that leads to the docked ship under the glistening night sky.

A storm forms in the middle of our journey, and the ship rocks hard against the roaring sea. The war of nature suddenly goes silent and moves almost in slow motion, as the ocean anticipates the streaks of white that flare in the air. The lightning crackles loudly as it spears down into the turbulent waves. The two facets of nature collide with an aggression that's both magnificent and terrifying. Captain Calloway bellows over the deafening thunder to his crew as they turn into a chaos of bodies running around to secure the ship.

I let the rain pelt down on me, the ceaseless drops chilling my bones. Tipping my head back, I stare out at the inky clouds veiling the night sky, the swirling storm within declaring war. The clouds roll, clashing into one another. I'm lost in their enchantment, briefly registering my name being called by someone.

Before I can break my trance, my eyes snag on a black blur gliding between the rumbling clouds, almost looking like wings. But it's gone before I can blink. I slam my eyelids shut and try again. Nothing. But I know my mind is not tricking me, not a second time. My eyes frantically search, staring up at the sky, hoping for another glance. A kernel of obsession rises in me as I try to find it.

"Emma! C'mon!" I hear Cora yelling, startling me from my reverie while tugging at my sleeve, desperate to take some semblance of shelter in the ship. But I don't dare hide the serene smile that crosses my face, because this storm is a beautiful ballad being sung.

A strong grip on my arm tugs me forward, jerking me from my trance. "You need to get inside," Aiden's voice penetrates through the vortex of winds swirling around. "It's not safe for you to be out here."

"It's not safe for anyone out here! But I can help. What can I do?" I feel like I'm screaming at him so my voice can be heard, but he just keeps pulling me forward towards the hatch of the ship.

"There's nothing you can do, Emma. You have no powers. You'll just be a risk out here, and you need to take cover. The crew needs to focus on making sure the ship doesn't split in half."

His words are a punch to the heart. Whether he meant to hurt me or not, I can't help but rein in the sorrow that wants to seize me.

I see the Fae using their powers to help. Those who wield water are doing their best to control the waves away from smacking into us and steadying the sea along our path. Those who are born with fire keep a heatwave floating around to shield the workers from turning numb with cold. Those who have the power that connects to nature grow more vines to tie the rope tightly to the ship, making sure they don't snap. All while the wind keepers are pushing against the storm, blocking its powerful force.

The crew members are usually the lower Fae with elemental powers. Not higher Fae, like Aiden, who has the ability to bend space around himself and do bursts of short-distance phasing.

But being told I'm useless, when I can feel my power constantly churning deep within the depths of my soul, begging to be set free, enrages me. My people simply think I'm powerless, but Aiden knows this necklace is the true reason. My power is there, and yet, I'm forced to be cut down into nothing.

Worthless.

I want to scream and rage and let my power burst out of me, but I don't. Doing that will only cause more pain and set fire to my skin. Proving even more that what Aiden says is true. I may as well be sent to the Mortal Lands of Helestria and live the rest of my days amongst those who hold no power.

His grip tightens as he keeps pulling me along, Cora offers me pleading eyes to get out of the storm. Her powers are minimal. She may serve in my father's palace, but she's learning to master her healing abilities. Unless someone gets hurt, it's nothing she can use to help counter the monstrous storm.

She trudges ahead, knowing I won't be able to fight her on this. I look up and feel the sting of Captain Calloway's eyes on me, promising my death. Before I can tear my eyes away from his and reluctantly follow Aiden, Aiden tosses me over his shoulder. I feel slight pressure as the air around us folds together, a blur of colors as he warps and teleports us to the other side of this ship, right in front of the door. A slight wave of dizziness hits me from the use of his power.

Setting me down on my feet, he lifts the handle and gestures for me to go in, even though every part of me is screaming not to. Screaming to let me be of use and help, that I won't break and am just as capable as any other Fae. But I don't. Instead, I give him one final aggravated stare, hoping to let him see how deep his words cut me and that he should know how they would make me bleed. I say nothing, knowing a retort would fall from my lips. So I wrap my cloak tighter around me and duck inside.

It's been hours, and the storm is still raging against the sea. Somehow, Cora is passed out on the bed beside me, even with her body tipping side-to-side with every smack of the sea's torrent. I internally smile seeing how this girl can sleep through *anything*. But most of all, she's sleeping peacefully. No monsters lurking in the depths of her psyche, waiting to claw their fingers into it and rip it apart.

I go back to reading the book Queen Zoraida gifted me. The pages are still damp from the rain pouring down and soaking through my cloak. But thankfully, the ink remains in place, and not one word bled through the paper.

I fold the corner of the page to mark my place before I flip through the pages. I never want to spoil the story, but I can't resist the urge of hoping to catch a glimpse of something good.

When I reach the end of the book, I pause. Opening the book fully and bringing it closer, the lanterns above swing in a steady rhythm like a pendulum.

A flattened black rose falls into my lap, marking the page where someone put a handwritten message inside. The black ink from the pen must be fresh, as it smears down the bottom of the page, leaving streaks of black around the lettering. I squint hard as I try my best to keep the message in the glow of the light that's swaying.

· · ·

When light and dark collide, your fate will be split in two.

I read it repeatedly. Engraving the twelve words into my head, wondering what the hell it means. Was it meant for me? Does the queen know something? Not only did she give me the book, but I recall the black roses on her crown, decorating the ball, and her placing one in her hair. Is this her way of discreetly telling me she wrote this? But what if it wasn't her? I lay back on the bed and stare at the distorted words smudged on the page, wishing I wasn't sailing home while I churn over every possibility.

PART III

CHAPTER TWENTY-NINE

Emma

We made it safely back to Asov a week ago now. The storm lasted for a long while, but it cleared up miles before we reached our bright shores. And as I lie in my own bed and look around my room, suddenly feeling even more out of place, I remember how centered I felt in the Court of Asiza.

I inhale a deep breath to prepare myself to speak to my father this morning. There must be some way I can get out of being betrothed, or at least push the wedding back until I figure out a solution. I know this will upset him, but I'm hoping if I approach him and stay collected, he will listen.

I make an effort to dress in a gown to his liking, even though the sight makes me nauseous. It's pink, as bright as a summer's day. The darkness in my soul wants to devour it, rip it apart with its sharp teeth, and destroy every piece of tulle and ribbon that decorates it.

The open hallways feel constricting as my vision tunnels and nerves dance through my body with every step towards his study. My palms start to feel clammy when the doors come into sight and I wipe them on my dress. Taking one more shaky breath in, I steel my spine to knock, but I hear voices carry from under the door. Their words slither through and make their way to my ears.

"What are you seeing?" My father's voice is hushed but demanding.

"Nothing, Your Highness. I don't see anything past a certain point."

I recognize that voice. A voice that sends every nerve ending in my body to become alert. It's Captain Calloway, who is not only my father's right-hand advisor but also happens to be my father's Seer. He seems all for my marriage to his son, but I always wondered if the reason he despises me so greatly is because of a vision he's seen. But even if that were the case, the promise of death in his eyes when he looks at me is extreme.

I inch closer, careful not to make a sound as I close my eyes to zero in on what they are saying.

"That makes no sense!" my father bellows. "You're a Gods damn Seer! Try again!" I flinch at the tone of his voice. I can feel my face pale at the memories of when it's been directed at me.

"Her future turns into a blur, a scramble of images I can't decipher," Calloway splutters. "Have you tried asking the Masiren?"

Silence follows Calloway's words. I bite my lip in anticipation. Whose future are they trying to foresee? Who is the Masiren?

I hear the sigh that I assume came from my father. "Yes, but the vagueness of its truths lately is not worth the risk of the aftermath I endure. Ever since we captured it, my anger and maddening thoughts have only grown with each year that passes. And every time I approach it, I feel like it's just waiting for me to give in, to fall prey to its whims. Just waiting for me to fail. For all I care, that thing can continue to rot at the bottom of the well, never to be free again." His tone is deadly.

"Do you think the Masiren has been filling its power into you all these years?" Calloway hedges.

An aggravated growl erupts from my father. "I'll kill it with my bare hands if it has been!" He seethes, until a tense silence fills the hall. "But never mind for now. We'll try figuring out what lies in Emma's future tomorrow at sunrise. Don't be late."

My hand flies to my mouth, silencing the gasp I couldn't hold in. Something else is trapped here, like me. And they're searching into *my* future? What do I have to do with anything? My thoughts are cut off when they start talking again. I gently place my palm against the wall beside the doors to hold me steady, my finger nervously digging along the dent in the stone.

"Any progress in finding the Liminal Stone?" my father continues.

Calloway clears his throat and any nerves he had vanish as confidence leaks from his voice. "My crew have made some progress. We're getting closer."

"What have they found?" my father hedges.

"We found that the last two Elders who know of the Stone and possibly its location live in the Court of Amihan to the north and the Court of Abhainn to the west," Calloway explains.

My father grunts. "We need to find them immediately and question what they know. I don't care what you have to do." The meaning behind his tone is clear. Take any actions necessary in procuring the answers my father wants.

I can't let him harm anyone else. They don't deserve to fall prey to his wrath. No one does.

"I already have a group of soldiers preparing to travel." Calloway sounds all too pleased with himself. Someone should knock him down a peg.

"Tell them to hurry. I don't want to wait any longer. I *must* have that stone. For when I do"—a dark laugh with ill intentions leaves my father, making the hair on my arms stand up—"I will be able to amplify my power and finally claim *all* of Deyadrum. Everyone will bow to me, and I'll even find a way to seize control of the Corrupted, to have those disgusting beasts under my command. It will be a perfect army, should anyone choose to rebel."

My eyes widen at the thought of my father wanting to disrupt the balance of rulers between courts and take over. I knew a vile creature lived in the core of his soul, but I didn't realize it wanted to raise its ugly head and rule over everyone. To spit its venom and sink its teeth into them.

I have to stop him, now more than ever. Having his hatred focused on me alone is one thing, but for others to fall into his grasp is something I refuse to let happen. But I need to figure out how to keep it from happening.

The sound of their voices dies off and I brace myself as I prepare to knock and make my presence known. They probably have resumed working or, I suppose, plotting against everyone, and I desperately wish Calloway was elsewhere. It would serve me better to have him gone and out of the room with the conversation I'm about to have. But it seems that's unlikely. It's rare when they aren't by each other.

I recite the words I plan to say in my head before I rap my knuckles against the door.

I can feel the tense pause, a pressure building as I wait for my father's response, "Come in." The order is deep and carries a wave of underlying anger with it. A voice inside me cautions me to turn away, but it's too late. They already know I'm here, and now I have to go head-to-head with the masked monster inside.

───

The door clicks shut behind me as both males stare at me, unblinking. I keep my chin high, not allowing their gazes to make me falter. My father's face contorts into a tight smile.

"To what do we owe the pleasure of your presence here?" The lighter tone ringing in every word sounds forced, but I steel myself regardless and do what I set out to do.

"I wanted to speak with you about the betrothal." My voice somehow comes out sure and steady.

A dark look flashes in his eyes and I can feel Calloway's gaze cutting through me. My father's jaw clenches before he speaks. "I hope you're not interrupting us for the sake of wanting to discuss petty things such as that."

"Well, actually, I was hoping to ask if we could postpone it."

"Why?" Calloway growls, adding himself to the conversation.

I keep my eyes set on my father, showing him that he has the higher power as I solely focus on him and dismiss Calloway. "Aiden and I have known each other awhile as friends, but it would be nice to have more time to adjust to being engaged and get to know him on a deeper level."

I really want to tell him I want the whole betrothal to be put to an end, but with the tension charging in the room, I might as well offer my death on a golden platter. At least by asking to postpone, it gives me a chance to find another way to end it, or at least a way to escape.

"You must think me a fool, my dear Emma." I balk at my father's words.

"What? No, I—"

"You can easily get to know Aiden once you are married. There's no need to waste time. In fact, we were just thinking about having your wedding in three months' time. But now, I think next month might be better, since you dared question my judgment." He speaks so casually, like deciding my fate in life makes no difference to him.

My mouth is hanging open, a thousand thoughts swarming in my head. "You can't!" I blurt the words out before I realize my mistake, dropping my head. "I'm sorry, but please." My voice cracks. "Please, allow me more time."

I can feel the panic rising when I bring my head back up, while his gaze morphs into one of excitement. His eyes promise pain for speaking out against him. Calloway chuckles softly as delight flares in his stare.

"It seems...my dear Emma, that you are in need of a reminder of what I *can* do." His eyes turn a molten red, his power slamming into me. The study I was standing in vanishes as he wipes it away and brings forth a different kind of hell. The type of hell he has created just for me with his powers.

With a flick of his hands, he creates an illusion, altering the reality of what's around him, making me see whatever he chooses. Dematerializing us from reality, vanishing us to outside eyes and into an alternate dimension of the world that he controls.

I feel the blood drain from my face as I'm thrown into the familiar grimy room, the room he always takes me to when delivering his punishments.

Past pain bleeds on these rusty brown walls, splattered in spots of red and layered amongst cunning words and silent cries. The room may be an illusion folded into time, but everything that happens within it is still real and will stay with me even when he releases me from his hold.

I stumble back as the illusion finally settles into place, the blurs of color coming into focus. Gnarled posts stare at me across the room. The same posts my wrists get bound to every time he brings me here, my arms spread for his demonic torment.

Fear bubbles in my throat. The stagnant air weighing heavily in the room floods me with its musty scent. The smell brings forth so many memories of him spilling my blood and painting the room with silenced screams.

The bricks in the walls are faded and chipped at the corners. One lantern hangs overhead, casting a dim light over the room, creating shadows all around. No windows exist, just brick walls, and a wood floor with dual posts standing in the center with a crusted drain placed right beneath. The one that steals my blood, forcing me to hear the vexing sound of each drop dripping into the pit below it. There is only one wall that's not bare. It holds an array of weapons for him to choose from to deliver his torture.

I begin to twist around, looking for a way out, but I know better. There's no escape. No way out of this hell. I wish I had my powers, so I could crack through his mind games and push his illusions away from me.

But I know they won't come.

I glance around and freeze when he appears right in front of me. His waiting hand is already airborne, slamming into me and knocking me back. Pain blasts through my cheek, a pounding pulse radiating beneath my skin. I can already feel a welt forming.

Rough hands take hold of my wrists, dragging me towards the beams. I force my heels into the ground, scraping against the dirty wood boards, fighting in my attempts to pull back. I know it's inevitable, but I try to resist him, because once I'm tied to those posts, I'm done for.

Hands ram into me from behind, forcing me to crash into one of the posts. My head smacks into it, causing my vision to blur for a second, making stars spin around me when I close my eyes.

My father takes hold of one hand, and he must have let Calloway in on the fun for he grabs my other hand, each securing them in place. I try to yank my hands from the chains, rattling them, but it's no use. I know by now I need to save my energy. The only way to be set free from this room is to suffer through the affliction I know will be is coming.

But I can't help the pieces of my soul that break off and fall to the floor, getting crushed under their polished boots.

Destroyed.

"I think you need to learn who holds the power here." The anger in my father's voice is attached to a short tether, ready to snap at any moment. "Any requests on what you would like me to use first?" A test. Another mind game to him. If I answer, then he'll deliver a harsher punishment for thinking I'd have a choice at all.

Choices aren't given to me. Ever.

I stay silent, keeping my head hanging down, my eyes taking in the all too familiar cracks that creep through the floor—claw marks that permanently scar the floor from when I was first brought here. A time when I tried to use all my strength to fight back, breaking every nail, feeling the sharp agony of them snapping from digging them into the ground while he would drag me by my feet across the floor.

I don't make that mistake now.

I can sense Calloway's presence lingering in the corner of the room, making the air feel more suffocating with each passing second.

My head gets yanked back, and the tight grip on my hair sends a rush of piercing stings, like a million needles stabbing along my scalp. "Don't feel like talking back now?" My father growls, sending chills down my spine. I hold his gaze as those crimson eyes slam into me with spiked ends. Puncturing my soul, only to rip it out and shred me apart. I can see the glee in the depths of his stare, relishing every piece of my soul he takes to terrorize and destroy.

He shoves my head back down, clearly anxious to deliver on his promise. Sounds of material tearing breaks through the silence, causing cold air to rush against the skin on my back as he rips the back of my gown in two. A broken canvas on display for him to mutilate even more.

Boots sound against the floor as Calloway walks to me. "I almost feel bad for my son, having to bed someone who is a far cry from beauty underneath everything." Calloway might not know it, but those words strike the shameful part of me that agrees with him, shattering me like a vase being crushed under his gait. I can see the tip of his boots a foot in front of me now as I keep my head down, refusing to let him see the broken parts of me in my eyes.

A dark laugh echoes around me as my father walks over to choose his method of torment. "Oh, Aiden can wear a blindfold if he needs it. It's worth it for the power it would grant him." My mind lurches. No. Aiden wouldn't want to be with me for just power, right? My father would never see me on the throne of Asov, married or not, unless his heart no longer beat. "But these marks are my own masterpiece, a reminder for my daughter to never forget who she belongs to."

Pain. A sharp lash slices into my spine less than a breath after he finishes speaking. I throw my head back at the unexpected snap of the whip, swallowing the scream that wants to thunder up my throat. Calloway's harsh glare connects with mine when I lift my head. Even through the pain, I force myself to smirk at him just to refuse any sense of victory he may feel over me. My chest is heaving in deep lurches, preparing for the next slash to target me.

"You will remember how to speak to me, Emma! I've had enough of your insolence lately." My father's voice detonates with a deep-seated pleasure as the crack of the whip sounds again.

I bite my lip hard enough to draw blood, the metallic tang saturating my mouth, refusing to let him have the thrill of hearing my agony. Lash after lash hits the skin on my back, slicing and ripping my flesh apart. I can feel the wetness dripping down my spine, a constant stream of red, and watch it slither towards the drain at my feet.

Crack.

Crack.

Crack.

The room cuts in and out around me, my vision turning fuzzy. My body is close to falling over the cliff and diving headfirst into the empty abyss of unconsciousness. I lose count of the lashes. I only wish I could call on my darkness, let it in to steal the pain and numb me from this moment. But I'm so weak, I can barely hear their whispers. My father grunts with the force of his next blow. The slice whips against the already opened wounds, tearing deeper into my body.

My back feels like someone lit a match on my skin and threw gasoline all over it. I can feel my limbs weaken, my body starting to shake. With every hit, my body slumps further, only being held up by the restraints on my wrists as I hang there helplessly. I feel the chains cut into my skin as my body pulls them taut.

The swoosh of the whip cuts through the air, and the final slice flays into my already bloody skin, cutting to the bone. He throws the whip across the floor, blood splattering as it hits the ground, raining drops of crimson. Calloway steps back as my father walks around to stand in front of me, grabbing my chin roughly between his stained fingers.

His eyes are full of satisfaction. "You brought this upon yourself." He spits in my face and I can do absolutely nothing to block it.

Suddenly, I'm back in his study, crumpled on the floor in a mess of tulle and blood. I've stained the torn gown I wore to please him, but it cursed me instead, sending me to my own personal hell. I open my eyes to slits, peering up, seeing my father's eyes change back to normal before the black around my vision swallows me whole.

CHAPTER THIRTY

Emma

I wake to the foul and wretched stench of my father's personal dungeon for me. Its the place I'm always hauled to when my body gives out and I get sucked into the dark. I'm locked in the box.

It's larger than an average coffin, with iron bars that cover the top, only tall enough for me to sit hunched over when I'm able. I'm locked away in the far end of my father's wing of the palace, a place where no one is allowed to venture. No light exists, leaving me alone to heal with only the company of my maddening thoughts.

I'm not sure how long I had passed out for, but when I wake, my back feels sticky, and I'm left lying on my stomach on the sodden wood surface. I can feel cracks on my lips. I lick them, hoping it will soothe the sting. It hurts to swallow. My throat is scratchy, and I desperately wish for water.

Vomit wants to pour out of me, but I hold my breath before shoving it back down. My body is uncontrollably shaking, feeling overheated, while chills pebble my skin. A *fever.* I always have to pray to the Gods that I don't get an infection because I'm not sure if I can recover from that. I almost think the pain that courses through me after my father's brutality is worse than the brutality itself, a constant throb of searing heat that flares like the hottest flame.

All I want is to break free from this box. I know no one will come for me. Not a single soul knows I'm here aside from my father, and now Calloway. When my father's rage takes over and I'm left in a heap of open wounds on the floor, he commands Cora to be sent away. Either to travel to another court or to her family. Kye is usually sent on duties across the sea. My father knows who I've grown close to.

One single, broken tear falls down my cheek, landing on the floor. I beg my eyes to stop filling with tears. It only makes me feel weak. But my body doesn't listen, as I'm left stranded in a pool of my own blood and filth. Alone, unable to fight my way out.

I will forever be nothing but a prisoner in disguise, chained to the evil soul that dwells in my father. I'm stuck living in a dark dream. Never to be set free from him or the nightmares that haunt me.

I wince when I try to shift my body. I'm able to manage a slight roll, now laying on my side. My wrists and ankles are bound together by chains, the cold sharpness of them digging into my skin.

More goosebumps rack my body as I feel the cold sweat intensify. My pulse races and I feel like I'm silently drowning, sinking deeper into the oblivion that wants to claim me, to render me unconscious. My mental walls are *weak*, and I feel ashamed for wishing I could bring the haunting darkness to me. I want to feel *nothing*. I want it to numb the pain. I want for this all to end.

I desperately craved for it to come for me when my father was breaking me down, to help turn off my emotions with every slash of the whip. But now that I'm alone, suffering on the floor with nothing left in me, I can't invite it in.

Even though I have to keep the darkness within me at bay, the silence brings a semblance of comfort. Offering a small reprieve from the memory of my father's vile voice and the cracking of his whip. The quiet holds me in its embrace.

I'm struggling to control the rage I'm never allowed to show, starving for revenge. The anguish building within cuts me deeply. A father is supposed to *love*, to care and protect, but instead, his deeds only sever my veins.

I want to scream until my voice gives out on me and release the fury that's demanding to be set free. But no one would hear. I'm alone. *Abandoned.* Not a single soul could help. My pleas would only echo back to me.

As I lay curled up on the frigid, damp floor, I have nothing to do but wait for my body to heal. This allows ample time for my thoughts to take over.

But clarity breaks through the empty silence. The Liminal Stone my father and Calloway spoke of…he said it would *amplify* his power. That thought alone twists my insides, since he is able to do such menacing things with his power already. I can't let him get stronger. But the only way I'll be able to stop him and seek revenge is to find a way to remove the barrier around my neck. I wonder… If I found the Stone first, could it amplify *my* true power that's trapped inside? Would it be enough to blast this wretched thing off me for good?

I need to think of where I could even start searching for such a powerful stone. They mentioned the Elders, so I could use that as my lead. But sneaking out and traveling to the other courts is still an issue. Cora would be able to help me break free of the palace, I'm sure of it. But everything that follows is unknown, and if I get caught… I curl into myself at the thought of the consequences.

I can't help but feel like I'm losing my sanity, thinking of going against everything that has been forced upon me. But I realize at this moment, as I lay stripped of my dignity, bloody on the floor, that I don't give a damn. So, I let the anger inside seep into my bones, allowing it to turn my heart into an impenetrable stone. Hardening itself to go against the monster of my father.

The more my mind swirls with different ways to begin this journey, the more it snags on one thought: *the Masiren.* My father's words race through my mind. *To rot in the bottom of the well.*

Whatever it is, I can't help but feel I need to save it. I know all too well what it feels like for no one to come save you. Lying here, I wonder if the Masiren is feeling the same. Withering away in the ground in a decrepit well, helpless to do anything but let its psyche eat away at itself. Maybe I was never meant to be saved, but rather, to be someone's savior.

I lose track of days and nights as I'm left in the dark space of the box, only to drown in my own suffering. Hours blend with days, and at some point, the chains binding me together are gone when I wake. My skin is rubbed raw where they had tightly restrained me.

I feel delusional, having no idea what day it is. Still shrouded in darkness, my body craves the warmth of the sun, even as I still battle a fever. I'm so cold that the dampness of the floor keeps me shivering, seeping into my dress, chilling me to the bone.

I slip in and out of consciousness, and when I wake again, water and a stale piece of bread are left beside me, along with the flicker of a candle. Its the only glint of light around me, teasing me with hope, only until the flame snuffs out. My eyes struggle to adjust to the small fragment of light, making me squint. I can feel the open skin along my back still throbbing, an endless ache that begs to be healed.

I drink the water in small sips to gently soothe the soreness in my throat. My mouth is still so parched from dehydration that the thought of eating stale bread makes me wince. So, instead, I gently dip the corner of the bread into my drink, letting it soak before I chew down the soggy piece of food. It's bland, but my body needs sustenance. Once I finish it all off, I lay my head back down and feel my eyes drift shut of their own accord.

When I come to again, I'm able to sit hunched over, with slow and careful movements. The burning of the wick eases some of the stenches that hang in the air, the smells that were beginning to cause bile to creep up my throat. My water has been refilled, and after drinking every drop, I force another piece of tasteless bread down my throat with a hard swallow, resting back on my side. I'm hoping to let sleep take over as my body heals more, because it's the only way time seems to go faster while I wait to be released from this cage.

Letting my eyes fall shut, I dream of standing aboard a ship at sea, staring up at the midnight sky that illuminates a full moon holding a crescent peacefully inside it. The sight brings a sense of calm over me as my mind falls into sleep.

CHAPTER THIRTY-ONE

Emma

When I'm healed enough, I'm sent back to my room. I do my best to stand upright and look unfazed, and by some miracle, I manage to walk back, albeit on shaky legs. I'm given a clean gown to change into and water to wash my hair. But the fabric of the dress scrapes against the scabbed wounds on my back, threatening to open them again.

When I make it to my bathroom on trembling legs, I wash the stained blood from my body and clean the wounds. Its a process that has become second nature to me, as I squeeze the rag and watch red swirl in the sink before washing away from existence. Much like I've done with the pain my father's caused me—washing it away and acting as if it never happened. The soap and water seep into my cuts and I have to bite my tongue to keep in the scream that wants to flood out of me. I brace myself on the counter as I squeeze my eyes shut, focusing on my slow and controlled breaths to keep myself from blacking out. My vision blurs and doubles as I count to ten before I finish washing away my father's abuse.

After I manage to clean the wounds I can reach, I carefully pat myself dry and grab the healing salve I keep stored away, rubbing it all over my back to the best of my ability. The contact of my fingers rubbing over the wounds has me grinding my teeth, but the salve quickly numbs the pain away. Its a temporary reprieve until I have to apply more later.

I slowly tug on a set of loose night clothes before walking into my room, where the smell of food waits for me. Drool pools in my mouth. I eat every piece of food on the tray before I lie down and fall into the deepest sleep I've had in a while.

I repeat the same routine for another week. Wake. Eat. Bathe. Apply healing salve. Nap. Wake. Eat more. Bathe and apply more healing salve. Sleep for the night.

Suddenly, a knock jolts me from my routine nap. I haven't used my voice in a while, so it sounds strange when I speak: "Come in." A slight rasp coats my words.

I watch the door open, wary of who's on the other side until sandy blond hair peeks through. *Aiden.* I welcome him in as I work my body into a sitting position in my bed, keeping the blankets tucked tightly around my waist. I watch cautiously as he closes the door behind him and comes to sit on the edge of my bed; the mattress dipping down with his weight.

"My father told me you aren't feeling well." His eyes assess me, looking for any signs of sickness.

I stiffly nod. "Sort of, just feeling under the weather. Nothing a little more sleep won't fix," I say, offering a soft smile to reassure him.

I see the slight squint in his eyes, like he knows I'm not telling him everything. "I know you can't access your powers to heal, but why not just go to the healer if you feel unwell?"

Shit. I need to deter him from this. A healer could easily make me better, but my father would redeliver my punishments and throw me back in the box if I went. The healer would be able to sense where my injuries reside, and it wouldn't be hard to guess what caused the long lines in a mangled mess along my skin. It would only create questions. Questions my father doesn't want anyone asking, or else he would silence them for good.

I shrug a shoulder. "No need to bother her. It's nothing, really. Just a little more rest and I'll be as good as new." I smile a bit brighter for him, hoping the lie doesn't seem too obvious.

His brows slightly furrow. "If you say so, but you're already weak, Emma. She's a healer for a reason. It's her job."

I wave a hand in the air nonchalantly. "And there's no reason to burden her. I'm good," I force out, even though, once again, his words hurt. He insinuated that I'm weak on the ship, a powerless Fae. But now, he's not even trying to skirt around it; he just says it right to my face.

He exhales a long sigh. "I don't know why you're so stubborn, but I hope when we marry that you will at least take my words into consideration."

"I already do, but right now, I just want to sleep."

I see the crease in his brows deepen, those green orbs never straying from me. "So it seems. Well, I'll let you be for now. If you aren't better by tomorrow, then you will be going to the healer. I don't like seeing you unwell."

All I can do is nod, not wanting to give anything away. Although, what he said sounded like an order, which churns my stomach. He leans forward to place a quick kiss on my cheek. Standing back up, he starts digging his hand in his pocket before pulling something free. I tilt my head in question and watch curiously when he gently places a pure white shell on my bedside table. He huffs a nervous laugh, swiping his hand through his tousled hair.

"I feel bad I've had to travel while you've been sick. But I'm here now, and I know how much you love the shimmering white seashells." His eyes flicker to mine, a slightly saccharine smile tipping his lips up.

My gaze falls on the shell sitting on my bedside table. Growing up, I always picked up the iridescent shells on the beach. I was always curious how they managed to evade the elements of nature, to escape the cruelty of life, as they blend perfectly in the sand. There is no darkness lurking to stain them, no matter what stormy waves crash against them. And this shell didn't reflect a speck of torment, not even on the inside, unlike my soul. It lays untouched, unharmed. And as I lay in bed next to it, healing from injuries I can not even speak of, I find myself wondering what that must feel like.

"Not a speck of any other color. Not even a spot of yellow, I checked," he says with amusement.

My eyes linger on the shell, stretching my hand out to trace my fingers over the ridged edge. "Thank you. I love it," I say when I bring my eyes up to his. A grateful smile lifts on my face.

He nods in relief. "You're welcome." He walks away from the bed, reaching the door and pauses with one foot out the threshold, looking back at me. "I know we aren't together, officially, until the day we say I do, but I consider you mine, nonetheless. Once we're married, you'll remain by my side and see the healer when you need it." His tone is light, but I don't miss the edge of seriousness. Visions flash in my mind of what a dutiful life would look like tethered to him. To this life.

It looks like he wants to either say more or drag me out of the room to the healer against my wishes. But relief flutters through me when he chooses neither, walking out and letting the door click shut behind him.

―――――――――――――――――

It's evening now. After letting my body claim more hours of sleep, I force myself to get up as the sun starts to dip in the sky. I pace around my room, unable to settle. Cora comes back soon from her break, and I was instructed to tell her that my time here was uneventful.

But I'm anxious. I need to leave, to escape again and follow through with the ridiculous plan I came up with in my delusional state. Unfortunately, it's the only plan I've got.

Tap. Tap. Tap.

Cora. I rush to the door and rip it open, startling her with my abruptness.

"Shit, Emma, you scared me," she gasps, slamming her hand to her chest like I knocked the life from her. With an amused shake of her head, she walks in and pulls me into a hug. I wince slightly, but I hide it as best I can. My back is almost completely healed, but occasionally hurts if touched. "Were the days without me so uneventful that you've taken a liking to trying to rip doors off their hinges?" She chuckles and I can't help the small lift of my mouth as well.

But then, the slight smile falls away just as fast. It doesn't slip her notice.

"I need out again," I blurt.

Her eyes widen in alarm, her posture changing to one of concern. "Why? What happened?"

I pull her forward so we can sit on the couches, needing to organize my thoughts. I leave out the punishment my father placed on me, but I dive in and explain what I overheard. I explain how I want to go after the Liminal Stone, because it could be the key to everything. To stop the Corruption, help the people all throughout Deyadrum, and release my powers so I can be free. But most of all, I want to keep the Stone out of my father's prying hands, knowing it won't be used for good. Deyadrum would be in serious trouble if he obtained it, and I need to keep that from happening.

"He wants to rule over *everyone*?" Cora asks, shock taking over her as her mind tries to keep up with what I've told her. "Sneaking out of the palace is doable, but how do you plan on crossing the seas?"

"By praying luck is on my side? I'm hoping to find someone with a ship I can hitch a ride on." I scrunch my face, unsure of her reaction.

Her eyes squint, clearly debating if she should question my lack of planning, but she ultimately decides to drop it for now. "I'm coming with you."

Shit. "I don't want something to happen to you. I have no idea how this will all work, and your family needs you here."

"No," she interjects. "*You* will need me. What kind of friend would I be if I let you go on this long journey alone? It sounds fun, the two of us going on an adventure and anticipating what awaits us. Think of the great unknowns we will defeat, like a pair of female warriors." I bite my lips to stop the chuckle wanting to bubble to the surface. "Plus, I may still be learning, but it would be good to have a healer with you." She gives me a knowing look. I know she's not just saying it because I can't heal but saying it in general in case anything happens to anyone, and I can't help but feel she's right.

Reluctantly, I nod. It would be nice to have some company, but I won't forgive myself if anything happens to her.

"There's one more thing…" I hesitantly say.

Her eyebrows raise. "And that is?"

I sigh. "I also overheard my father talking about a Masiren that's trapped here. I don't know what it is, but I need to free it. I know all too well how it feels to be confined and under his control, I won't let that happen to another for any longer."

She stands up at lightning speed and starts for the closet. Various items of clothing start getting thrown out and into the room. "Let's go save this Masiren and start our quest," she says excitedly. "Don't just stand there, get dressed. We need to gather our essentials and leave before the night guard comes to stand at your door." Her head peeks out and looks towards the balcony doors to see outside. "It seems we don't have much time. Hurry."

The orange glow of the sun is beaming brighter as it almost reaches the horizon. She's right, this is our only chance.

I grab the black leathers she tosses on the floor, running into the bathroom to hastily change. I ignore the small jabs of pain that pinch with my hurried movements. When I come out, she is wearing another set of my leathers but dusted in a midnight blue. They're the leathers Kye got for me as a gift, saying that anyone who has the skill to fight deserves to own some.

I grab the dagger from under my pillow and sheathe it to my thigh, both of us tossing cloaks around us as we turn to see the sun drop a few inches lower. We hurry to the door, but not before I grab my satchel and tuck away the book Queen Zoraida handed me, needing those hand-written words with me for the journey until I figure out what they mean.

CHAPTER THIRTY-TWO

Emma

We manage to make our way into the kitchen to grab some food for the road and water to fill the canteens we snuck from the guard's kitchen nook.

Telion is luckily not here, or he would be having a fit, but not without giving us a special dessert. When we make it outside, the rays of the sun have vanished, leaving a peaceful twilight glow of blues and purples to spread along over the sea. We trail down the side of the palace, creeping towards the side where my father's wing is located.

"Where is the well?" Cora asks on a hushed breath.

"A little farther down and around the corner. I've only seen the well a few times when I ran around here as a kid, before my father told me I wasn't allowed on this part of the beach," I say, remembering the way he scolded me for seeking refuge on this side of the palace when Aiden and I were playing hide and seek one day. Funny to think I would ever find refuge near my father. That day should have been my first warning of the villain within him.

We near the end of the wall and I peer around the corner, seeing no guards near. An odd sensation sweeps over me, not understanding why it's so deserted.

"Cora…where are they?" I whisper.

She steps forward to look. "Are you sure it's safe? It doesn't make sense. Why would no guards be out here?" Cora asks.

"Because of me."

Cora and I both jump back at the deep voice that interrupts us from behind. When I turn my frightened stare around, I see Kye standing there. His arms are folded, and a smirk plays on his lips.

"Damnit, Kye!" I teasingly smack his arm. "That's not cool. You scared us half to death."

"I hate you," Cora mumbles under her breath, trying to slow her beating heart with the hand she has on her chest. Two scares in one night. If she gets scared a third time, I don't doubt she would hurt someone.

I feel Kye looking straight at me in an accusatory way. "You think I'm going to let you sneak off into the night again, and without me?"

I go to start speaking, and then snap my mouth shut, racking my brain for a rebuttal. When I find my words, he holds his hand up in the air to stop me.

"Don't. I'm coming with you this time, and it seems so is *she*." His eyes drift down to Cora, who's glaring daggers at him, clearly still holding a grudge for sneaking up on us. He brings his brown eyes back to me. "I don't know what you're doing, or where you're going, but I have a hunch you don't plan on coming back for a while, and where you go, I go."

Tears start to build. I can feel them wanting to fall from the truth in his words. My heart aches, but not with the pain I'm used to. It aches with a deep beat, knowing these two are willing to risk their lives and walk through whatever unknowns await us.

I don't say thank you, because he can already see how grateful I am in my expression as he dips his head and lays a hand on my shoulder. "So, why are we sneaking farther into the king's borders instead of away?"

I bite my lip, glancing at the well before pointing at it. "I heard my father say he has something imprisoned in the well and I have to free it."

He tilts his head. "Why? How do you know it's not an enemy?"

Fair point. I keep my eyes trained on him. "That's a risk I'm willing to take. Nothing deserves a cruel fate like that, being left to bake everyday under the sun, and who knows what else." A twist of satisfaction rises inside me at the thought of taking something from my father.

He stares at me for a long moment. Cora twirls her hair between her fingers, watching our interaction. He sighs in resignation. "Alright. But we need to be quick. Someone could spot us from the windows above."

I quickly nod. Turning back to the source, the well sits in the middle of the beach, equal distance from the shore and palace walls. Blood drains from my face at the thought of how many days have passed where the sun beats down, making everything burn to the touch. Whatever is in that well has suffered tremendously.

With one final search of the area, Kye gives me a subtle tap on my shoulder, signaling for me to go. I take off with a burst of speed, no hesitation slowing me down. My boots pound against the sand as I dig my heels in, tossing the sand behind me with every step. Pumping my arms with the same speed as my legs, I hurry, for this is my only chance to free whatever waits before me.

My body slams into the hard rim of the well, breaking my pace. I gulp in a huge lungful of air before tipping my head over to peer down inside. My hair curtains around my face, leaving me a sliver of an opening to see the creature looking back.

Every muscle tenses when glowing gold eyes meet mine, baring its pointed teeth at me with a hiss. I take in its form, looking like nothing I've ever seen or read about. Webbed feet, a slashing tail, grey skin decorated in gills. It looks lethal. A nightmare of the sea.

Red stains are crusted around the inner walls of the cell, and the chains holding it prisoner look caked with rust and grunge. A foul, rotted scent wafts up to the opening, but I refuse to show that I notice. My only concern is how to get near without this thing tearing into me like dinner.

I hear Kye step behind me and Cora gasp. I whip around and face Kye. "I need you to rotate the handle and lower me down on the rope."

He stares hard at me. "No, Emma. That creature looks deadly. I'll go."

"Kye," I hiss, irritation bubbling in my blood. "You're too much of a brute to go down there."

Cora snickers. "She's right. You and your bulging muscles will snap the line."

Kye looks shocked as he stares at Cora. "My wha——"

"Focus!" I snap, cutting Kye off. "Cora's got a point." I slide my eyes to her. "But you're not helping." She shrugs with an amused smile but straightens up, determination in her eyes. I rest my hand on Kye's arm. "Look, there's no way you can go down there, let alone us bring you back up. If anything goes wrong, use that strong power of yours and all will be fine. You can just yank me back up. Either way, I plan to free the Masiren."

"Masiren?" Kye asks.

"That's its name, or so I think." I pause, wondering. "Do you have a master key on you with being head of the guard?" I ask, knowing Kye has earned that privilege from all the blood and sweat he's poured into his position to prove his place to my father.

He nods and graciously unclips it from the ring it was hooked to before setting it in my waiting hand. "Be careful."

"Thank you," I tell him, stepping up on the edge of the well, wrapping my fingers tightly around the rope hanging from the top. I look at Kye to signal when to let my feet fall from the ledge.

He gives me a stern nod and I let my feet pull away, hanging suspended. The rope loosens, inching me down carefully, the stench growing stronger. I dip my head down to look at the Masiren, finding it already watching me. Its eyes are blazing, tracking every movement I make. It takes a sniff in through its slitted nostrils, its glowing eyes slightly dimming. It cocks its head to the side like it's assessing me, but this time, it's not hissing. It's not baring its teeth.

It's waiting. For some reason, I have the distant feeling that this creature can sense I mean no harm, that I'm trying to help. The lower I am plunged into the well, the more the Masiren settles. Calms. Its tail stops whipping back and forth, but instead lays in the couple feet of water at the bottom.

It silently presses near the curved wall when I'm close enough to let go of the rope. Vomit wants to surge up my throat. The smell is pungent. My eyes burn, and it's hard to take a breath. I let my feet step into the water, soaking up to my knees.

I remain completely calm, holding my hands out in front of me. "Let me free you," I say quietly, my voice bouncing around the small space. I quickly glance up and see Kye and Cora watching intently, ready in case something goes wrong. Dragging my eyes to the gold ones before me, I take a small step forward. "I don't know if you understand me, but I'm going to unlock your chains now."

The Masiren says nothing, just watches me with interest. I steadily close the distance between us, the murky water sloshing around my legs. Fear wraps around me, screaming at me to keep my distance. But instead, I reach a shaky hand out, letting it brush against its grey skin. I exhale the long breath of air I had been holding. It's smooth where it soaks in the water, but the parts that don't are weathered. Singed from the heat of the sun when it sits directly above in the sky.

It jerks slightly at my touch at first, but slowly lets me explore. I find the keyhole in the chain latched around its neck, placing the master key inside and freeing it from its collar. I do the same to the cuffs on all four of its legs until the last one splashes in the water with a ring of freedom.

The Masiren stands up fully, bigger than me and more dangerous. I press my back against the mucky wall, looking up at it with rapid breaths. But it looks down at me with wonder. "Go, be free," I tell it, slowly making my way to the center of the well, grabbing the rope and tightening my grip on it.

It closes its eyes, and when they open, they aren't yellow, but a soft white, glowing in the dim well. I stare in astonishment, having never seen eyes change so drastically. "A gift for your selflessness," its voice rings out in a sweet tune beneath its words, creating a warmth in my heart that I didn't know was missing. "Your first step. You must find the one they call Shade, for he will help you."

My mouth falls open, and disbelief courses through me. Before I can say anything back, its eyes shift back to gold and it scurries up the wall of the well. Digging its sharp claws into the cracks and crevices, it hauls itself to the top. Kye and Cora move out of the way, giving the Masiren room to swing over and launch itself into a free life.

Kye hurries and starts tearing at the rope, heaving me up with powerful pulls. "You good?" Kye asks the moment my head crests over the well's opening.

"Yes," I breathe out. I slide my foot over to the edge and let Kye lift me back over. "It didn't hurt me." My mind spins, thinking about how that could have gone so differently.

"I heard it hiss something," Kye says with curiosity.

I nod as we race back to the side of the wall, getting out of view from the windows.

I wipe the beads of sweat lining my forehead with the back of my palm. "The Masiren told me to find Shade."

"Who?" Cora asks, confusion painting her face.

"I'll explain on the way," I say quickly, knowing we need to get out of here.

"Alright then, shall we start this adventure?" Kye asks.

All three of us share looks of determination before voices are heard nearby. We exchange nods of understanding before we quickly head off into the night. I know my father will spit hellfire into the sky the moment he finds out I've left, but let him fume. I'll get the Stone and make him wish he never laid a hand on me.

A twinge of sorrow tugs deep, thinking of leaving Aiden behind and in the dark. I left the shell behind, too, leaving it to rest on top of my pillow for him to find. But I have a gut feeling he would never understand these plans if I shared them with him. He'd never let me do this, and I *need* to do this. He may think I'm running from him and our wedding, and maybe a part of me is...if only to buy myself time. At least, that's what I keep telling myself. But that's not *why* I'm doing this. My father is an evil person and only someone who knows how his mind works can play against the pawns he's put into place.

I push off the ground and pump my legs as we run towards the front of the palace, and then to the border of woods beyond, never looking back.

CHAPTER THIRTY-THREE

Emma

*W*e walk down the street that leads past a tavern, once again full of laughter and music that drifts out into the night. We figured this would be a good place to start listening for any news on Corrupted sightings or Shade himself. Unfortunately, I don't have any coin on me. While being confined to the palace, I haven't been able to earn, or been given, any money, for there is no use.

Until now. I internally sigh as I realize I should have taken something from my room to barter off.

The smell of booze and roasted meat floats through the air as we keep walking and my stomach immediately growls. The seasoning of the food swirls around me, causing my stomach to rumble a second time. I slap a hand over it to shut it up, but it only growls louder.

Kye twists his head and raises a quizzical brow, but he's biting back a smile. "Something the matter, Princess?"

"I'm hungry," I say, and he chuckles knowingly. Cora covers her mouth as a laugh racks through her and I can't help but join in. "I was hoping if we go to the tavern, we might catch some information that could lead us to Shade. The problem is, we can't just go into a tavern and stand there like outcasts, and I don't have any money."

He slows his steps to nudge me with his elbow. "Good thing I brought plenty." He winks. "Plus, if you don't get fed, you might start nibbling on Cora over here." He jerks his head towards her.

Cora splutters. "Wha–what?! Emma would *never* do that to me. If anyone, it would be you, with all that extra meat on your bones." She snickers to herself, and I shake my head at their bickering.

My chest expands with relief that he's willing to use his coin to buy dinner and seeing the two of them going back and forth brings a sense of normalcy.

We step through the doors. A few couples are dancing in the middle of the room, their boots tapping against the scraped floor splashed with booze. Males and females clink their mugs, booze flowing over the rim. The three of us walk in and sit at an open table, as a few looks are cast in our direction, but not towards me or Cora… They're looking at Kye. I don't blame them, he's a beast of a guy, intimidating, and his presence is like a magnet.

Slurred words are tossed back and forth between the group of males at the table behind us as I glance over and notice the mound of empty mugs before them.

I lean over the table on my elbows. "Ears open for anything on Shade. That will be our ticket out," I whisper.

Kye nods but looks apprehensive. "It might not be so simple to find someone who doesn't want to be found." He stares down at me, clearly questioning the Masiren's words.

"It's the plan, big guy," Cora cuts in, goading him to see if he'll try and say otherwise.

I nod in agreement. "I have a gut feeling to trust the Masiren. I *felt* the truth of its words." I hold my hand over my heart, where I felt the spark of warmth. "Think about it. Shade is no one and someone all at once. We need a discreet way to leave without my father's notice, and I think he would be the best way for us to do that."

Kye stares at me for a moment, clearly thinking everything through. I know he could probably get us out of here, but we would be seen. Unlike Shade, who could probably shadow us. "Alright then," he sighs. "Let's eat first."

A huge smile breaks across my face, as he lets go of whatever objection was hanging on the tip of his tongue.

A girl approaches us. She's wearing a stained apron wrapped around a pale blue dress that falls to her shins. Brown boots are laced up her ankles and her hair is in a beautifully messy bun. "What can I get ya?" she asks, tapping her pencil against her notepad as she waits for us to give her our order.

"We will all have the roasted chicken and vegetables," Kye tells her, doing a quick order for us all. I watch in fascination as the server physically shivers when he speaks, like his voice detonated a flare of sparks through her.

She looks at him and a rosy tint fills her cheeks before she smirks appreciatively at him. Taking in the way his training leathers accentuate every bulge of muscle, his thick neck, and his hair that he hasn't tossed into a bun. It falls over his shoulders in a masculine and unruly way.

She clears her throat, completely ignoring us as she keeps her entranced gaze on him. "Alrighty, and anything to drink?" she purrs as she peers up at Kye from under her lashes.

He looks at us and squints before ordering us each a mug of beer. *Gross.* I could go for some wine, but any kind of alcohol will do. Just something to take the edge off of what we're about to do and the nerves I feel that we might get caught before we even begin.

"Sure thing," she says flirtatiously. With a slight wink, she saunters off and I have to bite my lip to hide the amusement bubbling up my throat.

Kye's head jerks to me and Cora, narrowing his eyes as he sees our faces turning red from the force of keeping our laughs buried deep inside.

"For God's sake," he rolls his eyes. "Let it out now, or you will both keel over before we even eat."

We cover our mouths with a hard press to muffle the sound of us bellowing over to the point of tears. This lady was so clearly enthralled by him, and Kye just ignored her attempts.

Once our laughter dies off, we all relax in our seats as we wait for the food to come. Our ears remain alert as we listen in on conversations in hopes of picking up some useful information.

Not much later, our food is brought out and the steaming pile of meat and vegetables makes saliva pool in my mouth. The smell of garlic causes me to lick my lips.

"Mmm, this is so good," Cora groans in delight, chewing a mouthful of roasted herb chicken. I take a swig of beer, the foam settles on top, and the bitter flavor bursts against my tastebuds. It's not the sweet wine I love, but it's enough to wash the food down and numb my nerves.

We keep quiet, eating and focusing on every word that falls from the mouths around us, until one catches my attention.

"Yeah, there was a Corrupted sightin' not too long ago, down by the south side of town. Heard them people got away when that Shade guy stepped in."

An older male sitting at the table behind us spoke, spilling the gossip to his friends. Kye leans back to make himself known as he butts in on their conversation. "Happen to know a more specific location to where the Corrupted was sighted?"

The male hesitates, eyeing Kye with his glazed-over eyes. His lips purse as he contemplates sharing the knowledge he knows. I lean over to speak. "It would be greatly appreciated," I say in a voice that's sweeter than honey.

No one recognizes me as their princess, but they still see me as a female with a pretty face.

He contemplates us, but then narrows his eyes. "Not unless I have a promise, pretty girl. No way am I having this come back to bite me in the arse after telling the lot of you, who look like you're up to no good."

I want to roll my eyes. A Fae promise is unbreakable. When one spills their blood, it binds them to the promise they state. I swipe the jagged dinner knife off the table before Kye can interject. I'm the reason they're here, so this should be up to me. Even though I know Kye will be pissed I didn't let him do it.

So, before he can intervene, I slide the sharp edge across my palm, letting my blood pool at the opening. "I promise we won't tell a soul you told us the Corrupted's location."

He squints his eyes and slices a small cut on his own palm, holding it out to me as he latches our hands together and shakes.

The booze-filled Fae looks pleased and maybe even a little impressed. With a nod and a quick wipe of his palm on his shirt, he reluctantly gives us the information we need.

"A few blocks down, behind the theater," he says so quickly I almost didn't catch it, but Kye would have if I didn't. "Heard there were a couple of 'em. Don't know if they're still there, but they said they were hangin' around there. No attacks yet, but if you go chasin' them down, then there just might be another death added to the toll tonight." He shrugs like it makes no difference to him and gives me an insouciant look. How very pleasant of him to say I might die tonight. However, I'm not scared to knock on death's door.

"I'll keep that in mind," I tell him, as I share quick glances with Cora and Kye.

We need to leave.

The theater.

I have no clue where that is, but I know Cora and Kye do. So we say our thanks, shovel the rest of our food down, and grab our glasses to drain the last dregs of golden liquid in them. It fizzes down my throat before settling in my stomach. My lips feel slightly numb from the mug of beer in my system, but I welcome it.

The throbbing in my hand starts to burn as evidence of my weakness. I stare at my hand that's leaking a deep ruby red and wrap my cloak around my palm before we head back out into the cool night air.

CHAPTER THIRTY-FOUR

Shade

There have been more Corrupted sightings than usual tonight. They are multiplying faster than they can be killed.

I'm crouching around the side of a brick building of the theater in the Court of Asov. For some reason, this court seems to be more flooded with Corrupted than any other. The cool, salty breeze drifts through the night air as I peer around the corner of the building. Two Corrupted are walking down the pathway, oblivious that their worst nightmare is lurking right behind them.

Waiting.

I take a moment to watch them and study their movements while they remain unaware. They aren't hurrying anywhere, almost like they're taking a casual stroll through town, but I know better. They're fast, murderous, and go straight for the kill. They can't help it. They have a need to spill blood.

Unfortunately for them, it's *their* venomous blood that will be spilled.

I wrap my fingers around the hilt of my sword, letting it silently slide free from its sheath. I bring it in front of me, about to make my first move to sneak up behind them, when they pause.

They lift their heads up with an unrestrained twitch, sniffing the air. A shriek erupts out of one, its spine bending back with the force of its scream, raging up to the sky.

They don't notice me, though, not as I cling to the shadows keeping me hidden, concealing their threat. As I begin to push my feet off the ground and make a run at them, they take off. I don't allow myself a second to be shocked by their change in behavior; I just chase after them. A hunter trailing its prey.

The streets around are mostly empty, aside from a few people wandering back to their homes. Until they start sprinting away at the sight of the vile monsters tearing through their town.

To my surprise, these Corrupted never look twice at the stragglers heading home… They're focused. Something has them possessed, enough to pull their focus to one target. It's like they are being drawn to something, acting like children being called back home by their mother, and maybe that something is the reason behind their existence.

As much as I want to pick up speed and drive my sword through their blackened hearts, I hold back. Curiosity has gotten the best of me, and I need to find out what has them in such a frenzy.

I trail them for a couple of blocks before another shriek steals the silence. A group of Fae around the corner slam their feet to a halt at the sight of the Corrupted. Two females and a male. I internally pray for them to fucking run. But they don't.

The Corrupted suddenly come to a stop, staring at them before they release another shriek. Only this time, it sounds like one of satisfaction, as if they've found what they were looking for.

I keep myself pressed into my shadows, waiting for the moment to attack before anyone gets hurt.

The male throws his arm out in front of the two females as the Corrupted slightly crouch, readying their stance to launch at them.

I see a whip of a blue jolt from his palms as he grabs his sword and holds it out in front of him. He shoots a blast of cobalt power towards the Corrupted, throwing them back as he uses that moment to dart towards them. *Strength*. This male has the power of strength as his blasts hold a weight to them.

The females behind him stay put as they keep into the shadows. They watch as he slams his fist into the one Corrupted's face before bringing his sword high in preparation to aim for its heart.

I notice the other Corrupted sneaking up from behind, claws and teeth out as it inches closer.

The one female must notice it the same moment I do, as she pumps her legs faster than the wind, while simultaneously drawing a dagger from under her cloak. The hood that masked her face flies back with her speed, and I stare in disbelief.

It's her.

I will never forget that brown hair or the storm that swirls in her eyes.

The Corrupted she's after stops its movements from attacking the male as he drives his sword in the other. It whips around and smells the air again, changing direction to charge straight for her.

She doesn't stop, never missing a beat as she closes the gap between them, raising her dagger. It's then that I notice the crimson liquid seeping from her hand, spilling against the hilt of her dagger.

Her blood. Is that what's consuming their focus and driving them mad?

Like a hunter's mark.

While she seems plenty capable fighting the Corrupted on her own, I can't continue to sit back and watch. I dive out into the glow of the night and throw my sword with forceful precision, and it soars through the air and strikes right into the Corrupted's heart. I watch its body jerk forward as the blade pierces through its back, causing it to lose its balance and fall to the ground.

The view opens up when it drops, a clear line of sight to the savage little female wielding a dagger. Her eyes are wide with confusion as she stares down at the body that's crumpling on the cobblestone road at her feet. Her eyebrows furrow as black blood pools around the body, but then her eyes catch on the sword going clean through it.

I see the fury storming through her, right before her eyes pierce into me, promising my demise. I smirk as I casually walk up to the lifeless body in front of her. I pull the sword back out, hearing it grate along bone before the entire body turns to ash.

"*You*," she seethes. "I *had* him. He was *mine* to kill."

I watch as the clouds darken in her eyes, building up to the hurricane she's about to unleash on me. But I seem to be drawn to the danger of her tempest.

"You don't seem happy to see me, little demon."

The rising anger coursing through her seems to draw back, calming the blood boiling in her veins. "Trust me, I'm not. That's the second time you've stolen my kill." She sighs, turning to look at the male who kills the other Corrupted as I watch her struggle to rein in every word, wanting to lash out on me. Taking deep breaths of resignation, her eyes are back on me. "But believe it or not, I was looking for you."

Her suppressed annoyance is amusing. She should be thankful for what I did. Most people would be, but she's not like *anyone* I've met before. She's standing here pissed that I intervened and helped. Curiosity stirs in me. Why was she looking for me? That question is now taking over any other thought.

"Need me to enlighten you some more on what's happening, while you stay living in a hole?" I can't help but want to get a rise out of her. I like when she keeps her eyes focused on me, unwavering.

"Need me to make you bleed again with my dagger?" she snipes back, but the thought of her doing just that makes my cock swell.

Her eyes are thundering with an impending storm as she stares at me. The harshness in her gaze makes me feel like she can see right through my shadows, even though I know she can't.

"I should probably mention violence turns me on," I say, watching her face turn red with restrained irritation.

She clears her throat. "We need your assistance." Waving her hand around her to remind me we are not alone. Both the male and the other female join her. I can't help but take in the brute who's now standing next to her, his eyes never leaving me. My shadows are drawn tight, not even a sliver of light can break through the darkness cloaking my face.

I bring my gloved hands up and wipe them along the blade, cleaning off any remnants of the Corrupted's foul blood from it. "Ahh, so you need my help. But it seems you don't like when I help you."

Her lips draw into a tight line, seeming to fight off a retort that's begging to burst free. "For this, I do. But I think it would help you as well."

That piques my interest. How could she possibly help me? "Care to clarify on that, little demon?"

Her eyes narrow and I know it's because the nickname I gave her burrows under her skin. "King Oren is plotting against Deyadrum. I believe if we work together, we can stop him and the Corrupted."

I know King Oren is a devious male who pretends to be the ruler everyone loves, but there's something rotten in him. Yet, why should I care about him? It's the Corrupted and the people of Deyadrum I'm concerned about.

"Look, I don't have time to play games, so get to the point," I growl. I'm not known for having patience, let alone associating with anyone. But this girl seems to be going against everything I say I am.

She looks around before noting it's just the four of us out here, not another soul in sight. "We need to find the Liminal Stone."

I rack my mind for information on this stone she's talking about, but from what I recall…it's only a myth. But maybe I'm wrong, and if that's the case, I need to see what this little demon knows. But staying near her is dangerous. She makes my cock twitch. For some reason, this feisty female might just snare me in her trap.

CHAPTER THIRTY-FIVE

Emma

"There's no poof the Stone exists. It's only a myth," he says as he sheathes his sword.

"Oh, but you're wrong." I laugh a little bit wickedly, if only to put this mysterious male in his place. "It does, according to a Seer, and King Oren already has soldiers searching for it. But we need to get to it first."

The hood of his cloak twists, and I assume he's taking in Cora and Kye. "Who are they?"

Kye takes a step forward. "I've heard about you, the one who lives in the shadows and leaves behind piles of ash in his wake. Much respect for what you've been trying to do, but this is bigger than that. This will either save Deyadrum or destroy it. It's just a matter of whose hands the Stone falls into," Kye says with a fierceness that settles deep in my soul. True loyalty shines there, and I can't help the grateful look I send his way.

"I'm Cora, by the way, and that mass of muscle is Kye. Can you help us or not? Because we really are in a rush to get off this island," Cora says bluntly. I realize she's right. My father or Aiden will figure out soon enough that I'm not in my room and a search party will be sent out. Plus, we need that Stone before it gets into his ruthless hands.

Shade is silent, assessing.

"A rush?" he questions, clearly not registering the tinge of urgency in her voice. Unless he's just that much of an ass and doesn't care. I'm betting on the latter.

I get into his space, breathing in his maddening aroma that I can't decipher. His shadows must mask his true scent, as those black tendrils of power swarm around me. Steeling my nerves as I stare deep into the endless pit of darkness under his hood. "Yes. A rush. Now, will you help us or not?"

I remain rooted in front of him, not backing down as I can *feel* the heat of his stare. "Why should I trust you?" he hedges.

A smirk sneaks over my lips. "You shouldn't. Just like I don't trust *you*. But I think we both don't want to face the outcome of what will happen to the people of Deyadrum if we neglect to get the Stone before King Oren."

He leans in, brushing the edge of his cloak's hood along the side of my face, as his warm breath feathers against my skin. "And what's in it for you?"

I don't hesitate giving him the most honest answer that pours from my heart. "Freedom."

His shadows dance around me, singing against my body. In the next breath, a surge of his shadows swarm around the two of us, cloaking us completely and wrapping us in our own shield of darkness.

"Emma!" I hear Kye yell as I'm blended into the night. Concern laces his voice as I disappear from sight.

"I'm fine! Promise. Please, stay back for a moment," I reply, hoping Kye hears the plea that's delicately dripping in my words.

I need to know what Shade will say, what he will do. I don't want to cower or ruin this chance for him to help. The Masiren told me to find him. There has to be a reason, which means at this moment, I'm at his mercy.

His head is still dipped close to my ear, his body so close to mine. "*Emma*," he repeats, testing my name on his tongue.

I realize I never gave him my name and the sound of it falling from his lips sends a rapid bolt of heat down my spine. I stand frozen, waiting for him to speak again.

"I'll help, but on one condition." The deep timbre of his voice calls to me, pulling on every nerve ending in my body.

"What's your condition?" I ask, doing my best to keep my voice strong, but I can feel my breaths picking up speed at his nearness. Stealing all the air between us, turning shallow while his shadows continue to curl around our bodies.

"Say you need me," he whispers.

My mind stutters, preventing any words from falling from my mouth as I gape at him. This ridiculous *asshole*! He's using a power game, a way to make me beg, in his own twisted way.

"That's insane! Why would I sa—"

He cuts me off as I feel his shadows pulling in tighter against us, threatening to force me all the way against him. "Say you fucking *need* me," he growls roughly.

I can't see his eyes, but I stare deeply into the dark void swirling in his hood, his words unlocking a deep hunger inside me. The fight in me suddenly vanishes, and only a desperate need to please takes over. But I tell myself it's because we *do* need his help to take on this journey and get out of this court.

"I need you," I tell him breathlessly. Giving in to his demand makes my conscious want to scream at me. But his command doesn't feel cruel; it feels seductive, with promises wrapped in unrestrained desires.

"Good girl," he praises. "That wasn't so hard, now, was it?"

The pleasure that overtakes me at his praise for doing what he asked grabs hold of me, but before I can relish in it, the shadows surrounding us disappear. The cool air rushes in, dousing every bit of heat that was stirring deep within me.

Kye and Cora are at my side a second later. "Everything okay?" they ask in unison, with worried voices.

"Yes," I turn to reassure them. "He's going to help," I inform them as I turn my eyes back to Shade. He's standing a few feet away, purging all the air from my lungs at the sight of him.

"Finally," Cora drags the word out to make a dramatic show. "Can we get the hell out of here, now that you're done showing off your shadow magic tricks?"

A bubble of laughter skirts up my throat, but I hold it back. I knock my elbow into her side, letting her know her lighthearted comment didn't go unnoticed.

I bring my full attention to Shade once the silence settles around us all. "So, Shade, have any ideas on how to get us off this island?"

A huff leaves him, as if I shouldn't even dare ask him such a question. "Follow me, but you need to explain everything you know. And I need to make a stop somewhere first."

I start to object, but decide to let it go. He's willing to help, and surely one stop won't hurt.

Before I can take a step, I hear a voice echo around the buildings, my head snapping to the side at the sound. Panic flares to life in my chest, terrified it could be one of my father's guards. My breathing becomes shallow as I listen for the sound again, anticipating one of his guards to appear from around the corner.

Shade clears his throat, bringing my attention back to him. I can *feel* him looking straight into my eyes, skeptically, probably noting my distress.

Without warning, he turns and takes off, absorbing his shadows, except for those around his face, allowing us to see his silhouette under the moonlit sky as we trail after him.

We follow Shade through the dead of night, silently drifting under the blanket of stars that shine around the pale crescent moon. He reminds me of a knight in chess, powerful and dangerous. One of the trickiest pieces to move, and the one most often overlooked. It blends into the board, waiting to strike, before bounding over another, holding them hostage until it makes another move. The Masiren knew I needed another piece in the game, one that purposefully stays under the radar, and one that will help me jump two steps ahead.

I discreetly fill him in on the location of the only two Elders who would know of the Stone and its potential location. I explain where we need to go first to start this journey and inform him of what King Oren plans to do if the Liminal Stone reaches his hands.

Shade doesn't offer much of a response, only what sounds like an angry grunt, but I let it go. He heard me all the same. He guides us to the southwest side, where there are a few ships tied to an old, crooked dock. He holds a hand up to halt us before slipping into his shadows, disappearing a second later and running towards the dock.

The three of us stand back and wait while he scopes it out. A part of me is wary he will leave us behind, that this is a trap to alert the king. But minutes later, he returns, wrapping the tendrils of his shadows around us all as he leads us to the ship.

"This is one of King Oren's ships," Kye states, noticing the wave symbol within a circle that is marked on the wooden boards of the ship.

"That's correct," Shade states with boredom.

"We can't just steal one of his ships!" I whisper in a hiss. He deserves to have one go missing, but I can't help the instant thoughts of how his docile daughter would behave. Immediately going back to thoughts of what will happen to me if I disobey.

"We aren't stealing anything, we're borrowing it," Shade says simply.

My heart picks up speed to a rapid beat. "Which court are we traveling to first? We can't delay any longer."

"*Patience*, little demon. I told you I have to stop somewhere, but either way, it will get you away from this court." His arms cross over his chest, waiting for me to talk back to him.

I narrow my eyes instead as he starts boarding the ship, jumping down onto the deck. Cora and Kye follow behind me, but she comes up to my side and leans in. "Just tell me when we can rip the shadows from him and shove them up his ass."

A laugh bursts out of me, such a contrast to the hushed stillness of the water and air around us. Kye raises an eyebrow at us both and I laugh even more, unable to stop visualizing us doing just that to Shade. But for some reason, my mind ventures to wanting to take his shadows and have them wrap around me, letting them do his bidding while I obey.

I immediately block out the intrusive thoughts, shaking my head to help clear it from drifting to a faceless asshole.

"How are we going to sail the ship without a full crew?" I ask. Only having been on a ship for the first time recently, I'm clueless when it comes to how to work one.

"I've got it handled," he says as whips of shadows take hold of the rope to untie it from the dock's post. "And I'm sure Kye here wouldn't mind lending a hand," he tosses in.

Kye's eyes watch Shade's shadows work, doing the tasks of multiple crew members at once. "Yeah, it seems we'll be good. You and Cora should go get some rest. It's going to be a long trip."

I see the meaning of his words, another way of saying they don't need us to help, which I'm totally fine with. I don't know a damn thing about sailing ships, and it would be nice to have some time to come up with more of a plan.

Cora and I let the guys do what needs to be done to get us out to sea. We start towards the far end of the ship and both gasp when a brush of shadows encases us completely. Veiling over the entire ship, now invisible in the night. We both take a calming breath because, for this moment, we can't be found. We continue on, walking away from where the guys are keeping busy.

"Give me your hand," she says, sorrow coating her words at my lack of natural healing shining through.

I place my palm in hers and she presses her hands on both sides of mine, closing her eyes as she takes a steady breath in. A soft glow cascades from her palms, sending a wave of tingling warmth into my wound, healing it completely.

She releases her hold, and I raise my hand in front of my face. "As good as new," I say cheerfully. "Thank you, Cor."

She waves me off with a swipe of her hand. "Don't thank me. Just feed me sweets and tell me I'm pretty." She gives me her bright smile and innocent doe eyes.

"You're ridiculous." I laugh. "How's your training going?"

Cora offers a genuine smile, loving to learn as much as she can. The more intricate the healing technique is, the more excited she gets to master it. "Really well. That trip your father sent me on was to the wintry Court of Amihan. While I was there, a child fell from the ridge of a mountain. He was too young for his body to heal fast enough." She turns her head to look at me. "His spine was broken." Her brows furrow in sorrow. "The focus for healing a spine is extremely difficult, but I managed to fix him, Em." Glee shines in her eyes, a slight sheen coating them. "That kid was running around like normal by the end of the week."

I rest my palm on top of her hand. "It's because you're amazing at it. That boy is lucky you were there."

She nods solemnly. "Another healer would have helped him, but that would have taken time to take the boy to them. I just happened to be walking towards the village. Right place, right time," she says, shrugging her shoulders.

"Fate," I tell her, smiling. "Will your parents be upset that you're traveling again when you were just across the sea?" I ask, feeling guilty for being the reason why she's been away from them.

"Nah. They love me, and they'll miss me. But distance makes the heart stronger, or whatever they say." She laughs. "I'll just steal one of Telion's cakes and give it to them when I see them next."

My chest shakes at how Telion would react to a whole cake missing, and it's a sight I wouldn't want to miss. "Count me in on the next dessert hijacking."

"Deal," Cora cheers with mischievous enthusiasm.

We both settle into an easy silence and lay down on the cool wooden boards of the ship's deck, resting our arms behind our heads for cushioning. The ship sways back and forth, luring us into a somnolent daze.

"You sure you're up for this?" Cora asks as we get more comfortable laying side by side.

"I have to be."

In my periphery, I see her nod in understanding.

I lose track of how much time passes as Cora and I let the tranquil night engulf us. We are enjoying every moment, not knowing when we will get another peaceful night like this. The undulation of the waves moves the ship beneath us as we continue to coast along the sea. We stay lying on the deck, gazing at the diamond-studded sky, the stars hanging onto our every word. They shine down on us, hoping to hear any of our whispered hopes and dreams. But they'll be disappointed. There are no hopes or dreams for someone whose soul is already tarnished and shattered in every way. It's irreparable, meant to stay broken until the wind sweeps every last piece of it away.

I eventually hear Cora's deep breathing as her body falls into a peaceful sleep. A smile graces my lips at seeing her so relaxed, with no creases of worry lining her face.

I turn my head back to look up at the endless sky, relishing in the feeling of the cool, salty breeze lightly brushing across my face. The waves lapping against the ship splash every so often. My eyelids start to feel heavy as I let them fall closed and listen to the soft rhythm of my heart.

"You sure you trust me enough to fall asleep?" Shade's deep voice startles me and makes my body jump before I even have a chance to let my dreams take me away.

I calm my nerves as I peek one eye open and see him standing above me, his shadows still clouding his face. I quickly peer over at Cora, hearing a slight snore escape her. Such a deep sleeper.

"I could kill you," he says quietly.

"You won't," I tell him, spitting his words from the first night we met back at him.

"We should reach the shore at sunrise," he informs me, the hood of his cloak now turned to look out at sea.

"Good to know." I pause. "Thank you," I force out a faint appreciation for his help. "Where's Kye?"

His head whips back in my direction, arms crossing in front of his chest. "He's at the helm."

Confusion takes over my features as I scrunch my face. "What the hell is that?"

His hood moves back and forth, making it clear he's shaking his head like the asshole he is. "The large fucking wheel that steers the ship," he huffs with annoyance. "Seems you are oblivious to everything, not just the Corruption, little demon."

I quickly make a mental note of what the helm of a ship is for future reference.

"I may have been once upon a time, but now I'm trying to do something about it, asshole," I blurt with barely reined-in aggression.

"Do you expect me to throw rose petals at your feet?" The sarcastic tone of his voice is edged with bitterness.

"You're infuriating," I mumble, slowly growing more tired as I feel the energy in me draining. I let the silence fall around us, hoping my tone is clear in wanting this conversation to be over. For him to go back to the other side of the ship and let me lay here in peace.

Maybe I do have a wish for the stars to hear, for him to leave me the hell alone.

It's quiet for a moment, but his voice turns curious when he speaks, as if something within him has settled. "You said you want freedom?"

I sigh. Clearly, the stars don't give a shit about my wishes. "That's what I said."

"Freedom from what?"

The initial urge to spit spiteful words at him surges forth, wanting to brush off his question. The need to defy and push against him is so close, but I don't. I keep my eyes locked on the stars, and it's like they're whispering for me to let go of the hate in this moment. That whatever I say under the veil of night, without anyone but us knowing, will bring me solace. To voice the heavy words that anchor my soul down, weighing it to the point of exhaustion.

I close my eyes as I push all witty retorts down my throat. "This life."

Two words.

Spoken in one breath.

Whether it's freedom from parts of my life or life itself and wanting to finally let my soul be set free, he will never know. I don't clarify, but for some reason, I have a distant feeling that I don't need to.

I shut my eyes as I let him absorb my words, but I can feel the heat of his stare warming my skin. A peaceful moment for my words to be set free, soaring through the midnight sky along the salty sea air, wishing that was me.

Another beat passes before his alluring voice cuts through the silent night. "Is he your lover?"

I falter before I jerk my body up to sit ramrod straight, staring at him with a stunned expression. This male is going to give me whiplash of the most severe kind. The bluntness of his words throws me off guard, and I think that's what he was hoping for. Another way to dig his nails under my skin.

"Who?" I ask as all train of thought about what we were talking about escapes me.

"Kye," he says with a slight tinge of uncertainty.

"No. He's just a very close friend who I *trust*," I say quickly, hoping to extinguish the assumption he was igniting right away.

"Do you have a lover?"

I narrow my eyes in a glare, trying to figure out where he's going with this. Prying into my personal life when we barely know each other, the nosy bastard. Maybe I should question him and ask if he's able to find any lovers as a faceless male.

"It's complicated," I say, shooting up from my spot to stand, not wanting to disturb Cora and to put some distance between me and the one wielding shadows before me.

I move on silent feet as I pad down the ship's edge, making my way to the shrouds that stretch high to the crow's nest. I feel his presence lurking behind me, clearly not done with the conversation like I am. I leap up and grab hold of the rope and start my climb to the top. The rope scratches against my palms as I force my muscles to pull my weight up. When I finally reach the top, I swing my leg over the curved edge of the open space and land inside the lookout.

Not even a full breath later and Shade is in the crow's nest with me, making the already small space smaller.

"That's not an answer," he growls.

"It's answer enough," I spit back. He's trying to dig into my personal life—into my world—when he can't even face his own. Hiding in his shadows and being invisible to *everyone*.

274

I can feel his shadows winding in a sensual dance around us. Barri-
cading us in as it wraps around the edge of the crow's nest, they only leave
an opening to see the half moon wide awake in the sky above. My pulse
accelerates, because it's also a way to keep me in.

His gloved hand snakes out and snatches my hand, flipping it over to
look at my palm. The smooth touch of his leather-covered thumb rubs
along the inside, taking note of the smear of blood left behind when Cora
healed me. I stare at the motion, wishing I could see his face to figure out
what he's thinking.

I feel his thumb pause before his voice cuts through the dark. "You're
not mated." I stare at my hand as a heart-wrenching throb pounds in my
chest from the thought of having a mate.

"Not in this life," I tell him. Honesty seeps from me as I share a small
part of myself. As much as I desperately want a mate, I'm not going to
keep holding my breath.

The heat pouring off him surrounds me, a welcoming warmth to the
cool sea air. His hand drops mine as he brings it up in a fast motion, grabbing my jaw and forcing my eyes to look into his vortex of never-ending
darkness. "What do you want in this life?" His voice is deep but hushed,
like a velvety caress.

My brows furrow as I contemplate his words. Questioning why he
cares. Wondering why this male, who speaks to no one, who hides into the
night, is asking me such a thing. Irritation spikes through me at him trying
to dig into my head. I jerk my chin, hoping to knock his hand free of my
jaw. But his grip is strong, and my attempts are useless.

"Let go," I seethe, giving a final effort to shake off his hold. He refuses,
and I start to realize he won't relent. A breath whooshes out of me,
suddenly becoming tired of...*everything*. "What I want in this life doesn't
matter. I've been dancing along the edge of death's tune for a while now."

He's quiet for a moment. "You should never have to dance to death's
song alone, little demon." The seriousness in his voice tugs something
deep inside me. The part of me that craves companionship and has never
known how it feels to have a true family that would burn the world
for you.

My soul-searching eyes dive deep into the dark sea of his hood, wanting to part through the waves and see the true treasure hidden inside. This irritating vigilante before me just repaired a broken piece of my fractured soul with one line.

The hand on my jaw begins to feel welcoming, demanding me to listen to his words as I become greedy in wanting to hear them. His shadows loosen as they shift slightly, allowing a breeze to blow through. I watch in fascination as the shadows in his hood spiral, but the denseness seems to lighten.

The stream of wind drifts past him and gently glides along my face, bringing his scent with it. No longer masked it behind his power. A *stronger* scent that drifts to me as he releases some of his shadows from himself.

I freeze. Every muscle in my body tenses as my mouth parts in uncertainty.

This can't be. I *have* to be wrong.

But his scent…it's familiar.

"*You,*" I sneer, venom dripping from my voice.

CHAPTER THIRTY-SIX

Emma

I watch with raging fascination as the swirls of black begin to recede even more. His gloved hand offers one final touch along my jaw before it vanishes, falling to his side.

I spring my dagger free without a moment's hesitation and lift it to his neck before he can register my movements. Pushing my hand into the warmth of his hood, I watch the fragments of his fading dark abyss swallow it whole. But I feel the softness of his flesh brush my fingers and his pounding pulse beat against the steel blade. I hold it there, challenging him.

Knowing.

Waiting.

The darkness within his cloak thins further, dwindling away as two piercing eyes look straight into the very essence of me.

Daring me.

I press the sharpened edge harder into his throat, as more wind brings the scent of cedar and maple from his body. The maddening smell makes sense now as it wraps around me with sinful promises, while two ice-blue eyes peer through the remaining shadows, glowing in the moonlight.

The Dark Prince.

I was expecting a smirk when the shadows clear away, but instead, all I find is Prince Draven looking deep into my being. Staring hard without blinking, not even a flinch at the weapon ready to slide along his jugular.

"Why?" I seethe. My nostrils flare at the truth standing before me.

"Because somebody has to do something more than just schedule gatherings that end in zero action," he says in a growl laced with such determination that it's overwhelming. He means it. Speaking straight from the depths of his soul. I can't blame him for it, but I understand even more why he despises my lack of knowledge.

I was worse than the rulers. The ones who claim to be doing what's best for Deyadrum but have no solutions.

"Why hide who you are?" I don't move my dagger, keeping it pressed snugly against his skin.

"Like how you hide who you are?" he questions back. I feel the anger boiling up inside me.

"I have my reasons," I state plainly, not wanting to share any more than that.

"And I have mine," he chides back.

I narrow my eyes at him, trying to block out the heady smell of him that twists around me with force, now that his barricade of shadows is gone. My body wants to melt into it. To drown in the waves of him that are crashing against me.

"Your voice sounded different." I narrow my gaze on him.

"My shadows can block out all sound, if I so choose. Same as how it can mask my scent. But I allowed my voice to deepen through it, not hard to change," he states simply, as though pretending to be a different person is completely normal. But I suppose for him it is.

"Why help us?" I ask.

The smirk I know too well from Prince Draven graces his face. "You *begged*, little demon." His words hold the cockiness that makes me want to drive my dagger deeper into his neck. But the name he calls me still stirs something deep down. Anger mixed with satisfaction. "Plus, if what you mentioned about your father is true, then he needs to be stopped."

I ignore his begging comment because I can't deny it. I need his help and his knowledge of the Corrupted. "You don't like my father," I state. I saw the way his eyes darkened when he mentioned him.

"You don't either." His eyes drill into me, challenging my own that I'm sure are full of vengeful storm clouds, raging within. I find truth in his words. So, I keep my mouth shut. There's no need to voice my feelings towards my father. They shine brightly in my eyes, with no way to hide them.

His eyes never waver from mine. "You going to drop your dagger, little demon?" His chest rises and falls in quick breaths. Then, a sharp reminder from earlier snags in my memory. Violence turns him on.

I try to brush aside the thought of him enjoying this. I shouldn't drop my dagger. It's my protection. I should just swipe it in one quick movement along his skin to prove a point. But I hold back. I need him, or else I wouldn't have fallen prey to his begging game. With one final glare, I remove the blade from his throat and sheathe it back in its holster.

"Next time, my blade will take pleasure in spilling your blood." I sneer, promising his death to be at my hands if he turns against us or tries to claim my life first. Only a small huff of amusement falls from his lips, and that spikes my aggravation even more.

I watch him shift his head to the side, catching the glint of his eyebrow piercing shining in the moonlight. "Where are we sailing to first?" I can't help but ask when I want so desperately to find the Elders.

His blue eyes shift to the side to glance at me before returning to the glistening water. "My court, Asiza. I need to discuss something with Fynn, and there's something I need to retrieve."

"Care to share?"

"I'd rather not." Now he throws my own words back at me from the night he questioned me about my necklace. Infuriating. I turn to the sea, hoping it will douse the flames threatening to burst from me.

"Go rest, little demon. Won't be too much longer until we arrive." With that, his shadows blanket him as he leaps over the edge of the crow's nest. I'm left standing alone at the top of the ship, staring out at the water swaying below. I stay there with so many thoughts racing through my mind, not sure how my life has taken such a sudden turn. The waves are soothing to watch, a steady rhythm I can focus on.

I squint my eyes, my heart thumping harder in my chest. Two gold eyes are set on me, peering just above the water's surface. Like twin yellow moons on the horizon. The Masiren. How can it see us when we are shadowed in power?

It floats along with the flow of the water, keeping its gaze locked on mine. I stare back, never faltering. A minute passes before it disappears, diving down into the sea below the ship. It's following me and I'm not sure why. But I'm grateful. The Masiren's presence feels *comforting*. Without its guidance, I wouldn't be miles away from my father, safely making my way across the sea.

CHAPTER THIRTY-SEVEN

Draven

The rest of the evening passes quickly as we sail through the night. Surges of orange and yellow crest along the horizon, the sun rising just as we reach the shore. I have my shadows drawn over me to hide my identity. The only ones who knew from the beginning were my father and Fynn.

Now, this aggressive, petite female is one of the few who knows the person that dwells under the mask of night.

I never planned to expose who I am, but I saw it in her eyes. The knowing glint of realization as it washed over her; and for some reason, I wanted to reveal myself at that moment. I felt the need to let her in on one of my secrets, no matter how frustrating this savage princess is.

Her feistiness sends heat licking down my spine and strains the ache in my cock whenever she gets mouthy with me. The stubbornness that challenges me. Those lips I'm finding harder to resist, to taste.

I never meant to go find her on the ship. I had made a point to keep my distance, but her scent was driving me mad. I told myself that if I just got close enough to her and inhaled as much of her sweet rose and honey scent as I could, then it would hold me over and satiate the craving that is turning all-consuming.

But I messed up. Because now, not only did she learn who I really am, but her scent has turned into a drug. One strong hit is not enough, and I'm left desperate for more, itching to have her close.

We make our way into the Court of Asiza, staying far from my castle to not draw any suspicious attention. I lead them into town to an inn that is comfortable enough for us to stay at for the night. The inn is built with stones covered in moss, camouflaging into the forest. The arched doorway welcomes us in, and sleek wooden floors cover the space. Chandeliers hang in rows down the arched hallway, lighting the rooms built throughout. The rooms here are cozy, offering plush beds with a wall of floor-to-ceiling glass windows looking out into the pines that stand tall like primal soldiers.

"I'll be back. You guys go get checked in and stay low for the time being. We'll start our travels early tomorrow," I say, leaving them standing just inside the inn as I make my way to find Fynn. I have faith they won't skip town, but if they tried, I'd know.

The forest trees tower over the town and streams of fog slither through the streets. Wooden homes are laid out between the pines, tucked into the growth of the forest. The morning sun casts a few rays of light that splinter through the grey clouds above. I pad down the stone road as I make my way to where Fynn should be. His home is made from deep, rich wood, nestled on top of a hill in the forest and only a few miles from town.

Once I get out of prying eyes, I let my shadows fall away and pull my hood back from my face. Once again, a prince.

I knock when I reach his door, seeing the puffs of smoke rising out of his chimney. I hear the pounding of his heavy footsteps before the door swings open. His face brightens at the sight of me as he pulls me in.

"Hey man! What the hell are you doin' here? I thought I'd just see you at training later, but I guess you couldn't resist all this sexiness, huh?" He waves his hands over his body, gesturing to himself.

I can't do anything but shake my head at him. He's always finding a way to tease me or talk about himself. That's one of the reasons why we're so close, because he doesn't treat me like a prince. We may have grown up together through our training at the castle, but he never walked on eggshells around me. No, instead, he would pull pranks on me, be my wingman, and never held back on anything he wanted to say.

He must have just gotten out of the bath, his hair dripping wet as he starts to pull some of it into a bun to get it out of his face. He's wearing a pair of lounge pants and nothing else as he kicks the door shut behind me, tossing his towel onto the back of a chair. His home has always been welcoming to me, with the red hues in the throw rug, and the grey sofa that blends in with the orange glow of the fire.

"You got me," I joke.

"What's with the visit, if not to admire my handsome face?" He raises his eyebrows up and down in a jibing gesture. When I don't react to it, he sighs. "You're no fun."

"She knows," I force out.

He freezes, and his eyes widen before they scrunch in confusion as he scratches his head. "Who knows what?"

"Princess Emma," I sigh. "The demon of a girl, who grates on my every nerve, *knows* that I'm Shade."

His mouth falls open, as both his hands grab onto his hair. "How?! If anyone finds out—"

"I know," I cut him off. "Not only will it put more of a target on my back, but on my family, too."

"Do you think she'll tell?" he asks, concern etching his voice.

I scrub a hand over my jaw and shrug. "I have a hunch she won't, but I'm not confident in that. But, either way, it's working to my advantage." I explain everything Emma told me about the Elders and why the Stone needs to be found. "She may be the link to it all, or secretly running the show. She said she wants to find this Liminal Stone before her father gets it, but what if it's a ruse?"

He taps a finger to his lip in thought. "My grandmother used to tell stories of a Stone so powerful it could change the rule of the world. Her stories always ended with a warning of how dangerous it is. Even though it's considered a myth, she believed it to be real. I feel people say it's a myth because the truth of it's existence is secret and untouched," he says with a shrug. "So, what's your plan?"

I pause, taking a second to consider what I'm thinking. "Keep her close and watch her movements. But if you truly believe the Stone is not a lie, then what's most important is to destroy it. I just need to grab the wyvern weapons." I've spent decades searching Deyadrum for all traces of Wyvern iron to hide away and keep it from falling into the wrong hands.

His face lights up with understanding. "From the caves of Tsisana?"

I nod. "We'll need it if we run into any Scavengers, as it seems that's the only way to kill them."

"We?" His eyebrows raise as he looks at me with amusement.

I shake my head with a small laugh. "Yeah, man. Up for some fun?"

A sly smile creeps over his mouth. "You mean…am I up for some mischief? Then, the answer will always be yes." He runs down the hall and ducks into the room on the left before reappearing with a clean shirt, new pants, and his boots. "What now?"

I sigh, knowing I have to do this next part, no matter how much I don't want to. "We go back to the inn I have them checking in at. Then, I'm going to have to show her friends who I am while we come up with more of a plan. I'll sneak out to Tsisana tonight and be back before we search for the Elders in the morning."

"Shit, okay. What about Emil and your mother?" he asks, while leaning over to shove his boots on.

"I'm going to stop by the castle and let them know I'll be away for a bit."

He stands to his full height with a mischievous glint in his eye. "Want me to tell your mother?" He winks.

I gag at his insinuation. I shove his shoulder in exasperation and can't help the small chuckle that leaves me. "You will go nowhere near my mother, you insufferable bastard."

He doubles over in laughter and braces himself on his knees. "Ahh, I'm just playin' man. That's a line I'd never cross."

I know it, too. Fynn has never lied to me, and my mother has treated him like her own. He just can't help but find ways to rile me up, making this long life a hell of a lot more interesting.

But my heart still cracks for him and I have to ask, "How are you holding up?"

The smile dancing on his face falls away and the pain he buries surfaces. "I'll be okay, man. But I won't lie, it's getting harder to wake up each day as I near the anniversary of her—" He stops. Squeezing his eyes shut, as if trying to push away the well of emotions that I know threaten to drown him.

"The anniversary of her death," I finish for him.

He nods, and when he opens his eyes, my own heart fractures at the sight of my friend. His fated mate died a century ago, when her ship was attacked at sea. He told me the pain he feels from the tear in his bond is excruciating, a part of him missing, and it seems to always be at its worst as he nears the day of her death. It's not impossible for him to love again, it just wouldn't be a love as strong as a mate's.

He told me a decade ago he was ready to open his heart again to someone who would understand and spark joy in his life. For a while, he felt like he was betraying his mate who passed, but he's come to learn that she would want him to truly live, to not let his heart suffer every day.

I pat his back. "I'm here if you want to rage and toss fists in combat. Just let me know what you need."

The agony in his eyes begins to fade, as he quirks a smile. "You'll let me win?"

"You're pushing it." I say on a laugh. A moment of silence falls between us, allowing him to gather his thoughts before I speak. When he stands to his full height and smirks, I know he's good.

I nod my head towards the door. "Ready when you are."

He smiles and grabs his weapons hanging on the wall. A small twinge of nerves bubbles to the surface at sharing my secret with a couple more people. Her two friends, who I barely know. I pray to the Gods they can keep a secret, because if not, my life will be at risk. It will taint my family name and drag my mother and brother down with me.

I make my way to the inn after stopping by the castle. My mother seemed understanding, like she knew I would be visiting her to tell her about the journey. Telling me to travel safely, stay alert, and to make sure I extinguish the flames. But I'm not sure what that last part means. My mind is still trying to make sense of her last request. Emil was not happy and wanted to join, but the unknown of the journey is too dangerous. I told him once he can beat me in our sparring, then he can tag along. But since our father is gone, I have needed to step up more for him. I will never be able to replace him, but my role as his older brother has shifted.

Fynn said he would meet me outside the inn within the hour, and he does. He walks in while I scurry up the side of the building to sneak in another way. If I walk through the door as Prince Draven, then everyone will rush over and the whole town will know of my location before I can blink. And if I walk in as Shade, then everyone will freak out and assume there is a Corrupted nearby. Either way, walking through the front door is a lose-lose situation for me.

The stone feels cool to the touch with a slickness as the moss blankets over them. I'm able to lift myself up a few ledges on the side of the inn before slipping into a window. When I make my way into the hallway, Fynn is already there, leaning against the wall with his arms crossed and one foot propped up behind him.

"You're getting slow," he teases.

"That wasn't a fair challenge," I say, shooting a string of shadows at him to shove him off balance. He curses with a laugh.

"Where to now, shadow man?"

I recede the shadows enough for him to see the narrow gaze I have pinned on him. Then, I take a deep breath in and catch her scent. I get a whiff of her sweet flowery aroma trailing down the hall and immediately start to follow it without a word.

I hear Fynn's footsteps behind me, knowing he won't question my direction. When her scent becomes overwhelming, I can feel my eyes dilate, darkening with a need to claim. But I shake off that unwelcome thought. She's not my mate, or the bond would have snapped into place the first night I saw her in the alleyway.

I pause in front of a wooden door, hearing hushed voices inside. It's them. Without a knock, I slide my shadows through the lock and push it aside, opening the door. Fynn's breath of amusement leaves him at my obtrusiveness.

The moment the door is wide open, three sets of eyes fall on me.

"You know there's a thing called knocking," Emma says, shooting daggers at me with her glare. The rage in her cloudy eyes only fuels me and stokes the desire that's building deep down.

I watch as Cora's eyes leave me and lock on Fynn behind me, widening at the sight. "Hey, what are you—"

She stops talking the moment I absorb every trace of my shadows and let my hidden truth hang heavy in the air.

Cora gasps, and Kye's eyes bulge just slightly at what they're seeing. I focus on Emma, though, her jaw clenching, looking like she wants to bury me alive. But if she does that, she should know that she's going with me.

A shoe comes flying across the room. My hand raises with quick reflex to snatch it out of the air before it can connect with my face.

"It slipped," Cora says with fake innocence. "Though you would deserve it."

Lies. Just like Emma. No wonder these two are so close. A growl slips up my throat as I throw the shoe on the floor.

"The ladies of Asov are feisty, aren't they?" Fynn muses behind me.

"Come closer and find out," Cora snarks back, opening her mouth before snapping it closed in a strong bite with a wicked smile.

In between their feud, I feel Kye suspiciously looking at me. I can tell questions are brewing in his head.

"You were at the ball," Kye states.

"I was."

"But there was an attack on the other side of the island. Rumor has it that *Shade* was there." A V deepens in his brows; he's trying to connect the events.

"I slipped out during the ball," I say plainly, not understanding where he's going with this.

"It was on the other side of the island, and you got there before any guards could." The skeptical gleam in his eyes drills into me, calculating. He's digging for another secret—one I'm not sharing.

I stare hard at him, not an ounce of concern etching my face. "I'm fast."

He squints, not quite believing me. But before he can say anything more, Emma pipes up to stop the interrogation, "Alright, that's enough. Shade is Draven and Draven is Shade. There is no denying it, the proof is clear as day. Right now, we need to find the Elders, who may have an idea about the Stone's location."

She's right. The more time we waste, the more time King Oren has to get his slimy hands on the Stone first.

"Why don't we split up?" Fynn chimes in, stepping farther into the room. "One group goes to the Court of Amihan and the other goes to the Court of Abhainn. Then, we can send word or meet somewhere to share the information we receive."

"That's not a bad idea," Emma says, focused consideration contorting her features.

"Who would go with who, though?" Cora questions. "The three of us and the two of you?"

For some reason, the thought of being separated from the little demon infuriates me, bringing forth the beast inside that wants to steal her away. The room flickers in darkness for a second as my shadows burst out in a flash before I suck them back in.

"No," I forcefully say. "You, Kye, and Fynn. The little demon is with me."

The turbulent waves roaring in her eyes come crashing down, trying to take me with them and pull me under. But I don't relent. I'd willingly be dragged to the depths of the sea, so long as she's with me. These thoughts are unbidden, and I don't understand where they're coming from. Anger courses through me because of it. I need to be rid of her, but I can't do that until I have the Stone and figure out if she's a part of the Corruption.

The darkness that came from her, the soulless eyes, and the black shooting through her veins is an image that never leaves my head. I can't forget what I saw in her nightmare, making me more curious about what she is with each passing day.

"Like *hell* I'm going with you," she snarls. Standing up, she storms right into my space.

"If I remember correctly, little demon, you're the one who was looking for me." I lean in, speaking quietly enough for only her to hear. "*Begging* me."

I don't miss the slight shiver that trails down her body.

"She's staying with me," Kye announces, standing up to his full height. His burly frame screams strength, which will match well with Fynn's teleporting ability to make warp holes. Plus, it will make things easier for us to meet if they are with him. Fynn can create a fissure in the air, a tunnel to connect from one point to another. He is one of the only Fae who doesn't have to travel by ship. It's a rare power that dates back far into his bloodline.

I weave around Emma, ignoring the flames flickering off her from the fury boiling under her skin, and block her from Kye.

I face him, explaining why that's not going to happen. "Look, from what I can tell, your power is a forcefield of strength. Fynn, here, can travel at the speed of light from different locations. You will clearly need Cora to keep the two of you in line, but you can travel to one of the courts and back at a moment's notice." I hold his gaze to show I'm serious. "This will be the only time it would be smart to divide us so we can hunt down the Elders. Your princess will be safe with me." I place my palm over my heart, showing him I'm true to my word. At least, for now. "I will be able to keep us hidden in my shadows, and have my own means of travel, but only for one extra person. Plus, she asked for my help, and here I am...helping."

The confusion settles on his face as his scar shifts from the way he purses his lips, his brows knitting further together. Always so serious. But then, resignation shines through, knowing Emma did seek my help, and even though she didn't know who I was at the time, I'm still needed either way.

"Princess?" Kye asks, moving his questioning eyes to the simmering female behind me.

She's silent. Nobody speaks as we wait for her response. But then, a huge, deep sigh exhales from her. "It will be okay. We'll split. But only if Fynn here will warp you both out of danger immediately and we meet up as soon as we're all done."

I turn to face her, finding silver eyes crashing into mine. "As soon as we each find and meet with an Elder, we'll meet back here."

"Damn straight you will," Cora snaps. "Or I'll haunt you in the after-life, once Emma sends you there."

Fynn's laughter fills the room as he bends forward to catch his breath. "And here I thought you were a ladies' man, Drav."

I shoot him a warning glare, but that only makes him laugh more.

"It's settled, then. We'll head out before sunrise," I state, giving one final look to Emma before I abruptly leave the room.

I need to head out to the caves of Tsisana tonight so we have what we need before our journey. The cave's existence is not known to any Fae; the knowledge of it fell away centuries ago, and only a few know of it now. But it's where the remaining wyvern weapons are safely hidden, away from the hands of those who yielded them against the Fae dragon shifters.

People of Deyadrum saw dragons as evil, sorcerers for death. Only viewing them as chaotic beasts who held power from up above. A mutated curse accidentally created by the God of Darkness, when a slip of his power left behind monstrous beasts. Yet, they never acknowledged the evil that was lurking right in front of them, walking amongst them in plain sight.

I hear Fynn's voice echo down the hall as he continues on in conversation, but I keep walking. I need time to think and get my inner beast under control.

CHAPTER THIRTY-EIGHT

Emma

*E*ver since we docked the ship early this morning, the rest of the day passes fairly quickly as we wait in our rooms at the inn. Nothing eventful happens, but I can't stop the unease trickling down my spine, worrying if my father will find me. I keep it to myself, and try not to think about it, but pray to the Gods we find the Elders.

Kye wants to get an ample amount of sleep before we start our travels to the other courts, but walking into a warp hole that sends them across the sea does not require hours of sleep. So, I joked with him, saying they barely have to travel if Fynn is with them and a shadow of a smile lifts his lips before concern creases the corner of his eyes.

Cora is getting ready to rest as well, in the room we're sharing, but I can't sleep. My mind is racing, and I just need air. I wished her goodnight and told her I'd be back in a bit for bed, but right now, I need space to sort my thoughts out.

I make my way up to the top of the inn and find a door that leads to the roof. I step out and almost forget how much chillier the air is here.

The fog lingers low to the forest floor, but the sky is clearer than I've ever seen it. Dusk is near as the twilight glow of oranges, blues, and purples begins to darken in the sky. Illuminating through the trees like a magical beacon to guide you to the sea.

I reach the roof's edge and sit down on the raised ridge, letting my booted feet hang over the side. I'm high enough to the trees that I feel adequately secluded to take a full breath of air. Filling my lungs until I can't anymore, then releasing it in a steady breath.

I forgo my hood, even though it would help lock some of my body heat in. But I want to feel the cold fingers of the breeze brush through my hair, making the ends of my strands dance. Something settles in me as the scent of fresh pine and cedar billows around, rippling through the wind with ease.

I close my eyes and think of the chaos that might be unfurling back home. My father is most likely boiling over in rage, threatening to tear apart every room in the palace. Then, Aiden…I wonder if he's just as angry, or if he worries more instead. But I'm slowly finding that I don't care. I'm *angry*. I feel like he's toying with me, using our friendship to excuse himself from his actions, from his *words*. Even with the comfort he has brought into my life, I fear I'm only a girl with a title in his eyes. A girl who is only good to follow orders and live quietly under the reign of men. A princess whose sole purpose is to sit on a pedestal and never to get her hands dirty.

He tore my trust for him in half the night of the ball, and as much as I can force myself to forgive, a part of me still cannot stitch the tear back completely. I have no doubt he would have held me back, but I don't want a future of remaining some quiet princess who never truly lives. A part of me still can't place what side he would be on if it came down to a war between me and my father. But I have a churning feeling in my stomach that it would be the latter.

The stress eats away at me as more thoughts of what I have to do take over. I need this Stone, because if I can't free myself from his leash on my neck, then I can't save my people. I owe them everything for all the years I've stayed oblivious to their hardships. The guilt gnaws at me, ever since Shade—

No, not Shade. *Draven.*

It makes sense now why I found both males incredibly irritating and couldn't hold my tongue around them. A sigh leaves me, everything hitting me at once. The backs of my eyes begin to burn as I feel a broken tear fall free, trailing down my cheek. I let a few more slip away as I tune in to an owl echoing in the distance and the wind rustling the leaves, weaving between the branches in a soothing dance.

I can feel the breeze erase all proof of the damp streams that mark my face. A weak, vulnerable moment, gone. Goosebumps rise along my arms, a stronger breeze whipping through, but this time…a hint of maple snags in the air. I bristle at the intrusion.

"What do you want?" Venom drips from my words, annoyance digging its claws into me. My moment of solitude is over.

I can feel his presence behind me, an all-consuming heat that drifts from his body. Hearing the scruff of his boots next to me, I open my eyes and see Draven sit down a foot away.

"Want company?"

I stare hard at the final beam of light glowing between the distant trees before us. "No," I say sternly.

He doesn't leave, just keeps his eyes focused in front of him as well, while we both watch the finale of the sun's descent. "Homesick?"

"Never." I sneer.

This time, I feel the sensation of his blue eyes assessing me, before I finally whip my head around to face him, forcing my dark gaze to his light eyes.

"You hate him." His words crash into me, like a riptide threatening to pull me under its current.

Narrowing my gaze, the anger in my blood begins to fester, threatening to burst free. I want to tell him I hate *him*, but I'd be lying. I know what true hate is towards a person. If anything, I'm unequivocally annoyed. I snarl at him to stop myself from spewing cruel words, and let my eyes harden even more to drive my point home.

His subtle laugh is barely audible over the wind, but I hear it, nonetheless. My frustration burns hotter.

"I'll be your villain if you need me to, little demon. But you don't hate me. And even if you did, you wouldn't be able to hang onto it for much longer."

"Cocky, much?" The nerve of this man. I let out a sigh of frustration. "Look, I already have to travel with you. I'd prefer not to deal with you now. So, *please*, just leave me alone, so I can have a moment of peace. Maybe you can pass time by finding your girlfriend and annoying her? I'm sure she's looking for you."

His demeanor shifts. A flash of a silver slit cuts through his irises and I see something shimmer over his exposed skin before disappearing a second later. I look at him in astonishment, unsure if whatever that was is real, or if my eyes are playing tricks on me. I rub the base of my palms against my eyelids before I look at him again. The skin I can see that's covered in tattoos on his forearms and creeping up his neck looks normal, no shimmer in sight. I raise my eyes up to his face.

I lose my train of thought when the hardness in his eyes hits me. Those blue flames sear into me, burning through my soul and into my skin. He leans in close, putting his face mere inches from mine. The intoxi-cating smell of him becomes overpowering. The sweet aroma of maple falling from his breath makes me unintentionally lick my lips. The thought of tasting him springs forth, but I shove it away.

"Girlfriend?" he questions roughly, his deep voice shooting warmth low into my stomach.

"You don't remember her? Blonde. Had her hands all over you. Her name starts with a K...?" I hedge, egging him on in hopes of infuriating him more.

It works. I can see the muscles pop along his sharp jaw. I internally high five myself with the ability to piss off the notorious *Dark Prince*. But I congratulate myself too soon, because in the next breath, his hand is grip-ping tightly behind the back of my head, careful to not touch my neck-lace. He yanks my face an inch closer until we share the same air. One small movement and I'd be able to taste the sweetness of his mouth.

"I don't do *relationships*, little demon. Unless that's what you consider a quick *fuck*." He drags his eyes down to my lips, which part in shock at his words.

The darkness of the night creeps around us, cloaking us in its embrace. If the air gets colder, I don't notice. The male before me causes heat to pool in my core and ignites every nerve ending in my body. His thumb strokes behind my ear and makes my breath hitch.

An unbidden kernel of guilt creeps in the back of my mind as thoughts of wanting to close the distance between us take over. How would he taste against my tongue? How would his hair feel in-between my fingers? How would it feel to have his hands on me…?

I feel awful, even though I don't fucking want to anymore. I hate the war raging in my mind, how I automatically feel the need to cater to how Aiden might feel. He's been the one person, the one *friend*, who helped ease my mind away from the abuse of my father during my childhood. I need to break free from that hold. I don't want to habitually cling to him any longer. All we have now is a fractured friendship.

I've had zero control in my life. But right here and now, I get to choose. I get to decide what *I* want, and a betrothal isn't it. But the darkness shrouding us makes me feel invisible. A secret that would cease to exist when the golden globe rises once again. Only us, the moon, and the stars would know. A forbidden chance to take what I want. A forever secret that will get lost in the dark.

I arch a brow, because I can't seem to help the joy that builds when I tick him off. "Or do they not want more because these girls of yours aren't satisfied?" A spiteful smirk creeps on my face as I stay put, never backing down or putting distance between us.

His grip tightens in my hair, a warning growl vibrating through his chest. His other hand shoots up between us and his thumb sensually rubs along my bottom lip.

"You have such a testy little mouth." The breath of his words fans across my lips as his thumb slowly falls away. His body never inches away from me as he invades my space, sharing the air. "Why don't I silence it and prove to you how *satisfied* they were when they screamed my name?"

"Fuck. Off." The boldness flows out of me, disgusted by the two-timing male before me. "I'm *betrothed*, remember?" It's a lame excuse since I left Aiden behind. Even the words taste bitter on my tongue.

A cunning laugh escapes him as he drags his nose along my jaw and up my cheek, sending intense shivers down my spine. "Where's your ring,

Princess? Because I don't see it, and you may have been told you're betrothed, but nothing is set in stone, little demon." He brings his face in front of mine, the ice in his eyes blazing brighter than I've ever seen them. Like crystal stars shining in the night. "For a girl with so much pent-up aggression, it's clear that the male on your arm at the ball isn't satisfying you."

I clench my teeth tightly together, biting back the curses I want to spit at him. Who the hell does he think he is? He knows *nothing*. Aiden may not have ever satisfied me, but I've never given him the chance to. It's not like I'm saving myself. I've just been trapped in a palace and always felt the need to hold back with Aiden. I couldn't have him seeing *all* of me, and I don't think I would have ever been ready to.

But I don't waver, letting my words roll off my tongue. "The aggression is only brought on by *you*. But yet again, you sound, dare I say, jealous?" I darkly tease. Anticipating his harsh, challenging words back. But then, something changes in his eyes. The ice begins to melt and the light in them dies down as they darken with sinful promises.

"Maybe a part of me is," he declares, catching me off guard with his honesty.

The air around us charges in a rush of heated energy and need. Our gazes lock on one another, crashing down the wall of our consciousness. A curtain of shadows falls around us right before I feel his thumb brush against the back of my ear again. My pulse begins to pound harder, faster, with every passing breath. All sane thoughts are forgotten as we both are unable to break the stare.

My lips part, gliding my tongue over them. That seems to be his undoing as he pulls me forward and fiercely slams his mouth to mine.

I match the vigor of his blazing kiss with my own, claiming his mouth with a frenzied need to taste him. Bourbon. The sweet, heady maple of him comes from bourbon, and I'm addicted. Needing to drink in more of him, more of his taste. This forbidden lust that's driving me deeper into him confuses me. I felt good during those heated moments with Aiden, but this feels like I'd willingly let myself drown in him. Never wanting to come up for air, unless he was air himself.

A soft moan unleashes from my throat and he kisses a heated trail down it seconds later before locking his lips on mine again. We're leaning into each other as we sit on the ledge of the roof, clinging onto each to get as close as we can. Kissing him feels like I'm free falling, letting go as if I slipped off this ledge to the drop below. The only question is, would he catch me? Or would he watch me fall to my death?

His other hand reaches over and clutches my thigh, squeezing tight, as if he needs to feel more of me. I allow myself this moment of being hidden in the dark to take what I want for the first time in my life. To take what I'm craving.

My free hand grips the rough surface of the roof as the other slides up to hold the side of his face. Shifting my fingers over the scruff that dusts his jaw—the very thing I wanted to do the moment I set my eyes on him —and it deliciously scrapes against my fingers.

His mouth devours mine in a sensual dance of tongues, matched with teeth clashing and lip biting. I swirl my tongue against his and a pleasure-filled growl works its way up his throat. My fingertips find the piercing in his brow, brushing gently over the cool metal.

Wetness pools between my legs, and the ache in my core grows to a deep thrum. His hand continues to roughly massage over my pants as his thumb dips between, brushing close to my center. It all feels so achingly good that my blood feels as though it's been lit on fire. My nipples harden, pushing against my top, and I can't help but to arch into him.

Draven must notice the need growing in me as his mouth pushes harder against mine, demanding more of my air. But right at that moment, the hand on my leg reaches the center of my thighs, and I suck in a sharp breath as my clit starts to desperately throb. He pulls back enough to curse against my lips, his fingers pressing and rubbing along my entire center, feeling the wetness through my pants.

He buries his face in my neck above my necklace as a low groan escapes him. "*Fuck.*" His fingers pause and we both pull back to stare at each other with heavy breaths and half-lidded eyes. His hand still grips my hair on the back of my head, as if he's afraid I'll escape. "You're so fucking wet." His scratchy voice is laced with lust, pressing his fingers harder against my slit. He takes a big inhale through his nose, and I see his eyes dilate when he releases his breath. "Your arousal drives me fucking insane, little demon."

I don't know what to say. A part of me is shocked. No one has ever touched me there, and I can't believe I'm letting him. But he's not demanding under my clothes, where I keep my most deadly secret. I don't need to hide my dagger from him, since he has become close friends with it. For the first time, I feel nothing holding me back to scream to stop. The throb in my core becomes unrelenting, ruthless, and I'd beg him again if it meant he could save me from its grasp.

I let my fingers trail up his jaw again and into his hair. Clutching onto the inky strands, silently telling him I need *more*. His nostrils flare as I notice his eyes change to those glowing silver slits I thought I dreamed up, before he lowers his mouth back on mine. Punishing. Demanding. Tasting every inch inside and along my lips as his fingers start to move. Finding my clit, he rubs against it in circles.

I whimper as the friction of his touch jolts through me, offering me some relief. I swipe my tongue across his again and again as his fingers pick up their pace.

My breathing comes quicker as more heat begins to coil tighter in my core. Racing against the rhythm his fingers have created as I desperately chase after my release. I can feel it building. I grip his hair tighter, pulling against the strands as my skin starts to flame.

"That's it. Come for me, Emma," he growls, demanding my body to do as it's told.

I want to refuse him, but I can't. The sound of my name falling from his lips pushes me over the edge of euphoria. His fingers circle faster as my inner walls tighten harder. Another moan leaves me. I'm his for the taking. Before I can suck in a full breath of air, my orgasm crests, hitting me with full force as my inner walls clench and spasm. Tingles rack through me as I stop breathing with every throb of ecstasy that pulses deep inside of me. Creating more slickness between my thighs as he continues his assault against my sensitive clit, letting me ride out the waves of pleasure.

A sated sigh slowly escapes me. As my release fades away, he removes his fingers. Wrapping his arm around my waist, he pulls me in a little closer. He places his lips on mine with a gentle kiss. "Atta girl," he mumbles against my mouth, as a strong sense of satisfaction in pleasing him ignites deep within.

He kisses me again and then brings his swollen lips to my ear. "Do you trust me?" he whispers.

"Not a chance," I say on a breath as my heartbeat begins to steady.

I wait for what he'll say next, but all I hear is a deep chuckle before his arm latches tighter around me and pulls me off the roof with him. A whoosh of cold air hits my face as we start free-falling down into the misty fog veiling the night.

CHAPTER THIRTY-NINE

Draven

This wasn't planned. None of it was. I made my way up to the roof to clear my head, the only place where I can freely sort my thoughts. The open expanse of the night sky feels comforting, allowing my mind to feel free and weightless. I didn't expect anyone to be up there, let alone the female who has been causing my cock to twitch with every snippy word she says.

That mouth of hers is what got her in trouble. She poked the beast in me, and I lost control, not able to hold back anymore. Her lips were just begging me to taste them, and when her tongue darted out to wet them, all rational thoughts left me. Only being consumed with the need to claim them would explain why I let my confession slip, about the stab of jealousy I felt.

The first time she arrived at my court and I took her to the library, I was able to see the pure, raw emotions that danced across her face. It left me speechless. I wanted to know what she was thinking, and I found myself hanging onto her every word.

I didn't trust myself when it came time for her to leave and sail back to her home. I made sure to not say goodbye because I needed to put distance between us. I saw how her body reacted towards me, but the bite to her words told a different story. All I know is that her savage little attitude makes my dick grow hard. When I left her in the library that evening, my cock was straining against the seam in my pants, needing some semblance of release. I could have taken a female to my bed, even Katrina, who was clinging to me with desperation, but the thought didn't sit well with me.

I had to take multiple cold baths that night, but it didn't help. I was left with my hand as I grabbed hold of my length, knowing she was near, somewhere in the castle. The forbidden thought of her had me fisting the sheets in my bed as I pumped myself harder, imagining it was her warm cunt I was thrusting into. Then again, even those sinful lips that curse me would take me hostage.

My breathing had picked up as my insides coiled tighter, shooting blinding pleasure down my spine. A few more quick pumps and I was spilling my release into my waiting palm. Cursing and roaring at the intensity of my orgasm. Just jerking off to the thought of her has made me come harder than ever before. I bet if I had her as mine, I'd black out the moment my release hit.

She makes me want to steal her away and punish that vicious mouth of hers. In a way, I suppose I am. Tonight I had planned on sneaking off to the caves of Tsisana that are hidden above the clouds in the Northeast, and be back before the light touched the sky. Yet, she has become a distraction that I can't resist.

Taunting me. Challenging me.

I take what I want because I can see it in her grey eyes, the swirls of desire filling them as our lips get stuck in a magnetic pull. Her lips taste even better than I imagined, sweet like honey that makes you only crave more. The little whimpers and moans of hers kept spilling into my mouth, making my cock stand at attention. Sending waves of desire in my lower back and down my length.

She's so responsive, so wet, practically dripping for me. I can feel how slick she is through her tight pants, making me want to rip them in half and feast on her right here and now.

The shock that washes over her the moment my fingers brush over her slit knocks me back. It seems like this is a new feeling for her, but I doubt that. Being betrothed to such a slimy fucker would have me guessing that he's already staked his claim inside of her. But I don't care at the moment, not as she pulls my hair in a silent plea. I can't stop myself from diving back in. Wanting to please her and see how her body reacts when it explodes.

I devour every shallow breath as her breathing picks up, her body's way of telling me she's close. I put more pressure on her clit as I pick up speed, demanding her to come for me. And like a good girl, she fucking does. Clutching me closer as she moans in my mouth, riding out her waves of pleasure as I control each and every one. My cock aches to the point of pain, and I feel a drop of pre-cum slip free.

She crumples in my arms as I pull her to me, making a rash decision in my need to have her closer. "Atta girl," I softly tell her against her lips before claiming them with mine. Once she loses her breath again, I trace my lips to the shell of her ear, inhaling her rose and honey scent. "Do you trust me?" I whisper quietly enough that I'm not sure she hears me as her heart starts to beat at a normal pace.

I feel her mouth raise against my cheek, as if a ghost of a smile is gracing her lips. "Not a chance," she says on an exhale as she still tries to catch her breath.

I expect nothing less. Even with losing herself in me for a moment, she still challenges me, and it only drives me more insane for her. A small laugh escapes me before I can stop it. Without a second thought, my arms tighten unforgivingly around her, as if my life depends on her, relishing in the warmth of her body against mine. I don't think as I willingly give her another secret of mine to hold against me as I pull us both off the roof.

We slice through the air as it rushes around us. I let us fall a few feet before we hit the ground, watching her reaction. But there's no fear as she faces death, just a peaceful look of acceptance that settles on her face. Like she's been waiting for it to take her, to strip her from this life. My mind drifts back to her words when she thought I was only Shade, an unknown male behind a mask of shadows. Her admission of dancing along the edge of death's tune made my stomach sink, but now it seems she's only waiting for the music to stop.

The storm that constantly rages in her eyes calms as the clouds part within them. Those grey irises seem thankful as the softest smile blooms across her mouth.

Well, *fuck* that.

She's not dying that easily. The music in her soul will not stop, at least not now. I will make sure her heart continues its rhythm, unless I choose to end it by my own hand. For if she is betraying me with her words of saving the people, I will make her death last longer than she will ever be able to handle.

I slide my other arm behind the backs of her legs as I pull her tighter against me, calling on my beast within, as strong wings flare out. I slam them down in a huge gust that thrusts us up into the air. Like an arrow shooting straight into the sky. I beat them again, with enough power to glide in between the trees and weave through the branches until we soar above them.

This time, her eyes widen as she stares into mine. I can see the silver glow of my eyes reflecting off hers. She doesn't say a word, just watches me in amazement as I wrap my shadows around us to blend into the midnight sky.

I call on my power some more, allowing us to glide through the air at lightning speed, as I take her to the secret cave of Tsisana.

CHAPTER FORTY

Emma

*W*ings.

Powerful black wings have us gliding with the wind under the glow of the moon.

I didn't mistake what I saw earlier. It wasn't me seeing things when I saw the change in his eyes. They *do* glow silver, with a black line cutting down the center. The tattoos on his body shimmer in a faint glow of silver scales. There was no blast of smoke as he changed; it's like he commanded the shift with ease. He still looks like himself, but minor changes resemble a beast that is not supposed to exist anymore.

Dragon.

I'm speechless as I stare up at him, looking at the same stunning male I was kissing. The only difference is the change of his eyes, like illuminating crystals in the night. I watch the longer strands of his hair I had my fingers clutching as they flow back with the wind. He embodies a different level of strength as he guides us through the night. I should be concerned about where he's taking me, but I'm curious. This prince keeps surprising me, along with eliciting a mixture of anger and awe.

He has me pressed tightly against his chest. We're moving so fast that I have to wrap my arms around his neck so I don't fall. The thought of letting go is tempting, but he has me secured so snug in his arms, a death grip of his own, that letting go wouldn't even be an option.

As much as letting my soul fly free to stop the suffering calls to me, I have to keep remembering what I need to do. If I don't take on my father or the Corrupted, then there soon won't be a life worth living for any of the people in Deyadrum. I must push forward and do what I can to help before my life can come to an end.

He's flying so fast that we are already past his court, drifting through the air over the sleeping sea. I shiver as the frigid wind cuts through my clothes, but then his shadows are there, blanketing me. A different kind of shiver racks through my body as he blocks the chilly air and sends warmth into me.

I am clueless about our destination, but I can tell it's getting colder. Small specks of white float around in the sky as we rise higher and higher. I reach my hand through the layer of shadows, feeling the cold bite against my skin. I twist my palm to face up as it catches a glittering piece of ice falling from the sky before it melts in my hand, like a frozen kiss.

I bring my hand back in and find Draven staring at me with wonder. So many thoughts seem to be flickering in his eyes that I can't decipher what he's really thinking. I tear my eyes away, feeling embarrassed to have been caught in a moment of naivety, having never seen *snow*. I've only ever been able to read about it.

I keep my gaze ahead as a large mountain becomes visible before us while he continues to climb higher in the air. His wings beat in powerful movements, sending us closer to the top of the mountain before us. An opening is revealed on the side near the summit, and it seems that's where we're headed as Draven aims for it.

The black hole swallows us as he dives inside, righting himself to land on his feet. His hold on me tightens for a second as his fingers dig into me before he loosens his grip. He sets me down on the damp cave floor and I slowly turn to face him.

I suck in a breath at the sight of him. Wet, inky black hair falls in front of his eyes as he stands before me. The metallic glow of his eyes sharpens, those slits focusing in on me and sending a thrill of adrenaline down my body. Dark, black wings span behind him, stretching to the width of the cave as they curve into sharp points, while his shadows ripple around them. His darkened silhouette is commanding, with the moon's beams shining through behind him, outlining his muscular frame.

I swallow hard as I take him all in. Now, I see.

He truly looks like a Dark Prince.

"Dragons are extinct," I say softly. "I don't understand."

He stalks towards me, blocking the light glow of silver behind him, his wings appearing larger as he nears. "Not entirely. I can't fully shift into a dragon, but I have traces of dragon blood racing through my veins."

I can't stop my eyes from roaming over his wings. They are massive shadows, morphing into the shape of a scythe, with long tendrils and curved spikes sticking out at the bottom. A silvery shimmer of veining travels over his wings looking as though it acts like a shield, while shadows still cloud around them. The moon frames his dark wings in a mystical glow. "But your shadows are your power…" I trail off as confusion makes me wonder about what he is.

I hear him exhale a breath before speaking. "That's a whole other story."

I don't tear my gaze away, keeping them pinned on him. "I'm listening," I tell him honestly.

Those glowing eyes scrutinize me for a minute before he crosses his arms over his chest, giving in. "Dragons weren't supposed to be created. It was a miscalculation from the God of Darkness' power when creating the first Fae. It was not only the cause of dragons but mutating one into having the power of shadows." He pauses, swiping his calloused palm over his trimmed beard. "You may have heard rumors of a cursed Elder, but I can tell you he wasn't cursed. He was the first dragon who manipulated the shadows. This power is the rarest. Only a chosen descendant in each generation from the dragon bloodline is born with it."

A shadow dragon.

He's like a knight in shadowed armor.

Then, suddenly, it clicks. The reason why *Shade* was able to be in so many different courts at once to take on the Corrupted. He could fly to them with ungodly speed and stay unseen from prying eyes. Then, I remember the day I met Prince Draven… When I was traveling to his court, I thought I saw monstrous wings soaring between the clouds, and now…I *know* I did.

It was *him*, heading back to his court before our arrival.

My heart starts pounding a little harder when I remember the confusion I felt when Prince Draven wasn't present to bid us farewell when we were leaving his court. But the image of blurry wings I saw darting through the stormy clouds above the ship flashes to the forefront of my mind. Maybe he did say goodbye, in his own discreet way.

His silver eyes burn into me, gauging my reaction to everything he has shared. I smile softly at how tense his body is. "So, you're the chosen one," I say bluntly. He nods, waiting for me to say more, seeming to know I have a question ready to ask. "Do the people of Deyadrum know?"

He sighs heavily. "No, they would demand my death."

I let his words sink in as I finally learn to understand him more. Instead of taking a step back, I take one forward, closing the distance as we stand an inch apart. Raising my hand slowly, I let my fingertips trace over the reflective silver sheen that covers the inked parts of his skin. It's not morphing him, but more of a transparent metallic shield of scales. They're firm to the touch, a smooth protective barrier of scales that seems impenetrable, feeling like steel. I bring my hands up and reach to his wing, and I gasp. They're made from his dense shadows, coming together to take their true form. My hand brushes over the top as the smoky black swirls around my fingers, welcoming my touch, and I notice Draven shiver at the contact.

I do it again, brushing over the top of his wing, and watch another shiver break free as his hands tighten in fists. I slide my eyes up to his and watch as they slowly shift to look into mine. The silver in them glows in the dark, like a spark in the night, a fraction of light tearing through the cursed darkness.

I'm caught in his gaze, staring at the true beast that dwells inside him. Enraptured.

The air around us starts to pulse as waves of heat crash between us, but I back away to look more into the cave and see…nothing. I can only hear the symphony of the wind and the stories that float with it.

"What are we doing here?" I ask, unsure as to why he flew us here after flinging us off the roof, which I should be mad at him about.

"Weapons," he says.

Apparently, we're back to one-word responses. A pity, really, because his personality is just so delightful. The sarcastic thought lights a tinge of amusement in me, but it dies away when I see him shift back into his Fae form. Nothing crazy happens. His eyes shift easily back to blue, his iridescent scales melt away, and his shadow wings vanish in a blink of an eye. Astonishing.

"Care to elaborate? We have weapons, or at least, I'm sure you have a whole room full at your castle." I make my way farther into the cave.

"Wyvern weapons," he tells me, like it's supposed to mean something. He makes his way over to the far side of the cave's wall and flicks a match to catch fire. I watch it dance as he lights the lanterns around the cave.

The cave expands far and wide, with lights that flicker around the border. This cave brings up memories of the one I hid away in back home, a place that would calm my soul. As the lantern illuminates the space, I can see it more clearly for what it is: a hideout. Much like my small cave back home by the sea. Except, here there is a sofa, rugs, and a few books scattered on a nearby table that faces the entrance to look out at the sea. The sounds of waves crashing against the mountain is nowhere to be heard, as the sea stands still, frozen. Yet, it still glistens with reflections of the mountains mirrored on the surface. A serene picture with the sparkles of snowflakes dancing above. We are in a different part of the world than I am used to.

My cave back home is more humid and damp. But here, it's warm inside, even as small gusts of the wintry breeze slip through. Various tunnels lead deeper inside the cave and my curiosity peaks, wondering what might be on the other end.

Rigid walls curve and arch around us as it shelters us from the outside. My eyes keep trailing around the space until they find their way back to Draven. Those pale winter eyes are already on me. Watching me.

Then, I remember what he said about why we're here. To get a special kind of weapon. A wyvern weapon?

"I don't know what that is," I tell him honestly. There's no point in holding back anymore. He knows I lack knowledge on certain aspects of this life.

Those piercing blue orbs narrow on me, but then a frown furrows his face as his eyes slide down to my necklace. "Your necklace is wyvern iron."

All the air rushes out of my lungs as confusion takes hold of me.

"I–I don't understand," I stutter, suddenly feeling my stomach twist in knots.

His eyes never leave mine, staring hard with a darkened look. "Wyvern iron is a thousand times stronger than regular iron. It's precisely why you can't use your power. Its effects on Fae are potent, but it's also the only iron that can kill a dragon."

My head starts to shake in disbelief. This makes no sense, none of it does. Why would the strongest type of iron be wrapped around *my* neck?

"How do you know this?" I demand as a feeling of uneasiness racks through me.

He stalks towards me, stealing all the air around us when he stands a hairbreadth away. His tattooed hand lifts, his fingers tracing above my necklace, never making contact with it.

"Because, little demon, since I'm part dragon, that night at the ball, this necklace of yours burned me when I touched it. Only wyvern iron can harm me. And I know it steals your power, because you couldn't heal a busted lip."

My eyes widen as I search his, trying to find the lie hidden under his words. But there isn't one. I force myself to remember that night, shifting through all the events that happened, until I land on our dance. Then, with stark clarity, the memory of him commenting on my necklace before yanking his hand back from it, hearing a hiss leave his lips… It had hurt him.

But now, everything clicks into place. It's the reason why he didn't ask if my necklace was why I can't heal. He already knew it was wyvern iron, he didn't need to ask.

Not wanting to talk more about my necklace, I try to bring us back to the present. Taking the attention off me and my lack of ability to heal. "So, why do we need wyvern iron if we aren't fighting dragons?"

He lets his hand fall as he turns away from me, heading towards one of the lantern-lit tunnels.

"Because it seems it can also kill Scavengers, which we might encounter on our journey. It's better for us to be prepared and armed accordingly."

A chill skirts its way down my spine at the thought of fighting the very thing that curses the Fae. Prowling in the dark as it hunts for its prey.

"But why are we *here*?" I ask again, questioning why we specifically need to come to this hidden cave in order to get these weapons.

His steps stop in their tracks, pausing as his back tenses. "This is where most of the wyvern iron was taken to keep it away from those who took it upon themselves to kill my dragon ancestors. There were others like me, who gathered as many of these weapons as they could in hopes of keeping our race from becoming extinct."

"Are there others like you now?" The air weighs heavy with my question, not sure if he will answer. I'm prying, I know it. But the words just flew out of my mouth, and now they hang between us and there's no way for me to take them back.

"I don't know," his deep voice says softly. "My father was the only one I knew of. He was part dragon, too. But he didn't control shadows. He was a mind reader, and that power grew stronger for him when he shifted. We are still half-Fae, but we can shift into this." He gestures his hands down his body, when he instantly brings forth his dragon form and my eyes slowly to drink him in. In the next breath, he shifts to his Fae body. "My father used to tell me that this power of mine, these shadows were a gift. That there is a reason I was chosen. But it has only ever felt like a curse."

Was.

Felt like a curse.

In this moment, I feel like we are more alike than I thought. My heart breaks for him. His Fae half has people he connects with, but his dragon half is isolated. Alone. The one person he may have been able to share this part of his life with is gone. I want to reach out to him, to comfort him. But I stay rooted to the spot, only wishing I could take his pain away.

To be the one to take on the ancestral bloodline, giving him the traces of dragon blood from his father, since it seems his mother and brother don't have it.

Fate chose *him*.

He continues walking again, heading towards the tunnel on the right as he lifts his arm and points to the tunnel on the left. "I'm going to be a while. You can stay out here, or there's a hot spring down that way." Then, he points to another tunnel down the center. "And a bedroom down that way if you want to rest."

I open my mouth to respond, but he's already disappearing down the path to wherever the weapons are stored. The finality of his exit echoes down the tunnel with every tap of his boots as they grow fainter. I sigh, looking around and questioning why I'm even here. I glance between the two tunnels and choose the left one. I couldn't sleep even if I wanted to right now. But once again, curiosity wins; I've never seen a hot spring before.

The rough, curved wall in the cave surrounds me as I travel through the tunnel, a small light glowing up ahead. A weightless swirl of steam floats around me as I near the welcoming warmth.

A teal, shimmering pool of water glows, as an opening in the cave lets the moonlight shine through from above. The flecks of snow falling from the sky melt when they reach the plumes of steam.

The water is still, undisturbed by any evil in this life. I dip my fingers into it and the hot liquid feels soothing against my skin. I quickly glance back at the tunnel's opening. He did say he would be a while… I should be able to do a quick swim. Nerves radiate through me at the thought of being seen, but the water is calling to me. The nerves in my body have been high-strung ever since I left my father's palace, and I'll do anything to settle them. I'm never able to have any bit of privacy to swim in water without my clothes, aside from a bath that's constricting and definitely doesn't count as swimming.

I bite the bullet. Only a few minutes, and then I'll get out and try to get some rest. Maybe this water will have voodoo powers or something that can offer me some momentary tranquility. To erase the worry and anxiousness of my disobedience from my body.

I slide my boots off and unlatch the holster for my dagger. I peel my socks off and start to slip out of the remainder of my clothes, leaving them in a pile next to the edge of the hot spring. As goosebumps pebble over every inch of my skin, I take another cautious glance behind me before I continue. It's empty and I hear nobody nearby when I strain my hearing.

I hurry with quick feet as I step into the water and dip down, letting it cover me to my shoulders. The heat of it soothes the chill away, settling against me in a gentle caress. I dip my head back as I let my hair float into the water, soaking it as a soothing breath whooshes out of me. With everything going on, this is the most relaxed I have ever been. Even with the beastly asshole kidnapping me to some unknown hideout.

I weave my arms through the clear water, letting it sway through the ripples I create. I swim back and forth from one end to another of the wide expanse of the spring, enjoying the movement and exertion on my muscles, even as it relaxes them. Just a few more minutes, I tell myself, and then I will get out.

But time slips away from me as I relish how the water laps against my skin and washes away the stress that hangs on my body. For the first time, I let myself forget about the necklace leashing me to my father, knowing he is most likely rampaging at my absence. I dive down under, trailing low to the pool's floor, pushing my feet off the bottom, and shooting back up to the surface with a smile stretching across my face.

The moment I break free from the water's surface, I freeze.

All warmth rushes out of me in an instant as silver eyes flare blindingly at me. Their luminosity burns into my skin as it traces every visible crevice.

I stop breathing and for a moment, time seems to stop with me.

My heart starts hammering against my chest, threatening to explode free.

"Who *the fuck* did that to you?" A guttural growl leaves him with the harshness of his words. He's blocking the entire entrance of the tunnel, as his shadows jerk and strike out around him, as if he's losing control of them.

I'm silent, not able to speak as shock and fear choke me in an unrelenting grip.

A blast of black smoke bursts out of him, shooting straight at me as his shadows wrap around me, pushing me to the far back wall of the hot spring and holding me against the rugged stone as it scratches against my back. Scratches against my *scars*.

"Little demon," he snarls as his eyes brutally stare into the depths of the mine, searching for answers I haven't given him. "I asked you a fucking question." His shadows constrict tighter around me, trying to squeeze the answer from my lips.

Anger flares in me at his aggression, at his demand to know something he has no right to. He's seeing me in my true form, one that's been ripped to shreds and put back together, only to be torn apart all over again. And I'm pissed at myself for letting my guard down, for not being more cautious, and for escaping into the feeling of serenity for a little while.

I grit my teeth and scowl at him from across the pool as I remain forcefully pressed to the stone by his shadows. "Let me go and take me back to the inn," I say, trying to sound intimidating as he keeps me in his hold. In his control.

The metallic glint in his eyes shines brighter, the muscles in his jaw twitching. He looks unhinged. One breath away from letting the dragon in him take over, as the storm of shadows still thunders around him.

He takes sure steps towards me, walking into the water with his clothes on, and keeping his steel eyes on mine. "You're not leaving until you tell me the truth, Emma."

Any time my name falls from his lips, it makes me weak as it settles something in my soul, brushing up against it with a gentle stroke. I give him a final glare, but he's not relenting, not giving in to my wants.

My head drops forward, a signal of me waving the white flag. Just a lone soldier that falls prey to the enemy.

"My father," I whisper on a breath. The silence around us has my words being heard with stark clarity.

"I'll kill him," he says in a such a calm voice, it sounds deadly. A promise. The water starts to ripple and his power vibrates through the air making his body shake with rage. "No one deserves to live if they lay a fucking hand on you." His words sound rough against the rising anger that wants to fully unleash.

I stay silent, unsure of what to say. A grip on my chin forces my face up, making me look straight into the lightning storms raging in his eyes.

"He doesn't let you heal," he says in a restrained voice, softening his tone, even though there's an edge of disgust lacing in them.

My heart cracks at what I'm sure is true: the disgust is for me and my gnarled skin. A monster in disguise. The sadness at that thought gets lodged in my throat, threatening to break free, but I swallow it down. Refusing to break in front of him. I give my head the faintest shake, no words need to be spoken, since he already knows I can't heal on my own.

"Revenge tastes sweet, little demon," he says with a maddening gleam creeping across his face.

Revenge against my father will taste sweet one day, and I plan to savor that moment for as long as I can. But I furrow my brows as I nod. Not trusting myself to speak without tears spilling free.

His fingers grip my chin harder. "You may not be able to heal your body, but you *are* able to heal your soul."

But doesn't he realize? I may have healed my soul, but every time I do, pieces of it get lost when my father smashes it to the ground. Losing a little bit of myself each time. But I'm promising myself in this moment, that he will never break my soul again, that this time, it will remain intact.

His shadows release me from their grip as he grabs my arms and twists my body around. I hear him sharply inhale a breath before I feel the feather-light touch of his warm fingers tracing along the scars on my back. Feeling the raised, mutilated skin that deems me repulsive.

I flinch the moment he touches my skin, not used to the gentleness. No one has ever seen my scars, let alone touched them. I'm glad I can't see his face, because I feel my heart and soul would fracture even more at the revulsion shining there. A nervous chill sweeps down my spine as I stand bare before him, dressed in scars.

I should feel embarrassed at my lack of clothes. He's the first to see me this way. But for some unknown reason, I'm not. Maybe it's because he seems more focused on the gruesomeness of me than the feminine parts of me, but my body begins to settle as the shock fades away along with the need to hide from him.

I just hope Draven keeps this his secret, too, because my father would tear the universe apart if he found out someone knew of his cruel deeds that slice through my veins. He wouldn't rest until Draven's death was reality.

The Dark Prince continues painting his fingers along my skin, following the damage left in my father's wake.

I've been hiding for so long.

And for the first time, I feel like I've been found.

Seen.

CHAPTER FORTY-ONE

Draven

This is the first time I've ever seen true fear overcome her. She never showed it before, not even when she thought I was Shade. But when her eyes connect with mine the moment she breaks free from the water, all the color drains from her face. Looking like a goddess of souls as her fair skin reflects against the water, her brown hair floating around her.

I immediately saw the red slashes covering her back when she was swimming beneath the surface, and now with her standing, my eyes dart to the lines marring the skin over her ribs. The dragon inside of me unleashes itself, fuming at the sight.

Guilt begins to churn my insides, for ever thinking she was a pampered princess who couldn't care less about anyone else. Yet, for once, I was wrong. She wasn't being pampered. She was being caged in a shiny palace, while suffering the wrath of a sinister king. No wonder she didn't know anything about the Corruption. How could she? She was too busy being hidden away and fighting her own battle this life has given her.

A distant feeling makes me believe the knowledge of these scars is a locked-up secret that I happened to find. The momentary light that was just shining in her eyes before she saw me was snuffed out when she realized she was no longer alone.

I clench my teeth as I try and fail to regain control of my shadows and the beast within thats roaring to life, unable to be contained any longer. I *knew* something was off on the day she first arrived at my court, with the way King Oren gripped her arm. Even then, I wanted to cut it off for thinking he could handle a female that way, let alone his own daughter.

I stand there, blocking the exit, leaving no routes for her to escape. And even if she did, I would have gone after her, enjoying the chase. Once I approach her, she seems to realize she has no option but to give in to me.

When I spin her around, my chest cracks. My eyes begin scanning every inch, taking in every scar, but I happen to catch the pain etched on her face before she fully faces the cave wall. The water soaks through my clothes, but I can't find a reason to care, as every thought was drowned underneath the second I saw her naked, marked skin.

Now, my fingers have a mind of their own as I trace each one, watching the shiver that racks through her body. Her tight, little figure is bare before me, slick with drops of water trailing down her skin. The water is shallower around the edge, leaving her top half in perfect view as the surface dances along the curve of her back. Her hair is wet and slicked back, like a siren luring in her prey.

My shadows still rage in a cloud of chaos around me, as my dragon shines through. My control is slipping as my imagination runs wild at everything she may have suffered through alone. The pain she had to endure. It's clear she's nervous of my reaction to her scars, by the way she is slightly hunching and wrapping her arms around herself. But it also seems she's...protective. Ready to snap at me like the little demon she is if I harm her scars.

I stare hard at every angry mark. Skin like this is not something Fae are used to, because our bodies heal and stay in pristine condition because of that. Only those who have been captured in iron and fought in wars bear such marks, but even then...it's nothing like this. Not like hers.

She goes against all of that, commanding her own kind of beauty that shows her bravery. These scars should never be seen as a Fae who has been abused or broken because, instead, they tell a story of every battle won. Every war her father unleashed on her that she didn't retreat from. She held her ground and never gave in, which is clear in how she's going against him now.

The part that triggers my frustration is that she doesn't seem to believe that she has the power to heal her soul. Not with the way she would welcome death if it came knocking on her door. Not in the way she closes herself off, like she's not worth a damn. Her skin isn't the core of her strength, it's what's inside her. If she doesn't see that, I will just have to make her.

I press closer to her. "I want to kiss and lick every single one until you see how beautiful they are. Until you realize that these fucking scars are raising their middle fingers and screaming *fuck you* to your father. They are proof of your strength," I tell her right before I dip my head and press my lips against a thick red mark that covers the top of her spine.

I hear her suck in a gasp as every muscle in her body tenses. Her posture stiffens as I kiss another scar over her shoulder blade.

"What are you doing?" she asks on a shallow breath, the water gently sloshing between us.

"I'm going to make you see, little demon," I say roughly between gentle kisses.

"Wha—"

Her words get caught in her throat when I twist her around and throw her over my shoulder. My cock grows hard at the feeling of her naked body laying over me, her ass right next to my face. A delicious temptation to bite into, and so, I do. I sink my teeth into her as a shriek spills from her lips. The beautiful sound rings throughout the cave. I lick over the bite, my beast elated with smugness from seeing the mark my teeth indented on her fair skin.

I trek through the water with hurried steps, unable to tighten the leash on my beast any longer as he breaks free. I gingerly drop her on the edge of the hot spring by her clothes, sitting her down before me as I spread her legs to stand in between them. I grip her thighs as I feel another gnarled bit of skin beneath my hands. My nostrils flare as anger courses through me, intensifying my dragon's rage.

"You'll tell me if you want me to stop," I say on a barely restrained breath, needing to make her see. Needing to devour her taste.

I drop down, water coming up to my chest and kiss the scars on her thighs, licking my tongue slowly along with them. I push her knees farther apart as I inch closer to her center. I hear her breathing hitch as I trail a hand up her side.

"What are you doing?" she asks again, her breathy voice edged with uncertainty, but the way her nipples harden betrays her.

I stop, only to look up at her. Confusion is painted across her face, as her eyes look frantic with how close my face is to her core. But underneath that, there's a flush to her skin, and the beast inside me rears its head at the sight. I know my eyes have shifted to silver slits, but it makes the dragon in me pleased she's not cowering away.

"Showing you that your soul is worth saving."

"You don't know *anything* about my sou—"

I slam my mouth over her clit, sucking hard as her spitting words fall silent with a gasp that echoes through the cave. A low growl vibrates up my throat, as I lower my tongue and lick her slit from bottom to top. I feel my shadows grow more crazed as her scent consumes me.

But her taste…

It's the sweetest poison and it will ruin me. It will travel through my veins and make me surrender, falling to my knees until I can taste her again. I need to be careful, only taking this dose of poison before my blood longs for it.

But she needs to fucking learn that her soul is worth healing, that she can *feel* more than pain.

My hand travels higher up her side as I reach her breast, tweaking the rosebud that's begging for attention. A high-pitched moan escapes her as she tries to close her legs, but I shove my shoulders between them, refusing her. So sensitive.

My hand continues to caress her breast as I bring my mouth back up to her clit, swirling my tongue around it before sucking hard on it. My other hand comes up to rub over her opening, feeling how slick she is. Dripping. Screaming to be filled.

I dip my finger in, causing her back to arch back as another moan falls from her lips. I can tell she's close as I keep a constant rhythm with my tongue over her swollen nub.

I press my palm between her breasts to lay her back on the damp stone, as my shadows slide up her body before I command them to wrap around her throat.

"Draven," her breathy voice is greedy with carnal desire, desperate to lose all sense of reason. Hearing my name spill from her lips makes my control slip. Her head whips up when my shadows tighten their grip, the beast in me wanting to steal her air. To have her life balance on the edge in my control.

Those storm grey eyes frantically search mine, hesitant with me claiming her breaths.

"You can always say stop, little demon." I remind her, waiting for her to do just that. But her eyes roll back when I go back to devouring her taste. She drops her head back down, her way of telling me *not* to stop.

I don't.

I let my fingers continue pressing against her opening, slightly dipping the tip of one in. Her hips arch and I wrap my arm over her hips, holding them down.

A whimper leaves her when I push a single digit all the way inside.

Fuck.

Her pussy grips my finger in a death hold, squeezing it tightly. I start moving my finger in sensual thrusts. I cut off her breathy gasp as I pick up pace. Licking at her clit with a precise onslaught, needing to feel her come around my finger and into my mouth.

I slowly slide a second digit in, as I let her have an inhale of air.

She's so fucking tight.

My cock is painfully hard as I work her to release, pressing her hips more firmly into the floor and putting pressure on her lower stomach.

I suck harder on her bundle of nerves as my fingers thrust in a steady assault, her wetness pooling more as her pussy squeezes tighter.

I claim her breath when I feel her hand fist in my hair.

She's surrendering.

Her back bows off the cave's floor as her orgasm finally explodes through her. Her knees quivering as they press hard against my shoulders, her hand pulling roughly at the strands of my hair. Her inner walls spasm, gripping relentlessly around my fingers, pulsing with every wave.

I let my shadows vanish as she sucks in a mouthful of air, chest heaving as she comes.

She's writhing before me, splayed out as I keep a steady pace with my tongue and fingers until every wave of her release is complete.

When her sated body comes down from its high, I slide my fingers out and clean her slit with a final swipe of my tongue. Licking up every drop of her orgasm as her taste becomes my new obsession.

She starts to rise up on her elbows as I bring my mouth back to the scar on her leg, kissing it again. Those vicious lips part, as she stares at me with half-lidded eyes.

I suck my fingers into my mouth, cleaning off her essence as her eyes widen, a red tint blooming across her cheeks.

"Such a good girl," I say, cupping her face as my thumb rubs over her bottom lip.

She heaves a sigh as if that pleases her, and I can't stop myself from saying the thoughts that fly forward.

"Shine like the moon, Emma."

Her brows furrow together. "The moon?"

"The moon has scars, too. But night after night, it glows brightly against all the darkness that tries to conceal it."

She opens her mouth to speak before closing it. I can tell she's struggling with what to say, confused with the gentleness in my tone and the kindness in my words. I don't let her suffer for too long before I step out of the pool and grab hold of her to set her on her feet.

"I'm going to grab another set of clothes in the room while you get dressed. I already have the weapons bundled up, so we should head back to get some rest before the sun catches up to us."

Those pools of grey are searching, desperate to find the words she wants to speak, but I turn and leave before she can. It's better to stop this, to put the distance between us, and focus on finding the Stone before her father.

I take a deep breath. I don't understand the way I lose all conscious thoughts around her, only knowing I need to be near. Maybe it's the way she bites back at me, or maybe I'll be bored and satisfied the moment I sink myself into her. Free of this uncontrollable thirst. I can't be hung up on a vicious female who's not my mate, I need to be rid of her.

I need to get my mind back on course, stay focused, and not get lost in the princess, who might just bring me to my knees.

CHAPTER FORTY-TWO

Emma

*D*raven flies us back to the inn in silence with the wyvern weapons in a sack slung around his chest. I allow my eyes to fall on his as he stares ahead, taking in the beauty of him. His eyes remind me of the sea, when the sand settles on the bottom, leaving behind the clearest blue under the sun-filled sky. But when they slightly glow…it looks like a sheet of ice shimmering from the luminescence of the moon.

He lands us on the roof with lethal grace and the coldness slams into me the moment he sets me down and steps back. I watch silently as he retracts his wings, letting his eyes settle into the iciness I've grown used to. I remain warily in place, for I'm not sure how to feel at the moment.

A part of me wants to pull him back, my blood buzzing with the need to have him touch me, but then the other part wants to stay far away. I'd never felt such pleasure spread throughout my body, growing hotter until my body had no choice but to detonate. Flaring to life as I shattered to pieces.

The broken parts of me have always been left forgotten on the floor, scattered for me to find in order to try and make myself whole again. But this time, I was put back together by the Dark Prince. Letting me fall apart in his hands so he could catch every piece of me.

"Get some rest, Emma," he says with indifference. I stare at him as he turns to the door that leads back into the inn. His shadows slowly start to creep around him so he can blend into the dark.

"The moon may shine brightly," I say, watching his steps pause. My voice cuts across the rooftop, disrupting the silence of the night. I tip my head up to see the moon glowing through the light fog, seeing its crescent shape hanging by a thread. Broken. Letting the darkness bury parts of it, stealing its light. "But it's not always whole," I say quietly, letting my words fall free.

His head whips around, those fierce blue eyes searing into me with keen awareness. His brows deepen, dissecting my words as his eyes continue to probe into my soul. Trying to find the darkness that lives within.

The silence hangs heavy around us as he gives me one last look before heading into the inn. I turn to stare out at the primal trees that stand like soldiers in the night, as I hear the finality of the door clicking shut.

I wonder if these trees hold many secrets, listening to the truth of words said under the veil of night. They seem to always be shrouded in darkness, and I can't help but wonder if they understand how the darkness slowly devours a soul.

With a final look at the distant midnight sky, I head back to my room, creeping in to not wake Cora as little snores escape her with every inhale. As I slip my boots off and slide under the covers in the small bed beside hers, an obtrusive pounding begins in my head with what I learned tonight and the exhaustion finally settles in.

Draven is a shadow dragon.

My father has sealed wyvern iron around my throat. The strongest iron made…and it's on my fucking neck.

I trace a finger over it, wishing I could rip it off.

But maybe Draven will be able to help me even more now. If he's willing. Maybe he has an idea or inkling as to how I can free myself from this weighted restraint my father placed on me. Especially now that he's learned the brutal truth of my life.

Much like I learned the truths of his.

Secrets unwillingly shared that now give us a shred of power over the other.

My body still hums with the aftershock of pleasure Draven demanded from me. Fantasizing how his lips felt against my scars, against my…

I bite my lip, knowing what his wicked mouth can do. Another first. I wanted to shove him away, but I couldn't bring myself to do it. I needed to know what he'd do and the pleasure he ignited makes me wet just thinking about it. He told me I could tell him to stop, but the words never sprung free. The way his shadows gripped my throat startled me. Images of my father's hand around my neck invaded my mind, but then Draven's lust-filled eyes met mine…clearing those memories away. He was promising me pleasure, not pain. I may have been held with his own swirls of night as he stole my breath from me, but he allowed me the comfort of having *control* if it was too much.

Control is something I've never been offered. But tonight, Draven made me feel like I sat upon a throne, with him bowing before me as he set my soul on fire.

I push away all thoughts of Draven as I gently pull free the book that holds a riddle from under my pillow. This riddle that is eating away at me.

When light and dark collide, your fate will be split in two.

I read it over and over again, racking my brain as to what it could possibly mean, but my conclusions fall short as I drift off to sleep.

I jolt awake to a pounding on the door and Cora screeches as she almost falls out of the bed from being startled.

"Beauty sleep is over ladies," Fynn's cheerful voice booms through the door. "We're meeting behind the building in the forest."

Cora grabs her boot on the floor next to the bed and throws it across the room, thumping loud against the door. "Asshole!"

I watch with tired amusement as I rub my palms over my eyes and Fynn's laugh bellows as he walks away. "Well, you're just a ray of sunshine, Cor," I say as she huffs with annoyance.

Her head snaps to me, her blonde hair wild as it tangles around her, and those deep blue eyes pin me in her gaze.

"Don't you start. Fynn is about to see how hot a ray of sunshine burns when I get payback." A devious smirk lifts on her mouth and that's the moment I choose to stay out of the crossfire between the two of them. Even so, I'm looking forward to seeing Cora's revenge on him.

We brush our fingers through our hair, slide our feet into our boots, and get ready to meet the guys. But my stomach growls furiously when we finally get ready.

Cora looks down to my stomach, with a laugh hanging on her tongue before she looks back up at me. "Food first?"

I don't want to be late starting our journey, but food takes priority as a sharp pain jabs my insides. "Yes."

Everyone else staying at the inn is still asleep as the hallways are quiet. The kitchen has a table of food left out, with snacks for anyone who needs something when the kitchen staff are not cooking.

We grab some dried fruits and nuts, eating them as we rummage through the rest of the food, taking some for the journey ahead. Once the hunger in my belly has calmed down, we make our way outside. The sun is not yet awake as we walk around the inn to the backside of the forest.

The chilly air cuts through my cloak and I can see Cora wrapping her arms around herself, trying to hold on to her body heat.

"Glad you could finally make it," Fynn says with a glint in his eyes as we step under the cover of the trees.

Cora shoots him a glare, no doubt plotting her revenge at this very moment.

"Sleep well?" Kye asks as he looks us both over, keeping his eyes on me longer than necessary.

"Not the best sleep, but I'm rested enough. Cora here slept like the dead, snoring loudly enough to scare off any ghosts lurking about."

An appalled gasp leaves her as she sets her accusing eyes on me. "Well, *someone* has to protect us from them," she says as she places her hand dramatically on her chest.

Kye's not fully smiling as he assesses me, searching for what I'm not saying. "Did you stay up late?"

I scrunch my face, not sure why the questions are flowing about my sleeping habits, unless he heard me from his room across the hall when I snuck back into my room.

"Enough, we need to focus and get a head start," Draven cuts in, his shadows engulfing every inch of masculine perfection under his hood.

He's the last to show, appearing out of nowhere as he emerges from the swirls of black he controls.

I stare at him, wishing I could see if he was looking at me. It was only hours ago that his mouth was on me, but now it feels like a distant dream. Another secret to pile on top of us when we die. I let my gaze drift to the forest floor as he continues to speak, scuffing my boot back and forth in the dirt, not wanting him to read any thoughts that might cross my face.

"The Elder in the Court of Abhainn is said to have lived at the end of the river that flows," Draven says.

"How do you know that?" Kye asks directly, as we are all curious about this new set of knowledge.

"I did some research right before we needed to meet. My healer gave me a book from her personal library and it said the Elder has never once moved, living in the same hut for centuries."

"And what about the Elder you two are in search of, the one in the wintry Court of Amihan?" Cora asks, hoping we have a clue of where to start our search.

Draven's hood shakes. "It didn't say. But I've heard of a Seer there who may be able to help us."

"Let's hope the Seer is willing to help," I say. I know it's our only option if we want to find the Elder. If we go around asking people, then it will draw attention to us. Attention that may also alert my father.

"There's only one way to find out," Draven says, and this time, I can *feel* his eyes on me, watching me from behind the darkness that hides him.

"Shall we get this party started? I'm anxious to go to the Court of Abhainn for some spring weather," Fynn chimes in, his voice cheery with excitement for adventure as he bounces on the balls of his feet like a child.

"Yeah, but first, take these." Draven tosses down the sack of wyvern weapons he collected last night in the midst of pleasuring me.

Stop it.

I need to stop letting my thoughts be consumed by what he did and how he made my body feel. Now is definitely not the time.

He opens the sack with gloved hands and starts handing out the swords and small daggers for us to strap on. Fynn gets a bow and arrows as well as a sword, admiring the sleek design of the arrows before slugging them over his shoulder.

"They can kill Scavengers and the Corrupted. Just aim for the heart," Draven informs everyone as he takes a double-edged sword for himself.

I decided to choose a normal sword, with another dagger that can be belted around my hips. The weapons I'm most familiar with. The moody shadow dragon better not piss me off now, because I have the true blades that will harm him if need be.

"Don't worry, we'll be back before anyone even knows we were there," Fynn says with confidence as a ball of yellow power radiates in his palm.

"Watch your back, Princess," Kye tells me. "Remember what I taught you."

I give him a stern nod, knowing I won't let him down. Fynn throws a glowing kernel of his power into the air a few feet away. It slams into an invisible force field before it slices through the air, making a cut in the land. It spreads wide, forming a circle that's shining brightly. A waiting portal for them to venture straight into another court.

"After you," Fynn tells Cora with a wave of his hand.

"You're insane if you think I'm going to be the first one to walk through something *you* created." She shakes her head in disbelief and I chuckle at her bluntness.

Kye looks at her thoughtfully, placing his hand gently on her back when he steps forward. "Don't worry, I'll go first."

Cora's cheeks flush the faintest shade of pink from Kye's show of chivalry.

He steps toward the light, and it pulses with a wave of power the moment he walks through, before returning back to its normal state. Cora looks at Fynn skeptically before giving us a final wave and blowing a good luck kiss as she steps through the golden void.

My heart lurches watching them disappear right before my eyes, praying to the Gods that nothing happens to them and that we will be reunited soon. Fynn looks at the two of us, bidding farewell with a salute to Draven and giving me a wink as he leaps through the fissure in the air, before it snaps shut behind him.

I hear a growl as I turn to look at Draven. He's staring at where Fynn just was as swirls of shadows shoot around himself with aggression.

"You have anger issues," I say as I stare him down.

His hood shifts to me and I can feel his eyes burning a trail along my body. "Seems my *anger issues* started when I met you."

I roll my eyes as I walk past him, making my way to the opening in the trees.

Draven's presence is all-consuming behind me, as his shadows flow around him, occasionally brushing along my back. I'm about to step into the opening between the trees when I'm yanked back, a shadow wrapped around my waist as I slam into his chest.

The hard muscles of his large frame pour heat into my chilled body from the early morning air, pressing against every inch of me. His hand slides up my throat, avoiding my necklace as he forces my head to tip back. His cedar and maple scent invades every part of me. I feel like I'm drowning as the pull towards him drags me further down.

Another growl vibrates up his throat and it sends shivers licking down my spine. "Roll your eyes at me again, little demon," he says, tightening his hold as it shifts up to under my jaw. "I fucking dare you." The deep baritone feathers against my cheek, his shadows caressing around my legs and tightening around my waist. Holding me harder against him.

I want to snap back at him, give him another eye roll just to see what he'd do, but he calls on his wings and launches off the ground without warning. Propelling us through the opening of the forest as he guides us closer to the glistening sky. He wraps his shadows around me as he blocks out the sting from the chilly air as we cut through it.

Twisting me in his hold, he locks his arm under my knees and places his other one behind my back. For some reason, I trust he won't drop me. Even so, I still secure my arms around his neck, twining my fingers together as I hold myself closer to him. The brown strands of my hair whip around me as we push through the sky.

I can't stop myself from looking down, so far away from life that is happening below. It feels like another world up here.

It feels *freeing*.

A feeling I've never felt.

I forget about all of the evil waiting for me as we leave the Court of Asiza behind, soaring over the gem-speckled sea. It's not long before a glow of orange starts to peek over the edge of the world as dawn signals a new day. Slowly illuminating streaks of light over the gentle waves.

I watch in awe and fascination as the sun slowly starts to push away the darkness, evaporating the deep hues of the night. Could it be just as easy to push away the blackness that stains a soul?

Is this possibly what the book Queen Zoraida gave me was referring to?

When light and dark collide, your fate will be split in two.

Does it mean when day and night collide? But that still doesn't explain anything, if that's what it's hinting to.

"We're getting close," Draven says, disrupting my thoughts as the rumble of his voice vibrates into me, sending a wave of heat crashing deep into my stomach. I look out ahead and see mountains in the distance as dense clouds blanket them from up above.

The wind turns colder, feeling like icicles slicing through my skin, but Draven immediately raises a stronger shield of shadows around us. A gesture I'm thankful for as we get closer to our destination, even though I won't tell *him* that.

But the view before me is something straight out of a painting. The brightening hues from the sun radiate through the mountaintops, as darkness fades and the moon drops. The beauty seems magical, with the untouched powder glistening. *Snow*. Flying so high as the wind whispers around us.

I have to close my eyes, because this peaceful moment will come and go. I don't know how smooth our journey will be, but at least in this moment, I can feel free.

CHAPTER FORTY-THREE

Emma

Gusts of white, fluffy snow dance around us when we land. I wrap my cloak tightly around me and pull my hood up to block the wind as Draven's shadows fall away. We're standing at the top of one of the snow-covered mountains in Amihan.

"What are we doing up so high?" I yell over the bustling whistles of the wind as it picks up the snow laying on the ground before spreading it around.

"This is where the Seer who might be able to help us locate the Elder, lives."

"All the way up here?!" I ask him, because I can't fathom why someone would willingly live at the top of a mountain. But then I think of the cave Draven took me to, and I hold back my tongue. That may not have been as harsh of weather, but the cave was beautiful. Gods, I hope it's warm inside, because I can feel mini-icicles forming along my eyelashes as the wind burns against my cheeks.

I look over at Draven, who is standing, unfazed, as if the cold yields to him, melting at his touch. Maybe the heat that blooms inside of me is not one of desire, but simply because he's made of fire. The traces of dragon blood running through his veins must be why he's staring at me like he's bored instead of as someone who is freezing to the bone.

He ignores me as he turns to head down the path that curves around the side of the mountain. I jab my middle finger up and curse him from behind.

"Don't you have a Seer in your court you can ask? You are the prince. Surely that holds some merit in obtaining the information you want?" I ask him while my boots crunch the layers of icy snow with each step, picking up my pace to catch up to him.

"Not all Seers are so willing to give out information. If I asked the Seer we have at the castle, then he would alert *everyone*. Our Seer may be good, but he enjoys spilling gossip more. He only keeps his mouth shut about anything concerning my mother's requests."

Interesting. "I assumed you enjoyed all the gossip that spreads about the notorious *Dark Prince*." I can't help but emphasize those last two words. Others may have seen him as the Dark Prince because of his cold exterior, never cracking a smile. But they don't realize how true the name fits him. For I got to see him in his darkest form, seeing the beast that lives within him.

He huffs as his breath flows in front of him. A puff of white swirls in the air before it vanishes. Draven takes a few more steps around the curve and pauses when we reach an oval door dusted with snow.

He bangs his fist on the door as we wait for someone to answer. I strain my ears, but don't hear anything inside, only the high tune of the wind whipping around.

"Maybe they're not home," I suggest as we wait.

He gives me no response, just the silent treatment as those icy eyes dart down at me. My breath catches when I see how light his eyes look in the wintry mix. Shimmering like frost under the rays of the sun. I fall still under his stare, overcome by the urge to reach my hand up and brush my thumb over his cheek. I clench my fingers together to restrain the unbidden desire to touch him. Our eyes are lingering on one another, only for the door to spring open and break the trance we were in.

"What brings you here?" A sultry voice dances around us as we both turn out heads to look at the Seer.

She's gorgeous, as she looks like the ice queen of this mountain. Pale, white hair falls straight to her waist. She's tall, with a lean body that's barely covered in a thin white dress that cuts a V down the center, the point stopping just after her belly button. Slits open the sides of her dress, all the way to her hip, allowing an easy glimpse at her long legs that peek through. Those violet eyes watch me closely before they trail up to Draven, who's letting his normal prince form show.

"Galeana," he states, letting the older Fae who healed me in his court's name hang in the air.

I whip my head to him in confusion, questioning what she has to do with this. But then, the female standing in front of us chuckles deeply and my gaze falls back on her.

Watching.

Waiting.

Her black-painted lips stand out against her pale complexion and white teeth. She clicks her tongue before she steps aside and waves us into her home. "Tell Galeana I prefer to be left unbothered."

"I doubt she'll listen," Draven says as we step into the middle of the room. I want to drop to my knees and kiss the floor. Her entire place feels like a summer's day, and all the snow on me instantly melts.

For someone living at the top of a mountain, she manages to have a lot of stuff filling her shelves. The room is open with a sleek design of white furniture against the dark interior of the mountain. Wooden shelves line the walls, holding different glass jars filled with... I squint my eyes and still am not quite sure what's in them. Small, decorative lanterns hang to give the room a cozy feel, and further back, she has a fluffy throw rug, which seems to be where her main room is.

She said she prefers to be unbothered. So, I'm assuming she lives alone. I can understand the lure of wanting to live alone, far away from everyone. The image is enticing. But I also know how being alone for too long can sink its claws into your psyche, shredding it apart in agonizingly slow slices.

Then again, maybe being a Seer allows her mind to stay sane because her visions never let her truly be alone. She can dive into the life of another if she wants to *see* someone.

She closes the door, blocking the harsh, freezing wind from blasting inside, and then refastens three sets of locks. Whipping her hair behind her, she saunters towards us, setting those blazing violet orbs on me speculatively.

"Galeana says you owe her a favor," Draven says, while she still stares at me with curiosity. Like a puzzle she can't figure out.

"Is that right?" she hedges. "She says that every time she needs something, ever since she healed me from the brink of death." She taps a slender finger against her lips. "And I'm assuming *you* are the favor?"

He doesn't answer. He just gives her that infuriating arch of his eyebrow like the answer is clear enough.

I watch her eyes narrow on him, while pursing her lips before she looks back at me.

"You are *quite* interesting. My name's Mauve and yours is Emma, no? The runaway princess," she says with a wave of her hand in the air.

I blanch, stiffening my back as my muscles tense in anticipation. Her eyes never sway away from me. She takes a step closer and Draven's there in a heartbeat, standing an inch in front of me.

She laughs wickedly at his actions. "Oh, my, my. Does the Dark Prince I've heard so much about have a heart? I thought it was rotting away with your lack of a mate." She turns towards her shelves on the sidewall, rummaging through them.

"We only need help to find someone, and then we will be out of your hair."

"Hmm, and whom do you need to find?" Mauve asks, while grabbing a jar of what looks like some kind of murky liquid.

"The Elder that lives in this court," Draven says without hesitation as he still stands in front of me, watching her every move.

Mauve sighs dramatically. "Tell Galeana that she needs to start keeping tabs on her own mother."

Draven goes to take a step forward but falters slightly from Mauve's words. "Her mother is the Elder?" he asks.

Mauve squints her eyes, before sighing in exasperation. "Yes. And it's becoming tiresome to hunt her down when she wishes to speak with her. So, make sure to tell Galeana that this is the final time I will search for her." She waves her hand towards the center of the room. "Come, sit down," she says as she takes a seat at her wooden table off to the side of the room. Draven and I both take the empty seats on the opposite side of her.

As soon as we're settled, she shoots her hand out, wrapping her long fingers around my wrist. I gasp in shock, as a wave of fear slams into me, not sure of what she's doing, and even Draven looks alarmed as his eyes go wide.

"Don't," Mauve says with a power booming from her voice as it paralyzes us in our chairs. Her eyes glaze over in a white film that causes my hand to tremble in her hold as her grip tightens. "What are you?" she asks, and my brows furrow at her question.

I'm Fae. But maybe the wyvern iron wrapped around my throat is blinding her from her seeing abilities, or at least at looking into my life.

"I'm sorry, but we really need to know where the Elder is and leave," I try to persuade her and remind her that she can be alone once again if she stays focused.

A hum buzzes up her throat, a purple flare erupts out of her as her head is thrown back, as she still remains clutching to my arm. "Your soul is torn between two sides of a war, and soon you will have to choose." Her voice sounds demonic as she speaks, but then her head snaps back forward, and the milky sheen is gone from her eyes as she lets go of my wrist. Her purple eyes pin me to the spot, and it looks like a semblance of unease flickers through her.

I cradle my hand up to my chest, unsure of what to make out of everything that just happened. But my mind is frantically racing at what the hell that means. It sounds similar to the riddle in my book, but it still doesn't give me answers.

"What does that mean?" I ask in a steady voice, trying to sound stern as I mentally take in her words and cover the tremble of my hand.

"I don't know, but for some reason, your future is blurry. Usually, I can see someone's life and all of the paths they can choose and what they will lead to. But for you…I can't see past a certain point."

Immediately, my mind races back to the words Calloway spoke in my father's office. That he couldn't *see* further into my future. None of this sounds reassuring. Does that mean I die? That my soul will finally become completely destroyed, with no longer any hope to save it as I leave this world? Let my last breath curse those who have hurt me. But I'm done questioning my future, because only death awaits there. I won't stop fighting against my father, or the phantom that appears in my dreams until my heart stops beating. I just hope that before that happens, I can stop the Corruption and seek my revenge.

"Enough about me, that's not why we're here. Can you tell us where the Elder is?" I ask, demanding her to focus on what we need to know, even though these riddles are starting to give me a headache.

I see Draven looking at me with concern, his eyes assessing to see if any harm was done by Mauve's power. Then, he turns back to look at her with predatory eyes. "Where is the Elder?" She scrutinizes him with malice at the tone of his words.

"Please," I say, hoping to lighten the heaviness in the room.

Without a word, she closes her eyes as she places her hands palm side up on the table. A few moments later, she opens her eyes again, looking straight at Draven. "The Elder you seek is living on the other side of town between the two lone mountains on the west side of the island. But you better hurry, it seems she may also have more company fast approaching."

Panic jolts through me as I instantly fear my father's soldiers might be the *company* Mauve is speaking of but not saying. "Thank you." I twist towards Draven sitting there with a serious expression. "Draven," I plead. "We have to go."

He stays still for a moment longer, staring hard at Mauve before he reluctantly nods. "Come on," he says. Those two words that I'm becoming familiar with as I push back my chair to stand up and follow him to the door. He opens it up, letting the freezing bite of the snowy haze rage through as I yank my hood up to help block the sting of the wind.

Mauve's voice halts my steps. "Nothing can protect you from yourself, Emma."

My grey eyes clash with her violet ones, as confusion deepens. A storm of dread and uncertainty brews between us with answers left unsaid. The power inside me rumbles to life, simmering deep with the feeling of trepidation coursing through me. I'm already plotting my pieces on the board, waiting to take down my enemies, but will I need to take myself down, too? Achieve my win and end my own suffering?

I tear my gaze away from hers as I stride out into the winter air, leaving her behind as her words sink under my skin and stay with me.

CHAPTER FORTY-FOUR

Draven

I scoop Emma up into my arms, as I push off the white powdered ground and jolt us into the sky. The sun that was peeking through earlier had all but disappeared once the winter clouds began rolling in, bringing a blizzard with them. The white flakes cling onto her hair, lingering as the warmth in her body fades. I blanket my shadows around us, their heated touch pressing against her shivering body as I pull her closer into my chest.

My wings force us through the wind, beating with strong gusts. Once we clear the core of the storm, I glance down at her, but she's oblivious to it.

Those fog-colored eyes stare off into the view below us, looking distant. She seems completely distracted in her mind, buried so far under her thoughts. It's not hard to guess that what Mauve told her unsettled her, even if she was trying her best not to let it show. It seems as if she's locking away her feelings deep down, like they're not important, and choosing to focus on the task ahead instead.

When Mauve took hold of her arm, a deep fire burned in me to rip it off her. The protective need to stop her mixed with a possessive urge to only want my touch on her. It froze me in that moment, the shock of how strongly I felt towards Emma. I was a second too late when Mauve somehow paralyzed us, not even my shadows were able to slither out of her powerful hold. It's a dangerous power that I wasn't prepared for, and I want to slam my fist into a wall because of it. I have never felt that feeling before, one where I'm forced into the control of another, unable to use my own power. My heart feels heavy in my chest as I realize that Emma has suffered through this her whole life, her powers being paralyzed in her very soul. Always there but never obtainable.

This beautiful girl in my arms looks anything but vicious at this moment. Her features are strained, and I can feel the stiffness in her muscles. A small crease forms on her forehead as she sorts through the chaos in her mind.

I still have yet to figure her out. Not fully trusting if she is with me or against me. I want to believe she stands on the same side as I do, wanting to seek the Stone before her father to stop him and the Corrupted. But I can't ignore what I saw that night during her nightmare, how she turned into darkness itself. And part of me still questions her true intentions when it comes to the stone, wondering if she's part of the Corrupted, but each second I spend with her is making that doubt become blurry.

I'm still wary of her true nature, even when a part of me refuses to believe that she would betray me and her friends. Even more so now that I'm starting to crave her, becoming blinded by the desire she lit with a match. I've been waiting for it to burn out, but it hasn't. The feel of her skin in the palms of my hands, the taste of her lips, and how addictive her orgasm tastes on my tongue.

I want to mark her as *mine*. To make her forget all the marks on her body but my own.

What the fuck?

Mine? Where the fuck did that thought come from?

She could never be mine. I wouldn't let that happen. Maybe play with her, yes…but anything more? Forget it. I haven't waited this long to find my mate to fuck it up by falling for another. I don't want just a relationship of surface-level feelings. I want the soul-binding love that consumes every part of you, ruining love for anyone else because all you can see is the one who is made for you.

Emma is one of the most stunning Fae I have ever laid my eyes on, with how sexy she is when she isn't even trying, or the way she snaps back at me. The way she bites her lip when she reads, the way her hips slightly sway when she walks, and the way those irises consume me like how the mist blankets over the sea before a storm, a veil of strength that hides her pain. They look innocent until I piss her off, and then they sharpen in a way that makes my dick hard.

No wonder Aiden looked so imperious and smug during the ball. Even through his mask, you could see the boastful smirk on his face as he had Emma's arms intertwined with his. Acting like he was showing off his possession, as if Emma was a prize he won. I wanted to wipe the floor with him, if only to see the high and mighty smirk fall from his face.

I can feel my irritation rising as I think back to that night but force it away as I notice Emma still consumed by her thoughts. I let my eyes trail over her soft features and let the press of her body against mine relax me.

"Do you want to talk about it?" I ask her, watching the crease in her brow deepen.

"Talk about what?"

Gods, this girl. She can't just make a conversation easy, always has to make it so damn difficult.

I keep my voice calm and steady when I respond, not wanting to push her away, "About what Mauve said, little demon."

"No," she says quickly, and I don't miss the way her spine stiffens in my arms. I don't think she's going to continue, but she surprises me when she does and her muscles begin to loosen. "She just…" She sighs. "The things she said just made me feel on edge." Her face looks strained as she admits how she's feeling. I want to soothe her worries and wipe away everything that haunts her.

I nod in understanding. "I'm here if you want to talk about it more."

She gives me a smile. "Thank you."

"Of course, but try not to let it consume you right now. My mother once told me to not worry about something that's not in your control, because if you do, you'll suffer twice. So, we'll deal with it when the time comes, together," I tell her, hoping that helps ease some of the thoughts churning inside her.

"You're right, I need to focus on what's ahead of us."

I frown, not wanting her to think I don't care, I just want to keep her from stressing over what Mauve said. "It's that stubborn head of yours that is confusing the damn Seer." I huff a laugh and notice the corner of her mouth lift.

I veer us right around a mountain along the edge of Amihan. I've been trying to keep us flying on the coast of the island to stay out of sight. Even with my shadows cloaking us, I don't want to take any chances.

"Gods, if my father has already gotten to the Elder…"

"He hasn't," I state.

"You don't know that," she snaps, finally bringing those stormy eyes to mine. Threatening to steal my breath every time they land on me.

"I have a feeling, little demon. Plus, it takes them far longer to travel than us." I let a cocky smirk grow on my face to watch her eyes harden on me.

She opens her mouth to say something, but snaps it shut and looks ahead again. I internally curse as I tighten my grip on her body. I want her to keep those eyes on me, even if she's pissed, in hopes it keeps her mind from getting lost within itself again.

Clenching my jaw, I raise my head and look up to see two lone mountains standing tall away from the rest of them. My eyes glow brighter as I call on my dragon senses, one of which allows me the ability to see for miles. My eyes pinpoint a small hut decked out in the snow as it's built against the side of the mountain. It must be the entrance that leads underneath. I hope so.

I brush my thumb along the side of her leg, seeing how her body startles and her breath hitches. I can hear the rush of blood in her veins and how her pulse starts to race.

"There." I nudge my head forward, towards where we need to go.

She turns to look, her mouth opens in excitement. "Please, hurry," she says in one breath, and I dive down, cutting through the wind as we approach. My eyes scan the area and, luckily, there's not a soul in sight, except the people out in the village on the other side of the mountains, but they won't see our descent from there.

I land on my feet, still holding onto Emma for a moment longer before she wiggles out of my hold and starts running to the hut. I keep pace with her as she pounds her boots in the snow, her hood flying back in her rush to get there. I make sure to have my shadows smooth the snow out behind us to hide our tracks, because Mauve's words of other company being here are still ringing in my head.

We make it to the wooden door under a torn-up canopy and I knock my fist against it. Only a few seconds pass before the door creaks open on its own and we step inside to see a tunnel that guides us further into the mountain. The door falls shut with a click the moment we step inside before I can close it myself.

We make our way along the dimly lit path. The tunnel grows wider as we walk through it and the end opens up to a huge room. There are steps that trail up the wall on the side, leading to other areas, but the main room has everything one would need to comfortably live. Books are shelved along the far wall, built into the mountain itself. Pillowed seats line a fire pit and orbs of light glow from the torches that expand around the room.

Small steps bring my attention to the left and I instinctively shoot my arm in front of Emma. When I turn to look, I see the Elder working her way towards us, slightly hunched with straggly, white hair. Her skin is leathered and her eyes are a chalky white, reminding me of how Mauve's eyes changed when she seemed to become someone else entirely as those purple eyes were veiled in white.

"I was wondering when you would show up," she says in a voice stronger than I imagined. She must notice the confusion on my face because she continues to talk. "I know many things, dear boy, I am an Elder. There are not many things I do *not* know." Her eyes peer around me to take in Emma. "And you're one of them, girl."

I can see Emma blanch beside me, but I try my best to drive the conversation to where we need to go, even though I'm sure this Elder already knows why we are here. "What's your name?"

"Edith," she says, walking over to the red and gold pillows on the floor, her all white robe trailing behind her, before plopping down as flames suddenly spark in the center and a fire roars to life.

We follow and sit down on the pillows next to her, letting the crackling fire spread its warmth around us. "I suppose you already know why we're here," I say, waiting for her to respond.

She turns her head to look at me and small a smile stretches over her face as she looks straight into my soul. "You want to know the where-abouts of the Liminal Stone. My question is why would the Prince of Asiza want the power the Stone would give?"

I'm not surprised she already knows who I am, as I'm sure she knows Emma, too. "The power is not of use to me, it's destroying it and keeping it away from King Oren that are the main priorities."

"Ahh but it seems *she* has some use of it," Edith says, as she slides her pools of white to Emma.

I turn to look at Emma, who is already staring unfazed at Edith. "I do," she says bluntly, with no sympathy in her words for wanting it.

I hide the anger that slithers through my veins, as Emma continues to not look in my direction. *Why* does she want its powers? Was I right? Has she been playing on two sides of the coin, wanting the power to help the king and rule the Corrupted? My hands clench tightly into fists, as a bitter taste sours my tongue. I'll have to deal with her later and force the answers from those wicked lips myself.

Emma stares at Edith, not backing down as the Elder assesses her. She must see something, because she drops her gaze towards the fire before she speaks. "You are entering uncharted territories by going after the Stone, and I'm not sure you will like what awaits you." There is uncertainty in her voice, but we have no options. The Stone must be found before it falls into the wrong hands.

"A journey's no fun unless danger is involved," I say in a lighter tone, hoping to ease the weight that's settling around us.

Edith humphs with exasperation, seeming to not care for my response, but either way, she decides to let it go. "The Stone was created by the Gods. One was the Goddess of Light, and one was the God of Darkness. It was a symbol of their undying love, submerging their powers into it with a drop of their blood to create balance and bind them together. The Stone is the reason they were able to create life."

I listen to her speak, remembering learning about how both Gods who were complete opposites were fated together, but I never knew the Liminal Stone was a part of that.

"That is, until one day, a true test was given on their love. None of the elders know what tested their relationship, only that it's one they failed. It was a way to grow that bond even further, but instead, the tether broke, causing them to crash apart from one another. They raged as enemies since, tearing the remainder of their love to shreds."

I stare at her in horror. How does something that is supposed to be an undying love…die?

"From what I know, only the Liminal Stone is proof that they bonded together. The Stone still exists as it holds a part of each of the Gods' essence within, making it *very* powerful. It has the ability to amplify one's power close to the level of a God, but…" She pauses. I hold my breath, waiting for her next words as Emma leans in close, our anticipation growing. Edith grows serious, as concern etches on her face. "But the Stone holds the power to see into this world, and the one beyond it."

I scrunch my face as I let her words sink in. To see into this world and the one beyond it… I snap my eyes up to find Edith already looking at me and nodding her head. "Death?" I ask. "The world beyond this…you mean the afterlife?" I say again to make sure what I'm thinking is matching what she's suggesting.

"Yes, my boy. It's the balance between both worlds, of life and death, and the one with the Stone controls what side they wish to see. But the stone is dangerous… If the one who holds the Stone is not able to control their own powers, they won't be able to control the Stone. It will ignite their power to a raging force and can consume them," she says gravely.

I sit there silently as I think about what that could mean if King Oren got the Stone and if Deyadrum could ever recover from the outcome if he did. We have to get that Stone.

CHAPTER FORTY-FIVE

Emma

We sit in Edith's home, listening to her explain what she knows about the Liminal Stone, but every so often, I catch Draven looking over at me. This Elder put me on the spot about needing to use the Stone, but I'm tired of lying, so I didn't. I had a feeling she would know if I did, which might ruin the chance of her trusting me with the knowledge of where the Stone may be.

But listening to her explain how the Stone came to be...it makes me feel more curious about it. It's a symbol of the beginning and end of the Gods, as their powers cling to the Stone itself. I never knew our two Gods were in love, but it seems moot now. All that matters is that the Stone still holds its powers, which makes me more anxious to ask if she knows its location.

Those milky eyes shift to me, and a chilling sensation sweeps through my entire body. I'm feeling more on edge than ever, especially since I have yet to fully settle after the words Mauve said to me.

"So, you want to know where the Stone is, girl," she says, not bothering with truly asking, because there's no point. She already knows we're here for the Stone, she gave us our warnings about its power, but now it's time to say our thanks and move forward.

"Yes," I say, never letting my eyes falter from her stare.

Smoke from the fire swirls around, springing water to my eyes as they start to burn. But the heat from the orange flames feels too delicious to move out of its path. The crackles of the fire echo in the massive room we're in, as Draven and I wait for her to speak.

"Nobody knows," Edith says with apprehension. I feel myself deflate as the words leave her mouth, like every organ inside of me is shutting down, ready to give up. But I can't. I have to remember that Kye, Cora, and Fynn might have answers that will help us, because if not, then... I'm not sure what we'll do.

I glance at Draven and he's clenching his jaw in what seems like frustration. But he's watching Edith closely, and then his eyes light up.

"But you have an idea," he says, staring her down with hope I wish I had.

She lifts the corner of her thin, weathered lips. "You're clever, boy." She stands up slowly to make her way to her bookshelves on the wall and we get up to follow her. "I may not know where the Stone is, but there is a book that might help."

She reaches a shaky hand up and grabs a dusty, old, red book, swiping her hand over it as the dust particles float in the air, threatening to make me sneeze as they tickle my nose. Could it be this simple? Does this book hold the answers we need? She opens it but there are no words on the yellowed pages, instead, a square is carved out in the center of them. She pulls out a sooty skeleton key hidden inside the book. A secret treasure buried in plain sight. She holds it out to place it gently in the palms of my hands and I'm shocked to feel the weight to it.

The design is hauntingly beautiful. Swirls weave around one another in an intricate pattern on the handle and I gently bring it closer to my face...noticing it almost looks like a skull.

Edith points to the key as she draws my attention back to her. "This key will allow you to enter the forbidden library." I stop breathing. I feel terror at wondering why it's forbidden, but also excitement at discovering a new library and a step closer to the Stone. "There is just one thing you need to know…it's located in the Court of Ashes."

"Shit," Draven says, running his calloused hand through the strands of his raven hair. I watch the way his eyes squeeze shut, as if Edith's words pain him.

Edith nods as she understands the issue, while my brain is still trying to catch up.

The Court of Ashes.

Then, it dawns on me. In the last training I had with Kye on my father's ship, he mentioned the Court of Ashes. He said—oh *shit*.

He said the Scavengers originated from there. The source of the Corruption lives in that court, so maybe we can find out how the Scavengers are being made and figure out how to end it while we're there.

Kye did say those who have wronged get sent there for their deaths. It looks like I'm walking straight into death's waiting arms.

The spiraling of my thoughts gets cut off when Edith speaks. "There should be an ancient book there called the Book of Kaimi. It holds an ancient power that only responds to those with blood that's pure."

"How will it help us?" I ask with curiosity. I need to know if going after this book will truly be beneficial for us if it means crossing into the Court of Ashes.

"With a drop of blood, it will communicate with you and lead you to an object you seek. But you must not—"

Draven's shadows whip out in a blast, coiling around us to lock us in. "Quiet," he breathes out. "We aren't alone anymore." He uses his shadows to press us further against the wall of stones between the bookshelves, being careful not to knock any over. Those blue eyes widen for a second like something dawned on him before he gives a flick of his wrist, letting his shadows extinguish all of the torches, only leaving a small fire crackling in the center of the room as it slowly starts to fade.

A moment later, Edith's door explodes open. I suck in a painful breath and hold it, afraid one small movement will give us away.

Armored males storm in with their swords and bows ready. I dart my eyes to their chests and see the wave symbol with a circle around it.

My father's soldiers.

I grate my teeth at their intrusion, storming into someone's home with such brutality. I'm thankful we got here first, but I hope they don't realize we are in the same room, as Draven blends us into the shadows, camouflaging us to be nearly invisible.

I watch as six of my father's warriors walk inside, shaking the snow off their cloaks before they turn to the door like they're waiting for someone. A second later, the blood in my veins freezes over. My lungs refuse to expand as I see Aiden step through the threshold.

He drops back his hood as his sandy blonde hair falls forward in front of those emerald eyes I know so well. It's hasn't been long since I left, but the last time I saw him was when I was still recovering, or when he thought I was *sick*.

I wonder what he thought when he found out I was nowhere to be found. A part of me hoped he would come searching for me and offer to help, and maybe that's why he's here. He's tracking me down, but I have a distinct feeling I have nothing to do with his reason for being here. Not as he steps farther into the room and narrows his determined gaze. Searching.

"Check everywhere." Aiden's voice fills the room as the males with him start scouring around and climbing the stairs. One of them stays at Aiden's side as he walks closer to the fire that only flickers with the weakest ember.

We stand hidden in the shadows, with our bodies locked into place. I can feel a bead of sweat forming on my forehead as I grow more nervous.

Time passes as banging is heard somewhere from above, the sound echoing from the opening at the top of the steps. Minutes pass before the soldiers upstairs start filing back down into the main room.

"It looks like the Elder's not here," the male next to Aiden says. I look over his face and I don't recognize him from the palace. But I never paid too much attention to all of the warriors who honor my father. Kye being the exception, because he helped me grow, trained me to be lethal, and has given me the ability to fight for myself. He's expressed his dislike for my father, but his honor and loyalty are to me. The ones who blindly followed my father were of no interest to me.

Aiden's quiet for a moment as his hand rubs over his jaw in thought, watching the lick of the fire burn out completely. "Hmm, there are no tracks outside though, and the fire just went out."

The guy frowns as he analyzes Aiden's words. "The storm is strong and could have easily covered any tracks. The torches weren't lit, so the Elder must know this fire will die out at some point after they left."

Nodding, Aiden starts moving around the circle of pillows bordering the fire pit. "You could be right." He stops, sitting down on the pillow Edith was using earlier. Bending his knees up, he rests his arms over them, still glancing around. Until his eyes snag on one of the pillows. He leans over and picks something up and I bite my lips to hold in my gasp.

Shit.

A long strand of my hair falls limply between his fingers as he twists it between them, bringing it to his nose. He inhales deeply, using his heightened senses, before his eyes darken. And then, in a flash, he warps himself back to the soldier at his side, standing next to him.

Chills race down my spine at the sound of his deep chuckle. "Seems my soon-to-be *wife* is playing games with me." He raises the strand of brown hair in front of his face again.

The male next to him seems confused by the way his face scrunches up and he leans a little closer to look at my hair.

"Rose and honey is the sweetest scent, don't you think, Bash?" Aiden asks the soldier beside him, whose name must be Bash.

"Yes, sir," he agrees.

Within a second, Aiden becomes unhinged as his knife is at Bash's throat. "That would mean you think my *fiancé* has the sweetest scent. Be careful with your next words and remember that she's *mine*." Blood leaks from the small slit along the side of Bash's jugular from Aiden's abrupt outburst. This version of Aiden I see before me is not the one I knew.

Bash gulps. "Yes, sir. My apologies," he adds quickly. Bash shows no sign of fear as he keeps himself standing tall, as if Aiden's rage is a normal occurrence.

Aiden holds the blade on his neck a moment longer before pulling back and running his fingers over the sharp edge as if he's holding himself back from slicing through the layers of Bash's skin, only to watch every drop of blood spill free. He combs his fingers through his hair in aggravation. A sting of hurt crosses his features when he pinches his brows together and presses his lips tight. He's lashing out, and a small part of me feels responsible, as though he's acting this way from me leaving him behind. Stabbing him in the heart and back. It's like he needs to take out his anger. His frustration.

He steps to where the fire went out, watching the glowing residue of embers among the ashes as he drops the strand of hair to watch it burn away from existence.

I'm staring at Aiden in shock from behind the shield of Draven's shadows. Guilt has been gnawing at me since the night on the roof when Draven first kissed me. I felt ashamed of my actions, for letting the desire that pulsed through me turn me feral and loosen my control. Even though, I felt more alive and seen than I ever have from what Draven and I shared in the cave.

But now, as I look at Aiden…it's like I'm staring at a different person. Someone who would harm another for no reason just because they were consumed by their own anger. The happy boy who I grew up with is gone. There may be a sliver of that part of him buried deep down, but I'm not sure if I could ever pull him free again.

I glance back at the blood dripping from Bash's neck, causing a painful memory of my father's blade against my throat when I was younger. I swallow roughly from how similar their actions are. He's looking for the Elder with my *father's* soldiers, suffering from his own kind of manipulative curse that my father's ruling has poisoned him with.

Maybe Aiden is more intertwined with the king than I ever knew. He's reminding me of my father, of *his* father. Both males are equally cruel in their own twisted ways, and now, Aiden is, too.

The sight turns my stomach as I see those lush green eyes that used to remind me of fresh leaves, but then the thought lights on fire, burning into nothing. I can feel the darkness in me stirring as my heart fills with disgust towards Aiden. The way he tries to claim me as his when he hasn't *earned* me.

I want to show him how I can play the game, how I can become his worst nightmare, and wipe him clear from this life. The whispers of darkness tell me they'll help, they say my power being locked away is of no use and that they will always be here for me, waiting for me to let go.

My imagination drifts, as a frightening vision flashes in my mind of Aiden and our fathers standing side-by-side, staring daggers at me as I wither on the floor under their control, and the image is enough to slam the barriers down inside me and welcome the darkness in.

Coldness slithers down my veins and I feel the rush of ecstasy as they slowly brush against my heart and my mind. It's painful as the biting feeling sweeps through me, but I revel it this time. My eyes close as I feel the anger dissipate. I open them again a moment later, with a smirk creeping on my lips, cocking my head to the side as I zero in on Aiden. I clench my fist as I begin to feel anxious about this power growing in me, not caring that it's slowly consuming me. I bring my palm up, ready to see what I can do.

But then, a heated touch burns against my cheek as my head gets whipped sideways.

Frantic blue eyes find mine.

In the next blink, his eyes glow silver, steeling against mine as our gazes stay locked. The hand of his shadows forces me to stay on him, as those metallic eyes burrow deeper into mine.

A gentle touch grazes my arm to find the Elder's hand on me. She's not scared. Instead, she looks at me with a sadness that makes my heart ache. A small flicker of green light leaves her palm, absorbing into my skin and shooting through my veins.

Every icy touch of darkness is flushed out with the power she pushed into me. My vision clears and I feel the cold claws digging their nails into my mind and heart pull out as warmth trails through my body. I stare wide-eyed at Edith, as she brings a finger to her lips, a signal to stay quiet. A reminder of the situation we're in, while I let myself slip, risking our cover.

I whip my head back and see that Aiden and his group are still here. I curse myself for not being able to control my own hatred towards him enough to keep the darkness at bay. I *wanted* to let them in. Their whispered words filled my mind and made me want to let them guide me. I cast my eyes downward as shame tastes thick on my tongue.

Thank goodness Draven has been able to keep his shadows tightly woven around us, dense enough to block everything from those on the outside.

I don't know what I missed in those few moments of being lost in the darkness, but when I look up, I see Aiden staring at us, but to him, we're just a shelf of books in the darkened room. Either way, the feeling of his sharpened emerald eyes sends chills down my spine and makes the hair on the back of my neck stand up.

"What do you want to do?" Bash asks Aiden, staying perfectly still as he awaits his orders.

Aiden shoves his hands in his pockets, squinting his eyes in our direction, and I hold my breath, praying he doesn't come any closer. "Let's go see if the Elder is meandering around town, and maybe the princess will be there, too. Seems she needs a lesson in what happens when someone deceives me." His gaze never wavers from where we are, and I worry he can *sense* we're here. But the one thing I never thought I'd say is that I trust Draven enough to keep us safe right now.

He finally tears his eyes away from us and takes one final glance around the room before calling to the crew of soldiers with him and leaving Edith's home with the door broken in their wake.

CHAPTER FORTY-SIX

Emma

*E*dith stares at me once it becomes safe to have Draven pull his
shadows away. She's not wary, but concern radiates brightly
from her.

"Thank you," I say softly. "I didn't mean—"

"I know," she says, placing her wrinkled hand on mine.

I hesitate for a moment before I speak as she watches me with patient
eyes. "How did you do it?"

She gives me a tight-lipped smile that softens the longer she looks at
me. "I have the purity of nature's energy, so I was able to cleanse you. But
the power I used won't stay in you, you need to figure out how to control
the darkness that lives in you. It would explain why I can't figure you out
or *see* you." She pauses, as those white eyes never leave me. "You best not
touch that Stone you're after, not until you control that power inside of
you." She lets go of my hand and starts walking away.

I nod, knowing I need to control the war inside of me, but I can't fully
do that until I get this necklace off me and know what I'm facing.

Draven steps forward, staring at the broken shards of her door. "I'll fix your door before we go," he says, as we watch her slowly begin to ascend her stairs.

"Don't bother, boy. I'll be long gone before anyone comes looking for me again." She stops in the middle of the stairway, keeping her hunched back to us. "Best be careful on your journey, the path you're traveling down is a dark one." With that, she continues up the steps and leaves us standing by her open doorway, with the snowy wind slamming into my face. Leaving me feeling as cold on the outside as her parting words did on the inside.

I stare up into Draven's icy gaze as we walk back towards the broken door. He holds his hand up to stop me, bringing his shadows around himself and disappears into the flurry of the storm. I impatiently wait, nerves dancing along my body, thinking Aiden and my father's soldiers are still out there. Waiting.

But I don't have to wait long before Draven is back, his full height towering over me when he appears inches in front of me. He stares down at me with his eyes slightly squinted, and I so badly wish I knew what he was thinking. I want to ask Draven more about what we just learned and his thoughts. But he doesn't say anything, he just sweeps me off my feet with alpha male, dominating strength, and launches us into the sky with pensive eyes as he surges against the flakes of snow.

We are heading back to the Court of Asiza and I'm anxious to get back. I hold onto Draven tightly, keeping my head tucked low as shame washes over me from my outburst earlier. I won't be able to handle the emotions flitting in his eyes if I look up at him.

It took us less than an hour on the flight here, but it feels twice as long this time, with the tense silence hanging between us. An eternity is more like it. I was itching to say something, but for the first time, I held my tongue.

We eventually make it back to his court, and instead of going to the inn, he lands on the roof of his castle. I'm assuming away from the prying eyes of his people, but I'm surprised when he says we'll be staying here, while he effortlessly shifts back into his Fae form.

He sets me down softly and steps back to put space between us. I feel my heart splinter from the action. I try to hide the prick of hurt. "Won't your family question why I'm here, or better yet, why I'm *hiding* here? They aren't going to want to have a runaway princess in their home," I tell him in a rush, as I fear my father finding out and sending his soldiers here to break down the walls of his home.

Draven crosses his corded arms over his chest. "Nobody will know. Fynn will bring your friends here, too, and you'll stay in the rooms in the tower. No one ever goes there, it's always empty." His eyes leave no room for discussion as he pins me with them. I choose to stay quiet once again, because I'm drained and don't feel like fighting back.

His brows furrow at my silence, like he's hoping for me to snap back at him or argue more reasons for why I can't stay here, and maybe later, I will do just that.

Somehow, the silence brewing between us turns loud as the foggy mist blankets us. Our eyes lock together with words unsaid.

Suddenly, a pop of gold light expands out of nowhere and I jump back, arms up in defense as my heart pounds frantically. I let out a huge breath of air when I realize it's Cora, Kye, and Fynn as they step through the opening. Fynn lights up when he sees us, and then his face falls, glancing between the two of us.

"Something wrong?" Fynn asks, while he closes the portal behind him with a swipe of his hand.

"Just tired," I say quickly. "How did you know where to find us?" I ask in confusion, because we never set a meeting place for after our travels.

His face brightens again as his teeth go on full display in a dazzling smile. "Pretty cool, huh? I can find those who I was recently with, with portal vision." He winks like it's the sexiest thing about his power. "It allows me a glimpse of them for a moment, and see what they're doing and where they're at."

Well, that's why he seems sinfully smug. "That sounds creepy, but helpful," I tell him with a laugh.

"Emma, it was so cool!" Cora shrieks. "It was like peeking through a window in his hands." Her excitement pulls a smile on my face, and I'm glad to have them back safe. Cora runs up to me and squeezes me tightly, whispering in my ear, "I was worried about you."

I hug her back just as tightly. "I was worried about you guys, too." Kye comes to stand next to us with a gentle smile on his face.

I let go of Cora and reach over to embrace Kye as he opens his arms up. "Glad to see you're safe, Princess." I smile into his chest at the overwhelming feeling of having people who care for me. I don't let go just yet, but then I hear a snarl vibrate through the air. I strain my neck around and see Draven vehemently watching me, looking about two seconds away from ripping me out of Kye's arms.

"Aw, Draven, need a hug, man?" Fynn chimes in, stretching his arms as he raises his eyebrows towards the male in question. Draven sends him a glare that would have anyone falling to their knees for forgiveness, but Fynn just brushes it off and belts a laugh. "One day, you'll beg me to give you a hug," he says in the middle of catching his breath as Draven still looks at him with a sour face.

The sight of it brings a small laugh tumbling from my lips, and Cora's, too.

"Did you find the Elder in Abhainn?" Draven asks, instead of acknowledging the laughter that's now starting to fade.

"After fighting off a damn river creature that wanted to shred us to pieces, we've got nothing," Cora butts in, wiping her hands down her clothes to smooth them out.

"She's right," Kye says, letting me go and crossing his solid arms over his chest. "There was no Elder there, because the Elder died a few days ago." I don't miss the concern in his voice.

"Died, *how?*" Draven questions, as it seems he's already guessed but doesn't want to voice it first.

Fynn heaves a sigh as he rubs his fingers over his eyes. "He didn't die the natural way, I can tell you that. Someone got there first, because the poor Elder was tied to a chair with his..." He stops talking as he quickly glances at Cora. Her face is pale, and instead, he looks back at Draven and mimics the movement of cutting someone's head off with his fingers sliding over his throat.

"Fuck," Draven curses as he starts to pace and brushes a hand roughly through his silky, raven-colored hair. "Well, we got to the Elder in Amihan in time. She doesn't know where the Stone is but gave us a hint of something that could help us find it."

"*Something?* Not someone?" Fynn asks.

"A key," I blurt. "To find the Book of Kaimi. She said it can help you find an object you seek." I grab my wind-blown hair and separate the strands into sections to do a quick braid while they process everything.

"So, where's the book?" Cora raises her eyebrows, seeming anxious to get it. The color slowly begins coming back to her face.

"That's the thing." I watch Draven's brows deepen when he stops his movements, seeing how his face looks solemn. "She said it's most likely in the forbidden library that's somewhere in the Court of Ashes."

Fynn curses under his breath as he stares at Draven, with his lips tightly pressed together. Unspoken words seem to pass between them, and I know I'm missing something. We are all aware of how dangerous the Court of Ashes is, but they don't seem scared about that, they seem to be filled with grief, by the way their eyes become weighted with sadness.

"Alright," Kye interjects. "If you're going off searching for this book, then count me in."

"Me too," Cora adds, as they both smile reassuringly at me.

My head starts to shake because they have both already done enough. "I can't ask you to do that, you've done so much already. It's dangerous." I cross my fingers, hoping they will stay behind so I know they will be safe.

"You didn't ask, Princess. Remember, where you go, we go." Kye and Cora look at one another and nod in agreement.

"Well, if we're all going, we need to eat and rest up." Draven looks off into the distance, the wind blowing his hair back, and it only reminds me of how my fingers felt running through it. "The sun's going to set soon. Let's take tomorrow to rest and offer some basic training," he says, his eyes sliding to Cora, "so we are more prepared. Then, we can meet here, and Fynn can transport us all there." He looks at Fynn with a nod.

We stand up there a little bit longer until Cora yawns. A clear signal that it's time to settle down for the night, the final glow on the horizon has started fading away, its orange light dancing along the veil of fog between the trees.

When Draven opens the roof's door to dip inside, his eyes connect with mine expectantly as I move past him. But once again, I'm too tired to snip back at him. We follow him through the castle as he guides us down one hallway before we hit a set of spiral stairs. When we make it to the top, the hallway circles around, and he shows us the three rooms that are up here.

Fynn and Kye get their own rooms and Cora and I agree to just share one again, and the company at night feels welcoming for once. Draven said he's going to sleep in his own room, and that is that. He brings up food for us all to fill our stomachs, and then we all go to our rooms to sleep.

When Cora and I walk in, we notice there is only one bed in our room, but Cora and I are small enough to fit with plenty of space still available. We both shrug, taking turns bathing in the separate washroom before we settle down.

I close my eyes and hope sleep takes me quickly, but the anger of Aiden's actions and my own come rushing forward. I feel the betrayal of his friendship bubble to the surface, stirring the darkest part of my psyche. I think of how easily I let the darkness invade me at the sight of Aiden. The acceptance of letting it slither through my body felt different this time, like opening a door that I had locked. As I picture how I lost control, that locked door comes to my unsettled mind again. But it's not locked, and slowly opens without my say.

My mind grapples with strength to close it, becoming more on edge, but I don't have time to re-lock it as I drift off to sleep.

Shadows twist around me, their icy fingers scratching against my skin.

"Emmaaa…" that deep voice whispers, and I can feel his breath against my ear.

I try to open my eyes, but they only peel open in my dream, and before I can see it coming, a blast of shadows fires at me with a phantom hand in the middle, aiming for my chest. Pain flares to life as I feel his hand wrap around my beating heart, squeezing. Staining my soul more.

I can't breathe as he holds it in his hands, and then I jolt forward with a silent scream, gasping for air.

I inhale greedily as I fill my lungs with air, pressing my hand against my chest to feel the beating of my heart underneath. Drops of sweat trail down my back as I squeeze my eyes shut to calm my racing pulse. This nightmare was intense, but not as long as they normally last. Maybe because I wasn't alone, with Cora snoring next to me. But I worry that, perhaps, he accomplished what he needed to do, tainting my heart with his mark, and then *let* me free of his hold.

I peel the collar of my shirt back and see a black painted circle on my chest. The spot he had gone through. I watch as the inky mark slowly begins to disappear. But I can feel my heart pounding in a frantic rhythm, not able to shake the feeling of his phantom hand holding my life in his palm. The way his cold fingers tightened against the pounding protest of my own heart. A chill erupts along my body, and I force the nightmare away, hoping the feeling will vanish as quickly as his mark on my skin.

I flatten my hand hard against my heart as I wait for my pulse to slow to a normal pace, while I look around the room. It's sometime in the night, but still a few hours off until sunrise. I carefully slide my feet out of the covers, not wanting to wake Cora as I work my way out of bed. With careful fingers, I slide my dagger out from beneath my pillow and strap it to my thigh. Then, I grab my boots and hug them to my chest as I tiptoe to the door. I manage to open it enough to squeeze my body through before shutting it silently behind me.

I yank my boots on and start heading toward the roof to clear my head, because I know I won't be able to sleep any longer after that nightmare. The cool breeze crashes into me as I open the door to step onto the roof, inhaling the freshness of the night.

Walking to the edge, I sit down and watch the trees sway to the wind's song under the light of the moon. The coolness of the air feels refreshing after waking up in a sweat. I thought my nightmares may have stopped, once I pushed the dark powers back against him, disintegrating the dream last time. It appears I was wrong. I fear I may have lowered my guard to let him back in, and the thought makes my head spin.

I have faith in Edith and her guidance, though, and I'm anxious to find the forbidden library. We have no idea what information my father's soldiers could have retrieved when they reached the Elder in Abhainn. I suppose only time will tell.

I close my eyes, and with my feet dangling over the side of the castle wall, I exhale a long breath as I let the silence of the night wrap around me in a gentle caress. That is, until I *feel* the presence of the male who irks me, while making me want to kiss him at the same time. The male who has made me feel things that no one has ever made me feel, and memories swarm me of the last time we were on a roof. I can feel a slight blush warming my cheeks, but I tell myself it's from the chilly wind.

Suddenly, I realize I never heard the door click shut, and I twist around to see him standing there under the moonlight as his silver eyes glimmer in the dark, his shadowed wings draped behind him.

"Where did you come from, shadow dragon?" I tease, letting the name run out of my mouth. Hoping to wipe away the tension between us earlier.

A wicked smirk kicks up the side of his mouth from it, as he starts to amble towards me. "I was searching for the forbidden library," he says casually.

I blanch. "What?! You can't just—"

He holds up a hand to stop me. "I can and I did, little demon. I wanted to see if the library could be seen from above." He sits down next to me, and I feel the warmth of his wing as it brushes against my back.

I tip my head to the side as I look at him incredulously. "It would be impossible to see that far to make out what would be there, even for a Fae."

His eyes glow brighter, almost becoming blinding against the dark. "Dragon sight is *very* different from Fae. I can see farther and zoom in on things in the distance." His words hold my attention as I stare at him blatantly in shock. He shrugs his shoulders like it's no big deal. "How do you think I can find the Corrupted so quickly?"

My mouth falls open. He flies and spots them from far away before anyone is aware. After I let my shock fade away, I stare out at the forest beyond us. "Did you find it?" I ask hesitantly.

"I did, there's not much there but desert and death. So, it was easy to see the location we need," he says with confidence as I whip my head back to him. He's smiling. My eyes drop to his dimple I love, and I force myself to look away again, before I lean into him.

I tap the heel of my boots against the stone, thinking of a way to change the subject. "You should be resting." I don't miss the huff of air that leaves him, but I can't hide the slight smile that slips on my lips at his irritation.

"So, should you," he tosses back.

"I did. Well, at least a little, and then——" I freeze, almost sharing the secret of the nightmares that assault me.

"And then…" he adds, waiting for me to finish.

"And then, I woke to relieve myself and couldn't fall back asleep because of our impending travels," I say, with a flit of my hand, hoping that will satisfy him enough.

"Lies," he says with a growl. I gradually turn my head to look at him and find those metallic eyes burning into me. "What happened earlier today?" he adds, holding his hard gaze on me.

"When?" I say with venom, feeling defensive at the way he's staring me down. I know what he's talking about—the moment I lost control—but I want *him* to say it before I admit to it.

"*When*, little demon?" I can see his frustration rising. "When those grey eyes that wrap around me like the fog of my home, blurring my vision of all sense of reason, turned black. Soulless. When the warmth of your skin that melts under my touch turned to ice. Lifeless. When your fair skin that begs to be touched had black blood creeping through its veins," he answers, with barely restrained rage.

I gape at him. At a loss for words, as he keeps me frozen under his gaze. The silver in his eyes glows brighter with every second that I stay silent. A sign of his rising frustration.

I make my face neutral and my voice bored, hoping to dissuade him from the effect the darkness has on me. "It was nothing."

His wings flare out as his control snaps. The shadows around him erupt before he reaches out, pulling me into his arms and tumbling off the roof.

But this time, he lets us drop only a couple of feet before he's swerving up to the sky, curving around the side of the castle. His arms are snug around my waist as I latch my hands behind his neck, our bodies pressed tightly together. I watch over his shoulder as his wings stretch wide, slowing his momentum as he glides down and lands gently on an open balcony that connects to a massive room.

I go to step out of his arms, but a growl vibrates through his chest as he squeezes me tighter. Refusing to let me go.

"Drav—" A squeal escapes me when he tosses me over his shoulder, and I see his wings, still burning with shadows in all their glory.

He walks into the room that opens up to the outside, the entire wall… gone. And that's when it hits me…it's *his* room. The smell of him is *everywhere*. Lighting every single nerve ending on fire as his cedar and maple scent slams into me.

I don't have time to take in his personal space as he flings me into the air and tosses me on the bed. I raise up on my elbows as I see the Dark Prince standing before me, completely unhinged, with the slight orange glow from the fireplace accentuating his masculine features.

Those eyes hold my breath, silence my voice, and control my pulse as they stay locked onto me in a silver stream of fierce power. "Don't lie to me, little demon."

"Why? You lie to *everyone* about who you are and what you do," I say with venom. Hating the way he's allowed to lie to keep his secrets close, but I can't keep mine.

Hypocrite.

His nostrils flare as he storms towards what seems to be his bourbon cart. *I knew it.*

He pours himself a drink of the dark amber liquid and swirls it once, twice, before bringing it to his lips. He turns back to me as he stays in the shadows of the room, sipping his drink slowly. I can feel the rage cascading from him, enough to make me break our gaze.

I glance around and notice his room is big enough for him to walk around comfortably with his wings, even his bed is wide enough to accommodate them. The whole one side of his room is open to the night, and a bookshelf decorates the corner next to the fireplace with neatly stacked books on it.

The obsidian silk sheets under me are smooth to the touch as I dig my fingers into them, pushing myself to sit all the way up. I slowly begin to inch towards the edge of the bed, feeling uncomfortable for being where he sleeps as he stands there, watching from the side of the room.

But I stop the moment he starts speaking. "I said, don't lie to *me*. Fuck everyone else."

My breath stalls in my lungs, as I feel the irritation that wanted to lash out at him begin to fade away. Taking in the seriousness of his face. His mouth opens again, but then he shuts it. A male, who never has to doubt anything, seems to be stuck on what to say for once. I can see in his eyes that he has so many thoughts hanging on the tip of his tongue as I hold his hard stare this time.

He tips back the rest of his bourbon, and I'm mesmerized by the way his throat works as he gulps it down, knowing how sweet he would taste with the drink fresh on his tongue.

The glass thumps when he sets it down on the cart, and he starts walking towards me again. I internally curse myself for not getting off his bed when I had the chance.

Placing both hands on the bed, caging me, he leans in so we're an inch apart and the maple of his breath wafts into my nose. The smell drives me wild as I feel my pulse start racing, the urge to lean in flares up.

"You're right, I lie to everyone. But not to you. For some *fucking* reason, I don't want to." The admission throws me off as I hold my breath, listening to every single word that spills from his lips. "Truths, little demon. I don't want you to feel alone when you're with me, because for some reason, I don't feel so lonely when you're here. I can't explain why, but you're consuming my thoughts. Like the sweetest poison that will kill me if I don't come back for more." His calloused hand comes up to my face as he traces my bottom lip with his thumb, his eyes glowing brighter. "I want to consume you, until I know every hidden part of your soul."

My mouth parts as his eyes drop down to my lips, where his thumb is still rubbing. The notes of his voice are music to my ears, causing my heart to race faster. I can feel the thrum of his heartbeat as he presses against my chest and the pounding rhythm locks away my fears. In the next breath, he closes the distance to claim my mouth with a bruising kiss. Igniting a burning passion as our two souls collide in a desperate need to claim. But before I can claim him back, he breaks the kiss, and a faint whimper escapes me.

A smirk settles on his lips when he hears my objection. "You still lied to me, little demon," he says wickedly, grabbing my hips to lift me up and place my back in the center of the bed. His shadows guide me to lie down on my back as he stands at the end of the bed, his eyes devouring me as they trail a heated path up my body. He pulls his shirt over his head, with one arm stretching behind him, and I'm fascinated by how it passes right through his shadowed wings with his control. My eyes take in every inch of his chiseled abs and defined pecs as his tattoos swirl over his skin. Mesmerized by how they shimmer with translucent scales like the stars in the sky.

He leaves his pants on as he moves towards me, straddling his legs over my body, and rests back on his knees to secure my legs between his. My breaths are coming faster in anticipation, and I feel heat coil deep within at the lust-crazed look in his eyes. He looks like a fallen God, with his wings draped behind him. He gradually lets his hands travel up my legs, making my entire body shiver at the contact. His fingers inch upward, but stop on my thigh, and I gasp when he unsheathes my favorite dagger and twirls it between his fingers.

Soon, nerves take over as I watch the blade dance around his fingers with precise skill. "What are you doing?" I ask, wary of what he has planned.

"Borrowing your dagger. It really is stunning," he says seductively, while his eyes are on me. He hooks the tip of the blade to the collar of my shirt and starts cutting it down the center.

"Hey! What the hell!?" I yell as he tears my clothes in half. I stop breathing the moment he brings the knife up to my mouth and presses the flat side against it to silence me.

"Shh…I didn't say you could scream yet." He slides the dagger slowly off my mouth and I bite my lip when it's free. I steady my breaths to leash the anger rising in me, even as my body starts to crave him, watching him expertly wield the blade in his hands. "Time to play a game, little demon."

CHAPTER FORTY-SEVEN

Draven

*F*uck. She looks so good splayed out before me, with a mixture of anger and lust storming in her eyes.

I don't know what came over me, but the moment the lie fell from her lips, I snapped. Without a second thought, I brought her to my room, wanting privacy, but also the space to show her what happens when she keeps her truths from me. Even though, deep down, I know that's a fucking excuse, I just want to find a reason to have my hands on her and my mouth licking against her skin. I wasn't lying when I said that she's the only poison I crave. A part of me feels like I will die if I go too long without a taste, now that I know how addictive she is.

I have her knees locked beneath my weight as I straddle them, staring down at her shirt that's falling open from where I cut it. I see her bra peeking through, and my cock instantly starts to harden at the sight. I tauntingly bring the sharp end of the blade back up and continue my plan.

But before I can play this game with her, I need her out of these Gods forsaken clothes, vulnerable for me. Nothing to hide behind when she gives me her truths.

Once her shirt is completely cut down the middle, I rip it aside and have her slide her arms out. She willingly complies as her cheeks turn a deeper shade of pink. Gods, she's so *fucking* beautiful. Knowing I'm the one causing her blush and the wetness I'm sure is dripping between her legs, her arousal invading my senses, is a heady feeling. She won't remember any pleasure that asshole Aiden may have ever given her. The thought boils my blood; I want to claim her as only mine.

But I can't. She's not my fucking mate, and that fact alone angers me as my beast wants to roar inside.

I center my thoughts back on this vicious female before me, knowing I have her in the palm of my hand. I let the side of my mouth tip up as I put the blade between my teeth and bite down, holding it there so I can grab hold of the waistband on her pants and rip them apart. A startled gasp leaves her, but I know she likes it because the scent of her arousal grows stronger, and I can feel my mind go hazy as the need to taste her grabs hold of me. I move to yank her pants down her legs and then crawl back up to her, watching her squirm beneath me as she fights the urge to cover her scars.

Her lacy undergarments are making my head spin, but I force myself to keep still. Grabbing the dagger out of my mouth, I start trailing the tip of the steel over her cheek and down her neck, before following the path between her breasts.

"Ready to play?" I ask her and watch as she nods her head. "I can't hear you, little demon," I say, with a little more aggression.

"Yes," she says in a breathy voice.

"Good girl." I watch the way my praise lights something in her eyes, and it makes me want to destroy the male who made her feel worthless. "The game is a truth for a truth," I say, and I don't miss the slight fear that flickers in those grey eyes for a moment. "Remember, little demon. I know when you're lying."

I watch her tongue lick her lips in anticipation, and fuck, if I don't want to suck that lip into my mouth. But I need her to learn, need her to open up to me. I can't explain why, but I hate the lies she's spilling and how closed-off she's being. After I saw how she reacted to Aiden blasting into Edith's home, working with her father, and claiming Emma as *his*, it reassured me that she is not working alongside her father. From the scars on her body by his hand, and the hatred that took over her because of Aiden, I feel confident in saying she would much rather watch them burn to the ground. And that thought rids me of some of the doubt I've had about her.

I let my eyes fall on her as I start our little game. "You are the only one who knows I'm part dragon, aside from Fynn and my family." Her eyes widen in shock.

"How have you kept it a secret for so long?" she asks.

"This isn't twenty questions, Emma. It's your turn to tell a truth."

Her nostrils flare and her eyes harden, pissed at me for not continuing the conversation. "I couldn't sleep because Cora was snoring," the lie falls effortlessly off her lips and I can hear the way her pulse picks up.

"Lie," I tell her. I press the knife down a little harder in the middle of her chest, just enough to nick through her skin and glide the blade down to make a small cut. A faint hiss falls from between her clenched teeth, but she makes no other sound as she looks at me with wide eyes. "Now, you know what happens when you lie, little demon," I tell her, bringing my face down to her chest and using my tongue to lick up the drops of crimson that break free from the cut on her skin.

Gods. Her blood explodes on my tongue and the taste of her shoots straight to my dick. She tastes so sweet, and the darker side of me wants her to keep lying, if only to keep placing *my* marks on her before I heal them with a salve. To lick every single mark I make and have her blood coursing through my body.

"Draven..." she whispers, and the shock is gone from her face as her eyes dilate at the lust igniting in her. She's endured so much pain and abuse, that she needs to see how pain can be turned into pleasure, and I have a feeling she's going to need the slight sting before her body gets high on desire.

"You owe me a truth," I tell her, waiting for her to remove one of the walls she has blocking her heart. Her soul.

She sighs with resignation. "I have nightmares." She stares deeply into me as I see her sorting through her thoughts, but she says nothing more. This, I know, is a truth, because I've somehow been in one of her nightmares.

Letting the blade travel around the swell of her breasts, I think of my next truth. "My father traveled to the Court of Ashes and never returned."

She sucks in a sharp breath but stays silent. Knowing that's not how the game works. I can see the realization on her face when she connects the dots from the conversation on the roof, when I told Fynn where we needed to go. But, like a good girl, she follows the rules and keeps her thoughts to herself right now.

"A phantom haunts me in my nightmares and…" She pauses to take a shaky, deep breath in. "He can hurt me in them."

A stronger wave of anger crashes into me, threatening to break the final wall holding me back from keeping her. To guarantee her protection, while I hunt down her father, and now, another monster who harms her. This must be the male I heard in her dream, the one who shoved a blade through her chest before she changed into what I imagine death itself looks like and disintegrated everything.

Now, it's my turn to share a truth as I continue the sensual dance of steel against her creamy skin. "The first time you visited here, I was pulled into one of your nightmares. I was on the roof and heard a scream that led me to you." I furrow my brows as I remember that moment. "The second I touched you, I was sucked into your dream."

Her eyes dance back and forth between mine, looking for the lie. But she won't find any. I keep tracing the blade gently over her skin as I wait for her truth. But minutes pass, and nothing. I drag the sharp edge to her hip and watch blood pool out when I press down to slice above her scrap of lace.

I hear her suck in a sharp breath that is followed by a soft moan as I swipe my tongue over the entire cut. She's watching in fascination as I bring my eyes to hers. I slowly sit back up and bring the blade that's slick with her blood to her mouth. "You took too long to share a truth, little demon. Now, taste how sweet you are."

Without hesitation, she opens as I put the blade between her lips. She twirls her tongue over the tip before flattening it and licking it clean. "Atta girl," I praise. My fully erect cock twitches at the way her eyes roll back when she tastes her blood, licking every drop off her dagger. A throaty growl rumbles from my chest as she hums her pleasure with the blade between her sinful lips that are now stained red. Heat shoots down to the base of my spine with the need to clean her lips with mine. But she still owes me a truth.

"A truth, little demon," I demand with a stern voice. "The one I want to know." I give her a deliberate look. I want the truth that she covered with a lie earlier. The one she brushed off as *nothing*.

She licks her lips as her tongue steals the rest of the blood that lingered on them. Her chest is heaving in quick little breaths. "There's a darkness in me that begs to be set free, promising to take all the pain away," she whispers. I keep the blade gliding across her body to keep her focused on the feeling as I see the hesitation in her eyes, her mouth parting to say more. "I fall into it sometimes, letting the coldness of its hold rush in and wash the pain away."

She closes her eyes to hide from her own truth, but I won't fucking allow that. I slide my hand behind her head, gripping her hair, and force her head up towards me. "Look at me," I growl. The moment her eyes open, the dense fog swirling in them once again slams into me, clouding all of my thoughts. "Don't you dare hide, little demon. When you feel like you're falling, I'll be your wings to help you fly." Her lips part at my promise and *Gods*, I can't wait any longer.

I take the blade under her collarbone and cut just enough to see her sweet poison leak out. I smear it along the blade and bring it to her lips again, only this time, I paint it on her lips before I toss the dagger to the floor and slam my mouth to hers. I swallow her gasp as she latches her mouth to mine.

The taste of her blood on her lips is addictive, and I groan in pleasure, licking them clean. I pull her bottom lip between my teeth, loving the sound of her whimpering at the slight sting. My free hand grabs hold of her breast as I roll her nipple over the lacy covering, while I continue to devour her mouth. She's just as needy as I am, with the way our tongues are tangling together and our teeth clash with eagerness.

I force myself away from her mouth and start nipping along her jaw and down her neck, carefully avoiding the wyvern iron constricted around her slender throat. I release my hand from behind her head so I can use both hands to slide her ebony bra over her head. The swells of her breasts and the hardened rose buds are *begging* to be touched. I sink my teeth into one and she yelps, grabbing hold of my hair as I start sucking it into my mouth. A moan of pleasure leaves her as she squeezes her thighs together.

I kiss across her chest to give her other breast equal attention before I lick down her stomach to the thin band of lacy material. The cut I made there earlier still bleeds lightly, and I lap my tongue over it, humming in pleasure. When it's momentarily clean, I place a feather-light kiss on top of it before I trail my mouth lower. Her breath hitches when I kiss her clit over the thin, layer of lace before I shoot backward to stand up.

"Take them off." My voice is raspy with desire, barely able to hold back long enough for her to do what she's told.

A wicked gleam ignites in her eyes as she bites her bottom lip. "You first," she says. My savage little demon is still challenging me, even as she's bare before me and most likely, soaking through that skimpy under-garment.

I keep my eyes on her as I unbutton my pants and slide out of them, leaving my briefs on that do nothing to hide my dick standing at attention. Her eyes immediately shoot down and widen when she sees how hard I am for her.

"Those, too," she adds, her eyes never leaving my cock. I smirk as I push them down my legs and my dick springs free, swollen and ready for her.

The way she's staring at my dick sends heat straight to the tip as I feel a drop of pre-cum leak out. She looks both fascinated, like she wants to swallow it whole, and wary, as if this is the first time she's seen a dick. But I doubt that, not with being betrothed to someone like Aiden Calloway. I plan on wiping every thought of him clean, every pleasure he's ever given her away. Making him nonexistent, so all she will remember is me and my name that screams from her lips.

She slowly removes the final barrier between us as I trail my eyes over every inch of skin before me, wanting to taste and lick all of it. But the beast in me needs to have her, needs to show her even more that there is pleasure in this world. My wings flare as I grow more desperate to please her, to claim her as mine, if only for a moment.

I climb over her, trailing burning kisses up her legs, taking a few minutes to lick her from ass to clit before I continue my ascent to those lush lips that drive me wild. My wings cascade around us, caging us in our own dark escape. A place we both can hide away from everyone, but this time, we aren't alone, but with each other. We are skin to skin, with my swollen cock between us, and my head starts to spin when her hips lift up to press into me.

I groan as the pressure squeezes my dick and I claim her mouth without restraint, pressing my hips down against hers. Our tongues swirl together in a sensual dance as I reset my elbows on both sides of her head. She slowly brings her hands between us and places them flat against my stomach before sliding them up to my chest and over my shoulders. Heat flares everywhere she touches, as if I've been lit up from the inside.

Her fingers brush over the inner part of my wing, and such an intense pleasure shoots down my spine. I rip my mouth from hers and nip her ear. "Little demon," I growl. "I won't last if you do that."

She stares up at me with such big, innocent eyes as I go to lay claim to her mouth again. But before I reach her lips, she starts talking. "Give me one more truth, Draven," she says. And the soft way she says it pulls something in my heart that makes me want to give her everything she asks.

"Is there anything you wish to know?" I ask her in a hushed breath that floats between us, wanting to switch the game up to please her.

Her head tilts to the side as she purses her lips in thought. "Why do you call me little demon?"

I hold back my laugh, because I was expecting something far more daunting. "Because when I first laid my eyes on you, you were fighting against a Corrupted like a savage, *little demon*." I close the gap to pull her bottom lip between my teeth. "And then, you spoke to me, and that vicious, little mouth of yours only proved the name suited you even more. The way you talked back and challenged me. Such a feisty thing."

She cracks a smile, and my heart skips a beat. "I have another truth," she says, and I watch her focus on my tattoos, avoiding my eyes as her fingers dance along with the black swirls that decorate my skin under the light sheen of scales. "I've never been with another in this way."

I tense.

Fuck. Guilt churns in my stomach with how rough I've been with her, how I've lost control on the roof and in the caves, needing to taste her.

I grab her jaw and force her eyes to connect with mine that I know are glowing brightly. "What *have* you done?" I say as the anger towards myself starts to take over.

She hesitates, noting the change in my energy. "You–you have been the first."

"Explain," I seethe.

"The first for everything, besides kissing." She bites her lip, drawing blood as she hears the building rage in my voice. My shadows flicker in a pending storm of chaos.

"*Fuck,* Emma! I've practically attacked you and—" I sit up, keeping my legs on either side of her as I run my fingers through my hair. "What has Aiden done with you?"

"Just kissing, I wouldn't let him go further," she says roughly.

"I'm sorry," I rush to say, hanging my head, not wanting her to think I'm mad at her. I'm pissed at myself.

"Don't," she snaps and I whip my head to hers. "Don't you fucking dare. If I didn't want anything to happen between us, I would have stopped it. I had doubts about Aiden, but for some reason, I didn't with *you*. And then, you saw me." She pauses, bringing her hand up to my cheek. "You *saw* me, Draven. Every broken part of me. Do you want another truth?!" Her voice raises. "*You* are the only one who has seen my scars, not even Cora knows about what my father does."

Shock slaps me across the face, that I've known her most hidden truth this whole time.

"You didn't look disgusted by me, or tell me to cover up." A small tear beads at the corner of her eye, as the storm clouds within start building. "No, instead, you made me *feel* something for the first time in my life, trying to kiss away my pain. So, don't back out on me now, because I *want* this. Even if it's just for tonight. Please, give me this."

The beast inside of me turns feral at the thought of being the first to claim her in every way, marking her as *mine*. I'm going to have to settle these thoughts later, because after tonight, she won't be mine, and I'll have to let her go.

I lean back over her and bring my mouth just a hair's breadth away from hers, just barely touching. "I like when you beg, little demon." Her eyes light up as I slam my mouth to hers.

There's no turning back now.

CHAPTER FORTY-EIGHT

Emma

*O*h, Gods.

Everything lights up inside of me when he frantically kisses me, not holding back.

I yelp in his mouth as he rolls my nipple between his fingers. A stinging pleasure that coils heat deep within.

The game of truths was freeing, to share my demons with him and admit the words I've been scared to voice. I wasn't lying when I said I wanted him. The last time he asked me if I could trust him, I said not a chance, but now, my views have shifted. I realized the moment I let him use my dagger on me, trusting him to mark my body, when my father has been the only one who has left his demented brand.

The realization shocks me to my core, but it also makes me feel safe for once. The nerves built when I was anticipating the pain from the blade. Pain like the kind my father has bestowed on me, but Draven…he made me see how pain can become pleasurable. He made me see that not all pain will leave me weak on the floor, as he picked me up by licking the hurt away.

My mind blanks when I feel his hand slide down my body between us, reaching my center as his fingers start circling my clit. My hips immediately jerk up at the intense sensation that surges through me, begging for the release I know he can give me.

He continues kissing me as his hand ventures lower, finding my wet opening as he dips a finger between my folds. "You're dripping," he growls in my mouth as he shoves his finger slowly inside of me. "*Fuck*, you're so tight, little demon."

My breath hitches as he starts moving his finger in and out. The heat of his body that was swarming me leaves, and a rush of cold attacks my skin, but then he grabs hold of my thighs. In an instant, he spreads them with a hungry look on his face and drops himself down. His tongue swirls around my sensitive bud as he dips his finger back inside, beginning a leisurely pace with his movements.

I move my hands down to his head and grab onto his inky strands as I feel my orgasm climbing fast, coiling tighter with every thrust of his finger and swipe of his tongue. The moment he picks up the pace and bites down on my clit, I'm gone. I scream out a cry of release as I clench around his finger and ride out the waves of pleasure, along with his tongue. Not stopping, until it completely fades away.

He sits back on his knees and brings his finger to his mouth, sucking off my essence.

I bite my lip, seeing the possessive look in his eyes as he keeps them focused on me, while he's on his knees, bare before me. All sin and muscle wrapped together.

"*Now*, you're ready," he says with intent as he climbs back up my body. I know my half-lidded eyes are full of lust as my body feels sated, but the moment I feel his hard length brush against my swollen clit, I feel a spark of heat shoot to my core again. He's right, I'm ready for more, as my body is begging for him to fill me.

He gently presses his lips to mine, but soon enough, he starts kissing me deeply, as if this will be our last kiss. This kiss slowly makes my black heart bleed red as he takes his time, like he's engraving this moment into his memory.

A forever tattoo of this moment is inked on our souls.

He lines his dick over my clit as he starts rubbing back and forth, sending tingles down my spine.

He breaks the kiss, staring deeply into my eyes. "Keep your eyes on me, little demon. I want to watch you as I enter you. I want to see your face when my cock fills you for the first time, marking this pussy as *mine.*" His husky voice turns into a growl at the end as his wings flare out, and the silver in his eyes turns blinding. The beast in him taking over.

I keep my eyes on him, but before he moves his hand, I shoot mine down between us and grab hold of his dick. Wrapping my fingers as much as I can around him as I feel his smoothness. His nostrils flare and a heated hiss escapes between his teeth when I grip him harder, moving my hand in slow-motion, like he was just doing a moment ago.

But my pussy is becoming wetter at the solid feel of him, and I'm too desperate to have him inside me as I line the tip of his cock to my entrance.

This was never supposed to happen, and I know Draven will never be mine, but at this moment, I want to pretend. Pretend that my life isn't a mess, and that we are just two lovers who want to escape the world together.

He slides the head of his cock a couple of inches into my aching core and pauses as we keep our eyes locked on each other. I feel him push another inch deeper, and I flinch when I feel myself squeeze around his thickness, resisting him.

"Relax, Emma," he says on a breath.

He starts kissing me tenderly, as I feel my legs fall loosely to the sides, and my breathing steady. As soon as he feels my body relax, he fills me with one solid thrust. A squeal leaves me as a sharp sting pierces deep inside and my walls wrapped around his cock burn. But I never close my eyes, never look away as his pools of silver keep me centered.

"Atta girl," he whispers. The praise brings a warmth of pleasure to my soul.

I give him a slight nod to reassure him, lifting my hips to tell him to keep going. He groans and slides out to the tip, and then thrusts back in, cursing under his breath.

"You feel so *fucking* good," he says with a grunt. "Such a tight, little cunt. Gripping my cock like it never wants it to leave." The burning fades away as a new kind of heat builds in my core, the kind that will ruin me for anyone else. The air around us pulses with magnetic energy as he keeps a steady pace with his thrusts. Grinding his hips to hit a deeper spot inside that brings stars to my vision.

"Draven," I moan as I feel my body heat up with anticipation.

He sits back on his knees and grabs hold of my hips to pull me all the way against him as he starts pounding into me. He slides one hand to my center and starts circling my pulsing clit with his fingers, causing my inner walls to tighten around his length even more.

"*Fuck*, you take my cock so well, it's like you were made for me," he groans, never slowing his pace. The slits in his eyes sink into my soul as he's buried inside of me. He presses his fingers harder on my bundle of nerves and it spills a guttural moan from my lips.

"Don't stop," I breathe, feeling myself drip down my thighs as the heat that was building starts to boil, threatening to crest over.

His shadows shoot out and grip my jaw. "Come for me, Emma." My name falling from his lips is like a sinful prayer, a promise that he'll be here to catch me when I fall from this high.

He slams into me harder, faster. My inner walls tighten around him as the pleasure grows so intense, that I'm not sure if I'll recover. My breathing becomes frantic as my mouth falls open, keeping my eyes on his. His fingers continue their assault on my clit as his cock hits that spot deep inside of me.

"Oh Gods, Draven!" I scream as my back arches and I dig my fingers in his silk sheets, clawing them into the mattress as my orgasm wrecks me. Each tidal wave of pleasure squeezes around his dick tighter and tighter as all the air leaves my lungs. The high of my release hits hard and makes me break our eye contact as mine roll into the back of my head, while I continue to moan in pleasure.

The darkness that lurks inside of me, the one that is always pushing to break free…clears away. For a moment, the whispers stop. The feeling of its claws raking inside my mind and inside my soul fall away. Silence. Draven's touch, his words, and his body against mine rekindle the ember of light in this vault of nothing. Like a burn of a torch spearing through my cold frame, a beacon I can cling onto. Igniting the entity that illuminates inside, making me feel alive for the first time in my life.

After a couple of thrusts into my climax, Draven falls on top of me, sinking his teeth into my shoulder as he roars, reaching his own release. Spilling into me as the muscles in his body tense, the one hand he left on my hip tightens in a bruising grip as he falls over the edge. Pride bubbles up to my throat at seeing him so undone because of me. The Dark Prince.

At this moment, I pretend that I was made for him. I wonder if he's struggling with how he feels about us as much as I am. A conflict of emotions at wishing for something that will always be out of reach. But I know he's been waiting years for his mate, and I won't get in the way of that. I won't be hoping for more than one night, because he deserves to find his mate and have every night with her.

So, this will be it. This will be the only time I can pretend he's mine, until we have to go back to reality. Working together for our travels ahead, but keeping our distance before I fall deep into him. And I have a feeling that if I fall hard for him, he won't be there to catch me and be my wings, like he said before. Not if he finds his mate, because when he does, I'm afraid he will watch me fall, until that tether between us snaps, so he can be free of me. A distant memory of tangled sheets, pleasure, and nothing more.

He stays inside of me as we both float back down from our high, keeping each other grounded. After a moment, he pulls out and lays down on his side to face me, shifting back into his Fae form. He brings his hand to my mouth and rubs his thumb over my bottom lip, watching as I swirl my tongue around his thumb and suck it into my mouth. His eyes darken before pulling it free. I only smirk at him as my own body rings with sated pleasure. My eyes grow heavy with every passing moment, and the last thing I see is icy blue eyes looking at me.

As I fall deeper into sleep, I swear I hear his distant voice say, "You're ruining me, little demon."

I can feel myself waking to the most delicious feeling. My body is still humming from earlier as my legs have a faint tingle and the need in my core continues to ache for him. I can feel myself growing wetter as I come out of my dream state, desperate to have him take care of this desire that's growing stronger. Heat pools deep in my belly and a moan slips from my mouth.

My eyes fly open as my breath hitches from the powerful wave of lust that racks through me. I lift my head from the mattress and find Draven settled between my legs, with his arm draped over my stomach to hold me down. He's licking vigorously over my bundle of nerves that he has aching for release, before flattening his tongue and licking from hole to hole. Worshiping my body like a morning prayer.

A throaty moan works its way free as he slides two fingers inside of me, curling it upward. It only takes a few thrusts, and I'm coming around him. Falling from the high he built as I crash hard into the feeling of ecstasy. Wave after wave rolls through me as he continues to prolong my orgasm. My thighs tighten around his head when I can't take it anymore, and he lazily licks me clean.

"We have to leave soon, little demon," he says as he slowly climbs up me and rests his weight on top.

"How long have I been asleep?"

"Not long, but I figured you'd want to take a bath before we meet with everyone for breakfast." That's…thoughtful. It would probably soothe the soreness that feels heavenly at the reminder of the way his hips slammed into mine and the way his fingers demanded my pleasure. "I just needed to watch you surrender under my touch and come all over my tongue again."

I blush at his words, but a different kind of need rises in me. The kind that wants to watch him surrender at my touch, to give him the same kind of pleasure. I push him over so he's on his back, and I straddle him, as I'm still completely bare. At some point when I was sleeping, he tossed his pants back on, but that just won't do.

His blue eyes darken as he sees the intent in my eyes, and I slide down his body, tracing my tongue over his tattoos as I lick down his torso. I fiddle with the button on his pants and yank them down as he lifts his hips up to help me. His already hard cock stands straight up when I free it, making my mouth water at the sight.

"I've never done this." My voice is husky as the thought of him on my tongue makes me impatient.

"I'll enjoy anything you do." His voice is deep and strained. "Look at me." I raise my eyes to him instantly. "Good girl," he praises me as I follow his command. "You don't have to do this. I didn't please you to have you do the same back. I just needed to taste you again."

"I want to do this," I say, with lust lacing my words. Before he can say anything more, I grab hold of his length and swipe my tongue from base to tip, tasting the salty drop of his arousal as I suck the tip into my mouth.

"*Fuck, Emma,*" he groans.

I lift my eyes to him, and his pupils are dilated with lust, as he becomes greedy with need. I plunge him down my throat and he grunts in pleasure as his hand wraps around my hair, taking control of my head. He starts moving me up and down, hitting the back of my throat. Gagging me to tears as he deprives me of air.

"Just like that," he says as he keeps up the pace, and I swirl my tongue around him when he lifts my head up before thrusting back inside.

I bring my hands to his chest and scratch my nails down his torso in lines of red. A pleasurable hiss leaves him as his breathing gets harder, panting as he reaches his release.

He's becoming unhinged, as I take back control, working my mouth over his dick at the same pace he was going. I want to suck his sins away, to heal the coldest parts of his soul, as he did with mine. I pull him into my mouth harder, deeper, at a punishing pace as I lock my eyes on his, a silent command to not look away. I want to see him come undone.

"I'm gonna come," he growls, the hard muscles in his abs tightening as he gets closer. I don't stop, I want everything he can give, and the moment he sees that shine through my eyes, he grunts a loud curse as he spills himself down my throat. Exploding into his climax as he pumps himself, until every drop of his orgasm is free.

I swallow it all down, loving the bitter taste of him as I continue licking every inch of his pulsing length.

I lick my lips as I sit and find him watching me with an adoring expression. A warmth that settles in those wintery eyes. He lurches forward and grabs me by the nape of my neck before capturing my mouth with his. I kiss him back with a longing that buzzes through my veins, a craving for his touch, that will have me obsessing if I don't tread carefully.

"What are you doing to me?" he asks with a hoarse voice.

"I could ask you the same thing," I say as the air around us transfixes us together in the dark. I feel drawn to him, my body singing in delight with him being so near.

But the time for pretending is over.

I'm not his mate.

I pull away from him and slide off the bed. A deep crease forms on his forehead as I retreat, like he knows this is it. This is all we can be. Just a moment that flashes by, and will soon be long forgotten.

I feel the lie of my thoughts sink its teeth into me, knowing I will never be able to forget what he's made me feel. To never forget *him*.

But I can pretend…

I can pretend to be okay.

CHAPTER FORTY-NINE

Emma

I had only dozed for an hour, so I still had about an hour to spare before sunrise. Draven somehow scrounged up one of my outfits from my luggage. It was my black training leathers with a matching top, and I'm thankful I wasn't wearing this when he decided to destroy my clothes. He must have blended into his shadows to discreetly get this for me, and I silently thank him for it.

I grab my dagger that was now sitting on a table next to his bed and strap it back to my thigh. The same dagger that coaxed my sinful desires and demanded my truths.

I planned to sneak my way back into the room I share with Cora, while Draven washed off and got dressed, but instead, I want to see the library again. I step out of his room and stay close to the edge of the walkways. The corridors are still cast in shadows, since the sun is still below the sea. But I need to hurry, so I'm not found. The problem is, I don't fully remember where the library is.

I keep my boots silent against the stone floors, traveling down multiple

383

walkways, turning left, then right, without any hope in sight. Then, I turn a sharp corner and gasp.

Emil stands in the middle of the hallway, knowingly, his hands clasped in front of him as he gives me a sly smile.

I bow forward, greeting him as I call on my years of being a dutiful princess. "Prince Emil," I say, slowly standing back up as I fidget with my fingers while my nerves rack their way through my body.

"My brother is sneaky, but I'm better," he says warmly, and I can't help but chuckle at that.

"So, it seems," I say, wondering if he will alert everyone of my presence here.

"Your father has put out a search for you in every court, wanting you returned immediately to him, because *apparently*, the Princess of Asov has been stolen," he says, while fighting the urge to laugh. His eyes lift on the corners as he waves a hand in front of me. "You don't look stolen to me." His eyes dance with amusement.

I bite my lip in thought, as I can't imagine how many soldiers my father has sent out to find me, spinning a tale that I was taken, when he should know better than anyone that I escaped.

"Please, don't tell anyone you saw me." I bring my hands together, pleading for him to keep this secret.

He tilts his head to study me for a moment. "You don't have to worry, I would never give away your whereabouts to that pigheaded king. No offense," He adds quickly. "I liked you the moment you challenged my brother, and I know he likes you, too, even though he will never admit it." Emil rolls his eyes and I smile at that, because that's a gesture I love.

I maintain a calm face, but my sated body says otherwise in reaction to how Draven feels about me, at least for a moment. "Your brother is only protecting himself. He wants his mate, and I understand that," I say honestly. "But, since you've busted me, would you mind showing me to the library?" I wince as I know I must look completely lost right about now.

He laughs as he looks down the hallway I just came from. "I feel like I have to help you." He chuckles. "Because you're heading in the wrong direction." He laughs some more and points behind me. "The library is back that way."

I bite my lip to hold back my amusement, even though my smile breaks free. "Thank you for pointing that out so clearly," I tell him in a joking manner.

"Anytime," he cheers. "C'mon, let's get you to the library and make sure no one else sees you."

I follow him back down the way I came, but he takes a different turn that leads down a set of stairs. After peering around corners to make sure the coast was clear, and trailing down long hallways, we finally make it to the most beautifully designed doors I remember so well.

He opens the door with a wave of his hand. "Have fun." He smiles as I walk in, letting the door slowly close behind me.

Before it clicks shut completely, I whisper-yell through the remaining crack, "Thank you!"

I walk farther into the library that's still veiled in the lingering night shadows, but there is a painted brush of orange that is softly glowing. The morning sun waking up to shine a light on a new day.

My feet pad along the smooth floor as I let my fingertips trail lazily over the spines of books lined on the shelves, hoping to find some that are useful before we go to the forbidden library tomorrow.

The room slowly glows as the sun rises an inch higher in the sky, slivers shining through the clouds above the glass dome ceiling. I know I need to meet with everyone soon, but take advantage of this extra time as I walk down every aisle of shelves and step on the wooden ladder attached to each one so I can read the titles on top. It feels like an eternity before I find a few that pique my interest, and I gather them in my arms and walk over to the sitting area.

I lose track of time as I read through the various books. The first book, which discussed some history of the Gods, didn't hold any special information. It told of their love and everything I have already learned, but it did briefly mention their split and how it rattled the world with their rage towards one another.

Then, I got drawn into a book that held details of every library in the land of Deyadrum, including the forbidden one. It spoke of how the castle in the Court of Ashes was blown apart during a war centuries ago, and now only three separate ruins are left behind. Broken like the souls that are left across its land. Apparently, only two keys were ever made to open it, and I have one of them. The weight of it feels heavy in my pocket as I made sure to grab it from my torn clothes that were lying on Draven's bedroom floor.

I continue to read more about the library, but there's not much left to be said, since not many have ventured to it or made it back alive after attempting to gain more information on it.

I toss the book on the table and grab the one that I've been itching to read.

Legends of the Dragon.

I let the pages fan in front of me as I see an image appear in the middle of the book. A drawing of a massive dragon with wings, standing on four legs is staring back at me, looking incredibly monstrous. A note at the top of the page says it's called a Wyvern. My mind connects the dots on the wyvern iron, that it's the only kind of weapon that can harm them. It's because it's made from their scales. Iron fused with the scales of the ones who were full dragon shifters, since regular iron isn't strong enough to cut through a wyvern in it's true form. I think back to the ebony sheen of scales that glimmered over Draven's tattoos, the way his skin felt harder. Tougher. His very own shield.

I flip to another page, where it explains that the main reason for them being hunted was to take their scales to forge such powerful weapons. The different courts hoped it would give them a stronger advantage in wars waged against them, but then realized it hurts the dragons they were fearful of. So, instead of using the weapons for their own blood-shedding battles, they soon began to hunt dragons with the hope of ending the species permanently.

People considered them to be enemies that could kill a person instantly in their full form. Yet, it breaks my heart to think about it. What about the children that were born? Were they attacked as well? I bet the dragons raged back in anger at being used for weapons that were ultimately made to take their lives. To take their *children's* lives. Then, the painful thought of wondering how Draven feels, to wield a weapon made from his ancestors, I would assume he's disgusted. Hating to even look at them, but if it helps end the Scavengers, then he wouldn't hold back on using them.

I keep flipping through the book in hopes of seeing if there's any other knowledge of a wyvern clan that may have survived, feeling the desire to find more for Draven to connect to. Even if it would lead to finding his mate.

"Interesting book you've got there." The familiar deep voice rumbles through the room and sends a spark of heat down my spine.

I keep my nose buried in the book, refusing to give him a lick of attention as I feel his presence inching closer. The thuds of his boots grow louder as he walks across the floor.

"It is interesting," I say as I read the words on the page before me.

I hear the clink of a glass and the sound of liquid pooling inside it. I let my eyes peek over the top of the book when the chair in front of me softly creaks. The sight dries my mouth out, and I think he's the only one who can quench my sudden thirst.

Fallen pieces of hair drape over his forehead as he reclines back, his muscled legs spread apart as he holds a glass of chilled bourbon in his hand. The amber drink that makes him taste like maple.

"Isn't it a little early for a drink?" I say on a shallow breath. My eyes hungrily zero in on his chest. His black shirt is undone, hanging off his shoulders, and he's wearing nothing underneath, just toned abs and tattoos on full display.

I bring my eyes back up his body until they land on his icy ones. He's already looking at me, watching me with a dark expression. As if we're both just as consumed at this moment, wanting nothing more than to claim the other and give in to the spellbinding storm lighting between us. I'm instantly flooded with images of him moving along my body, drinking me in, tasting me. His nostrils flare, and I know he can smell me, because I can feel myself growing wet with the memory of every single act this male committed to my body.

He ignores my question with a smirk. "Come here, Emma." The need in his voice sends more heat pooling to my core.

As much as I know I shouldn't cross this line with him again, I can't help but oblige him. Listening to his command and giving in to the feelings that beg me to go closer.

I gently shut the book and walk slowly over to him, loving the way his eyes devour me with one look as they trail down every inch of my body. When I stop before him, standing in between his legs, he carefully sets his drink on the table beside him. I watch the muscles in his jaw jump right before he grabs my waist and pulls me to him, as his hands deliciously slide down to the back of my thighs. He spreads my legs wide before he pulls me all the way on top of him, straddling him.

He holds me tight against him as his breath fans against my jaw. "Find anything interesting?" he says in a sultry voice, drunk on desire.

My breath hitches as goosebumps pebble down my body at the feeling of him underneath me, and the sweet scent spilling from his lips. "Hmm," I hum along the shell of his ear. "I did learn that dragons are notorious for being stubborn and domineering," I tease.

His stomach dips as he huffs a laugh, and I lean back to see his dimple showing, the one smile that softens his features. "Did you, now?" he says with amusement.

I nod at him with a smirk. "I did." I bring my lips a breath away from his, taunting them. "I also learned that from personal experience."

His grip on my ass tightens, as I'm sure he's remembering the pleasure we created between us. In the next second, his mouth is on mine, making me moan, feeling the instant lust that ignites in me. His tongue forces between my lips, but I willingly open them, as it swirls with mine. His hips raise as I roll mine down, feeling him harden beneath me. I'm high on him, and only him, as I continue the sensual roll of my hips, grinding against him as he ravishes my mouth.

With a bite of my bottom lip, he pulls back, and I can't hide the frown that creases on my face. "Everyone's waiting in the tower. You weren't there, so I had to come find you. Plus, I brought breakfast up for everyone."

My eyes widen as I snap my head to the windows above, seeing the hazy fog blanketing across it, hiding every ray of the sun now, so it's impossible to see how high it is in the sky. I know I've been down here a while, but I didn't know I'd let a full hour slip away.

At that moment, my stomach decides to protest against me for not feeding it, rumbling through the silent space between us. I slam my hand over it, hoping to shut it up.

Draven chuckles and the sound just melts me inside. A rare sound that not many people get the chance to hear. "Let's go, before you waste away." My stomach gurgles again and he shakes his head. "Maybe I should bring a second plate for you," he goads.

I start to argue that I don't need that much food, but then he smacks my ass and lifts me off him. He downs the rest of his drink before walking towards the library doors, jerking his head for me to follow.

And once again, I do.

CHAPTER FIFTY

Emma

$\mathcal{A}$fter Draven came and got me from the library, he walked me to the tower before disappearing to get more food. Apparently, he wasn't joking about getting me a second plate. When he came back, we devoured the cinnamon bread rolls and fruit he brought before inhaling the sweet sausages. We discussed our plans for tomorrow, and I quickly explained what I had read about the forbidden library in the book. It's not much, but it also explains my absence this morning. I really did want to find information, which is why I tried to sneak down there, but I also didn't want to face everyone while the taste of Draven still lingered fresh on my tongue.

We ended up having a relaxing few moments of easy conversation, and I did, in fact, eat the second plate Draven brought me. We laughed, watching Fynn crack jokes at Draven, while I sat back against the wall, my body feeling ready to pass out. I think I may have eaten so much food that it was putting me in a food coma.

Fynn tosses a grape at Cora and it knocks off the side of her head, bouncing to the ground and rolling away. Her glare is instant, the stillness that floods her body is like a lion ready to pounce. Fynn's eyebrows raise.

"Oops. It slipped," he teases with a smirk playing on his lips, popping another grape into his mouth. "But now that I have your attention, I have a question for you."

"Depending on your question, I *might* answer," she quips.

His lips purse to the side in thought. Then he shrugs, brushing it off. "You're a healer. So, why did seeing the Elder's head chopped off make you almost spill your guts? Surely, you've seen some gruesome things."

Cora's mouth falls open in disbelief. "Because his head was chopped off!" she shrieks. "I mean, the male's eyes were still open, and his mouth was wide with critters in it! I don't heal dead, rotting, corpses." Her whole body shudders at the memory.

"But you'd heal me, right, babe?" Fynn winks.

I laugh at the bluntness of his flirting, knowing Cora is acting annoyed but is secretly relishing in it. Kye's knees are bent, with his elbows resting on them, as he sits next to me on the floor, back against the wall. His eyes flick back and forth between Cora and Fynn, keeping tabs on their conversation.

I nudge him in the side with my elbow. "How was the journey to the Court of Abhain? You know, before the dead body."

A smile softens the hard features on his face as he shakes his head in amusement. "I think you would have liked it," he says, turning his head towards me. "Miles of rolling hills that you could run through and roll down. There were no trees, so everything was open and it felt like you could see across the whole land. Blankets of pink and red roses decorated sections of the grassy knolls, and small rigid cliffs with waterfalls scattered along the river, creating a rainbow of colors in the mist." Kye gives me a pointed look, but it seems to hold the weight of all the emotions I've tried to bury. "Everything just felt freeing. You wouldn't feel confined there."

He pauses, letting his words sink in, and I feel a sudden burn behind my eyelids from the well of tears wanting to break free. A tender smile lifts his lips and he finishes speaking when he notices the moisture gathering in my eyes. "Just past one of the waterfalls was a wooden bridge along the river that ended up making the journey to the Elder's home quicker. But despite the view, like Cora said before, there was a nasty creature in water, worse looking than that thing you freed from the well."

Suddenly, a grape comes flying and smacks me in the face. Fynn sits with a satisfied grin from hitting his mark. "You saved a creature?"

I narrow my eyes on him, but it's pointless since I could never be mad at him. So instead, I give in to his question. "Yes, before we escaped my court. My father had it chained to the bottom of the well under the sun for who knows how long. I couldn't leave it behind. But thank goodness I did set it free because it led me to you." I directed my gaze to stare right at Draven.

His handsome face contorts as he furrows his brows in confusion. "Me?"

I simply nod and wave my hand in the air. Not wanting to make a fuss since it's over and done with. "It told me to find the one called Shade and that he would help. By *he*, that means you."

Draven remains still, staying silent, like he's trying to understand what that all means. Maybe this was part of his path as the chosen one, but I can't say for sure, it seems this is the first time I know just as much as he does.

I let him stew in his thoughts as I face Cora, who is sitting cross-legged on top of the bed. "So, tell me more about this creature."

Her eyes widen, ready to give me all the details. "Emma, that thing slithered out of the water like it wanted to drag me under. It was dark blue, but also had green eyes that looked at me with hunger like it wanted to *eat* me. And not in the way I usually like. But Kye managed to knock it out, and then Fynn transported us a little farther away from the river, just to be safe," she says.

A coughing sound erupts from Fynn as he pounds his fist against his chest as he hacks up a grape. "Please explain how you like to be eaten," he says with restrained amusement after he catches his breath.

Cora ignores him with a dramatic, yet playful roll of her eyes, and I can't help but notice a slight smirk to Kye's lips before he chuckles, tossing a piece of cinnamon roll into his mouth. "If the monster did eat you, it would have allowed us to get by without a hitch." I watch him hold in his laugh while attempting to chew his food.

Cora yelps in surprise. "How could yo—" She stops speaking and squints before tipping over to her side, grabbing her belly and laughing. "Kye! Did you just make a joke?" Her laughter turns almost silent, wheezing to tears as she tries to calm herself. Completely forgetting about her horrendous encounter with the river creature.

"Don't get used to it." But his voice holds no threat, just a hint of playfulness.

Draven sits across the room, legs stretched out with his ankles crossed. His empty plate rests on the top of his thigh. He's still quiet, but now I can see a glimmer of joy in his eyes. Watching the conversation play out, he seems relaxed. Like he's soaking in this brief moment of not having to protect and guard Deyadrum. To simply just be a male with his friends.

We sit around for a while, bonding and sifting through more books that Draven found in the library. Still, we glean nothing useful from the books, no way of knowing what we are truly in for.

When we call it quits on sifting through the pages that lack information, it is agreed that now will be a good time to train Cora. So, Draven shadows us all and leads us to the training room. I watch with words of encouragement as all three guys do their best to help Cora learn some basics of combat, how to hold her sword, the position of her arms when she swings it. They go through every detail of footwork, and what cues to look for in assessing her opponent. Even going so far as having her stab a tree outside at the end to show her how much strength she will need in order to stab through the bones in someone's chest.

She takes in every word and puts all of her effort into learning what she can. Periodically, Kye joins me, offering a duel of swords when he isn't needed. And by the end of training, we are all exhausted, ready to replenish ourselves with food and water.

After dinner, we play a few card games to ease the mood before our impending journey. Of course, that quickly comes to an end when Cora and Fynn start bickering about who won. I find it entertaining. But it made us all agree to settle in for the night before we meet at sunrise to leave.

I toss and turn around in bed as Cora, once again, is able to pass out the moment her head hits the pillow. Her little snores fill the quiet room. I pull the blankets back to get out of bed, sliding my boots on loosely, then snatch the lantern we left burning and carry it with me out of the room.

My boots are out of place with the pajamas I'm wearing, but I toss on a cloak before I slip out, knowing where I'm headed will be chilly.

The door creaks faintly on its hinges when it opens to the roof, but my feet stop short, seeing Draven up here alone. My steady heart already picks up speed at the sight of him. The cool breeze wafts his scent over to me, overwhelming my senses and disrupting my thoughts.

"Can't resist me now, little demon?" His voice carries sensually across the expanse of the roof.

I pad my way towards him, setting the lantern down next to me once I'm beside him. I kick my unlaced boots off before I sit down, letting the cold air nip at my feet. "I know my boundaries, Draven. You said as much," I say calmly, staring out into the night.

He doesn't say anything, but I can feel the heat of his eyes on the side of my face. I get a glimpse of his mouth opening to speak out of my peripheral, but I turn to look at him, talking before he can respond, "What does the tattoo on your finger mean?" I ask. The question has been silently burning in my head since I first saw it, and the curiosity is eating me alive. Making me remember the dream that brought comfort to me when I was in the box. "I'm only curious because all your other tattoos are the same swirl design, but that one"—I point at his finger—"that one is the only tattoo that is different."

His head dips down to his hand, rubbing his thumb over the tattoo in question. Whatever he was going to say is snuffed out. Clenching his jaw, he furrows his brows in thought. "I'm not sure." His voice is quiet, while he continues to stare at the ink on his finger. "I kept having these dreams, the same ones that would have this symbol glowing in the sky. I don't know what it meant, but I felt drawn to it." He lifts his head, looking up at the night sky, hooking his eyes on the moon, shifting between the moving fog. "It looked like two parts of a moon meshed together. Like one was a full moon but hollow inside, and the other was broken but shined the brightest. The two coming together to balance the other, to become whole."

My breath stalls from my lungs, his blue eyes sliding up to meet mine.

He stares at me, his gaze darting back and forth to each of my eyes. Like he's trying to find an answer to a question he hasn't asked. The moon glows against the angles of his face perfectly, so much so, I have to look away. It's too much. My heart already aches with knowing nothing more can happen between us.

We sit there in peaceful silence for a little while longer. Two vulnerable souls embracing the melody of the night.

CHAPTER FIFTY-ONE

Emma

In the morning, we freshen up and collect our weapons. Cora and I make our way to the roof of the castle and find Kye and Draven already waiting. Two males, who have somehow managed a place in my heart in different ways. I smile at the sight of them together as I tighten the strap across my chest.

My wyvern sword is slung across my shoulder and the extra dagger hangs on my waist. I feel more prepared having weapons that will harm the Scavengers, but my heart still aches at the thought of why they were made.

Draven must have put a healing salve on me the moment my eyes shut the other night because only a few small scratches remain, and my heart warms at the thought that he made sure I wouldn't scar. I'm starting to realize that maybe he's not as *dark* as he makes himself be, but I know he struggles. It seems like he's been taking on the world all by himself for years. Carrying the weight of every death taken by his hands as he protects the people. Not just of his court, but the people in *all* of

Deyadrum. I see how the light in him flickers, how he struggles with not finding his mate, the loss of his father, and living in the dark. Keeping who he really is hidden away from everyone, forcing him to be alone. I know all too well how loneliness can eat away at you, slowly, destroying you from the inside.

I look out in the distance to where the forest meets the shore and see the sun blazing in the distance as Fynn appears from mid-air, stepping out of his own glowing portal.

Cora stands to the side and seems unimpressed this morning as she looks half a second away from wanting to go back to sleep. She glares at Fynn with annoyance. "Should I lay out a red carpet for you next time when you make your grand entrance through your golden gateway?" she snips.

Fynn is unfazed as he smirks at her. "That would be a nice change, babe," he says with a wink and walks towards Draven to pat him on the back in greeting. Cora blanches at what he calls her again, and the look on his face shows he does it on purpose. Knowing it will rile her up.

"Why didn't you take the stairs?" Draven answers as he shakes his head at Fynn's childlike nature.

"Well, since everyone here knows what I can do...that means I can be lazy with my travels again." He shrugs, acting like Draven should already know this.

"Everyone have their weapons?" Draven asks, looking around the roof. I keep my eyes everywhere but on him as I drop down to make sure my boots are nice and tight. Time to pretend nothing happened, but the feelings stirring in me are pounding against my chest, wanting to do anything but pretend. Demanding to feel worthy of being seen, instead of burying them away and becoming a shell of who I am again.

I feel the warmth of a hand on my shoulder, and I whip my head up to find Kye next to me. I rise on steady legs as he stares deeply at me. "Is everything okay?"

"Yeah," I tell him. "I'm just nervous my father will beat us to the Stone." It's not a lie, but it's not the full truth either. Guilt gnaws at me for keeping another secret from Kye, but at this point, there's nothing to tell.

He gives me a reassuring smile as he rubs his giant hand over my shoulder. "We'll get it, Princess. Just focus on your surroundings and keep your senses alert. I don't know the layout of the land in the Court of Ashes, but I'll still protect you with my life."

The backs of my eyes burn as I look up into his amber ones. The voices of the others mingling in the background fade away as emotions get lodged in my throat. "I'll protect yours with mine, too, Kye. But don't worry, you've taught me well." I wink at him, resting my hand on his that's still covering my shoulder.

"How do we know where to start looking once we get there?" I hear Cora ask.

"I know where we need to go," Draven cuts in.

I feel Kye's hand squeeze my shoulder. "How do you know where the forbidden library is? Unless you've been there before?" he asks, with a suspicious edge to his voice.

"The Elder," I cut in. My heart seizes the moment to cover him from having to reveal using his dragon form to fly along the borders of the Court of Ashes. Feeling the need to hold his secret close. I know my friends would keep his secret of being part dragon to their grave, but if he's not ready to share, then I can respect that. It's his secret to tell. Like he said, we lie to everyone, just not to each other.

I grab hold of my hair and start casually braiding it. "She gave us a general location for where it might be, and there was a scribbled map in the book I read." Another lie falls from my lips, cursing my soul even more as I take another step further into hell.

I can feel the touch of Draven's eyes scorching me, but I refuse to look at him. Refuse to let those icy blue orbs freeze the rain that wants to fall from the storm clouds in mine. Then, I hear an enraged low rumble, coming from his direction. The beast in him rises above the surface. I'm unsure if it's from me ignoring him or if it's because Kye's hand is still on me.

It takes all my willpower to ignore him, and I want to hug Fynn for breaking the tension pouring from Draven's direction. "Let's do this thang," Fynn's voice cuts through. His hands go out in front of him as a fissure in the world opens, forming a gilded circle that radiates his power.

I rush forward, desperate to get to the forbidden library.

"Emma!" I hear Kye and Draven's voices yell, but they fall away as the gentleness of Fynn's power brushes against my skin.

I had to go through it first. I needed to be the one to walk into the unknown that awaits us, because their lives mean more than mine. My life was doomed from the beginning, but theirs are still vibrant. I will do everything I can to keep my tainted life from staining theirs. I can't lose any more people who I hold dear to me, the thought makes nausea stir in my stomach.

The brightness is blinding for a moment, and as I step through, I feel tingles sweep over me. It only lasts a second before I step into the Court of Ashes.

My breath stalls in my lungs when my eyes adjust to the land before me. No colors exist. It's like everything was stripped of life and left to rot. The air is still, unmoving, with not even a whisper of a breeze. It's like a desert as hard, black sand stretches far beyond what my eyes can see, cracks decorating the top. Dead, greying trees stand tall in random spots on the outskirts, never having any hope of growing.

The part that really catches my attention is the charcoal mounds that litter the obsidian ground. I crouch down to look more closely at it and gasp.

Ashes.

Piles of ashes are everywhere, never being able to blow away without any wind. They lay dead to the world. Stranded. Stuck here forever.

A thick layer of clouds veil the sky, casting everything in a murky gloom. The whispers scrape hard against the barrier I made to block them. Growing louder, the darkness inside me becomes restless, wanting to be set free. I seal it within a deep well, but the seal is weak. Small fissures exist that can snap if it pushes hard enough. If I lose focus. I wonder if this court calls to it. Calls to me.

I push its promises away, even as nerves trail up my spine. I fear the longer I stay in this court, the more restless the darkness in me will become. Scared that it will grow stronger, and I'll sink into its icy depths as it swallows me whole.

I hear the hum of the portal behind me as Kye steps through, looking furious, his eyes landing on me. "You shouldn't have gone first," he says in a deep tone that could rattle the ground below our feet. "Don't pull a stunt like that again, we don't know what to expect here, Princess." His eyes start scanning around us and taking notes. He seems to come to the same conclusion I did.

This place screams death.

"Won't happen again," I tell him as I blink up at him with big eyes, while simultaneously crossing my fingers behind my back. I can't afford another slash on my soul as the lies continue to add up.

He goes to speak but decides to let it go as the rest of the group follows through, with Fynn coming in last. "Wow…" Fynn whistles. "This place could use a little work." I bite my lip to hold my laugh. The most ridiculous stuff comes out of his mouth; he never misses a beat in trying to lighten a situation.

"This place smells like burnt skin and something…foul," Cora says, wrinkling her nose, looking like she might add to the smell if she decides to bring up her breakfast.

"How do you know what burnt skin smells like?" Fynn turns to her with intrigue.

She rolls her eyes. "I'm a *healer*, I learned what it smells like during my training. Not that I liked it." Her face pales slightly, and she swallows thickly before walking towards me.

"Sorry to cut in, but I think we should focus on getting to the library," Kye says, facing Draven and watching his every move.

Draven looks around, seeming unconcerned about where we need to go, but I can see the emotions he's burying inside as he takes everything in. Seeing the land that his father stepped on. The land where he took his final breath. I can tell by the way Draven's face is set in harsh lines, the flicker of silver in his eyes as he focuses on keeping his dragon tamed. Seeing him battle the need to tear this land apart makes me want to wrap my arms around him. To kiss away the pain, to take his struggles from him and burn them to ash, only to leave them here to rot so he can have some peace.

I see the way he comes back to himself as he stares out at the open black desert and mounds of ashes throughout. "This place is empty, except for the castle, where the ruler of this court lives, and the library. The tricky part is that they are both located in the deep valley in the center of the island." He rubs his hand over his jaw, and I can't help but think about how those hands were on me, *in* me. That my hands were rubbing where he is now, and I have to look away from him before I forget myself. I curse internally, needing to focus on what we need to do.

I rub the outside of the pocket in my pants and feel the key safely tucked away. A deeper pocket is sewn inside my top, big enough to fit the small book that still holds a mystery I can't seem to figure out. I didn't want to leave it behind.

I hear the sand crunch beneath boots as Draven steps forward, turning to face all of us. "Fynn will get us to the library, and I will try to cast my shadows around us all to stay hidden. But we will have to be quick about it and try to find the doorway as fast as possible, because I'm unsure if this court affects powers. The air feels…*off*."

Kye nods as he stands tall next to me. "And we don't know *what* will be over there."

Kye's right, there could be Scavengers and Corrupted roaming in the court's center. But there's also the ruler no one has seen that lurks somewhere. For someone who has an army of Corrupted, you would think they would be everywhere, but I see and hear nothing. Not even an insect buzzing by, or the sound of anything prowling nearby.

"Have your weapons ready, and the key." Draven's eyes grab hold of mine, and I think I see a hint of worry in them, but I doubt it. Most likely just my mind wishing he may feel a portion of what I feel for him that's slowly taking root in me. Roots that are intertwining around my heart, encasing it so it beats for nobody but him.

We all take hold of our weapons and stand close together, waiting for Fynn to open the door to the unknown. "Let's find that book," I say with a determination that fuels the energy around us, ready for whatever is to come.

"Fuck yeah, let's do this," Fynn chimes in, lighting a smile on my face as I watch him open up a new opening in the air before us.

The warm touch of Draven's shadows glides over me and I can't hold back the shiver that dances down my spine. I want to drown in it, let his shadows own me, but I force myself to rein my desire once all of us are cloaked beneath and step through the portal to whatever fate awaits us.

CHAPTER FIFTY-TWO

Emma

*I*t's darker here. An eerie silence that holds the power to death's song.

Hidden beneath the touch of shadowed darkness, I look ahead of us and see that the valley is bigger than I imagined. It's deep, as if everything has sunk below with the weight of the sins that lie here. In the distance, there are three broken stone buildings, which are spread out on opposite sides of the valley, sitting on raised mounds of black sand. Almost like they are the points of a triangle. It's like a raging power blew a castle apart, only to leave it in pieces. Fissures dance along the hardened sand as more piles of ashes are scattered, but no dead trees are here. It's empty, aside from the ruined buildings.

The biggest section of the castle is in the center, which must be where it originated. Fynn opened his portal to be on the east side of the three ruins, per Draven's direction. The one in front of us must be the forbidden library that Draven found scouting the lands the other night. Its chipped stone and uneven structure sit a little higher on the land. Resting on top a mound of black sand, or…is it ashes? The thought sends an uneasy chill down my spine. But there's a third, smaller building in the distance, skinny and broken like the rest. As if all three are pieces of a puzzle that was never put together.

We all glance around, anxiously, to assess if there are any threats near, but there's…nothing. Only the sound of our breathing and our boots crushing the specks of sand to dust with every small movement.

Draven's eyes scale up the building and back down. "Say it. I can see you struggling to hold in whatever you want to tell me." He gives a pointed look to Fynn.

Fynn's body rocks back and forth on the soles of his feet. "If you're wrong about this being the right one, I get to say I told you so," Fynn quips.

Draven huffs. "I'm never wrong," he says with all the cockiness I remember so well from when we first met.

Fynn rubs his chin with a smug look. "*When* you're wrong, you'll have to beg me to use my powers to take us to the next building," he says teasingly.

Draven swipes a palm down his face in exasperation, but I don't miss the slight glimmer of amusement in his eyes before he masks it. "Not gonna happen," he says with a wave of his hand for us to start moving as he keeps his shadows around us.

We inch closer to the stone structure in front of us, and I hope to Gods that Draven is right.

We scale up the side of the sandy terrain, my boots sliding in the obsidian grains, as Draven's shadows match the ground beneath us. I look up to the sky, and not even a sliver of sun peeks through from behind the heavy clouds, a forever darkness blanketing the land as the grey plumes stay in place, unmoving. It makes me wonder if sunlight has ever touched this land.

We keep digging our heels into the side of the sandy hill to reach the building. My feet continue to slide with each step, but I push through, my calves burning with the force. It's not too far up, but it's steeper than I thought as I take my final step.

We make it to the top, and I look over to Cora to see Kye holding her elbow as she glares at him. But there's a small bit of what looks like relief on her face in between her winded breaths. A few steps farther on top of the mound, there's a stone covering, a broken piece of a slab that hangs on the edge. We all crowd under it, clinging closer to the shadows it provides. I scan my eyes around, still seeing no signs of life or anything lurking in the distance, but that doesn't mean we're alone.

"There's no door here, let's try walking around," Kye says with a slight wave of his hand. We follow him around the perimeter of the building on silent feet, staying close together as we reach the far side. Slinking slowly, pressing close to the warped exterior. "This has to be it." He points down a few deteriorated steps that lead down beneath.

"There's only one way to find out," I say on a breath as I place one foot on the first step, but Kye's hand grips my arm before I can put my weight on it. I turn around, looking at him in confusion.

"You promised," he reminds me. Bringing up earlier, when I said I wouldn't put myself at risk by going first. But I *have* to. This is my battle to fight. My guilt I need to repair in helping the people.

"I'm sorry, I have to," I say softly, hoping he understands.

I rip my arm out of his hold and rush down the last few steps. I reach for the key in my pocket and pull it free. Brushing my thumb over the rough metal in silent prayer all goes well. But I should know better, because my prayers are never heard. Rejected and turned to ash, left to waste away like the piles found here.

I balance the key between my fingers, assessing the iron door before me that is tightly sealed shut when I try to push on it. I slide the key into the hole, and with a little resistance, it goes in. A breath whooshes out of me with relief as I start to turn it and hear the click as it unlocks. I don't want to question how Edith had this key, but it makes me think that the books inside here are powerful, meant to stay hidden away, or to keep someone locked out.

The door creaks and scrapes against the stone floor as I push it open, getting hit in the face with dust floating in the air. I place my arm over my mouth as I yank the key free and tuck it back into my pocket. I grab hold of the hilt of my sword over my shoulder, ready to pull it free as I walk inside.

"Wow, talk about ancient," Fynn says between coughs as he follows behind Kye. The room is clouded in dust particles. It's hard to see inside, as no windows exist, just stone that conceals everything within.

"Stop being such a wimp," Cora teases him, walking past him to get a better look inside.

"Says the one who looked like she was going to pass out just walking up a mound of sand." Fynn smirks at her as he attempts to blow dust away from his face. "If you would have asked nicely, I could have carried you." He winks. "Or I could have portaled you to the top, if you really begged." His mischievous smile is on full display.

Cora just narrows her eyes on him. "You have a begging kink?" she taunts.

"Wanna find out?" Now, his smile looks excited as his eyes drink her in. Only, Cora rolls her eyes and ignores his blatant flirting.

Draven is the last one in, removing his shadows when he comes to a stop, and an emptiness settles inside my chest without his touch. His eyes drift around, until he walks over to the side and grabs what looks like a torch, dragging it against the rough stone to light it like a giant match. The orange flame flares, spreading throughout the room, and that's when I notice a few more torches on the walls. We each grab hold of one and do the same, making the fire come to life.

The flames dance against the dark space, illuminating the forbidden library below. I step down the rest of the stairs, holding my torch close. Cobwebs cling to the railing, and I cringe when I feel one brush against me. I take each step with steady feet, fearful a trap lies in my path and will either send me to my death or tumbling down to the bottom.

A cracking sound makes me pause, freezing my breath as I shoot my head upward. A streak of orange light cleaves its way slowly through the dark, a line of fire igniting around the ceiling of the room. I twist my head back and see Draven holding his torch to where the line starts, a pit of oil must fill it. But I'm even more thankful for the extra light, as I can now see the rest of the steps more clearly.

My eyes gradually adjust to the brightening light, as I make it twenty feet down to the bottom. The air feels alive down here, primordial energy pulsing around as I reach the bottom. Almost like the books have a life source of their own. Worn, decorative books climb up the stone walls on jagged shelves. A mix of leather and the musty smell fills the air.

"Wow, look at this place," Cora muses as she comes to stand beside me. "How are we going to find this book the Elder told you about?"

"I don't know, I think we're just going to have to go through each one." My stomach sinks as I take in the thousands of books stored underground, a sea of hidden power and ancient stories.

"It's called the Book of Kaimi," Draven's voice carries down the stairs.

"Did the Elder give any more details on what the book might look like?" Kye asks, wanting to have all the information to get straight to work.

"No," I say with a sigh. "In fact, she wasn't fully sure if it *was* here, just that it was likely." I wince as the admission falls from my lips, but it's our only shot at finding the Stone. Not one person says anything about how ludicrous it is to come here on a whim, on brief words told by an Elder, but I think everyone realizes this is our only option. Our only chance of procuring the Liminal Stone before my father.

Fynn claps his hands together and rubs them excitedly, causing a puff of dust to swirl in the air. "Alright, the race is on." He hurries over to the first stack of books and begins to rifle through them. I can't help but let a small smile slip at his enthusiasm.

We all go to different sections of ancient books and scour through each title. Trailing my fingertips over the spines, I carefully read their titles. While I search, I can feel a scorching heat kiss down my spine from time to time, causing a need to burn in me. I *know* he's looking at me, watching. Those frozen blue irises do nothing to make me feel cold, they only make my insides melt. Urging my body to go towards him, to close the distance between us. The thought of him watching me brings up memories of how he tunneled his attention on me when I came undone under his touch. The image makes me long to feel that again.

Stop it.

I can't fall into the thoughts of him, as a wave of desolation washes over me. Threatening to anchor me beneath the surface, sinking to the bottom to drown alone. He wanted my truths, but they mean nothing now. *We* mean nothing now.

I lose track of time as the outside world becomes nonexistent. We keep searching underground, brushing off cobwebs and climbing rickety, old ladders.

"I think I found it!"

I whip my head around, and a sharp pain stabs me. Hours of hunting for this book have made my muscles ache and my neck stiff. I grab the side of my neck and put pressure on the source of pain as I see Kye standing at the top of his ladder, holding a leather-bound book in his hand. He slides down with ease, but I squeeze my eyes shut, too nervous that the ladder might snap with the giant male zooming down it.

I hear the thump of his boots and we all make our way to the small table, stacked with more books in the center of the room. He lays the book flat on the cracked, wooden surface, and I swipe my hand across the top of it, revealing a streak of brown beneath the white layer of dust.

My palm tingles when it makes contact with the book, the power inside pushing against my hand. My blood buzzes as Draven stands beside me, his arm brushing against mine. "Let me open it." He looks around at all of us. "Just in case."

The brown, leather-wrapped book is etched in a gold design, with a strap that keeps the book shut. It's heavy, with the number of old, yellow pages that are stacked inside the binding. Draven carefully opens the book, and we all stare with slack jaws.

Blank. Every page is blank, with no words to be found.

"She did mention a drop of blood," I say, my eyes rising to meet his, remembering her words. I take hold of my favorite dagger, the one made of regular iron, and hand it out for him. His only weapons are wyvern, and if he uses one of those, it may bring attention to his inability to heal from it.

But he doesn't take the blade from me. Only holds his palm out over the book and keeps his pale pools of blue frozen on mine. "Care to help me out, little demon?" the tone in his voice is daring, as his eyes darken with excitement.

I feel my heart skip as my pulse begins to race, remembering the way he took pleasure in using the same dagger to draw blood from my skin. I lick my lips as if I can taste it, the taste of my blood mixed with the heady taste of him. I know he's thinking the same thing as his eyes darken, and he swallows roughly. I shake off the trance we both got sucked into before anyone starts to question it, and tighten my grip on the hilt.

A spark ignites inside me at the contact when I grab his hand, holding it still as I slide the blade against the center of his palm, keeping my eyes on him. The pain is pleasure to him, I can see it in how his pupils dilate, in how they trail down to stare at my mouth. I wonder if everyone else can feel the rivers of heat coursing around us, the current that grows more intense the closer we are to each other.

I hear the dripping of blood splattering on the pages. I tear my eyes away to look at the open book, wondering what we need to do next, but…

"What's supposed to happen?" Kye asks as Draven's blood begins to steam away off the pages, vanishing before my eyes.

"Maybe ask it where the Stone is," I say hopefully, as his blood slowly stops falling when the cut on his hand begins to heal on its own. I stare, mesmerized. Fascinated as his skin repairs itself, the blood clotting.

I rub my wrists, remembering the time I cut them, watching all the blood spill free from my veins. The way I started to feel weak, and the blackness edging around my vision. I would have died, leaving this world without a stitch of my body healing itself

"Where is the Liminal Stone?" Draven's baritone voice cuts through my thoughts and brings me back to focus. But nothing happens, the remaining ruby liquid on the pages fully evaporates, returning to empty pages once again.

A few moments pass, and still, nothing changes, not even a flare of power from the book.

"Now, what?" Fynn asks, as it looks like we hit a dead end.

"Maybe try again," Cora adds, keeping her hopeful spirit alive for all of us.

I smile at her, and what could it hurt to try again? If anything, the same thing will happen, and we'll be back at square one again. I raise my hand and do a quick cut across the center of my palm. The slight sting burns as the blade sinks beneath my skin, wishing Draven could lick the pain away. I hold the dagger in my other hand, seeing how both our blood blends together against the blade.

Crimson falls in the center of the book, painting it red as I continue to bleed.

I wait for the steam to come, for my blood to fizzle into nothing, but instead, it starts to move. It comes to life, slithering across the stained paper, every single drop forming its own pool of red. My breath catches as it moves, and I cover my hand to stop any more blood from hitting the pages.

"Where is the Liminal Stone?" My question hangs in the air, all of us silent, waiting.

My blood starts moving, until it shifts to letters dancing across the page, becoming words for us to read.

"What the—" Fynn's eyes watch in amazement as a sentence is displayed before us.

The stone of light and dark lies with death.

I read over the nine words, repeatedly, until the bloodied words steam away and disappear into the air. *The stone of light and dark lies with death.* My mind can't wrap my thoughts around the words, they just fall away in confusion.

"What is that supposed to mean? Do you guys have any ideas?" Cora asks as she scratches her head in thought.

"I–I don't know." I look back down at the book and wonder if the risk to come here was worth it. A deep crease forms between my brows as I feel the whispers of my darkness stab through me, deafening me as everything around me fades out. Not even Kye's moving mouth cuts through their intense voices. Stirring with restlessness, as if they are excited, anxious about something.

Kye's trying to talk to me, but I can't hear him. My focus is unsteady, with every bit of energy I wield to build the barrier between me and the darkness, attempting to rebuild its strength.

A burning touch ignites against my chin, blending its energy into mine, as I shove more strength into the shield to lock the whispers away.

My eyes peel open from squeezing them shut to find Draven's hand holding my face to his.

"I've got you." I stare wide-eyed at him as his voice pours into my head, filling the instant silence as I finish slamming the wall up within. But Draven's mouth, it never moved.

I must have imagined it, then, wishing that would be something he would say to me. He stays quiet, his sharp eyes assessing me, seeing into my soul and the darkness that tries to consume it. But the way he's looking at me, it doesn't seem like he spoke into my mind. Or if he did, he doesn't realize I heard him.

I pull my head away and glance around the table. "Sorry," I brush it off with a light chuckle. "Just got a little light-headed, you know me, a bit of food will do the trick," I say, hoping it's enough to reassure everyone.

Kye watches me carefully, but I didn't let the darkness override me, and I kept my eyes shut, in case my darkness showed through, like when I trained with him.

He lets any of his wandering thoughts go as his teeth show, knowing how much I love food. "Well, maybe we should head back and feed you, while we try to figure out what the book means." That sounds like a good idea to me, to get out of this land full of desolation, which causes the darkness in me to pound against the cage I'm trying to hold it in.

"I could go for a drink," Cora announces.

We laugh at her bluntness but freeze when a growl rattles through the stone, instilling fear into each of us as we frantically look around with wide eyes. Draven pulls his double-edged sword free, keeping his hands in the center, away from the wyvern iron blades. I follow suit, sheathing my red-stained dagger and unleashing the sword I chose from the caves of Tsisana.

"Stay down," Kye whispers, stepping in front of me while putting his hand out behind him, motioning for us to crouch as he nears the battered stairs. The scraping of nails echoes through the door above, causing a chill to sweep down my spine. The hair on the back of my neck stands on end as I stay on alert, mentally preparing for what's outside these walls.

Draven is beside me, focusing ahead until his head jerks to me, those blue eyes zeroing in on my hand. He grabs hold of my wrist and holds it out in front of him. *"Shit,"* he mutters. "Cora, heal her, now," he commands with a seriousness that makes her follow his order without demanding he ask nicely.

I stare at him in confusion, because this is not the time to worry about a little scratch on my hand. It's meaningless. But the stiffness in his posture tells me he won't back down on this, he will have her heal my hand, no matter what needs to be done.

She holds my hand between her palms, just like before on the ship. Closing her eyes, she lets her power spill free as a warmth settles inside the cut, closing it entirely.

My hand drops from hers when the door bangs open and a shriek tears through the silence. A nightmare coming to life as a Scavenger stands at the top of the stairs. Its red eyes glow brightly, battling against the orange light streaming dimly from the fire. Its body moves like the wind at night or the sway of a flame. I remember the way Kye described them after our training session, and his descriptions were right, but I didn't imagine how massive they would be. For a monster that size, it moves with lethal grace as it slowly descends the stairs.

The blood in me freezes at the thought of not having another way out. Only up. But one Scavenger against the four of us won't stand a chance, not when we hold the weapons that will end its existence. I slowly rise to my full height, not wanting to cower in front of the beast of death. The Scavenger's head twists towards me, sniffing the air before its eyes flare to life, like scorching twin flames beaming in the dark.

"Get back down!" Kye's voice booms as he tries to block me from the Scavenger's sights.

"If you fight, I fight." I refuse to back down as I inch closer to Kye, readying my weapon for any sudden attacks. Another shadow of a beast prowls in next, two of them against us four now.

"Fuck," Fynn swears as a few Corrupted follow behind the Scavenger. They look disheveled in tattered clothes, their black veins bulging in their arms, rage boiling in their blood. Black blood that trails down from their eyes, like they're crying their rotted sins.

We all wait in heavy silence for one of them to attack, to make the first move. We stay frozen in place, watching their every move. Their every breath. Footsteps pound outside and the darkness in me bangs on its walls, begging to be set free. A flicker of shadows streams through the door, pressing against the walls as a male steps in, blocking the entire doorway. The power radiating off him threatens to cripple me.

He stays, lingering in his shadows, not yet revealing himself. But something about the energy rubbing off him, the coldness radiating from his shadows, has my psyche screaming, clawing at my mind to listen. To *follow*.

"Emma," the familiar deep timbre of his voice freezes my breath, causing fear to lodge in my throat. That's when I realize, I never stood a chance of escaping my nightmare. It currently stands above me, branding me with his eyes.

CHAPTER FIFTY-THREE

Draven

I notice the terror that fills Emma's eyes, the way her grip tightens on her sword, turning her knuckles white. Her jaw clenches as I watch in fascination when she turns that fear into aggression that wants to strike out and slay the nightmare that haunts her. I remember his voice from when I was sucked into her dream, and the way she let her darkness spread through her to force him out of her head.

"I should have known you would come right to me." A demonic chuckle leaves him as his shadows twist further around him, bringing a chill to the room. He steps into the open, letting the soft orange light flicker over his features. Grey-toned skin with black eyes and slicked back raven hair. He brings his hand up to his jaw, scraping over the bare skin, as his shadows dance with the movement. His hands are stained black, as they fade back to grey at his elbow. He wears no shirt, and he stands there with an unvexed posture, a murderous glint in his eyes.

Emma raises her sword higher in front of her. "Who are you?" She sneers at him.

He clicks his tongue as his shadows float him down the stairs, his black pants blending into the darkness of his power. "You come into *my* court, break into *my* library, and dare to ask who *I* am?" His power surges as the flames on the torches flicker with the gust of energy that blasts from him.

The beast in me slams forward and I have to resist the urge to let him out as I stare at the ruler of the Court of Ashes. The same one my father came to face and never returned from. My eyes track up to the top of his head, seeing the black spiked crown hanging crookedly. It shimmers against the flame, the twists of silver that band around it, with red crystals shining in between. My mind begins to sort through everything we know as I stare at the ruler of this court. Looking like death himself, as if he rose from the ashes. I grind my teeth to refrain from launching myself at him, which will only cause an uproar and chaos to unfold with us being outnumbered.

A wicked smile spreads across his face, as he looks at every one of us before landing those soulless eyes back on Emma. "I'm afraid you won't be leaving here, though." His smile snaps into one with cunning intent as he shoots forward, dissolving into thin air before appearing right in front of her. I blast my shadows out in front of her, blocking off his attack right as the Scavengers and Corrupted sprint towards us.

I realize that the Corrupted have swords as they clash against Cora and Kye, but I notice how Cora struggles with her fighting skills. She's not putting enough strength into her swings and delays her attacks, but it's not her fault. It's the shock of a real fight and not having enough time to prepare her, at least not until she felt comfortable in defending herself. Kye takes the brunt of the attacks, going back and forth from fending off the Corrupted male leaping at him, while spinning and kicking the chest of a Corrupted female launching at Cora. They are savage, feral in their attacks, and I know Cora and Kye may need my help.

I curse under my breath as I feel the weight of this ruler before me weakening the wall I've created around Emma. I grit my teeth as I try to throw more of my shadows at him.

Fynn has two Scavengers circling him as he holds out his bow and arrow, cocked back and aiming straight for whichever leaps towards him first. I know how good Fynn is at fighting, especially when he uses his power to disappear and surprise his opponent from behind. But we're still overpowered, if only we left a moment sooner, we could have safely escaped back to my castle before we were found.

We should have healed Emma's hand immediately. They sensed her and whatever is in her fucking blood. It calls to them, calls to *him*. Just like the book didn't respond to me or my blood, it only responded to whatever power is running through her veins. Whether it's the darkness she told me about or the power that is chained away, something about her is connected to these beings.

I want to let my dragon out, to give me more strength and fly Emma somewhere safe, but I can't. There's no room in this library and I wouldn't be able to make it through the stairwell and out the door. They would easily catch us.

With a wave of the ruler's hand, a Scavenger comes to life that wasn't there before, already hissing with its teeth pulled back as it crouches before me, lowering on its haunches. He fucking creates them. I spin my double-edged sword in front of me to hold it off, but my shadows are starting to slip in front of Emma. She backs up a step, seeing my hold slipping between my fingers.

I hear an ear-piercing screech fill the air. Fynn must have killed one of the Scavengers, but I refuse to look up as the beast before me stalks closer. I try to keep my power focused on Emma. But I can't hold onto it for much longer.

I hear the rough sneer of his voice vibrate against my weakening shadows. "You were never supposed to be born, *daughter.*" The moment the words fall from his lips, my shadows unwillingly drop and the Scavenger launches itself at me, snapping its razor teeth as I duck out of its way. The Scavenger regains its footing, spinning towards me again and we stand off facing each other as that one word keeps echoing in my mind.

Daughter.

I don't have another second to question it as I'm fighting the Scavenger again in low kicks and swipes with each end of my sword, twirling it to hopefully hit my mark. One quick glance tells me the others are still fighting, holding their own as a few piles of ash litter the floor.

Ducking low as the Scavenger on me leaps high, I drive my body upward with the blade in tow and ram it through its belly, making sure to angle it towards its heart. Its body slumps over me, the blade sliding deeper into him before smoke spills free and the black, fiery shadow turns into fragments of embers that dissipate. I turn in time to see Emma standing in shock, lightning flashing in her stormy eyes as she stares at her nightmare. The darkness hovering around him starts to whirl and twist, forming into a vortex, snapping out to wrap its icy arms around her.

"Emma!" I yell to grab her attention, to get her to *fight*. She's frozen in fear. In shock that her nightmare is not just a bad dream. I push off the ground hard to reach her, but a sword appears in the next second, held by a phantom hand that slices towards me. Panic seizes me by the throat. There's no time. No way to block it. A blinding pain sears inside of me as the blade strikes through my chest, my blood spilling free. I choke, trying to suck in air. My mouth falls open, still trying to yell her name again, to beg her to run. But nothing comes. The burning in my chest invades my entire body, feeling like I've been lit on fire from the inside.

A scream rips from Emma as she reaches for me, her eyes locking on mine in a desperate plea. The fear filling them breaks me, I've never seen such terror shine so strongly, just as a tear falls down her cheek. I try to reach for her with a shaky hand, but her eyes are still on me, not seeing the monster behind her. My eyes widen. I open my mouth to speak again, to try to warn her, but blood gurgles in my throat instead. One second, she's there, and in the next, she's swallowed whole, gone to wherever hell has taken her.

CHAPTER FIFTY-FOUR

Emma

A glimmer of light starts filtering in as I begin to peel my eyes open, blinking against the brightness invading the darkness I was lost in. My head pounds relentlessly, taking in my surroundings when I regain some consciousness.

Where am I?

Fear grips me as visions flash of the last few moments before everything went black. This powerful male, who has been haunting my dreams, claims that I'm his *daughter*. The thought makes my head spin as I raise myself up on an elbow, finding myself lying on a cold, damp floor. I'm grateful to not be stripped bare, but I shiver as an unknown liquid on the floor seeps through my clothes, turning my skin colder with every inch as the wetness spreads. I do my best to ignore it, as I try to focus on where I am and the state I'm in. I immediately notice that my weapons are missing. I knew it without checking for them, their absence feeling like an extra limb removed from my body.

Shit. I feel for my book and the key to the forbidden library, but both are gone. I curse internally, my jaw clenching in aggravation.

I press a hand to my head as my vision wavers. He shrouded us in a tornado of shadows, the strength of it made me feel dizzy until everything around me became a blur of motion and the blackness dancing around my vision consumed me. Now, I'm in some type of cell, with chains decorating my ankles. The cuffs cut into my skin from how tightly they are bound, and the irony doesn't pass my notice. The fact that the two males who have claimed to be my father have bound and caged me like some worthless animal. Worst of all, I'm still not any closer to finding the Liminal Stone before my father, or I suppose, I shouldn't call him that anymore. Now he's *only* King Oren.

I wish I could deny the phantom ruler being my father, but the way I felt a piece of my broken soul come alive in his presence says otherwise. Like it found him *familiar*. The way a part of me snapped into place, connecting a bond of long, lost grief that I didn't realize was weighing on my heart. A kiss of recognition in my blood. I just assumed King Oren was my father, but it would explain the distance I always felt towards him, even before he started hurting me.

I glance around the cell again, grinding my teeth together. I want to slam my fists against the stone floor in frustration, letting him get the upper hand. Letting myself fall prey to his trap, even when I heard the distant yell of Draven's voice calling to me, I was already lost in a haze of confusion. The rug swept out from beneath me, my whole life turning into more of a lie. But the pain that tore my heart in half was seeing Draven get a sword shoved through his chest. I *felt* a faint sting and the wavering pulse of his power as if it was calling out to me. I saw the agony in his eyes, how the light dimmed in them before I was ripped away.

I scrub my hands over my eyes to hold the tears at bay. Not knowing if he's alive or not has my soul fracturing with the thought. I push the grief down, thinking about the final words I heard. If the words that the ruler of the Court of Ashes says are true…then who the *fuck* am I?

Am I even *related* to King Oren? Does he know?

So many questions race through my mind. One being how is it

possible for my life to get any shittier? Apparently, it can, as I see the true rot surrounding me when my eyes are fully adjusted. The room is cold and musty, the stench of urine and something rotten makes bile creep up my throat.

What looks like ashes are scattered in the corner opposite of me and I curl in on myself, bringing my limbs together to hug my core. Old, tattered brick walls stained with what I can only assume is dried blood take up the three walls, leaving an open section of rusted iron bars trapping me in on the other. The charred remains keep me company in this cell, making me wonder what victims were captured before me.

Alone once again. Trapped in filth and left to be consumed by the tainted power that wants to rise inside me. Stripped of weapons and cuffed around my ankles by chains hooked to the wall. I give a hard yank, rattling the iron shackles with a clanking sound, but they resist. The hooks remain locked to the bolts in the wall as I stop my attempts, letting my limbs fall limp. My muscles shake with weakness from the extra iron secured around me. I stare blankly at the floor, the harsh truth of my situation settles like an anchor in my chest, which feels like it's being crushed by stone.

I don't know how many hours pass as I flicker in and out of awareness. Fear takes hold of me as I fully come to, worrying about the others as I was taken in the midst of them fighting. I should have done *something*; I should have protected them. Guilt gnaws at me with a feeling of worthlessness, as I lay powerless on the frigid floor. But I can't just wallow here in my own self-pity, I have to try to find a way out of here before he comes back. I need to *fight*. Maybe I can still do something by figuring out what the book said about the Stone, or maybe I could even find the meaning of the words in the book Queen Zoraida gave me. I keep those thoughts at the forefront of my mind as I attempt to stand.

On wobbly legs, I push myself up as the iron cuffs tighten even further around my ankles, their sharp edges digging into my skin. I unsteadily wobble up to the sturdy iron bars, slamming my palms roughly around them in a tight grip to stop myself from tumbling sideways. I regain my balance and stand up a little higher, pressing my face between the bars to peer down the hallway. The faint sound of liquid dripping from the ceiling and splashing to stone echoes down the dim corridor, but I'm unable to see what lies at the other end.

A clinking sound snaps my attention to the cell adjacent to me, and I inhale a shocked breath. A female older than me stares back with wide eyes, curled up in the corner. Her threadbare clothes are torn and covered in dirt, pale skin peeks under the filth coating her as if she hasn't seen the light of day in years. Decades. Her body looks haggard from whatever suffering she has endured, her golden hair is dull, her cheeks are sunken in and dark circles cave in under her fear-filled eyes.

Carefully, I lower myself to her level and try to get some answers out of her. "Are we still in the Court of Ashes?"

She stays silent, and it makes me wonder when the last time she spoke was, especially if she's been locked away here all alone. I sink lower until I hit the ground, crossing my legs on the floor and try again. "I'm Emma, what's your name?" She opens her mouth to speak, but nothing comes out. She tries again, only to close it with a wince and scrunches her face in pain. As if it hurts too much to speak. I take her all in as I keep my eyes on hers. She is so beautiful for someone diminishing right before my eyes. I try in a final attempt at getting any kind of information from her. "Are you able to tell me where we are?"

She swiftly glances around in fear of someone listening, but a whisper so soft slips from her lips that if I wasn't focused on her, I would have missed it. "In the dungeon of death itself."

Confused and in need of clarification, my jaw falls open, but before I can speak, darkness slithers into the room, freezing the air. I shoot to my feet, demanding the muscles in my legs to hold me up straight. Pain lances through my limbs with the quick movement, but I ignore it. The phantom from my nightmares, who is very much real, stands before me.

The one who said I'm his daughter.

His coal-black eyes snag on me, waiting for me to speak. "Are you comfortable?"

I disregard his question, letting it hang in the air. I hold my chin high to help shove the fear down. Keeping my spine straight, feeling it protest with the slight quiver in my muscles. In the next breath, a tendril of his shadows shoots out, wrapping tightly around my throat. Squeezing above my necklace as he stops air from entering my lungs. I try to inhale but my airway is blocked off completely, and my lungs continue to demand oxygen.

"You know how much it angers me when you ignore me," he seethes. Standing casually on the other side of the iron bars with his hands in his pockets, the icy claws of his power doing his bidding while I suffocate in silence. "Enlighten me on where you've been all these years?" His eyes are hostile, his tone is threatening.

The coils of shadows lift enough to force out an answer. "Asov," I gasp, inhaling deeply before I choke out the rest. "King Oren says he's...my father." No sooner do the words leave my lips does his power curl around my neck, tearing the breath right from my lungs. The name of King Oren seems to have sparked a darker kind of flame that twists around the shadows engulfing his hands, a hellfire that wants to unleash itself and destroy the world.

His eyes start to swirl in a chaotic abyss of black flames, latching onto my necklace. A phantom finger forms in front of me to trace along it. "So, *this* is why I couldn't find you, my own *blood*. King Oren, who declares himself as your father, is a fraud, hiding you away to keep you all to himself. To have your *power* be in his control. Probably keeping you alive until he could use you as a weapon against me. Against the world." He relinquishes his hold on my throat and I gasp for air. My body wants to heave forward, but I force myself to stay tall, to keep my eyes on him.

The black-stained skin on his arms grows darker, black veins shoot out through his body, tracking over his chest and up to his neck. I need to know more. I need to know what everything he's saying means because I know he's not bluffing, or spitting lies as the phantom hands of his power scrape down my neck and trace the barrier of my psyche, causing my entire body to seize in panic.

"If you wanted to find me and this *power* so badly, why not come searching on your own? Why all the mind games? And why would King Oren want my power if he trapped it?" I spit off a rapid fire of questions, hoping he'll answer at least one. I don't know what he has planned, but if he chokes me again, I won't be able to ask. It doesn't make sense for someone as cruel and malicious as him to not do his own dirty work.

I have to ask about my power, since the worst thing King Oren ever did was prevent me from using them. He took my protection, my pride of being *Fae*. The thought of him not being my biological father brings a sense of relief with it. Yet, the idea of this male before me being my father is a whole new nightmare that I am not prepared for.

The whispers grow louder again, as the phantom claws trailing along my mind beckon them. A faint vibration brushes through the air, and my eyes trail up, trying to find the source. It snags on his head while he glares at me. I swallow, forcing my eyes to meet his gaze quickly.

He pulls a few of his shadows back into himself, the power radiating in his palm simmers to nothing. "The darkness is your friend, Emma. Death is untouchable. It's why that thing on your neck could never sense it. But I know *you* feel it, hear the whispers of my power trace along your mind. Comforting you," he says with such gentleness that I almost believe him, but I've seen his darkness and the destruction it causes. "You should know, you're not Fae."

I blanch, feeling all the blood drain from my face, while he remains standing outside my cell as if we're having a casual conversation.

"In fact, this is quite a reunion. You see, your mother is the Goddess of Light and I am the God of Darkness, Whiro. It seems King Oren wants your power in his grasp, in his court, because he found out *who* you are and took it upon himself to steal you away. He knows how powerful you are. But if you need more proof that you are, in fact, my daughter, the Book of Kaimi you found only accepts pure blood." He pauses with a smirk. "Pure blood of the Gods."

I stare at him in disbelief, opening my mouth to say something, but he shoves his shadows down my throat to silence me. "I'm not done," he growls. "I don't like having the power of my blood existing in another's veins. It's why I've been residing in the Fae lands instead of my own realm, refusing to return until I succeeded in ending you. You were never supposed to be born, but your mother went against me and hid you before I could find you. Now, I finally have what's mine back, and I plan to spill every drop of your blood."

My lungs burn with his power sealing my airway, but he suddenly clears the shadows from in my throat, and I force my broken voice before he can stop me. "Did you kill her? Did you kill my mother?!" My voice is gruff, but my rage fumes with a gut-wrenching need to kill him myself if he took my mother away from me. The person who I have never met, yet still left a gaping hole in my heart, never to be filled.

"Why don't you ask her?" He grins savagely.

I scowl harder, not understanding what he's talking about. "Who?" I seethe.

He steps back and the female across the cell comes into my view, her grey eyes are filled with tears that grip my heart. "Mariam, your *mother.*"

My breath catches, feeling my heart slam to a halt in my chest. The storms raging in our eyes crash against each other, and I *know*, at this moment he's telling the truth. The way she's looking at me, with so much undying love in her eyes shrouded with sorrow, consumes me. My defiant reserves deflate, crippling into nothing. I drop to my knees. Chains rattling. My kneecaps crack against the floor.

"Mother?" I force out with enough emotion to suffocate me. My eyes burn as I feel the storm cloud within me break, with an overwhelming surge of rain that floods down my cheek. My heart bleeds as I stare at her, letting her see every raw emotion cutting through me.

One moment, she's there, and the next, she's gone. Whiro blocks her from my sight, his stream of deathly shadows form a wall behind him. Leaving just me and him. "I found her only months after she *hid* you. I kept her alive to play with, but mostly to have her witness your death, which she tried so hard to prevent." He sneers. "She fought hard, but still didn't win. But since you came so willingly, I'll let you have one night together to catch up before I take my power back. The portion of my power that left me and now runs through your undeserving veins." With a twitch of his lip, he glares, promising to stay true to his word. He waves his hand up, engulfing himself in darkness, disappearing into thin air. Final words echo through his funnel of night, those whispering words that haunt me. "Sweet dreams, Emma."

I stare at the empty space, replaying his words, she fought for me. But I feel bile resting at the base of my throat, learning that he kept her so she could watch her own daughter's death. My stomach convulses once, but I shove the nausea back down. Breathing through shallow breaths, still in a state of disbelief, I dart my eyes up to lock on *hers*. My mother.

"You've been alive this whole time?" I say softly, my voice cracking at how I could have saved her if I only knew. I would have suffered any punishment placed on me if it meant I could free her. She's been suffering down here for so long, all alone and in the hands of death himself.

I can already feel my heart shredding apart even more. A hurricane of anger whirls to life towards the male who's never been my father. The one who's kept me locked away, clueless to everything in this fucking life. The one who *took* me from my only family. The next time I see him will be the last time his eyes look upon me. King Oren's sins will fall upon my sword until I hear the very last beat of his internal drum. This I can promise.

My heart aches as I watch her pull her body closer to the bars. Closer to *me* as she grunts in pain. When she reaches the bars, she rests her shoulder on it, tipping her head towards me. Her eyes take in every feature on my face, a soft smile stretches across her dainty face, but then it falls away.

"I was so afraid he had found you when he brought me here, but then, I soon realized that my heart can rest in peace so long as I was in this cell. It was the only sign that you were still out there and *free*." Her voice scratches from lack of use and, if I had to guess, minimal water. The anger that cuts through me, making the maddening thoughts come alive in my head.

That is, until I register the word she said, shaking my head at the word *free*. "I was never free. I was in another kind of prison." My head falls forward, realizing how screwed up everything has become.

"Emma," her voice gently soothes something inside of me as I lift my head. Her eyes well up as I see the watery sheen to them from across the cells. "I never wanted that for you. I never wanted to leave you. But I knew he would eventually catch up to me. We're bonded, so I could never truly hide from him. And that meant if you were with me, you would have always been in danger. But I won't let him hurt you, I can't bear the pain. You deserve to *live*, Emma. But I want you to know that I have thought about you with every passing second of each day, I've never stopped loving you."

My heart throbs at the love pouring from her words. The emotion that cracks her voice. Wishing I could wrap my arms around her for the first time, to learn what she smells like, and feel her motherly touch. The touch of pure love. The love of *family*.

A warmth blooms inside me, at hearing her say she loves me. Something I haven't heard since I was a child living with Aunt Lyd. Even though we never got to spend a day of our lives together, deep down, I know my love for her has always been there, giving me strength when I felt like I had none left. Like the strength she had to leave me behind, to *protect* me.

I never thought I'd ever be able to see her, so I don't hesitate. "I love you." My voice shakes as more tears fall free, staining the stone floor. Letting those three words fall from my lips. Words I've never said before to her, never voiced to a single person since I was taken from Aunt Lydia. Three words I never thought I'd tell anyone again. It's almost like they were always meant to be said to her first. Waiting for this moment.

Her lips tremble. "I love you, my darling Emma."

A sob ripples out of me for the way fate likes to toy with us by finally bringing us together, only to tear us apart again. But maybe our souls can dance together in the world beyond this one, finally shedding our chains and be free. Never alone.

Unless I can find a way to kill the one who is death itself.

My eyes widen on a gasp as clarity slams into me, my entire body freezing as my mind spins with all the pieces laid out before me. The words that were written in crimson from the book spring forward.

The stone of light and dark lies with death.

I bring my eyes, sparking with realization, to my mother, who's watching me with interest.

"The crown," I say in a hushed breath. Remembering the ruby stone swirling in the crown on his head. The faint hum of power pulsing inside. It lies on the head of death.

My mother tilts her head, not understanding where my mind has run off to in the middle of our conversation.

"I need Whiro's crown," I state, and now I may be the only one close enough to retrieve it. I just need to find a way to get us out of here.

CHAPTER FIFTY-FIVE

Emma

The evening passes as my mother and I converse back and forth, but only for a little at a time. Her body is so weak she can barely manage to stay awake for very long. I start telling her about how I got shackled in this cell, but my words die off. My voice strains the more I try to talk as it gets lodged with a million different emotions, worried of Draven's fate. His eyes held such fear, and when I broke free of my shock, all I wanted was to rewind time. To dart in front of him and take the hit to protect him, like how he's protected me. A tear trails down my cheek as I clench my teeth together, doing my best to pocket the sorrow ripping through me and failing. I'm desperate to know if he's okay or not.

My mother watches me silently, giving me time to process my thoughts. When no more tears slip free, she speaks. "It sounds like you love him."

I turn to look at her with blurry vision, rubbing my palms against my eyes to clear them. "I can't," I say with a small shake of my head. "He's not mine to love."

She presses her lips together, as if she wants to say more, but I'm grateful when she lets it go. She changes the subject and tells me more about Aunt Lydia, and I tell her what I can remember before everything becomes fuzzy. I can only recall bits and pieces from that time in my life, and the ones I do remember bring a spark of joy to my heart. But most of my memories start after King Oren took me as his.

King Oren took me.

King Oren, who is not my *fucking* father.

Grief lodges in my throat, the thought slams into me as I feel another fissure crack deep through my heart. If King Oren took me away, then he must have taken Aunt Lyd's life. I've never connected the dots before, always hoping she got away once he took me and a stronger wave of heartache makes my chest cramp. It hurts so much I have to claw at the spot, demanding it to settle while I attempt to hold back another round of tears.

My mother slowly fell into sleep, curled up in her fragile state as scraps of food are on her plate. She still has not woken since we were given the bits of moldy bread. The distorted color and spots of growth was enough to make my stomach constrict and dry heave. I shoved mine away, but sorrow plagues me at wondering if this was all she was ever offered to survive on. I wish I could take away her pain, and the guilt of being so oblivious to everything as it continues eating away at me.

I sit against the tattered stone wall, facing the bars of my cell, and rest my head back against the cold surface. I rock my head back and forth against the wall, in a daze of defeat. No light creeps in the small sliver of a crack in the stone ceiling, the constant gloom in this court leaves me unaware of what time of day it is. My heart feels heavy in my chest, not knowing what's happening beyond these walls, once again, cut off from the world outside. I want to say I'd pray to the Gods, but I can't anymore. My parents *are* the Gods, which makes me…a *Goddess*.

Is that why King Oren used wyvern iron for my necklace, for he knew the strength of the power that flows through my veins? Is that why he abused me and mutilated my body? In hopes of having the strength of a Goddess on his side and in his control? With years of his torment, it may have ripped apart my soul, but he made the heart he ruined stronger, turning it to stone. The emptiness of never being *enough*. Never knowing why I was punished, then left to rot alone in a box with no love to cling to. Like a star lost in the vast darkness beyond, that can't find its way home.

But then, pale eyes flickered in the oblivion that swallowed me, a glowing compass guiding me back to life. With soft kisses that erased the pain of each scar, along with words of open truths splintering cracks against my hardened heart.

I can't deny the feelings that buzz along my skin when Draven is near and the jolt to my heart when he touches me. My mind flashes to the shocking pain that filled his eyes before I was swept away, and I squeeze my eyes shut to block it off, but I can't. I somehow felt a piece of his pain as I saw his blood spill down his chest, and the way his power left him. A sickening worry makes my stomach lurch. This time, I fully heave all over the floor next to me, the bitterness from it coating my tongue.

I wipe my mouth with the back of my hand and make my way to the far corner of my cell to get away from the stench of my own stomach contents, and pick at the specks of dirt that are on my clothes. A shiver runs through me while I stare at my mother, fast asleep on the floor. I hate to see her so weak. I make promises in my head to free her from here, but I can feel my eyes drifting shut before I can protest.

A kiss of warmth caresses my cheek, eliciting a pull to the vines wrapped tightly around my heart. My eyes flicker open as I see a black spiral glittering before me, blanketing me in a warm embrace. I reach out to brush my hand through it, feeling like I'm in a dream, but then it vanishes, clearing the view that leads through my cell. I inhale sharply at the male standing behind the bars.

Draven.

His eyes darken when he sees the state I'm in, the muscle in his jaw jumping with a flare of his nostrils. His body is vibrating with anger, looking dangerously close to having his beast break free and blowing this dungeon to pieces.

He inhales deeply with restrained fury, his chest expanding before exhaling slowly. "Are you hurt?"

My heart slams in my chest at hearing his voice. "No," I say, to help reassure him I'm unharmed. To help smooth the crease forming between his brows. I shoot up on my legs, which are still not fully awake as they try to give out. I flatten my palm up on the wall beside me to hold myself upright.

I bite my lip, staring in disbelief that he's alive. My eyes frantically scan every inch of his body, searching for any injuries, any sign of the wound I saw before I was torn away from him.

"You're okay," I whisper, too choked up to use my voice as a well of tears glisten in my eyes. "I thought you might have died," I confess as I stumble to the bars, standing inches in front of him. Desperate to have him near me, to know he's real.

He reaches his hand through and grips my chin, rubbing his thumb over my bottom lip in the way he always does. In the way I love.

"I'm not that easy to kill, little demon." That delicious dimple appears when he smirks, and I slip my hand through the bars to trace my fingertips over it. "Only wyvern iron can kill me, remember? So, I was able to heal."

I exhale a sigh of relief. "What about the others?" Nerves rack through my body as I wonder if they are here with him.

"They're safe. Only a few scratches, but Fynn transported them away to safety and will be returning in less than an hour, enough time for me to get you out of here." He looks at the door of my cell, frowning at the intricate lock on it.

"How did you get in here?" I ask, figuring this place was guarded like crazy, impenetrable. My eyes dance back and forth between his, still in a state of shock that he's *here*.

He grips my chin harder, pulling my face to the space between the bars as he inches his own closer. "Did you forget who I was when you first met me?" There's amusement lining his voice as I think back to that night, even when I didn't know who he was at the time. Just a shadow of a male who vanished in the dark.

"Not a chance," I say, watching the way his eyes darken because I could never forget him. I felt drawn to him in every form he was in.

His hand falls away from my face, letting his shadows twist along the bars and around the lock, before it explodes, breaking apart as he starts to slide the door open. He does the same thing to the lock on my chains, snapping them open, making them fall free.

"They aren't made of wyvern iron," he says, if only to help make sense to me of how he can do that. I push my wobbly legs forward as I race into his arms. They wrap around me tightly as I press my cheek against his heated chest, hearing the steady rhythm of his heart beating.

"Thank you," I mumble against his shirt. "I'm not used to someone saving me."

He fists my hair and pulls it back. He rears his head back, glaring at me with intensity. "You might not be my mate, but you have become the broken rays of light that fracture through every lonely night. I will fight through every crashing wave just to make my way to you. You will never be lost to me, for I will always find you." The sincere promise falls from his lips and I feel the spark of his truth as it lights inside of me, begging to burn brighter. His promise is sailing on a shooting star that crashes into my chest.

He rips the top of his shirt aside, displaying his chest, the spot where his heart beats. Freeing a wyvern blade, he carefully cuts a line over his heart, his blood trickling free.

"Draven!" I whisper yell. "What are yo—"

He leans in and presses his lips to mine, placing my hand over the cut on his heart. His blood runs down his chest, coating the palm of my hand. "You remain here. A scar on my heart that will never leave," he says against my lips.

I feel the burn in my eyes as I watch his blood continue to spread between my fingers. He'll scar there from the wyvern iron. A permanent declaration, for me. My lips tremble when his cut doesn't heal. He may say these things, the words that make my heart race and have a sliver of hope, but I know I can't cherish them as strongly as I wish to. For the moment his fated mate comes into his life, I will just be a burned-out star in his midnight sky, dwindling to nothing as his soul aligns with another.

I want to tell him none of it matters, but I don't. "I will always find you too, for you have marked my heart with the only scar that I will ever cherish," I say instead, knowing my heart may never truly let him go. Not unless I find my own mate, but my future seems to end soon with no hope in sight. The Seers couldn't even sense what my fate will be, but death may soon become a close friend.

He grabs my hand in his and wipes the blood off with his shirt, but his pools of blue remain on mine. Deep emotions are flickering in them, but I can't pinpoint what he's truly feeling. All I know is that I don't ever want him to stop looking at me that way. Like he really would search the whole world to save me.

My heart swells and I turn my head away before the organ pounding in my chest bursts. I step back, slipping past him and stand in front of the cell across the hall. I wrap my fingers around the cold bars and twist my head back to look at Draven. "She's…" I take a deep breath as I shove the emotions hurtling through me back down. "She's my mother," I whisper in the dark space, keeping my gaze on the floor next to his boots.

He moves to stand next to me with wide eyes as he takes in her fragile form. Without questioning me, he slips his shadows into her lock and snaps it off with a surge of power. I slide the door open and walk to her. With shaky hands, I brush a fallen piece of golden hair out of her eyes. Even with all the dirt painting her face, she looks peaceful when she rests. Her breaths are steady. I see Draven's shadows work on breaking her chains from the corner of my eyes.

"Mother," I say softly, continuing to rub my hand over her head.

My eyes shine back at me as she slowly wakes, seeing myself within her. Her eyelids flicker briefly as the tiredness fades from them, but she just looks at me like I'm a dream she hasn't woken up from yet.

"Mom?" I say again, worry tumbling through me that she might tell me to leave without her. But that will *never* happen.

Her eyes brighten, finally realizing that I'm truly this close to her. Me, in her cell, and *real*. A sob escapes her when she looks to my empty cell and down at her ankles, noticing we're not chained. She rolls her marred ankles around with another sob, covering her mouth with a trembling hand. She pushes herself up with more strength than I thought she would have and throws her arms around me, pulling me in close. Aside from the earthy, damp smell of the dirt that coats her body, her scent is like lilacs on a sunny day. The fresh morning breeze that glides across the sea. I gently wrap my arms around her, nervous I'll hurt her. She feels so frail.

"My baby. I never thought I would be able to hold you again." Her voice is strained as she takes a deep breath in, like she's nervous to let me go now that she has me.

"I'm here. Are you able to walk?" I ask as she slowly leans back to look at me.

She nods, bringing herself to stand up and her eyes immediately dart to Draven, taking him in from head to toe. "Thank you," she tells him with more power in her voice. "But I can't go."

My heart stutters, darting my eyes back and forth between hers. "What do you mean?" I can feel my panic inching closer to the surface.

"He'll sense me. And if I'm near you, then he will find you again." She takes a weak step back.

My arm darts out before she can take another retreating step, latching my fingers around her wrist. "Please. I can't live another day knowing you are trapped in here." I feel so many emotions smothering me at picturing her here, or worse. Him killing her. "Is there somewhere you can escape to?" There has to be, I will give my life to get her there safely.

She's quiet for a moment before softly nodding. "Helestria. It would cut off my power and block him from using it to track me. I could escape to my own realm, but he could still track me and would destroy it."

"Then, it's settled. We will get you to the mortal lands," Draven says with a swell of emotions in his eyes when they quickly peer at me. I bite my lip. He just keeps surprising me. Every word. Every action. Everything. He dips his head in respect before quietly waving his hand to lead us out of the cell.

"I can see why my daughter looks at you the way she does," my mother says with tender amusement. I roll my eyes because Draven doesn't need anything else going to his head.

He chuckles softly, giving her a warm smile before looking at me, the look in his gaze darkens and I wonder what he's thinking. "I feel the same." My pulse picks up until he looks back at my mother. "Do you need me to help you out of here?"

A freeing smile breaks across her face. "Thank you for the offer, but I'm good. I can feel my power inside growing, giving me strength."

Draven nods before guiding us down the tunnel. "We should hurry."

Time is not on our side as we rush to get out of here, traveling through a maze of pathways. It's silent, save for our footsteps tapping and splashing against the damp stone. Draven throws his shadows over all of us, dancing together to blend us into the dark, silencing our movements. Scattered piles of ash decorate the walkways. I lose count of how many there are, and I have a feeling Draven slayed every single one of them.

My eyes dart to Draven's chest, watching the way it still lightly drips his crimson promise. Noticing my stare, he places his hand over his chest, like a soldier taking an oath, a gentle smile gracing his lips. We both keep our movements at the same pace, my mother doing well in staying right beside us.

The walls are grimy, until we pass a certain point. The stone is still worn, but it's dry and *clean*. The scent is not nauseating, and I have a feeling we are nearing the main area of this broken castle. The section where Whiro resides.

We reach a split in the path and Draven halts, holding his hand up for us to remain back. He peers down each corridor before he signals the coast is clear and guides us down the left one. It's dim down here, only a torch lit every so often to cast a soft glow as we stay close to the walls. The glow does nothing to bring comfort. No warmth to settle the fear in my bones. It flickers at us like a warning; a threat that will burn us.

At the end of the corridor, there's a rusted grate. When we finally reach it, Draven crouches down to push it outward, opening it enough for us to crawl through. I go first as Draven keeps a lookout from behind, but I want to make sure the coast is clear outside these walls before my mother comes through. My knees scrape against the bottom of the grate before they sink into the sand on the other side.

I stand up and brush my hands together to rid them of the black grains stuck to my palms before dusting off my pants. I lift my head up and see no stars, none can be seen as the dense clouds remain over the land, cursing everything below. Not even the moon can be seen, unable to shine with its scars, because here, it's forever living in the darkness that swallows it whole.

I still can't get used to how still the air is, how it feels like nothing, but everything horrible all at once. I turn back towards the grate with a racing pulse in fear of Whiro finding us and see the petite hand of my mother as I help her through, followed by Draven, who has to use a little more force to get his muscular frame through the opening. Once he does, he softly slides the grate shut behind him before he stands up.

Draven turns back to look at the both of us. "We just need to run for it until we hit the edge of the valley. That's where Fynn will portal back in to meet us," Draven says in a hushed tone. "My power is wavering from getting injured earlier, and I used a lot of energy to heal the wound. Cora couldn't help me until we fought off every Scavenger and Corrupted, but my body still took a hit. My power is too drained to shadow us anymore." I remember that moment all too clearly, and it made me realize just how strongly I feel for the Dark Prince.

I bite my lip anxiously as I look around, a sea of black as the ground blends with the sky. "Can you run that far?" I look at my mother and see her eyes widen as she looks around, a serene look washing over her.

She bends down to touch the ground. It hits me then, she probably hasn't been free from that cell in all these years, forced to stay locked away in her own personal hell. The sight chips away the stone encasing my heart, as she lets the sand slip through her fingers. Watching it fall before her feet.

"Yes, Emma." Her eyes glisten when they shine up at me. "My power is barely there, but I can feel it now that I'm out of that iron cell. I'll make it." The sureness in her voice causes a smile to lift on my face.

"Let's go, then," Draven says in his confident way.

My mother rises and nods to me in reassurance. I smile softly at her strength and give her a subtle nod in return.

We take off, cutting through the stale air, my feet sinking when they pound on the sand. My lungs start burning as we make our way to the lip of the valley, protesting for me to stop.

But I don't.

I won't.

We run and run, halfway there, when the strain in my legs begin screaming, begging me to rest. I twist my head to look at my mother next to me and see she's keeping pace. Her strength is truly replenishing, and I note that her hair is not dull anymore, with it flowing behind her in a golden wave as she runs to her freedom.

Our breaths are hard as we force our bodies to pump harder, never looking behind us, for it will slow us down. But a few feet farther and silhouettes dance along with the high lift of the valley, standing above us and blocking the way we're headed. More line up around the curve of the edge and we rear back, halting our movement. A wall of soldiers holding their weapons, leaving no gaps between them. Blocking where we are soon supposed to meet the others. Their iron blades scrape against each other, like a final formation signal.

"Shit," Draven mutters, holding his arms out as he gently eases us behind him.

The land is ominously quiet, save for our breathing. The threat above has me on edge, scanning the length of the valley. If we turn back, we'll doom ourselves to the fate Whiro promised.

A single war cry wails above, one sword raised in the air before it slashes down in one swipe. The bodies above begin running down the dip towards us, entering the belly of this hellhole. Like an avalanche of dark souls gliding down a mountain, floating along the waves of a black sea.

We start stepping backward, but once they reach the bottom, their movements stop, as the male commanding them holds his fist in the air. Every single soldier behind him begins to regain their formation.

I squint my eyes around Draven, taking in the details of their uniform. The golden emblem on their chest drains the blood from my face. The soldiers in the center split apart, until a male dressed in all white steps out. Walking towards us with promises of death in his dark eyes that hold a slight sheen of red.

The one who made me believe he was my father.

King Oren.

A growl erupts beside me, and I see Draven's body coil tighter as the king nears. But his eyes aren't solely on King Oren. I follow his line of sight, and it's on *Aiden*.

A raging charge of fire ignites deep inside of me at the sight of him beside my father, confirming who he chose. He's dressed in a white armored top with black pants, the two of them standing out in this dark court. My eyes track up to his face, he looks like he's balancing on a rope between pain and anger, all directed towards me. I left him behind, but I had to. He still saw me as a girl whose only purpose was to be a tamed princess to warm his bed. I'm not sure he ever looked hard enough to see the part of me that was dying inside, slamming its fists against a wall, begging to be seen. To be free.

The green in his eyes looks almost frightening, with the way there's no light to bring warmth to them. Instead, they look dark, like a haunted forest at night. The green that once shined with hope now stirs with a mixture of envy and resentment. Eyes that never leave me. The male I knew is no longer my friend, not anymore. He's changed and crossed the line to being my enemy.

"Well, well, it looks like we made the right choice." My father's voice grates through the heavy silence as he stands feet away.

"You don't know what you're up against," I tell him, putting aside my disgust for him just to get us all the hell out of here. Since I've learned that he will be trying to take down a *God*, not even having double the amount of his army will help tip the scales.

"Ahh, but that's where you're wrong. Because I do know what I'm up against, and now I've learned that my own daughter is against me." I feel the blood in my veins heat up as my pulse pounds relentlessly in my ears.

"I was never *with* you, and I am *not* your fucking daughter," I seethe, watching his reaction, and for once in my life, I see shock rattle through him. The slight widening of his eyes I would have missed if I wasn't looking vanishes a second later when he lets them fall back to neutral.

A sly smirk smears across his face. He straightens his white tunic with gold accents I despise so much. No armor covers his body, assuming no one would dare harm him. "As long as that collar is around your neck, you are *mine*. I should punish you for sneaking off and disobeying, whip you until you can never stand again, but it seems you hold some use for us." He huffs a forced laugh, raising his arm to pat Aiden on the shoulder before bringing his malicious eyes back to me. "You see, Aiden here found something interesting in the Court of Amihan. A beautiful strand of hair. It also just so happened to hold your scent that he loves and knows so well." I don't miss the way King Oren's eyes slide to Draven who is fuming beside me, and I drag mine to see Aiden smile with mirth when he looks at Draven. I wait for shock to slice through me at the sight, but it never comes.

But then Aiden's eyes shift slightly to King Oren beside him, a slight frown contorting his snide smirk. A flicker of what looks like confusion flashes, and I wonder if he's confused why the king speaks of punishing me. Whipping me. His nostrils flare when he snaps those green orbs to mine, a glimpse of hurt and pity filling them. He swallows roughly, dragging his eyes over my body, looking for the truth he can't see.

I realize at this moment, I don't like pity in someone's eyes. Pity makes me feel like I've lost, like I'm weak.

Aiden's gaze hardens again, and I snap my eyes back to King Oren, right when his eyes fall back on me. "Now, I want to see all of your blood spill because, you see, one of my most cherished conquests was freed. One that I spent *years* searching for," he seethes, with flecks of spit flying from his deranged mouth. His red eyes of bloodshed flash momentarily. He closes them, inhaling once. Twice. "Anyway, once I realized you were looking for the Liminal Stone, I decided to have my Seer have another go at finding you. Luckily for us, we were able to see the briefest glimpse of you here, before it went dark."

My jaw clenches as I prepare to take a step forward, ready to unsheathe Draven's sword on his back. The whispers in me tell me to inflict as much pain on King Oren as he has on me. Yet, I almost don't want a slow death for him. He deserves to die before he can even say a final word. Before he knows he's taken his final breath.

I bring my arms up to claim his weapon, but Draven's hand shoots out to stop me from attacking. His blue eyes pin on King Oren. "She will never be *yours*," he snarls, and I'm not sure if he's speaking to King Oren or Aiden.

A faint hum draws my attention as I feel my mother slip her hand into mine, a glow of light sparks before it fades away. I watch in fascination as her eyes dimly glow white. Like two crystal stars in the night.

My mother juts her head up sharply, flaring her nostrils with years of rage begging to be released. "You are the one responsible for stealing my daughter." She keeps her voice steady and stern, but the power behind it raises the hair on my arms. And I see so clearly her love for me shining through.

King Oren gulps as I look back at him, this is the first time I have ever seen him nervous, as he realizes who the female beside me is: the unleashed Goddess. "You should be thanking me," he spits. "She wouldn't have lasted another day longer with the weak girl you left her with. I did you a favor."

"You took my truest friend from this world," my mother seethes. "You will pay for taking her life." The promise in her words punctures through the night, cementing into the land itself and taking root until that promise is delivered. So much power is held in those words as she regains her strength, the iron no longer holding her back. But I can see the slight shake in her legs and the shifting of her feet in the sand.

She's tired.

She may be holding her own right now, but this spike of adrenaline is going to drain her soon. No matter if her power is beginning to rekindle its light, it won't be able to keep up with her wavering energy.

"Emma." I snap my head up when Aiden's voice penetrates my thoughts. "Let's head home." His words are soft as he holds his hand out, expecting for me to follow his demand. But I stay standing in place, searing him with the painful rejection in my eyes.

"That place was never my home. It was a prison," I tell him, refusing to go with him and refusing to ever step foot in that fucking palace again.

His jaw clenches, hands fisting. His eyes turn darker as he goes to take a step forward, but Draven cuts in front of me. Aiden barks a harsh laugh at the action. "Where do you plan to live, Emma? With *him*?" He sneers, pointing at Draven, mockingly. "You're my betrothed and you're mine to have. He's not *anything* but a prince without a heart. He can't love you, not in the way I do."

My breath slams to a halt at his words.

Love?

He may have truly loved me at one point, before everything. Before the betrothal. But his deceitful love cracked like porcelain, and while his eyes beg for me to glue the pieces together, I refuse to repair something I didn't break.

Because what he feels now? It's toxic. It's *possession*, the need to win some type of game to boost his ego and possibly please his father and King Oren. Even gain him a higher position of power, but that's all a lie now since, I suppose, I'm technically not a true Princess of Asov. No, I am a Goddess of Deyadrum.

A wicked smile spreads across my face at the realization. I step around Draven, putting a foot between Aiden and me. "You know nothing about his heart," I say, feeling Draven slide a dagger into my hand from behind, letting me take control. Offering me his trust.

I wrap my fingers around the hilt, a sense of calmness washing over me, clearing my head of everything around me but him. Him and his inviting scent that envelopes me, centering me.

Before Aiden can even finish releasing his breath, I swing my dagger up. Aiden's eyes widen in fear when he sees the metallic glint appear in my hand. He stays still in shock when I swing my hand up and throw it. But I let it fly past him. Straight into my father's heart.

CHAPTER FIFTY-SIX

Emma

I watch in delight as my dagger slices its way through the air, hitting its mark with perfect precision. King Oren clutches onto the hilt, his eyes bulging as he pulls it free. His blood drips down his pristine white tunic, staining it crimson.

"You bitch!" he roars. "You will die for this," his strained voice snarls as he throws my blade to the ground, but he's not healing so fast. The iron of the blade seeps into his skin as his blood struggles to clot. Hunching over, he braces his gloved hands on his knees. Aiden whips his head to me, stunned, as he stares at my murderous expression. Another wave of confusion overcomes him, looking at me like I'm a stranger to him. As if wondering how the domestic princess he's always seen me as could kill a person. To wish death on another.

"Heal him!" Aiden barks, his eyes focused behind me. I spin around to see Cora there, with Fynn and Kye by her side. I never heard them appear. Never heard or felt Fynn's power ripple behind me. They must have transported back, like Draven said they would, at the top of the valley, noticing our predicament from above. Seeing us trapped down below. Now, they've joined us in the midst of a massacre.

"No," Cora's voice is unwavering as she holds her ground, finally seeing Aiden's mask slip and the male that lives underneath.

"Enough, Aiden," King Oren says roughly. "Just find the Stone. I'll deal with them." With one wave of his hand above his head, another war cry pierces the night. His soldiers start charging towards us, hundreds of them eating up the desert floor as they brace their weapons out in front of them. Their pounding feet vibrate through the ground as they kick up sand, creating a black cloud hurtling behind them.

Aiden nods to his king before giving me a searing promise with his eyes that he'll be back for me as he takes off in a sprint, warping every ten feet as he heads towards the forbidden library and away from the stampede.

King Oren stands upright, keeping his hand pressed to his heaving chest, grunting with the movement. "I should have killed you the moment I found you." His tone deepens as his lip curls up.

I lift my chin high, grinding my teeth as I speak in a controlled tone. "But then you wouldn't have had your secret weapon." I glare at him with a knowing look, hardened by all the pain he's delivered in my life. "If you want to kill me now, you have to get in line."

I watch the vein in his forehead pulse as he starts trembling with anger, his skin slick with beads of perspiration. I see his foot shift, anticipating when he rears back to lunge at me. But then, a deafening boom echoes, and a blazing bolt of lightning strikes between the clouds. The army racing towards us slams their feet, skidding to a halt against the sand.

A coil of black writhes in the air as Whiro appears, making my heart sink. Dread grips me knowing we didn't get out of here fast enough, out of the boundaries of his court so he can't follow. My eyes trail up to the crooked crown on his head, zeroing in on the red stones placed around it and the faint pulse of energy stirring within.

His soulless eyes show a sudden interest in King Oren as his ink-like veins spread further over his skin. I can feel the wrath Whiro is promising him with that one look.

He tilts his head to the side with a purse of his cracked lips. "You're like a pest that keeps disrupting my plans, keeps *taking* things that don't belong to you," Whiro says with unnatural stillness.

King Oren's eyes tighten, setting his jaw in a sinister smile that creeps over his mouth. "And I won't stop until I have it all," King Oren says in a harsh tone. He's still clutching at his wound, but the bleeding has lessened.

I feel the warm brush of Draven's hand gripping around my wrist, pulling me back as a storm cloud of obsidian power springs to life, surging in a hurricane of fiery shadows that rage above Whiro. A summoning. Death's mark in the sky. Calling on the Corrupted as they rise from behind. Around a hundred balls of shadows disperse on the ground behind him, a Corrupted stepping out of each one, being transported in the same fashion as Whiro travels. His black-stained hands whip out around him, creating Scavengers from nothing beside him, the beasts of his power.

This is his army that's been lying in wait. My heart aches at knowing each Corrupted is a Fae who used to live a free life before death's poison flowed through their veins. Before Whiro *Corrupted* them.

Draven hands me an extra wyvern sword he has strapped on his waist, a silent signal that we will have to fight as a war hangs on the edge of a precipice. I see King Oren trying to use his power that sucks someone into another void of his making, the red glows in his eyes before it blinks out, the iron still blending into his blood. It's an inopportune time to feel the slight surge of joy, but seeing his power work against him only gives him a taste of what he has done to me for all these years.

Whiro commands a section of the Corrupted to surround us, waiting to strike at any sudden movement. A tendril of Whiro's dark power snaps out, firing close to King Oren. "Your soul will taste bitter, but it will be a pleasure to watch you crumble beneath my hands," Whiro says to King Oren before he disintegrates in the air, sucking into his shadows before reappearing in front of one of King Oren's soldiers, the one leading the army, grabbing hold of his throat. The male's feet dangle, his fingers clawing at Whiro's hand.

Whiro's black veins grow even darker around his eyes, bulging as they pulse with power. "Let me show you, *King Oren*"—he sneers—"what fate awaits you."

In the next breath, the blur of the soldier's essence is ripped from his body as the God of Darkness consumes him. His soul is pulled out in a visible ghostlike wave, until the soldier's wide eyes lose their light, those fighting hands falling limp to his sides. When the last sliver of his soul is gone, Whiro's black fire ignites over the dead body, turning the male into a mound of ash. Left to sit untouched, like the rest that adorn this court.

My lungs stall in my body as I realize *why* there are piles of old ash everywhere; they are the dead left behind after Whiro feeds on their soul. The thought shoots bile up my throat and the bitter taste is overwhelming, but I shove it down. Taking a careful step back to not catch the attention of the Corrupted surrounding us, I pull my mother with me.

"Now!" King Oren yells to the rest of his army, even as they stand there with fear filling their eyes at the loss of their comrade. I startle at his booming demand, watching them obediently follow their king's orders as they charge forward. With a wave of Whiro's hand, the Corrupted shriek and race headfirst into the wall of soldiers. The ones surrounding us stay unnaturally still.

Bodies are coming at us from every direction outside of the trap we are stuck in. King Oren's soldiers are made up of lower Fae, wielding either water, fire, earth, or air. They hold their weapons high, while using their other hand to blast their elemental power. Spurts of water, balls of fire, shields of sand, and vortexes of wind are being thrown at the Corrupted. It won't kill them, but it will throw them off balance and stun them momentarily.

King Oren spins and slams his boot into the Corrupted waiting to pounce behind him. Setting off a reaction in the rest, making them shriek and close in on us. A grunt sounds next to me as Fynn gets knocked back, grabbing his sword to plunge it straight into its chest.

"Cora!" Kye yells with wide eyes as another Corrupted lunges behind her. Kye dives forward, knocking her down as he kicks the Corrupted in the chest. He swings his sword out and leaps on his feet in the same movement.

Draven spins and starts knocking back and slashing down the Corrupted charging at him, wielding his double-edged sword with powerful strokes that cut clean through its victims. The sword sings through the air with the promise of claiming their deaths.

The air leaves my lungs when something heavy slams into my back. I fall forward, only to be caught by my mother, who throws her hand up so spurts of arrows made of light penetrate one of my father's soldiers. Not liking the thought of fighting against my own kind, I'm torn about fighting King Oren's army, the ones who don't need to die if they leave his rule. It would be better if all of our focus was to go after the Corrupted, but I have no choice if they attack me.

My mother helps steady me with a worried look, one I understand completely, because we are finally reunited. Her eyes narrow in determination as she nods, throwing what she can of her power out into our attackers. I'm weaponless as my dagger still lies by King Oren's feet, and it would be a risky move to get it.

Fynn tumbles in front of me as he avoids a Scavenger. "I can't portal out of here without risking them following us through!" he yells over the chaos of madness unfolding. The clashing of metal, the killing wails and pounding feet.

Another Corrupted races toward me and I duck and dive out of the way, swinging my arm as I spin around to clock it in the jaw. Pain radiates like sharp splinters in my knuckles from the impact. I only have a second to glance at my dagger, the risk is worth it to be able to kill. To defend myself.

The Corrupted I hit screeches, losing its final tether of sanity, sprinting at me with uncontrolled ferocity. I turn my back to it and push the balls of my feet hard into the sand to launch myself forward. I pump my legs fast before sliding into the ground, my stomach scraping against the rough grains, swooping up my sword the moment I'm close enough.

I scramble back on my feet to face the Corrupted, but instead, I see King Oren coming for me, his gilded blade in his hand slashes out towards me. "You are *mine* to kill," he seethes, spit flying from his mouth. "You were supposed to obey *me*, so I could use your power. We could have been a team and ruled the lands, but you had to rebel every step of the way, never falling in line."

I block his attack and hold my dagger out as his blade clangs against it.

His eyes bulge in shock, staring at how our weapons are pinned against the other. Until realization of what that means registers in his mind, him learning that I know how to fight. Suddenly, a flicker of red surges in his irises as anger consumes him. Reaching out with his free hand, he latches onto my wrist and grabs hold of me when he manages a surge of his power. I feel the tingle of his illusion prickle over my skin, and I try to yank my hand out of his before it's too late.

"Emma!" I snap my head to Draven's voice as he slides a sword across the ground. His eyes widen with fear but I also see his confidence in me that I'll be the one making it out of this fight. Without hesitation, I release my dagger, letting it fall to the ground. I drop down and quickly wrap my fingers around the sword right as King Oren sucks us both away into a void of his own making. An illusion, vanishing the sight of us from everyone.

Suddenly, we're in the same room he torments me in, the two of us alone. No one to call out to, but I won't bow down now. I refuse to hold back. I am no longer setting the pieces on the board, but instead, I'm playing my final moves. He may think me a pawn, but an overlooked pawn can always become a queen.

He walks to the wall of weapons and sets his fashionable dagger down before reaching and grabbing his own sword. The vile smell burns the back of my throat, but I grind my teeth together to try to not let images of the past filter into my head.

His boots scuff on the stone as he begins circling around me with a devious grin. "You really think you're more powerful than me, thinking you can take me on? You forget, dear Emma, that my gift is still wrapped around your breakable neck. You're *powerless*," he says with venom.

His words cut deep, but I need to make good on my promise and my mother's. For my Aunt Lydia, for my pain, for the lives of those he's ruined. He's once again ripping me away from my family, my mother, who is now faced with a battle she didn't ask for, while she's still too weak to fully access all of her power. My heart beats faster with the high adrenaline pumping through my veins. The anticipation of combat.

This has to end.

This is my only chance to seek revenge.

I hold my sword steady in front of me, tracking his movements and the placement of his feet. The way his eyes travel to certain points—a tell of his next move.

As expected, he launches himself towards me but aims his sword at my left leg, where his eyes had darted to, hoping to make me drop before him and remove my ability to move around the room. But I whirl away as his sword slices through nothing but air. I twist around behind him and slam the heel of my boot into his spine, reveling in the feeling of causing him pain. He stumbles forward but maintains his balance as he spins around, charging at me with pure, unhinged hatred.

He's not focusing on strategy; he's fighting clumsily and without calculated movements, as he lets his anger consume his decisions.

He jabs his sword towards my stomach, but I leap back, landing on a patch of uneven stone that makes me tip forward. The motion allows for his fist to collide into my face, crashing against my jaw. I feel the beginning of blood trickle from my lip. I tumble to the other side of the room, shaking off the specks of white dancing across my vision.

"Come fight me, *daughter.*" He sneers, pushing a fallen strand of hair back away from his face. He looks like the true sinister king he always hides under his perfectly kept appearance.

I leap forward, clashing my blade against his as it sparks in the dim room. Both of us push against each other. I feel his strength overpowering me, so I give one final force of my weight before I jump back. He falls forward with the unexpected move, his weight driving him forward. I bring my blade up at the same moment. His eyes connect with mine as he loses control of his footing, watching the look of satisfaction I hold in my eyes. Without a second thought, without allowing him to take that final breath, I slam my blade up with all my strength as my muscles strain with the impact.

My sword makes contact as I feel the resistance of bone, but in a second, his head is rolling across the floor. His bulging eyes remain open as his blood spills and stains the stone beneath my feet. The irony of his blood painting the room, like a final farewell, doesn't escape me.

"Checkmate," I whisper to the soul that leaves his body, watching the way his eyes grow dull and his pulse ceases to exist.

In a blur of motion, the room vanishes, and I'm staring at King Oren's cold body lying in black sand. Shouts and clattering of steel against steel draw my attention as everyone still rages against one another.

Cora is fighting to the best of her ability, her back against Fynn and Kye's as they help tell her when to duck or when to drive her sword forward. A smile is etched across her face with pure pride as she watches a Corrupted she killed disintegrate into ash. I watch as they both stay near her, a shield of protection, while they take down one Corrupted at a time. The Scavengers are still attacking throughout, tearing pulse points from necks with each person they pass.

I feel a pull in the distance and see Draven battling against three Corrupted at once, driving his blade through one's chest and effortlessly swinging around to dodge the others' sharp talons. His body moves with such powerful movements that they stand no chance as he swipes his blade down one in the center, cutting one in half. I can see from here how his eyes keep fighting to change, the glow of silver warring to break through. But if he lets his dragon side out, they will tear apart his wings, shredding them to bits. It would do no good for him to attempt flying anyways, he can only carry one person at a time. It would draw attention the moment his feet lift off the ground.

I want to race over towards him. Towards my friends. But panic takes over as I look for my mother, praying she's still alive. I just got her back. I can't lose her again. I *won't* lose her again.

My eyes travel around the mass of colliding bodies until I finally find her. She's wielding a sword of light, a creation from the kernel of power that's burning in her as she fights off the Scavengers Whiro keeps sending at her, a game of torment.

I don't think, I sprint.

I charge towards her, needing to help, needing to protect her.

Her glowing sword eliminates the beasts with one touch, burning them into thin air without needing to pierce their hearts.

My heels dig into the sand as I push against it, pumping my arms as my sword swings back and forth with the rapid movement. I force my lungs to keep up until I finally reach her. I hold out my weapon, still dripping in crimson, and shove it through the Scavenger's heart that leaps at her from behind.

Whiro blasts more soldiers out of his way as they lunge at him. He glides a few steps closer to us when he spots me. Those pits of black pin me with a look that promises death. A couple of his Scavengers obediently stay by his side, prowling next to him with every movement as he continues to command the other ones to attack.

He stops a good distance away as he shakes his head in annoyance. "Like mother, like daughter, it seems," he says with false amusement in his voice. "You both thought you could escape my court when you left your cells, but not even in death will that happen."

His head slightly drops, making him look sinister as a hardened smirk lifts on the side of his mouth. "This ends now." The tone in his voice sends waves of unease though my body and warning bells ringing through my head. "I will take my power back, and this world will be mine to control." He slams his hands forward and a gust of shadows blast into us, scattering us apart before we have a chance for defense.

We regain our footing and stand side by side, both of us locking eyes on one another. My mother grabs my hand and squeezes. "I love you."

I bite my lips together as they start trembling, squeezing her hand back. "I love you."

We nod to one another and ready ourselves as Whiro sends more Scavengers running towards us. Pounding their shadowy paws into the sand, they peel their lips back and open their mouths with the need to fight and tear into flesh.

One after another, we exhaust ourselves in fighting them off. Taking hits when they slam their bodies into ours, only for us to work as a team and cleave through their chests. My mother's power is killing them way easier than I can with a single sword.

I lose count of how many we fight off, until my mother's light flickers, her body beginning to sag. I'm at her side when I catch her from falling over at the last second as she blasts a spear of light into a Scavenger's chest a foot in front of her.

A demonic laugh bellows through the sky when there's a momentary pause in the onslaught of Scavengers stampeding towards the two of us.

Shrieks continue to swarm the air with an ear-piercing melody around us. "Surrender now, *daughter*, let me claim your life and I'll let your mother live," Whiro's voice is coated with trickery, but the choice is still tempting. Maybe he will hold onto his promise, after all, it's *my* body that carries his blood.

"Don't, Emma." My mother's voice snaps my eyes to hers as she shakes her head.

"You don't need to suffer anymore," I say softly, trying to get her to understand that her fight is over, this is not her war, it's *mine*.

Whiro wields a massive sword made out of shadows, looking like a blade of midnight fire. He swirls it around the air as my darkness whispers to obey, to walk to him, and to do as he commands. It grows louder, drowning out the scrapes of metal and swirling wind from the vortex in the sky. I take an obliging step toward him, letting the whispers guide me. I feel my wall falling apart brick by brick.

"Emma?" I hear a gentle feminine voice far off in the distance, reaching me, but the whispers are roaring through me as her voice gets muffled underneath.

A shrilling scream blows through the fog of hushed voices in my head, clearing away their desire for death's hands, and snapping me back into focus. I spin around and feel my heart get sliced in two. I watch with help-lessness as Cora slams to her knees. A Corrupted tears its claws through her stomach, protruding through her back as it tears down to her navel before pulling its hand back. Her blood splatters out before her as she stares at nothing in the distance. Her voice is lost to the pain as she falls fully to the ground. I choke on a sob as my eyes light on fire, my chest cracking in half.

"NO!" I hear Kye yell, racing through the mass of Corrupted as he tries to get to her, cutting them down one by one. Determined to save her. The three of them must have gotten pushed apart as the number of Corrupted kept growing.

Fynn portals to her side, not caring that a Corrupted goes through it with him as he shoves his blade through its chest, only to spin around and kill the Corrupted whose hand is covered in Cora's blood. He pulls his sword out of its chest as it falls away to ashes, mixing into the sand. Fynn

ALI STUEBBE

drops to his knees, scooping Cora up in a rush, gently holding her to his chest, and whispering words in her ear.

Tears cascade down my face, dripping off my chin.

My fault.

She wouldn't be here, hurt, bleeding in my father's court if it wasn't for me.

I lurch back around to face Whiro, to get that Stone and end this. To return the pain he's inflicted. I just need to fight off the voices that want to listen to his call, to listen to his darkness.

I white-knuckle the hilt of my sword, my nostrils flaring with grief and anger that pumps through my veins, boiling in my blood. I bend my knees slightly, digging my feet into the sand and charge for him, blade in front of me while I focus on his movements. Pushing my legs with all my strength, I beg the stars to hear my plea to not let Cora die. To for once listen to a wish I have for them.

A wicked gleam fills Whiro's black eyes. He's ready for our final fight. A fight to the death. A new game I'm forced to play, but he doesn't know I already have my bishop lying in wait. Ready to cut across the board and claim his crooked crown.

Right before I go to leap in the air at him, a streak of blonde flashes past me. My heart sinks into my stomach. My feet stumble beneath me. The momentum I was running with throws me off balance with my lack of focus, but I manage to keep myself upright. When I come to a stop and steady myself, it's too late.

My mother speeds past me to launch herself at him. Her blazing weapon of light in her hand, ready for a killing blow. But it dies out, her body too weak. My heart hammers in fear as I begin to sprint towards her. But before I can, Whiro sharply pins his eyes on me.

"You could have saved her," he says before he raises his powerful weapon. Driving his arm forward, his shadowed blade tears through her, making her body press to the hilt as it sticks out of her back.

My throat shreds with the scream that leaves my body, tearing through the night. Overpowering the sounds of the battle as my lungs burn with pain.

I watch the way her body jerks from the impact, before it becomes still.

Her head dangles forward as Whiro lifts his sword higher, bringing her body with it. I notice a twitch in her hand before her head lifts slightly.

Turning to look at me with love in her silver eyes, a promise she will always be with me. "I will be waiting for you in the world beyond this one," she chokes out.

I shake my head, another guttural sob ripping painfully from my chest. Tears wet the sand as they fall to the ground, flooding my eyes, blurring my vision. Even as her blood keeps spilling, she gives me a tender smile. One full of love that holds a note of finality to it.

Her hand raises in a final effort to attack, and Whiro looks slightly pained from breaking their bond. But then, shock jolts through him. In one final swipe, she takes hold of his crown. It whips through the air as it comes flying towards me, landing a few feet away.

My heart lurches in understanding. She's the only one who knew I needed the crown. She never asked why but sacrificed herself for it anyway. Tears keep flowing freely down my cheeks as I wipe the back of my hand to clear them away.

I take a step forward, reaching down to grab hold of the crown of darkness. It feels like ice in my hands. I let my fingers brush against the red stone in the center. It buzzes under my touch.

"Give that back," Whiro growls, relinquishing his sword, letting it vanish as my mother drops to the ground with a thud. My heart splinters even more, and before he shadows himself to me, I need to use the stone.

Right as I see his body get swallowed by his shadows, I slam the crown on my head. A burst of power flares inside of me, sending a shockwave of energy outward.

CHAPTER FIFTY-SEVEN

Emma

A surge of energy tears through every inch of my body, sparking against my nerve endings and ripping them to shreds with the force. Pumping torrents of unknown power into me, it crashes into my bloodstream. My back arches as my arms snap out without warning. My feet slowly lift off the ground. The strength of the Stone's power ignites and twists around me, feeding into my own well of power that's buried deep within.

Rivers of fire amplify inside of me, burning everything in their wake, and the well of emotions from battle explodes in an instant. They flood through my mind as I replay the image of Cora, my mother, and the rest who are fighting against such an impossible battle.

A sense of grief washes over me and blends into the darkness that desires to be set free inside of me, to come to life after being locked away for so long. But a feeling of longing electrifies inside, feeling the loss of love that I am not destined to have with Draven. The love of my mother that was stolen from me my whole life. Losing the love I had with Aunt

Lydia. The love of friendship I feel towards Cora, only for it to be ripped away.

My power erupts inside of me, the Stone's energy crackling against my skin. A combination of light and dark swells within me. The light power King Oren trapped when he sealed this necklace around my throat blazes against the iron on my neck. The darkness that has been begging to surge forward, to be fed and take control of me, slithers to the surface. Both collide against one another with the strength of the Stone. Threatening to surge until they detonate. Streams of black and white power rush out of my body, screaming against my skin. The backs of my eyes start to burn through me in a battle of wills.

Suddenly, I understand.

When light and dark collide, your fate will be split in two.

The light and dark is *me*. I'm losing control, as both parts of me push against each other. Tearing me in half as they try to consume the other. Dividing my soul.

The question I'm scared to know the answer to is what fate will be waiting for me? My life is in the balance of what feels like a simple flip of a coin. Only, there is nothing simple about this as I grind my teeth together, bracing against the constant onslaught of searing pain.

A scream shreds its way up my throat as a flare of blinding heat erupts around my neck. It singes against my skin as the necklace tries to fight against the overflow of power. The pain becomes infinite as I attempt to reach for my neck, but the whirlwind of energy has me stuck in its current. Unable to move my body with its intensity as I hang in the air. Another scream that wrenches itself from me is swallowed by the buzz of power radiating through the night, seizing my body.

The unrelenting torture threatens to make me faint as the burning pain blazes hotter.

And hotter.

But then, it shatters. The force of the Stone's energy merging with my power pries it from my neck. I cry out in agony. My back snaps farther into an arch, bending in an unnatural angle. My head is thrown back from my power being set free, at last. My body is spasming. The blood under my skin boils, the immense power absorbing fully into my body. It's too much. I can't handle this much power so quickly. The streaks of black and white continue to rocket out of me, multiplying and cracking against the midnight sky.

Flashes of light and dark tangle in the air, whipping around me as the clashing of metal slowly comes back into focus. My hair swirls in a maddening dance in the vortex that courses from me. The pounding beat of my heart softens its echo and hum as the power in my veins gradually becomes content. The pain fades away, but the surge of power continues to snake around my body. I can feel my internal candle burning down, dwindling into a mere ember.

I'm able to lift my head and look around, straightening my spine as I still hang in the air. The intense weight of the energy raging through my bloodstream grows more satisfying with every breath. I glance down to see the battle is still ongoing, but Whiro is staring at me. Even death is forced back from the waves of power flowing from me. His beasts continue consuming souls that aren't theirs to take. Demanding them to fight to the death.

So much death.

So many lifeless bodies are strewn over the desert land, their blood seeping into the obsidian sand.

The funnel of power storming around me stirs a breeze against my hair, whipping back and forth across my face. My eyes find my mother's unmoving body. Lying abandoned on the ground. Like a sunken ship at sea, while the waves continue to thrash rampantly around it, sealing its fate. Just like she chose to seal hers by giving her life in exchange for mine, leaving me again.

Except this time, it's a forever goodbye. One I don't want to accept. Her physical body remains here, but her soul is out of reach. Far away in a world beyond this one. The blood that flows through my veins is the reason I've been plagued by grief my whole life, longing for a love that never fades. Forcing me into a lifetime of desiderium.

Another stab of pain infects my heart. I want to rip it out and bury it in the sand with her. I clench my fists as tears stream down from my eyes. I'm alone, with no time to get to know her, leaving me to grieve her once again.

I force my eyes to drag away from her and see Kye holding Cora tightly in his arms. Cradling her head to his chest as she stares faintly at him, her mouth parted in silence. She blinks slowly, but her breaths are shallow. Fynn unleashes himself, fighting the Corrupted around them, keeping them safe from harm. He roars a promise of death with every slash of his sword.

Cora.

My best friend.

Her light in a world of darkness is fading and I'm to blame. She never deserved this fate. Never deserved a life that would be ripped away from her like this. I wish I could rekindle her flame with mine to keep hers from going out.

A sudden spark of heat pulls me like a blow to the chest. My eyes find Draven in a heartbeat, knowing exactly where he is. I feel something monumental shift between us. Like the world shifts just to join our paths. Our souls. An earthquake breaking through the barrier separating us. His eyes are blazing as he stares at me, his mouth open in what seems like disbelief and awe. Like I'm the only tide that will bring him to shore, the only one to keep his head above water.

He slams his blade in the Corrupted next to him before he digs his heels into the sand and races towards me. I can see his mouth moving, but I can't hear him. The hum of power surges louder around me, silencing everything beyond.

So much devastation is scattered out before me, so much blood. A blast of black fire slams into the current of light and dark power that continues to swirl around me as they battle for control. I latch my eyes on Whiro, my *father*, as he tries to break through the forcefield.

A maddening need to seek revenge against him, like I did to King Oren, consumes me. A need for vengeance so strong that it further ignites the darkness in me, eating away at the light as it starts to smother it down, to seal it away.

This overwhelming wrath and grief swims through me, freezing the warmth of light inside my soul. It injects itself into my veins in a desperate need to take. I can feel myself slipping into the darkness, as it numbs the grief, the pain, and the heartache from everything around me. Rooting a brief fit of deep-seated anger in me to consume more power, to take Whiro's and rise above him. But then, it's gone in a flash, questioning why I would want to harm him when this power bows to him, answers to him.

Coldness blankets my eyes, and I know they're black. I can see the inky veins running all through my body, up my arms, slithering along my skin as it feeds into my heart. Into my soul.

I scour through the sea of bodies, of life and death, and see Draven below me. Finding him with urgency, because I know I can't stop this. I can't fight the force of this darkness. It's turning me into something cold and detached. Those blue eyes steal my breath as mine plead for forgiveness. My eyes are begging for him to let me go. It's the only way to end the destruction. To protect them.

I quickly lift my hand over my heart, the meaning only for him. That he holds it. An unseen scar that I never want to fade.

I cry out when a final fissure sears its way through my heart as the vengeful shadows emerge to welcome me. Their black waves crash against my mind as its turbulent storm strikes, like a final warning bell ringing in my ears.

The energy coursing around me starts to recede as the light of my power is almost completely snuffed out. About to be buried away again, and I hope one day I can find a way to free it. To free myself from this internal prison I'm falling prey to.

A tidal wave of desolation slams into me. The darkness covers the entirety of my heart.

A finality.

My body lowers. The soles of my feet hit the ground as I feel my thoughts go blank, a numbness filling my body and soul. The girl I am is drowning, chained to an anchor as I get dragged deeper inside myself.

But this power, it's like a pitch-black sea. A pretty poison.

It unleashes my deepest, most sinful desires of revenge. *Hate.*

Draven stands in front of me, with his crystal eyes frantic. He grabs hold of my face with his calloused hands. I stare blankly at him. "Emma," he breathes. His eyes dart back and forth between mine, searching.

My heart pounds in a steady rhythm, I cock my head to the side as he waits. It seems like he's waiting for me to fall into him, to *feel* for him.

Yet, I feel nothing. Only a coldness that tips the side of my lip up wickedly. If he saw me as vicious before, then the world's not ready for the disaster that this darkness in me craves. The disaster the whispers demand.

I keep my eyes on him, holding his stare for only a moment before I jerk my head away. Walking to where the whispers are telling me to go. Guiding me. Whiro stares cautiously at me as I walk through the ashes blanketing the ground. I reach up and grab the crown off my head. An uncontrolled burst of my power flares out, creating a fiery black shadow that singes the edge of the crown.

I watch in fascination as embers fall from the edge of the metal, feeling a resemblance as I look at the broken crown hanging between my fingers. Shattered, with pieces of itself drifting away to never be whole again. Much like my soul.

I feel the presence of the God of Darkness before me, and I look up. His black eyes assess mine carefully before a crooked smile darkens his face.

Only a beat passes before he sifts through his shadows and stands directly in front of me. "Well, looks like I might not need to kill you after all, *daughter*," he says as he waves his hand and relinquishes the Corrupted and beasts that were fighting for him, vanishing them in bursts of shadows. The act leaves the valley deserted, except for injured soldiers that look confused, and a few who stare at me with sorrow in their eyes.

I tilt my eyes in confusion but turn back when I hear my father's voice, "Come, Emma," he says and opens up an orb of shadows for us to walk through.

The whispers scurry in my mind, excited to be free. Telling me I *want* to follow. To go *home*. I listen to them as I step forward and walk into his black void. Following him. Never looking back.

CHAPTER FIFTY-EIGHT

Draven

*E*mma looks like a beacon floating in the sky, a queen of power with that crown on her head. The light and dark swirl together, blasting magnitudes of energy through the valley as the sand picks up and whips around. A power so strong it has my knees threatening to buckle and willing to submit.

Her hair flows around her in a flurry of glowing strands, like a Goddess in the night. But then, I feel my heart pull tight, a magnet drawing me in. The moment the collar around her neck breaks free, a bond snaps into place. A bond so solid it sears into my very soul, branding me to her. My body lights up inside, flaring to life with a feeling of euphoria and *love*.

I want to kiss her. To hold her. To claim her.

Until I see the light around her weaken. I watch helplessly as she begins losing its grip, when she notices the disaster happening before her. The devastation of a battle going to hell.

I see those grey eyes I've come to cling onto, break. I see the way they grow heavy with sorrow when she looks at her mother. At Cora.

But then, she looks at me, and what I see there feels like a blade to the heart, twisting itself deep before being yanked free. A plea for my forgiveness. I can tell with the way they burn into me, begging me to understand. And my heart cleaves at how they speak so many words in one look.

No. I refuse to accept and forgive.

I'm screaming at her, my voice cracking as I try to have her hear me through the power whirling around her. But she can't... She can't hear me.

She can't do this.

She can't leave me.

She's *mine*.

I want to release my dragon, but it's too risky. My wings will be ripped to shreds in an instant, keeping me from getting to her. I can feel the dragon in me roaring in pain as I watch her become consumed in a matter of seconds. But I'm sprinting to her, pushing past the exhaustion in my muscles. The moment she floats back down, I'm there. Waiting.

I grab her face and she's so cold. Her skin stings against my hands.

"Emma," I whisper. My voice is rough as I shake my head, seeing how her eyes have turned completely black. Dark veins twine through her body. I can barely hold myself together seeing the way she's looking through me and not at me. As if she can't see me at all. Like she's truly lost inside herself, with no compass to guide her back to the surface. Back to me. She's drifting further. I can't see the girl I've come to cherish. The one before me is something ungodly as she smirks at me.

Without a single word, she tugs her face out of my hands. I feel the bond crack when she walks away, slipping out of my grasp to leave me behind. The beast in me cries out in agony as I watch her retreating form, making her way to Whiro and leaving a wake of power behind her. A black shadowy fire singes the ground beneath her feet.

The darkness has completely taken her over, making her soulless with a frozen heart.

So cold she could make death bow before her.

The valley clears when Whiro reins in his army. The Corrupted and

Scavengers answer his call and disappear. Emma turns to look at us while Kye, Fynn, and I stare at her, but her glacial face holds no emotion. She let herself be completely consumed. I saw the fight leave her, as if she knew this would be a way she could end this. To protect us. To *save* us.

She turns around again, continuing to close the distance between her and Whiro, but instead, he transports himself directly in front of her, smiling cruelly.

"Come, Emma," Whiro says with a wave of his hand, commanding shadows to burst in an orb of black flames for her to step through. His portal of shadows. The same way he stole her before.

She stays still for a moment, and my heart races with the hope I'm clinging onto. Hoping that she will turn back around and sprint into my arms.

I take an uneven step forward. "Emma," I call to her. My broken voice ringing clear through the now silent night, wishing I could will her back to me.

Instead, she takes a step forward, following him through his swirling portal.

I take off, racing towards them. "NO!" I roar with all the air my lungs will allow. When I'm only a foot away, the portal disappears and they vanish into nothing. Never looking back. Leaving me behind with the ashes.

I stop abruptly and drop to my knees. Pain blasts through my heart as it desperately strains to reach for her.

I feel a hand on my shoulder grip me tightly, when I manage to stand back up. "We'll find her," Kye's voice chokes out, as he stares off into the empty space she was standing in just seconds ago. "This is my fault. I told her I would help her with this darkness in her and failed. I vowed to always protect her, and I can't—I *won't* fail her again."

I nod in understanding as the same guilt eats at me when I turn to look at him, his eyes red with a watery sheen. Fynn is holding Cora in his arms as he walks towards us. His chest is heaving with endless emotions flickering in his eyes and I hear Cora grunt in pain. Blood coats her body, soaking into his clothes. I don't want to leave, but Cora needs a healer, fast. I can already see her pulse point ticking slower. We can't lose her too.

I clench my jaw as I stare hard at Kye. "Don't blame yourself for something unknown and out of your control. But we will find her because I won't stop until I do," I tell him, choking my words out as a surge of sorrow floods me. I shake my head, refusing to feel sad when she's not gone. Not completely. I *will* get her back. I force out a barely restrained growl as I clench my fists in a death grip, letting him see the look of determination in my eyes. I don't care if I have to break through the gates of Hell to find her. The relentless waves of darkness think they have stolen her away, but I have her chained to my heart, anchoring her to me. I will tear this world apart for her.

For Emma.

My mate.

To be continued...

*She's like a black rose,
with darkness that holds beauty and power.
And I found myself wanting to be her thorns.
Her protector,
with promises to make those who dare touch her bleed.*

-Ali Stuebbe

ACKNOWLEDGMENTS

I've been sitting here, staring at my screen, trying to wrap my mind around how to write these acknowledgments, but sometimes, words are hard. I do know all of you who are reading this are the ones I wish to thank first and you have my gratitude. Your support has been constant since before this book even had a name. You all were my backbone in helping me through this writing journey.

To Stevi, my amazing editor and fellow ninja, who was my partner in crime when bringing this book to life. You always understood the jumble mess of words I would write, the half-asleep mix-up of my thoughts, and I always appreciated that. The support and encouragement from you, knowing I could always message you about anything brought comfort and joy throughout the entire journey. I truly believe I would not have enjoyed the entire editing process if I worked with anyone but you. I mean that. You shared your knowledge with me and truly guided me with this book. Even teaching me some of the ins and outs of editing, your kindness is truly felt. We have spent months together to turn this book into a master-piece, and like I said before, the separation anxiety was real when the final editing stage was nearing completion. But just know, you are stuck with me and that I can't wait to work with you again.

To Tay, I don't know what I did to deserve you as a friend and to have met you, but I am forever grateful. You are a Goddess. You were the first person who got to read this story, and in its earliest form. So early, that I was sending you chapters as I was writing it. You powered through the first draft of what we now refer to as a mish mosh of words and I still laugh about it. You gave amazing feedback and thoughts on each chapter, and every single one was helpful. You are my fellow grandma, who likes to be in comfy clothes before dinner and snuggled down for the night before the sun sets, and I am so incredibly thankful to know you.

To Raquel, I remember walking down the airport steps. Okay, not walking, pretty sure I was huffing and puffing, but your face was the first I saw. I am so thankful to call you a friend and to have met your beautiful soul. You have been so supportive throughout this entire journey, cheering me on and helping with any indecisiveness I have. I love all of the knowledge that just hangs out in your brain and how you made me feel not as short in person. Our late night talks on our girls trip when we were supposed to be sleeping—those I will always remember.

To Fay, my nocturnal best friend whom I love. You have been with me since this book was only 8,000 words. You helped me navigate how I would want a scene to play out, how I might connect plot points, and more. I can always count on you for anything. You always knew whether I needed support, advice, something funny to cheer me up, and everything in between. You have always been there. There were times that I felt so defeated, but you pulled me back up and said I could do it. You're my best friend, and as Kevin Hart would say, 'My bullshit is your bullshit.' And that couldn't be truer as we have become closer and gotten to know one another. I am so happy we got to meet in person and share such amazing memories together.

To Abbie, Ashley, Liz, Krystal, and Ashleigh, the five of you were the best beta readers I could have ever hoped for. The feedback, your honest thoughts, the conversations, just all of it. I am so incredibly blessed that you wanted to do that for me. The reactions from all of you had me cackling so hard I was put in tears. I rave about you all so much, and how you made that round of editing so incredibly fun. Thank you for everything, I am beyond grateful to have had you a part of the team and helping shape this book into its final story.

To Taylor, my proofreader, you are amazing and thank you for being so flexible with me. Your comments in the manuscript made me chuckle and I'm appreciative for your extra eyes in helping me get this book to its final stage for everyone to read.

To Jaqueline, my cover designer. I will forever say that I am in awe of your talent. You transformed my vision into something that was more than I could ever imagine. The cover speaks for itself, it's stunning in every way.

To Zoe, thank you for creating the beautiful map of the land of Deyadrum, as well as character art that will be shared and drooled over by me and the readers. I know I've said this before, but your talent breathtakingly beautiful.

To my family, always checking in on me and asking every phone call how the writing was going or how the book was coming along, it was always appreciated. You have given so much unconditional love and support and it means more than you know.

To my husband, Chris—you have told me this book is meant to be out in the world, that it was always supposed to be written. Much like us, fate knew we would be together before we did, writing us in the stars before we ever laid our eyes on each other. I told you a couple years back that I don't think I could ever write a book, and you looked at me and told me I could. That was all it took. You helped me outline this story, by taking the chaos of my thoughts and writing them down on paper, organizing them for me. Your faith in me is endless, always there to embrace me when I'm unsure. I may have written this book, but it is solely yours, my permanent declaration to you. Proving that the brightest love can be found, even when it's too dark to see.

ABOUT THE AUTHOR

Ali Stuebbe grew up in the state of Ohio, near the city of Cleveland. At the age of 21, she married, becoming a military spouse, and has called three other states home. She studied English Literature at Cleveland State University and American Public University. She began writing her debut novel when she grew confident in her writing and felt ready to bring this story to life. When she's not writing, she can be found at the gym or sitting on the couch with her nose in a book and a large coffee in her hand. Ali is the author of Blood of Desiderium, and currently lives in Texas with her loving husband and two beautiful children.

To get updates on book 2 in The Divide series, follow me!

    Instagram: @bookedbyali

    TikTok: @bookedbyali

    You can also find me on Goodreads!

THANK YOU

I appreciate you taking the time to read my debut novel, and I hope you enjoyed Blood of Desiderium!

It would also mean the world to me if you could leave a rating/review on Goodreads or Amazon because that helps tremendously for new authors.

Thank you again for reading my story.